WITCH WAY TO THE GATE - PART 2

WITCH WAY CHRONICLES #05.2

KIM & JIM NEXUS

This book is for my wonderful and loyal readers.

Thank you for giving me your precious time,
for letting my characters into your hearts,
and for telling your friends about my universe.

You're the best!

CONTENTS

CHAPTER ONE

SERGEY\\ UNEXPECTED COMPLICATIONS

When Sergey informed Felicity about the incident on the plover, her face briefly turned ashen, then immediately rushed into ripe tomato territory.

"You assured me this was perfectly safe!" She punched her index finger against his solar plexus with surprising force.

"Nothing in Ms. Yun and Ms. Delacroix's files would have led me to believe they'd be snooping around, playing amateur detectives, and riling up trouble," he pointed out. "Especially given the exhaustion and hunger that should have taken up just about all their waking thoughts by now. Besides, how could I have known that there even was any trouble to rile up? It's a voidforsaken cold storage facility, not gangster central!"

Oh, he would have a good look at the people running that facility. With two of his own attacked, getting their cooperation should be laughably easy.

"I trusted you on this!" She delivered the low blow with all the righteous fire in her luminous eyes he'd come to expect.

He let her take the high road. After all, she had good cause to be angry. Just like him. But where she could afford the luxury of openly displaying her dismay, people expected him to always be in control. Running around like a raging madman wouldn't impress anyone or get anything done.

Sergey caught the good doctor's hands in his and squeezed gently as he said, "I'm sorry, Doctor. This should not have happened, and I'll find out exactly how and why this went down so it can't happen again. Now, would you like to accompany me to the station to confirm that your patients are all right?"

Her shoulders moved back a few centimeters. Was it this hard to believe that he accepted responsibility, even when there'd been no way of predicting this incident and even though it had occurred through no fault of his own? After all, it was his operation.

Her eyes narrowed. Suspicion rang in her voice as she asked, "Why?"

"Why do I want you to accompany me?" he asked for clarification.

She nodded. "You would have preferred me never even knowing about this 'test,' and you only showed me the medical logs so I wouldn't pester you about it. So what changed?"

For some inexplicable reason, the fact that he couldn't get things past her unnoticed made her even more attractive.

He decided to play it straight, saying, "There's a decent possibility that this is an inside job. Since I don't know half of it yet, I'd like you to provide a second opinion. Might be that you see something I ought to know and which the station medics won't tell me."

"You think they're involved?"

"It seems improbable." He smiled. "But I like to cover my bases. Besides, you don't seem to have any patients at the moment, and I'd enjoy the company. It's a long flight."

She gave him that look.

"Don't fret, Doctor. We won't be alone."

When she raised an eyebrow at that, he elaborated, "I'm going to take a provost and a few troopers along, maybe even one of my sergeants. Wouldn't want anyone to think I'm not taking this seriously."

Besides, he didn't yet know the kind and size of hornet's nest those two troublemakers had kicked. They might need protection. Pulling them out would give the wrong impression to everyone involved, so that remained a last option.

Felicity bit her lower lip and gazed at her almost empty desk. Void, how he envied her that workload. But then, maybe she just kept it all in AR. Given her subtle bodily clues, a lively discussion occurred in the pretty doctor's head.

Once it was decided, she rubbed the bridge of her nose and announced, "Fine. When do we leave?"

"So, what happened exactly?" Provost Eisengaard-Diaz asked as soon as they'd all settled into the comfy seats on the *Lady Godiva*'s main deck. If he minded being ordered to accompany them, he didn't show it. Though officially, he was off-duty, Sergey had decided to ask for him anyway. It was a nice chance to see if the former criminal investigator had retained his edge. Not that the colonel doubted Naddi's assessment of the man. But as they said, 'Trust, but verify.'

Should this little exercise reignite Diaz's interest in his

former occupation and/or help him train for the recertification, Sergey could always claim intent and palm it off on the old fossil as a small favor.

Win-win for everybody.

While Henri, the veteran pilot the colonel had 'picked up' a week ago, launched them out of the hangar and punched the engines for all they were worth, Sergey explained to his passengers what allegedly transpired in cold storage about two hours ago. Then he selectively forwarded what information station security had sent up to this point and singled out the provost to meet him in VR in an hour to look at the crime scene. Time enough for Diaz to peruse the rest of the material he'd been given and for Sergey to discuss the mission parameters with his sergeant. Felicity, meanwhile, excused herself to catch up on some digital paperwork of her own.

"This was a rush job," Pro. Eisengaard-Diaz commented as he met Sergey in a private VRE to study the 3D holo provided by the lawmen on call.

The colonel squatted to take a closer look at one of the downed assailants.

"You mean the holo or the attack?" he asked, only half-jesting.

The sensor shadows blurring out details on this side were especially deplorable. Most likely, the crime scene scan's rough edges and limited scope just about covered the minimal demands set by procedural instructions.

"Both, I'd say." Diaz consulted the preliminary report the scan had been attached to. "Even with the perps wearing self-heating long underwear, they would have had to get those guys out of the cold quickly. Probably had no time to take proper scans."

"Could also be intentional low effort," Sergey pointed out.

"Sure, but I doubt it." If the unspoken suspicion that one of his own might be involved miffed the provost, he didn't show it. "Here, see this guy's fingertips? Looks like he was heading toward frostbite severe enough to cost him digits. With them all sprawled on the cold floor—no hats, no gloves, no nothing—they would have been dead within the hour. But that's just my assessment. You might want to refer to Dr. Fox for an expert opinion."

Even though subtle and in VR, the knowing glint in the provost's eyes and voice was unmistakable.

"Besides," he continued, "on a backwater place like this, you don't need to pay off half the crew. Most are private security, three provosts at most for the 'real' crimes on this plover. You don't necessarily need to pay off one of them if you can control the flow of information. One beat cop and one administrator are usually enough to keep most things under wraps. The two guards responding immediately were ours, so even if the first responder from station security, this Pro. Maj. ...," he rechecked the report, "McEntire was close at hand only because he'd been warned that something was going to go down and even assuming our guys were too preoccupied with rushing the penals to medical, his two colleagues from the private roster arriving at the scene only three minutes later would undoubtedly have prevented any attempts at a cover-up. Not much point in it, in any case, given that these guys absolutely needed medical attention."

"And is that your expert opinion?"

Diaz nodded, his dark eyes still roaming the downed figures. The way he shifted into different positions, as if measuring distances and running theories in his head, reminded Sergey of an almost forgotten day long ago when he'd accompanied his father to work. Only now, he was the one testing the other's aptitude for observation.

"So you don't think they were moved? Or that they had weapons which were removed from the scene?" he checked.

"I wouldn't think so. Their arrangement adheres to Ms. Yun's statement. The only thing missing," the provost squatted down for a closer look, then pointed at a perp's neck, "is whatever did this."

In the air to Diaz's right, a close-up picture and an in-depth scan from the perp's medical examination popped up for the provost's inspection.

Sergey pulled up the same images, saying, "Yun reported having used a rope."

"But there's no rope around now." Diaz gestured. "No need for one, either. And the pattern of subdermal hemorrhaging looks more like the effect of a whip curling around an object, except it's not tapered."

"You could swing a rope at a pole and have it curl around several times," Sergey pointed out.

What was Diaz driving at?

"Sure, but not like this. It would rapidly lose force. This almost looks like it adhered to the man's neck."

Well, a provost should know about that.

"And that's what you find most interesting about the incident?" the colonel asked dryly.

"Actually, the fact that this fight even happened is even more remarkable, in my opinion," Diaz said. "Even assuming they were stealing from storage frequently and had gotten somewhat accustomed to the cold, these perps must have already been starting to suffer physically. I just talked to Dr. Fox about the effects of extreme cold and the stages of freezing to death. Given the distances and time frame in question, they should have been sluggish and mentally impaired at the start of the fight. And that our penals were able to fight back as hard as they did in their weakened state... One has to salute that. Not to mention Ms. Yun pulling a larger, heavier woman onto a hover cart and rushing her outside for help."

Indeed, Sergey thought, somewhat grudgingly. *They definitely passed their stamina test. Too bad that's not the important part.*

Given what supposedly happened here, Yun had already passed the other tests as well. How Delacroix would react once she woke up might just tell Sergey all he needed to know about her disposition and usefulness. That's why he'd told the station's medics to keep her sedated until they arrived. Maybe it wouldn't be necessary, though. Given his pilot's flight style and the power of his shuttle's engines, Delacroix might still be in the OR once they did.

Diaz gestured away the images and stood, saying, "But back to the point: You don't have any real reason to doubt Ms. Yun's depiction of the incident, do you? Might I ask why we're taking such a deep look into this? Why not just pull our people out and have station security clean up their own mess? We have no jurisdiction there, and they know it."

"No direct jurisdiction, no." The colonel shrugged. "But I have a ship full of soldiers lining this plover's pockets and a way to cut them off not just from that but from all business coming from the dock and the *Voidhammer* fleet. At this point, all it takes are a few pointed inquiries into their trustworthiness."

The other man nodded his understanding, and asked,

"So you want me to try to get these guys put into our custody once they're patched up and cleared by the medic?"

"You think you can make that happen?"

"Not through official means, no." Under his face shield, the provost seemed to frown. "My options depend on the details. If this turns out to be a robbery turned bad, station security could claim jurisdiction, should they want it. The fact that a semi-military operation was disturbed by the crime could weigh in. Still, since the victims are neither part of the Plutonian military nor accused in an official Plutonian trial nor subjects to a plea bargain yet, that might be a hard argument to pull off."

"Legally speaking, they're foreign nationals with lawful status at best," Sergey clarified.

Damn, he hadn't considered that.

"Exactly," his expert agreed. "Also, we can't force military jurisdiction on a civil matter. Might still be that station security isn't interested in working this case. Then, they could hand it over to the local provosts. Should the attack turn out to be attempted murder, it would squarely fall into their jurisdiction anyway."

"And could you then claim it from them?" The colonel had always been somewhat confused by the 'who's who and what trumps what' dance provosts had to engage in whenever other law enforcement entered the picture.

"No." Diaz shook his head resolutely. "Pro. Maj. McEntire has more points than me, so I'd have to convince him to hand it over. I can try talking my way around obstacles, but if McEntire is the one taking cuts, that might not work. And even if it would, given the severity of this perp's head trauma, the medics might decide to put him into a brief artificial coma, just to be sure, and won't hand him over anytime soon."

It was tempting to have Diaz try and see how good he was at 'talking his way around obstacles,' but Sergey already had four more penals on his hands than he knew what to do with. He hoped to pawn those off to the Crimson Chain Gang as soon as possible. Except for Suzy Magecraft, obviously.

"Your enthusiasm is noted," the colonel said, waving the offer aside, "but I'm not interested in more problems to solve. No, this is solely about ensuring our people's safety. I'm not pulling anyone out. So I want to be certain our penals are safe and unbothered for the remainder of their trial."

The other man considered this, then nodded again, saying, "I see. Well, in that case, with your permission, Colonel, I'll call ahead and interview Ms. Yun and the first responders myself. You *are* allowed to start your own inquiry, no matter whose jurisdiction this ends up in. And if it just so happens to uncover individuals taking a cut to look the other way, the evidence of it will have to be forwarded to internal affairs."

"And it's always nice to get rid of the bad apples before they spoil the whole bucket, isn't it?" Sergey baited the other man.

"Certainly," Diaz returned. "So do I have your permission, then?"

It would be interesting to see if the calm, collected control in the provost's voice prevailed in his face.

"Granted," Sergey allowed. "Still, if you feel there's something to share, I expect you to share it with me first."

"Naturally." The provost's answer came without hesitation. Almost too smooth. Had Garin told him about her dealings with Sergey? If so, how much did he know? Well, if there turned out to be something worth sharing with IA, the provost's handling of it would no doubt prove telling.

"Also," the colonel added, "you do understand the second reason I brought you along, yes? You're acting provost major, and this can't wait until Garin returns. If anyone shirked their duties, punishment has to be swift and decisive, so it won't happen again."

Diaz showed no visible signs of unease as he answered, "I've already checked the personnel files of the troopers standing guard at the time in question. No mentions of previous tardiness. But, of course, I'll have to interview them to see what exactly they were doing, what they've been told to pay attention to, and how much of it. This might turn out to be an error in the dissemination of orders as well as bad adherence to protocol. Do you have a copy of the original orders you issued to the guards?"

Sergey nodded. "Of course. I'll send them to you."

CHAPTER TWO

WIRE\SERGEY\\ GRAVE INJURIES

"Ms. Delacroix, can you hear me?" A male voice, calm and professional, pushed back the veil of darkness overlying Wire's thoughts.

A strange sound echoed in the distance.

"Hecate be blessed, she's awake!" Yun's comment made Wire realize it had been her groaning like a zombie.

And something else.

Warmth. Beautiful, incredible warmth surrounded her, filled her lungs, and seeped all the way to her bones.

She pushed away the dizziness and blinked open her eyes. Dull brightness prevailed all around. The feel of something hard underneath her back. Not like the metallic floor. Rounded. Padded. She swallowed to relieve the dryness in her throat.

"Where am I?" she croaked. "What happened?"

A man examined her face, shining a light first into her right eye, then into her left, as he asked, "Do you know your name? What year it is?"

Without thinking, Wire rattled off her name and old service number before supplying the current date. Since, at the moment, she counted the days down to the minute, that was easy enough.

The man in surgical scrubs nodded with satisfaction and explained, "You're in medical. Your fight in storage left you incapacitated. Your left clavicle was fractured in several places, and two of your ribs were partially cracked. You also sustained subdermal hemorrhages, as are common with blunt force trauma like this, ... oh, and you got a good bump to the back of the head, so I'll have to keep you under observation to rule out a concussion. We've already operated, set and reinforced your clavicle, and introduced healing agents to facilitate a quick recovery. For the ribs, we'll have to fit you with—"

Panic rushed through Wire and pushed aside the fuzzy feeling the warmth—and probably the painkillers—induced.

"I have to go back to storage!" she gasped and tried to rise. "I can't leave! Why did you take me away from there? I have to get back, or I'll be executed!"

"Nononononono." Xinyi's hands flew to Wire's chest, but she obviously didn't quite dare to push. "It's fine! You're fine! Relax, or you'll aggravate your injuries! Besides, you didn't leave; I carried you out. If anyone's at fault, it's me. You're in the clear."

"You carried me out?" Wire stared at the other woman. "Are you fucking mad?"

"I couldn't leave you in the cold, injured as you were." The strange symbols in the mage's eyes churned wildly. "He fell on you, and you stopped breathing for several seconds! I didn't know how bad it was. So I got you on a hover cart and rushed you outside as fast as I could."

"No ... Luna, no." Wire fell back in sudden horror.

Fear, not just for her own skin but for her unexpected savior, made her insides tremble.

"I'll be fine." Xinyi nodded to herself. "We'll both be fine."

She didn't sound at all convinced.

"How ... how did you deal with that guy?"

"She just about bashed his skull in with a pipe," another voice, harsh and cold, chimed in. Federov stepped into the tiny sick room.

Xinyi's eyes widened, and she whirled around, pleading, "Colonel, I ... I didn't mean to kill him! I didn't kill him, did I?"

"So what if you had?" He gave the smallest of shrugs, like a life really didn't matter much in his eyes. "He attacked you two first; you defended your comrade. Nothing wrong with that in my book."

She swallowed but didn't say anything. He stopped so close to her that the mage almost flinched away. But with the sick bed at her back, there was nowhere to go. As his eyes bore into hers, he enunciated every word of his next question. "What exactly did you see?"

The woman's lower lip trembled. "I ... I'm ... not sure you would believe me, Sir."

"That's my decision to make, Ms. Yun. Your psychological assessment paints you as remarkably calm and collected. So what did you see that made you react this violently?"

Golden eyes jumped over to her fellow prisoner.

"It's all my fault, Sir!" Wire's mouth rushed out before her mind could stop it. "I went looking for them. I didn't pay enough attention and they jumped me. I called for help. Ms. Yun only—"

"Yes, I read her statement," the Plutonian cut her off. "I'll take yours later."

He turned his attention back to Yun. "Now, tell me

what you saw. I'm the one who has to be convinced that you're not a loose cannon, after all."

"I ..." Her shoulders sagged in time with her head. "Her aura vanished. I thought he'd killed her."

"Her aura?" His brows furrowed slightly.

My what? Wire thought.

Xinyi pointed at her eyes as she said, "Sometimes I see these colors around people. They are like ... feelings, maybe. State of mind or ... I'm not sure, exactly. But I always see hers."

She did what, now?

"She could merely have been knocked out," Federov countered.

"No. I saw her being knocked out once. She still had a slight grayish color surrounding her, then. This was the first time I couldn't see anything. It frightened me. I ..." Xinyi stared at her hands. "I didn't know how much force to apply. I just struck him, hoping for the best."

"And how did you know how to use that rope?"

The mage blinked, stuttering, "I ... ahem ... I just did. It just ... felt right."

"And where is the rope?" Federov's voice sharpened. "I surveyed the scene, and I couldn't find anything matching the marks on that perp's neck. Where did you get it, and where is it now?"

The object of his inquiries swallowed hard. Then, she slowly, hesitantly lifted her right arm and pushed back the sleeve. Translucent light emerged from the tattoo on her wrist and a golden rope slipped out of it, glittering and ethereal. Federov studied it. For a suffocating minute, the rings in his artificial eye were the only thing moving. Then he prodded it with his augmetic hand before feeling it with his flesh-and-blood fingertips.

Finally, he pulled back both and delivered his verdict.

"You had your comrade's back. As far as I'm concerned, that's what counts. All other details are for the provosts to sort out. You did nothing wrong."

As the mage pressed her lips together, her eyes downcast, Wire could almost feel the guilty conscience wafting off of her. Luna, this really wasn't the stone-cold killer who'd gunned down Kurt from behind, anymore. Without the constant cold and hunger bogging down her mental faculties, the Spartan finally understood what had been in front of her the entire time: This new Xinyi Yun was a good person, kind and considerate to a fault. She'd never meant the other any harm. On the contrary, she'd been there when her fellow prisoner needed her the most. Even while facing the same harsh conditions Xinyi hadn't snapped or lashed out, unlike her cellmate. And now, she'd reluctantly revealed what had clearly been a well-guarded secret. If she hadn't used the rope, she would have never needed to explain. Now, it was on record. All because she'd helped Wire. The least she could do was get Xin's burning question answered.

Wire met Federov's gaze and asked, "So, is he dead?"

The man smiled, and his tone shifted into an almost warm register. "No, but he's got a skull fracture, as well as a decent concussion, and will enjoy some long and uncomfortable Q&A sessions with the local provosts, thanks to the investigation the two of you kicked off. Seeing as how the two of you apprehended four criminals on your own, I'd say you've both earned yourselves two days to recover." He held out his hand, and the two women shook it, still stunned from this sudden reversal in his demeanor. "So enjoy the warm beds and hot showers while you can. Afterward, it's back to cold storage. You still owe me another eight days of labor."

The ray of unexpected sunlight dimmed somewhat at the prospect.

"Aye, Sir," they answered in unison. "Thank you, Sir."

Fuck, Wire thought. *I almost died there. How the heck am I supposed to go back to that place now?*

She looked up to find golden orbs studying her. No, not her, her aura. Probably.

As soon as Federov had left, Xinyi reached out to gently grasp the Spartan's hand, saying, "Don't fret. The worst is over. We'll manage the rest."

Something warm engulfed Wire's heart. Gratitude. When had she last felt that? She couldn't remember. And what had she done to earn Yun's friendship and loyalty, anyway?

Enjoying the unexpected windfall, she squeezed back. "Yeah, I think we will. Thank you. For everything."

"And?" Sergey asked Felicity, who'd continued watching the exchange on a monitor in the adjacent room. "What do you think?"

"I think they're cooperating with each other now." A mixture of surprise and rancor filled her words as she had to admit, "Your test actually worked."

"We'll see if it sticks. That's what those last eight days are for."

"Is it really necessary to send them back? And for the whole eight days?" she pleaded. "They already endured more than they bargained for."

"True." He leaned against the wall and studied the two

women on the monitor. "But I have to make sure. Besides, there are no shortcuts on my watch."

Felicity sighed. "Too bad."

He kept his smugness out of his following words. "So, what do I win? Maybe you'll let me take you out for a drink while we're on the station?"

"Maybe." She picked up her satchel. "Excuse me, I have to check on my patients now."

"You know, Doctor," he called after her, "I'm not normally one who lets himself be strung along by pretty 'maybe's."

The tantalizing mess of her hair wafted in a stray breeze from the nearby ventilation outlet as she stopped in the doorway and turned her head, returning, "Then why don't you stop asking?"

"Void knows." He shrugged. "Why don't you just say 'no'?"

"Would you take 'no' for an answer?"

He gave her a lopsided grin. "Maybe."

With a snort, she walked out the door.

After another minute of watching the relief her sudden appearance sparked in the adjacent room, Sergey shook his head. He'd better go see how Diaz was faring with his local colleagues.

CHAPTER THREE

RUFFA\\ CONTACT

LIGHTBEARER, *EN ROUTE TO THE KUIPER BELT*

"I'm not sure you fully grasp the complexity of this struggle." The dimwit's hologram twisted his wig in his hands nervously. "The Outer Systems Alliance and the Plutonian Republic have been at war for a long time. And it has been obvious for a while now, to everyone involved, that the current conflict can ultimately end only one way."

Ruffa leaned forward. "Then why are they wasting people and equipment on ongoing fighting?"

"Exactly my point!" Senoxes shook his head. "This is not a Velorian struggle, Commander. Humans are very different from us. Judging them by our standards will only frustrate your expectations in the end. I strongly discourage—"

"Noted," Ruffa cut the ambassador off. "Now, can you get me in contact with the Outer Systems Alliance or not?"

Senoxes threw up both hands in an all-too-human gesture. "Which part of them? This is not a single entity,

Commander. The OSA is composed of thirty-five small states clinging together for dear life! Any negotiations you wish to start with them must be brought before an assembly of clan or family leaders, guild masters, and station commanders! It's a voidforsaken mess that even most Plutonian secret service agents don't seem to be able to make heads or tails of!"

Ruffa took a deep breath and kept his folds clamped down tight so as to not show his disgust for the other's blatant incompetence as he argued, "Someone has to be replying to Plutonian missives and handling negotiations, don't they? There have been ceasefires and prisoner exchanges brokered. Someone opened the holos on those!"

"Well, yes ...," Senoxes agreed, then stopped and sighed. "I'll see what I can do."

"Good. You have two Human days to set it up."

"But—"

Ruffa disconnected the call.

Now that he wasn't expected to tiptoe around in Thallamon's diplomatic shadow all the time, he felt the deep need to finally get things done instead of relaxing his folds. Just because Senoxes had all day to come up with arguments and objections didn't mean Ruffa had the same luxury.

CHAPTER FOUR

GLEN\\ OLD WOUNDS

Glen sat in his office, reviewing the latest reports with his XO, when his right hand jerked unexpectedly. A small stack of dataslides tipped over and spilled across his desk.

Nick reached down to pick up the ones that had sailed to the floor, asking, "I thought it was getting better?"

"It is," Glen replied, pushing the rest back into a rough stack. "Ever since Eve started having me do those workouts and GaSIn took over advising me on my diet, I'm having fewer and fewer spasms. Still happens from time to time."

He closed his hand into a fist experimentally. His muscles strained against the motion, and he could barely close it all the way. This had been a bad one. He started massaging the limb.

Nick set the collected slides onto the stack, asking, "Do the Plutonians know?"

"I don't think so." Glen frowned. "Certainly hope they don't."

"Don't want to seem weak in front of Federov?" The lad winked as he stood to refill their mugs.

"He already thinks I'm weak." The admiral shook his head unhappily. "Too weak to deal with my ship's problems."

"I'd say that's an exaggeration. He seems to respect you well enough. Maybe even starting to like us."

"Liking has nothing to do with it; you know that." The captain felt the first knot grudgingly dissolve beneath his fingertips. "I can't afford to have him think I'm a sentimental old fool with medical problems."

"So, don't have medical problems," his XO countered. "It's easier than solving the old fool part. Eve offered you a solution. Just take it."

"If it were that simple..."

"But it is! So, cut the crap, Glen." His friend placed the refilled mugs on the table. "This isn't about the technical details, and you know it. The question you need to answer is: Do you trust her enough to let her in?"

The admiral sighed. "It's not just about what I'm comfortable with."

"What else could it possibly be about?" The lad sat back down and crossed his legs.

Aye, what else was there?

Glen licked his lips. "If Federov ever finds out that she was in your brain, he might think you're compromised. If I let her mend my hand, he could argue that she left some nanites behind, that they made their way into my brain, and that I couldn't tag you as compromised because I might be too."

"Oh, please!" The lad's voice rose in exasperated volume. "After all we've been through, you can't possibly believe she would do that!"

"This isn't about me; it's about what could be construed against us!"

Nick leaned back in and narrowed his eyes, saying, "Because if controlling us with nanites is all she wanted, there's no other way to get some in our systems, right? It's not like she couldn't hide them in our food, the air, or apply them directly to our skin with a subtle touch?! Glen, you're trying to rationalize an irrational fear. Besides, you made *me* go to her. If you didn't trust her, why would you have left my life in her hands?"

"You were dying; there were no alternatives. This," the old man waved his hand, "is merely an annoyance."

"No, by your own argument, it isn't! Either you care about the Plutonians' opinion, or you don't. If you do, then this wound makes you look old and broken. It comes with its own risks to keep it. And after what Eve did for me, you really have no excuse to postpone this. Didn't postponing stuff cause enough trouble for you already?"

Glen glanced away, and Nick leaned over to open a desk cabinet drawer. His nimble fingers found the bullet and slammed it onto the table before his friend. "Do you trust Eve? Do you trust her with your life?"

"Yes, yes, I do." The Scotsman's voice turned sheepish as he stared at the pointed piece of metal, which might have exploded his head if not for his alien protector.

"Well, then you really have no reason not to trust her with your hand, do you?" The lad picked up his slides and mug and stood.

"Where do you think you're going, XO?"

"I'll go to my office to get this sorted out," Nick waved the slides, "so you can figure out where your priorities lie and do something about it while we still have time. Besides, I have another training session with Lt. Ludmilla to prepare for."

And off he went.

"One devil's advocate you are," Glen murmured as he stared at his wrinkled, callused fingers.

Nick was right, of course. The real question was regarding trust, not technicalities. He and his instincts had grown quite comfortable with having Eve by his side. But have her rework his insides, as well? Having no good excuse didn't exclude him from being apprehensive. And given how much Nick had suffered ...

After a few minutes, Glen shook his head in disgust. If Federov could see him now, he would laugh at the silly old coreworlder. Not even half the admiral's age, he'd already lost his entire hand and gotten it replaced with a metal one. What was a bit of internal surgery to get some nerves stitched back together, compared to that?

Glen threw the bullet back into his desk drawer and walked out to ring the neighboring office, calling, "Eve, are you in? Do you have a minute?"

The last words hadn't entirely left his lips when the door slid open, and her voice rang out, "Sure, come in."

Eve sat at her desk and gestured to the chair across from her. "What can I do for you, Captain?"

A glimmer on her hand caught his eye, and as he sat down, he found himself staring at the engagement ring in puzzlement.

"Oh!" Her cappuccino-colored cheeks darkened slightly as she slid the piece off. "It isn't mine. I gave the ring to Maj. Thompson, but as you know, he declined to use the thing and returned it. I was just wondering whether I could find some fault with the design."

"May I?" He stretched out his hand.

"Sure."

She let the ring fall into his palm, and he studied the jewelry more closely. If the opportunity had arisen in his wife's lifetime, he would have bought it for Amanda immediately.

Gosh, she would have loved the understated craftsmanship and combination of materials.

"There's nothing wrong with this," he said with a gentle smile. "It's beautiful. Did you design the ring yourself?"

"Yes. I had my shuttle create it."

"Even the gem?"

"No, I have some of those lying around," she admitted. "When I first came to your system, I found that precious stones were a good mode of payment since I could easily locate and extract them from unclaimed asteroids. They're almost untraceable in raw form, and their value-to-weight ratio is excellent. I always carried a few inside me when visiting Human outposts."

"This one isn't raw."

He wasn't an expert, but the cut seemed bloody flawless.

"No," she admitted, holding out her hand. "I learned that most Humans see more value in a cut gem, so I had a large quantity processed by an expert craftsman. He charged a premium to leave the gems unmarked, but since it was all free money, I didn't mind."

He returned the ring with a grin. "And there I thought you only exchanged knowledge."

"On the contrary." She stood and walked over to the back wall. "In this solar system, knowledge is hard to barter with. Most Humans have a much clearer sense of the value of money than of the value of information."

She gestured, and a small section of the wall disappeared, revealing a sleek display case. Eve stepped aside and opened the glass front, allowing her visitor an unobstructed view of a translucent jewelry bust showcasing a necklace and matching earrings. Next to it, a delicate, translucent hand sat, its wrist adorned with a tasteful, high-end bracelet —a silver chain dotted with tiny charms—while its cupped palm cradled several glittering trinkets.

After a brief pause, Eve slid the ring onto one of the fingers and closed the case. But it was the drawer beneath that caught Glen's attention. A translucent compartment, roughly ten by fifty centimeters, positively stuffed with an impressive array of cut gemstones in every imaginable color and size, their brilliant sparkle impossible to ignore. The sheer volume hinted at a fortune carefully concealed within. Glen's throat dried up as his eyes widened. So this was how she paid for their mission ...

As the *Gateshot*'s owner turned, the faux wall blinked back into existence.

"Why did you show me that?" He stood to get a glass of water. And maybe to turn his face away from her scrutiny.

"So you know where it is." Eve walked back to sit behind her desk. "Just in case."

Glen thought back to the jewelry. He'd never seen her wear any. "That necklace—it's from Mars?"

"A parting gift from the governor." The chair creaked ever so slightly as she leaned back comfortably. "Maybe a bribe ... I'm not quite certain, actually."

He filled a second glass. "Seems you and Marshall had a much more complicated relationship than I realized."

"Actually, I found that all relationships I truly value are much more complicated than I could have ever imagined." Her tone of voice made him glance her way. Eve was studying him intently as she asked, "Tell me, why do I have to prove yet again that I can be trusted? What is it you came for and that you now avoid addressing?"

Bloody hell, she was starting to know him too well.

Setting the glasses down on her desk, he kept hold of both.

"My hand," he confessed. "You said you might be able to fix it?"

Eve's fingers slid onto his. Her gray-blue eyes looked up to ask for permission, and after a second of tentative hesitation, he let her lift it off the cool, translucent surface. He stood motionless as she studied his palm like an old-world fortune teller, and then turned it to scan the other side.

"It's slightly better," she finally judged. "I've learned a great deal from my mentor's treatment of Nick. I think I can manage this in two sessions of two to three hours each. But I would like to involve Dr. Fox to double-check my progress."

"I ... ahem ..." He cleared his throat. "I'd like to keep this off the logs."

"Obviously." Eve nodded. Holding his gaze, she commed their chief medic.

CHAPTER FIVE

SERGEY\\ THE CAMEL'S BACK

"What do you mean, you won't take Ms. Yun?" Sergey did his best to stare down his unexpected opponent.

"Exactly what I said, Colonel." Brigadier Major Stenson stared right back, completely unruffled, showing not even the slightest rise in heartbeat. "The Crimson Chain Gang can't take on magic users. No penal brigade does. It's in the rules and regulations."

Right, the fucking rules and regulations, of course.

Sergey took a deep breath and tried again, calmer now and with his 'I'll make it worth your while' voice. "And can't you make an exception? This is a special case, a special mission. And she only ever made a shield and maybe some brass knuckles. That can hardly be considered high risk."

"Well, that and—according to your report—" the older man tapped a dataslide holding the aforementioned document, "some sort of whip-like weapon, which she used to take down several opponents of larger size. So even if it were allowed, you can hardly blame me for refusing. Who knows what else she can do."

"Her psych evals show she's about as far from being a threat as I am from being a pacifist," Sergey tried.

"Irrelevant," Stenson declared.

"And what am I supposed to do with her, then?"

"Not my problem."

"Now, listen." Sergey leaned in closer. "There must be a way to come to a workable solution we both can live with?"

The brigadier major smiled ever so slightly, and for a moment, Sergey thought he had him. That his coworker had only been holding out to get a request for better equipment approved, or something.

Instead, his mother's former lover followed it up with a resolute shake of his head and said, almost phlegmatically, "No. Now, if you'll excuse me, Colonel, I have another appointment in five."

"Well, what did you expect?" Yelena asked when she dropped another stack of slides on his desk, less than two hours later.

More procurement forms. Great.

"To be honest, I didn't think it would be a problem," Sergey grumbled and slid them over to Lev's pile.

His second's dark eyes twinkled with subdued amusement. Then her expression shifted. She frowned and reached out to pinch his uniform, asking, "Did you lose weight?"

"Hey!" he slapped her probing fingers aside.

Had he? Sergey pulled at the same section of empty cloth.

"Would have thought I'd gain some, seeing as how I'm almost chained to this voidforsaken desk by now ..." he murmured. "Must be all the file lifting."

"Well, you did develop an unhealthy habit of missing meals," she pointed out. "Maybe you should get a second aide."

"No, I haven't. And I don't need another aide. Lev is doing fine! He was basically born for this logistic shit. ... Speaking of doing fine ..." He fished in the 'current reports' stack. "Do we have word from Diaz? It's been two days; he must have uncovered something by now."

After dealing with the two guards, who'd been tasked with keeping an eye on the prisoners, Sergey had left the former CI and four troopers on the plover.

"Here." His second slid a slide out of the stack and held it out to him, summarizing the content. "Says he delivered the punishment, then finished the interviews. He's made contact with the local provosts and received mixed cooperation with his investigation."

"As is to be expected if one of them really is dirty," Sergey conceded as he glanced at the report. All very neat and factual.

"Right. Well, seems Diaz thinks one of them is taking kickbacks, but he's yet to discover who," Yelena continued. "He's almost had an accident, so I guess you insisting he keep those troopers around was a good idea."

The colonel grunted.

"Don't worry. I called him. Whatever happened, he's downplaying it, but I believe him when he says he can handle it. Just let him do his job."

With a small sigh, her friend and superior leaned back, saying, "Right."

Damn, why did everyone else have all the fun while he was stuck behind a desk?

"So, what was the deal with the guards you had on that detail, anyhow?" his second prompted. "Those 'slaps on the wrist' punishments suggest they weren't completely at fault?!"

"Failure in the system mixed with tardiness," Sergey explained. "Since most cameras in cold storage are busted, they had to use the drones to keep an eye on the two penals. They also monitored their BCIs, but only for the purpose of placement verification. No one told them to keep an eye on the other entrance, so that's my fault for not considering the possibility someone might come in and steal stuff ..."

Yelena shook her head, interjecting, "Nonsense! We're not security for cold storage; there was no valid reason to expect intruders."

"Right." The colonel knew this, but he was still frustrated by the fact that all of this shit had transpired during his operation.

"So the guards had shitty tech but also didn't pay enough attention?!" his second clarified.

Sergey nodded.

"Damn..." She went to refill her mug.

When she came back, he was staring at his desk, unsure which fire to put out first today. An unexpected weariness settled in his bones and dragged down his mind.

"I need a to-do list," Sergey murmured.

"No, *you* need R&R." His second held out a hand. "Give me one of those procurement forms; I'll request some extra leave for you."

"I don't need extra vacation days," he said with a sigh, gesturing at the two stacks of shit he was expected to read and sign as he continued, "I just need people to bother someone else with all this nonsense for a change."

"Right." She picked up his mug from the desk and replaced it with her own. Winking, she said, "Why don't you go welcome the fossil and her charges back, and I'll take over here? Once you're in the hangar, you can wing it, yes?"

Sergey smiled.

CHAPTER SIX

SERGEY\SUZY\\ A DAY OFF

THE TRANSPORT SHUTTLE TOUCHED DOWN SO GINGERLY that the colonel briefly considered having the pilots scanned for residual alcohol and drugs. But they might just be considerate of the number of raging headaches and queasy stomachs they were ferrying around. As several squads' worth of mostly newbies stumbled out of the vessel, they quickly tried to right themselves and look at least somewhat presentable for their superior's inspection. Sergey waved them on, his mind too preoccupied with his own need for R&R to care.

Garin and her charges were the last to disembark. To Sergey's surprise, Jamaal Robbins was the only one of them looking like a wet rag. And while the provost major had surely had her fill of the celebration, her system was way too used to her preferred poison to care. The only person completely unencumbered by the residue of inebriation turned out to be Suzy Magecraft. Carrying her companions' packs as well as her own and a small box with holes in it, the ship's witch looked around the hangar with fresh, clear eyes.

In those eyes, the relief of returning mixed with the dread of unfinished work.

"Why didn't you party with the rest of them?" he inquired as soon as the salutes and such were done.

Magecraft blinked. "I ... ahem ... I did, Sir. I just ... ahem—"

Sergey looked at Garin, who shrugged.

"Well, you obviously did it wrong," the colonel cut her off. "And that's unacceptable. Come on, I'll show you how to do it right. Robbins, get some rest and report to Acting Maj. Vestergaard at the start of Prime Shift."

"Sir, yes, Sir!" The dark-skinned Spartan's voice and salute seemed significantly slurred.

Magecraft, meanwhile, looked toward the provost major for help, but of course, the fossil merely gestured for her to get going. She was probably happy to get them off her hands and return to her quarters for a decent sleep cycle. Dozing on a transport remained one of the lesser ways to refresh oneself.

"Sir?" his ward asked as her heart rate shot up.

Void, was she still afraid of him? That needed to be addressed. Maybe this would be more than a good excuse to get himself back to that plover for some fun time. With a brief thought, he reassigned all his appointments for the next twenty-four hours to Yelena and instead entered this 'teambuilding exercise' into Magecraft's calendar and his own.

"Well, don't just stand there, Ms. Magecraft," he said, marching off toward his personal shuttle. "Keep up!"

"A-Aye, Sir!"

Sergey heard her scramble to hand over any extra belongings and follow.

What in Mars' name was going on?

Had Suzy done something wrong? Had her conduct on the mining vessel not been up to par or whatever? Or had she done something stupid on the space station? She could barely remember stumbling onto the transport eight hours ago. And there were some blank spots before that. Had she been arrested? Had Garin pulled strings to get her released, and now Federov would rip her a new one for ... ahem ... whatever? Or had she done something that had only been discovered after she'd left, and now he was taking her back there to ... well, what, exactly? Shit, would she have to work it off in cold storage like Xin and Wire? Suzy hugged her pack closer.

Federov led her to the shuttle he and his void walkers had stolen ... ahem, sorry, *acquired* on the pirate station. It looked ... cleaner. Someone had changed the name and had repainted the voluptuous woman lounging on top of it. They'd mostly kept her as she'd been, except for extending her dark tresses. With several strands of luxurious hair now covering up the decent minimum of her nakedness, she looked infinitely more tasteful. More like one of those old-world pinup girls than a cheap canvas for jerking off.

Federov noticed that she noticed and raised an eyebrow, asking, "You like it?"

Was this a trick question?

"Sure." She quickly glanced away. "But why *Lady Godiva*?"

"I like a lady with conviction. Besides, it was an easy change to make."

What kind of reasoning was that?

"Right."

"Well, get in!" He gestured at the open airlock.

Marsdust, did she have to?

"I ... ahem ... have so much to do, Sir," she dared to try, "and—"

He merely gestured again.

Suzy swallowed hard. With a last look back at the main entrance of the hangar, she stepped into the next transport to take her away from home. And her super-important work of figuring out the gate.

Marsdust, she hadn't even really arrived yet.

Home ...

Hey, was that Glen back there? Before she could be sure, the door closed and cut off her view. The engines rumbled into subdued life, and the shuttle hovered up.

No. No, it probably wasn't. No reason for the captain to be here, and if he were, he certainly wouldn't just let Federov take her away, would he?

"We've got permission to disembark, Colonel," a welcome but utterly displaced voice echoed out of the loudspeakers. "Small window, though. Are you ready to leave, or shall we wait for the next one?"

Both passengers looked up in sudden confusion. Federov drew his knife and headed for the cockpit. Before she'd realized, she'd half-barred the scary dude's way.

"Nick?" she called.

Silence. Then a monitor on the wall next to them blinked on, showing a pleasantly surprised look on her former training partner's face.

"Suzy, it's you. What are you doing here?"

Federov eased the knife back into its sheath. Kept his hand on the handle, though, as he sidestepped the young witch and continued to the cockpit, saying, "I could ask you the same question, Commander. What are you doing on my shuttle?"

The door slid open, revealing Nick in the pilot's seat, an older man in the copilot's, and Lt. Ludmilla strapping into a fold-out seat at the back. Nick spun around to face the vessel's owner.

Oh, my ..., Suzy thought, *He's been hitting the gym hard! I'd totally kick Lady Godiva off my bed for a piece of* that ...

"Piloting lessons." Nick smiled broadly. "You agreed a few weeks ago that I could use your shuttle for that purpose. Don't you remember?"

"Right." Federov eyed Ludmilla, the stranger, and finally Nick. "Your teacher likes my ship. But doesn't the *Gateshot*'s first officer have better things to do? We'll be away for three shifts at least."

"Not really, no." Aforementioned XO typed in something with his right hand. "Besides, it's my day off, and I haven't done any long-haul shuttle flights in quite a while."

"Henri?" Federov glanced at the stranger again.

With his graying dark hair, light five o'clock shadow, and several small scars adorning his slim face, the man looked like a battle-hardened veteran. Had kind eyes, though. And a pleasant, resonant voice.

"We'll get you there in one piece, Sir." He gestured at Nick and indicated a blinking light. "You won't even know they're here."

The XO immediately responded by flipping several switches until the light flashed out. So, at least one of them was thoroughly enjoying himself ...

"Got another minute to leave, Sir." Nick wiggled his thumb at the hangar door sliding open. "Or we'll have to wait fifteen minutes for—"

"Fine," Federov cut him off with his voice as well as his hand. "Let's go!"

The pilot spun his chair back to the front with a childish grin and set both hands to flying over the controls, saying, "You two better strap in."

Suzy did a happy dance on the inside. At least she wouldn't be alone with Mr. 'Intimidation Incorporated' now. The colonel shooed her out of the cockpit and into one of the comfy chairs in the gloomy main room. No sooner had they sat down than the shuttle just about jerked upward and into instant forward motion. Federov muttered a curse under his breath as he snapped his straps closed.

Several screens mimicking windows flickered to life, providing a 360° view of the outside. Then they passed the transparent blue energy field, and the hangar fell away. Dockworkers, drones, and load-bearing vehicles came into view, swarming this way and that. As Nick swung the shuttle around with a flourish, Suzy could see the whole length of their beautiful bird rush by underneath her feet. Harsh points of light blinked on and off as drones and workers fused new parts into place.

"Does this mean they've finished the inside?" she asked. "Is the structural damage taken care of?"

In her peripheral vision, Federov nodded. "As I understand it, what they're doing on the inside now is mostly redecoration. Work on the bridge level is finally starting in earnest, and people are being moved into their new offices and quarters as we speak. All new security measures have been integrated; everything's moving along nicely. Dr. Lustig and Ms. Baileywick seem to know what they're doing."

"Yeah, they do. Woooooow," the girl whispered as their shuttle performed a lazy corkscrew and the *Voidhammer* completely filled one side wall. Their course seemed purposefully chosen to pass the giant ship's entire length, thereby providing the passengers with an amazing view of the tiny lights and outcrops on the dark blue hull. The sight of several large cannons gave Suzy a sudden case of the queasies. But Nick obviously maintained the correct distance, and nothing happened.

Just when she'd decided that Mama Tasha's flagship had no end, the enormous zeppelin shape tapered to a sharp tip. Suzy turned to watch it and the dock enveloping the *Gateshot* on the back wall until they'd become too small to distinguish from the stars in the distance.

Such a beautiful sight ...

CHAPTER SEVEN

GLEN\\ PLUTONIAN RESISTANCE

"And this is supposed to work better?" Glen asked as he studied the new VR setup of the *Gateshot*'s scanner section.

Three consoles facing each other in a triangular arrangement; a fourth set on a higher tier would be able to monitor only two of them.

"It did in the first few simulations," Eve returned with a shrug. "It seems to be a good setup for them to learn to work together, but I doubt it will be the final solution."

"So, let me guess." Glen rounded the VR furniture. "Ms. Rivers sits on this console, where no one can look over her shoulder. Lt. Montoya oversees the other two, and her team works in parallel with Rivers. Whoever spots something first gets bragging rights?"

His ship's master smirked. "That's the idea. Or as Ms. Rivers put it: the Plutonians *are* her redundancy."

Glen sighed. Was there no end to this nonsense?

"Unacceptable." He shook his head for emphasis. "It's going to slow down performance in critical situations. They're not learning to work together like this!"

"No, they're not. They're training their understanding of what each side can do and what it can't." Eve stepped closer and gently squeezed his shoulder. "Glen, you gave me the responsibility to advise you on your crew. And I know there's still much to learn before I can meet your standards. But trust me on this. We can't crowbar them into a working unit. We have to let them take one step at a time. Give them a few more days to get comfortable with each other. Then we'll pile on the pressure, and they'll come around and understand that this won't work in a stressful situation. They'll develop another iteration, and we'll do the whole song and dance again. Until we get it right."

"Eve, we don't have time for this!" The captain gestured at the virtual space. "Even if we allow a slow schedule for the training, this has to be made real! The refurbishing of our bridge has to be completed before we can go anywhere; the Plutonians won't wait for us! As we speak, the Velorians are fortifying the gate; every day we delay could mean more ships barring our way!"

"I'm aware. After all, I'm the one coordinating with the dock, Dr. Lustig, and the drones. I'm the one calculating all these timeframes." The mildest touch of rebuke vibrated in her clear voice. "And I'm telling you that we still have time. We're proceeding as fast as Humanly possible. But I can't work our people to the bone, and there's a physical limit to our drones as well. Relax, Glen. As it stands, we're well ahead of schedule, and I calculate that it will take the scanner team two weeks at most to get themselves sorted out. We'll be in the dock for at least another three. We have those two weeks. We can finish this section last."

Glen crossed his arms. "We don't know that. We might be called out of the dock sooner than we like. We need to have a working bridge by then. Are the other shifts shaping up any better?"

"They are, but ... Wait." Eve's bonny blue-gray eyes narrowed as she studied him. "What do you know that I don't?"

For a moment, Glen thought about the implications of telling her this. With military intel, one had to be cautious, especially when ...

"I'm still unclear on how this connection with the rest of your kind works," he sidestepped the issue. "Do they know everything you know?"

"Yes and no." Probably sensing that this was an important issue to resolve, the alien robot's whole demeanor focused on him with renewed intention, as she continued, "In theory, everything I know and experience gets uploaded into the Great Neutrality, but I have a subroutine sorting private matters from raw information, and I'm not under constant supervision. In addition, my mentor checks up on me occasionally."

"But everything you know could be asked for by a third party?" Glen clarified. "Like the fact that we're trying to go through the gate and how we plan to do so?"

Eve relaxed visibly. "Oh, that. Yes, in theory, someone might ask for it. However, I'm the only guardian on this side of the gate, and no Velorian wanted to ask me anything. That's how this whole mess started, after all."

Right.

"And what of the Velorians and guardians on the other side of the gate?" he asked.

"I put in a request for any guardian who encounters a Velorian to ask them about their plans for the Human women they take through the gate. So, if any Velorian asks for your battle plans, they'd have to answer and might render the very battle unnecessary."

That was smart.

"Besides," Eve continued, "as a neutral party, we don't make a habit of giving out information that could directly cost lives or decide large conflicts. Only on very rare and specific occasions has this ever been done."

"Wait," the admiral clarified. "So once we make it through the gate, the Velorians can't just go to any guardian and ask for our whereabouts since they would have the intention to destroy the ship and kill everyone aboard?!"

His teacher fortified herself with a deep breath before saying, "Well, since I know that's likely their intention, and so this would be transmitted to the guardian being asked, I'd expect them to decline answering. But you keep missing the most important point."

"Right." Glen leaned back against a console with his arms crossed. "Your kind is exceedingly rare, and meeting you is like winning the lottery."

"At least in terms of probability." She mirrored his easy smile. "Maybe not so much in terms of enriched happiness in some cases ..."

"Please forgive an old geezer; I keep forgetting how special you are." He wiggled his eyebrows. "You do seem so dreadfully boring and normal most times."

"'Boring'?" She puffed up her chest in mock indignation. "What did I do wrong to deserve that denominator?"

By way of an answer, Glen merely grinned. The resonance of their shared laughter provided a relieving oasis in the desert that was the stressful urgency of their situation.

Finally he said, "All joking aside, you'd better keep up that facade until we're through the gate."

"For the Plutonians' sake, I know." She dabbed away a

tear with her thumb, then stared at the glistening liquid as she asked, "Now, what was it about the run on the gate you wanted to tell me?"

He, too, turned serious again. "They're sending a marshal and two or three more man-of-war class battlecarriers like the *Voidhammer*, each probably with their own escort attached."

Eve crossed her arms and leaned back against a neighboring console, saying, "Sounds more like a war fleet than a ship's escort."

"Aye." The admiral gazed off into the distance, dark anxieties gathering at the edge of his mind.

"Plutonians are known for taking military matters very seriously." She wet her lips. "This might not be your fears coming true."

"Aye."

Besides, even if they were ... what else could he do but try to stay in control and shield his crew from any kind of backlash?

"Glen, we're not the ones starting a war here."

While Eve's words mirrored Nick's youthful folly, her tone declared it an honest wish.

He sighed and murmured, "Doesn't mean one won't get started."

The guardian reached out a hand to gently squeeze his. Whatever the coming weeks might hold in store, it sure felt nice to have an indestructible fighting machine with a direct line to the largest deposit of knowledge in the universe on his side. Somehow, that actually made his anxiety recede somewhat.

"Either way," he decided, "I can't risk looking even more indecisive than I already do. You have one week to make it work, or I'll have to remove Ms. Rivers from my bridge."

CHAPTER EIGHT

SUZY\SERGEY\\ CHILD'S PLAY

Suzy must have dozed off at some point, because suddenly, Nick's cheerful voice announced, "We're on final approach, ETA: ten minutes. All passengers, please return to your seats and strap in for docking."

When Suzy blinked open her eyes, the station grew rapidly larger on the front screens. The lighting in the shuttle's main room had changed. Since she'd just spent time on a Plutonian vessel, she knew to identify this slightly lighter gloom as a kind of relaxed working and reading environment. And, really, when she glanced over, Federov just put down his feet from the table. He slipped a dataslide into a holding pouch and his feet back into his boots. A mug steamed away merrily on the tabletop. He'd also changed into another uniform, this one less utilitarian, more ornate and flashy.

As if he'd felt her gaze, he looked her way. Suzy remembered the instructions concerning station leave with that *déjà vu* of cold panic flashing up her bones.

"I don't have my dress uniform with me," she blurted, like she'd already done a day earlier.

But Federov only scratched his chin and waved it off, saying, "I expect the provost major already gave you an earful for that oversight."

His eyes briefly lingered on the patch covering the telling symbol on her left breast. It featured a generic company logo. Eve had issued these to every crew member before the first dock workers arrived aboard the *Gateshot*.

"Oh, yeah," Suzy fibbed. "I've been thoroughly scolded."

One of the rings in his augmetic eye whirred half a circle to the right, and he snorted lightly. Heat rushed up the girl's neck.

"ETA: five minutes, taxiing into docking position now," their charming pilot announced.

Federov drained his mug, then said, "You're terrible at lying. Did your parents teach you that?"

"Did they teach me to be bad at lying?" Suzy wasn't sure what answer he expected to get to such a question.

"*Da*." He secured the drinking vessel. "I found that too many parents endorse their children's truthfulness to an unhealthy degree because it makes their job easier. When they're also very forgiving or just don't care, their children rarely find themselves in situations where they can practice this essential skill. Makes it harder once life demands a lie. You should work on that."

Suzy blinked.

"I lied to my dad," her mouth revealed without checking in with her brain first. "A lot, actually."

The corner of his lip ticked up briefly. "Then maybe you should think of your dad before trying to deceive."

Suzy coughed and glanced away. On the forward-facing screen, the station's hull swooped in closer.

"Docking now," Nick informed.

Tiny blue flames shot into view, mainly on the cameras in front and at the side facing away from the station, as their pilot aligned the shuttle with an airlock clearly marked with those universal symbols even Suzy could read. As soon as they touched down, several docking clamps reached out, magnetic locks engaged, sending slight tremors and *clonks* through the hull. The *thump* and *hiss* of the airlock connecting followed. PUs powered down with a distant hum. The door to the outside beeped and the light on its control panel turned green.

"Docking procedure complete," their pilot reported in good spirits. "Thank you for flying with Sheridan Space Lines. We wish you a pleasant stay and—Umph!"

The mic cut out. Suzy bit back a laugh. Federov shook his head slightly, as if to himself, and unstrapped.

"Let's go!" he said.

With one last, longing look at the cockpit door, the witch hurried out after her warden.

"Where ... ahem ... where are we going, Sir?" Suzy gazed around with growing apprehension. "If you don't mind me asking?"

Federov had led them through the outskirts of the bustle near the docking area to an elevator and up several stories. Although still wide, the hallway they traversed now lay almost empty. The advertisements, AR and otherwise, had significantly reduced both in number and obnoxiousness, and the storefronts they passed weren't filled with people but decidedly less sexy wares. With the sole exception of one—for Plutonian standards—brightly lit lingerie shop, most offered everyday necessities. Considering the primary income sources on this station, though, lingerie might actually be regarded as an everyday necessity here ...

"There should be a bar facing that square up ahead." His eyes tracked their surroundings, as if he were searching for something. "One frequented by the locals. A friend recommended it. Considerably cheaper and more private than the establishments downstairs."

"More private?" she echoed.

"*Da.*"

They reached the end of the corridor and stepped into a vast circular space lined with shops, bars, and restaurants. Each of those eked out ground from the common area, claiming it with extra tables, chairs, or displays.

At the center, two playgrounds, distinguishable by the size of their respective equipment, sat next to a large, open lot. Following painted indicators of different colors, one group of teenagers chasing a soccer ball kept to one half of the area, while the rest was divided about equally between six smaller kids playing basketball and a mixed group trying to impress each other by performing tricks or feats of agility and speed on hoverboards and the like. In the time it took Federov and her to skirt their section, Suzy had gauged the skills and weaknesses of all eight of them. Her feet started itching, and she suddenly missed people she hadn't even thought of in months.

She only realized how distracted she'd become when Federov stopped, and she just about walked into him. He gave her that look.

Gulp.

With a slight shake of his head, he held out his hand, the echo of an amused smile dancing over his stern face as he said, "Give me your jacket and show them how it's done. I'll go ahead and secure us a nice table."

"Oh. Ahem ... okay. Thanks!"

Before he could change his mind, she shrugged out of her jacket and ran off.

Watching Suzy Magecraft mingle with the kids was an eye-opener. Within six minutes, she was accepted and invited to show off her skills, laugh, and play with the others. The group leader had the barely tolerated kid from the admin family lend her his board. She held herself back when racing the alpha, but couldn't resist winning. Made it a close call to spare the boy's feelings, played all coy and nice afterward. Probably told them she just had more practice. Her empathy opened up the group, and soon they were actively seeking her input.

So this is what it looks like when you're not out of your depth, Sergey thought as he sipped his tea. *Or believe that you are.*

This was clearly what Felicity meant when she claimed the young woman to be 'just a kid'. Magecraft herself thought of herself that way. At least part of her did. That part made it easy for her to blend in, to be accepted by the teenagers. But she couldn't fool herself entirely. There was a certain something in her stance, a dominance asserting itself in this company only. The knowledge that she'd seen shit they hadn't, that she'd done things.

Leaderboy realized instinctively that she would have an easy time taking his place if she wanted to. How he danced in and out of her space mirrored the unconscious conflict. Should he confront and try to drive her away to uphold power, or would that be the surefire way to lose it? Surely she would leave on her own time. Until then, he could learn a move or two from her, which would help him stay on top later.

So what does it take to make you step up and take control, Suzy Magecraft? Sergey thought. *Overpowering adversity?*

The restaurant's owner could read his wishes as astutely as he could the power dynamics of most groups and slipped a short menu onto the table as she refilled his mug.

"Today's offers" were designed for people like him: hungry but with no mind to peruse a long list.

He smiled appreciatively at the graying woman. "I'll have the fish soup and two bean bread rolls. Thanks."

That playful wink and the sway of her hips as she walked away left no two guesses at what she'd been doing before opening this joint. Smart woman. Some occupations one couldn't do after a certain point, and she'd apparently left at the right time. Still retained enough beauty and energy to charm her new customers.

When Magecraft finally joined him at the leftmost of the two-person tables out front, he was just finishing up his meal. One look at the last morsels of bread disappearing into his mouth cued her stomach to growl like a circus lion, and her purple eyes widened into pitiful puppy versions.

With an inner laugh, he slid over the menu.

"You really are a strange combination of traits." Sergey shook his head, but put on a soft smile to keep her at ease. For the same reason, he'd shrugged out of his jacket and folded it onto the chair next to him.

She combed back the sweat-soaked purple tresses on one side of her head. The other side was freshly braided. And not by a device, too many minuscule flaws for that.

The design was rather artful, but the execution lacked polish. Someone had had time on their hands and a good idea of how it was done, but not much prior practice. Magecraft's eyes lingered on where the long sleeve of his shirt hugged the lines underneath, where the metal of his artificial lower arm met flesh. Was that the cause of her reservation? She was friends with a robot from outer space, and an AI governed her planet. She shouldn't feel queasy about a few replacement parts, right!?

Her slim fingers picked up the menu, and she asked, "What do you mean?"

That self-conscious tone in her voice, like she were just waiting for an unseen trap to snap shut around her. What was it about him that kept her on edge like this? Sure, he'd put in some effort to give her a bit of a scare that one time in the brig, but he was just a guy. He wasn't that scary ... was he?

"I mean, you're a giant chicken until someone hands you a hoverboard or a reason to use your magic." He put some challenge into his smile to draw her out. "You stand apart, all reclusive and self-conscious, until, suddenly, you're the heart of the party. Your earnestness disarms people, and I think you know it."

Magecraft sucked in her lower lip and started to gnaw on her piercings as she studied the menu.

"One minute you're the typical snotty teenage brat, emotional and raw, just bashing through with your magic like it's a jackhammer, then you try to solve the gate like a professor, studying it for months on end. You can take a beating, but you can't take sitting in an office all day."

"You mean, like you?" She slapped down the menu and met his gaze head-on. He didn't blink. Her bravado ran out again, and she glanced back down, murmuring, "The office part, I mean?"

Now he saw it. "You're not really afraid of me. You're afraid of netting yourself more trouble, so you're holding back."

Her pulse spiked briefly. Her gaze went in search of their hostess.

Sergey chuckled. "Well, you don't need to. It's my day off. The only thing I'm going to do to you is get you thoroughly drunk so you stop being such a stick in the mud," he caught the graying lady's attention and lifted two fingers. Got a nod in return. Magecraft's rather stupefied blink made him add, "Maybe show you a good brothel or two afterward. You seem to need it more than I do."

She blanched.

It took a surprising amount of strong spirits to get the girl to loosen up, especially considering she was a coreworlder. So this was that heightened mage metabolism in action. She also ate like two miners her size.

"So," Sergey asked, "you split asteroids with magic. How does that work?"

"I just ... look at them and think of what I want, and then I invest the energy." She shrugged.

A sudden terror ran down his spine, and he voiced the unpleasant thought, "Could you do that with people?"

"What?" She shook her head like she didn't understand the question. Like she'd just woken up from a dream she hadn't shaken off fully.

Even with the danger of making her defensive once more, he repeated his question.

"No idea." She shook her head some more. "And why would I ever want to try it out?"

"Don't know." He mirrored her head shaking. "Just a dumb thought. I guess it could come in handy."

Their hostess, exchanging her empty bowl for a full one, broke the oncoming silence before it could fully assert itself.

"Oh, damn," the lady murmured under her breath. "Is it that time of the week again?"

Sergey and Suzy followed her gaze.

The girl frowned, probably unsure what to look for, and asked, "What time?"

"Ration day." The Plutonian had spotted the small group of workers shambling out of a side corridor, heading for a nearby shop.

"*¿Cómo?*"

"Right, they don't have rationing where you come from." He gestured for a refill of his glass. "Around here, people get ration slips once a week, then go shopping for food. See?"

"Why? I thought you Plutonians had enough food?" Magecraft glanced at her plate in sudden apprehension. Like her taking extra might leave someone lacking. Her naivete was adorable at times.

"We do, most of the time," their hostess agreed as she poured Sergey's next drink. "It's to ensure everyone's needs are met. With the ration slips, you buy cheaper. If you want more, you can have it, but it comes at a higher cost. This ensures an affordable basic living for everyone, *daniete*?"

A woman hugging a box full of groceries left the shop just as the other group reached it. Something about the image prompted the void walker to engage the magnification on his artificial eye for a better look.

"Then why do they look so glum?" Magecraft named

the suspicion ghosting around in his mind. "Shouldn't they be happy to get cheap stuff?"

Right.

And wouldn't they bring something to carry it home?

The woman with the box looked around nervously, then hurried down the length of the room and into another grocery shop. At least that's where Sergey suspected she'd gone, since she didn't appear on the other side of the colorful climbing wall attached to the kids' slide, and there didn't seem to be any side corridors or other entrances around.

"Well, that has to suck," his tablemate declared around a mouthful of stew. "You can't even decide what you want to get with your ration slips? We could, back in the war. Well, kinda."

"Hmm?" he asked. His sight briefly split between Magecraft's entire face and a close-up of that tiny wrinkle on her forehead, until his augmetic readjusted itself.

"You know, that big war ten years back, the one just about everyone but you participated in?" Her tone grew sharper with every word. "Kinda strange seeing as how you're eager to fight all the time. I was just a kid back then, but I remember the blockade of Mars. I know what rationing feels like—the real kind meant to keep people from starving when there's just not enough—thank you very much."

Her sudden aggressiveness gave him pause, and he cleared his throat before asking, "What did you mean just now? About not getting to choose what to buy?"

Her eyes narrowed for a second, like she was trying to figure out if he'd actually meant to belittle her experience or if he'd merely been distracted.

Finally, she shrugged and pointed at the first shop,

saying, "They all got in, got a box full of stuff, and walked out again. So it's pre-packed, no choice of what you get, right?"

"That's not how it normally works. Preorders are common, though." As he swung around to look back at the first shop, the woman reappeared, walking back the way she'd come. Her hands stuffed in her pockets as if she were hiding fists, her head and shoulders drooping. She passed by the group with the pre-packed boxes and looks were exchanged. As Sergey zoomed in, he thought they all looked very unhappy. Like they acknowledged some shared suffering.

"This isn't right." He frowned.

"Better not think about it too much," their hostess murmured. "Trust me."

A mischievous feeling bloomed in Sergey's chest and jumped onto his lips as a smirk. He would have to talk to his godmother about her venue recommendations and how his late mother might not appreciate her best friend purposefully steering him toward trouble. Again. Not to get her to stop it, of course, just to get a bargaining chip out of it.

"I need a better look at this," he mused.

"Sure," his companion murmured around a spoonful of her food. "I'll wait."

"Actually, I'll wait and you'll go."

She blinked. "Huh?"

"They know my face around here; yours is fresh. And you look like a tourist rather than uniformed trouble." He folded his hands on the table and smiled. "You can stream me what you see."

"But ..." She gestured at her half-empty bowl.

"I'll keep it warm for you, Sugar." Their hostess winked. The smile on her face said she'd gotten what she'd wanted.

Sergey studied his fingernails as he proposed, "We could also go and check out those brothels ..."

Magecraft stood abruptly. "Fine! So you want me to go into that shop they're getting the boxes from!?"

"*Da*. That one and the one behind that playground. See it?"

She leaned over to better share his POV, squinted, then nodded.

"Good." He sent a shared-vision request to her BCI. "You can decide which one first. We'll want a closer look at those boxes and the interactions at the counter."

"Right ..." She accepted with a hand-eye gesture. "Marsdust!"

As their hostess gave her a sidelong glance of reevaluation, Sergey shook his head, saying, "Stop mentioning drugs all the time. Someone might take you up on it."

"I don't ... I mean ... Where I come from ..." She stopped her wordflow, paused for a crestfallen second, then bent forward to quickly brush some bread crumbs off her pants. Might also have been to hide her reddening face.

He considered her getup. Without the jacket, it was just a pair of blue pants. Those sweat stains heightened the sense of civilian casualness her dark purple t-shirt and hairdo propagated. "Here," he slid over two coins, one for each shop, "go buy a little something for yourself. Browse the shelves for a while, look around like you're not sure what you want. Just don't be too obvious."

"Yes, Sir," she murmured, pressed her lips into a thin line, and left, coins vanishing into her pocket.

As she headed for the second shop, the one he couldn't see from this vantage point, the slight sway in her gait aptly transmitted her tipsiness to everyone.

Perfect.

CHAPTER NINE

SUZY\\ STRANGE OCCURANCES

SUZY STRUTTED DOWN THE PATH THAT ENCIRCLED THE central area, huffing and fuming inside.

Why the fuck was this happening to her? When had this outing turned into a spy vid of all things? And just when she'd thought this might be all right after all. Now she'd upgraded from Federov's amusement to his gofer.

'*Aren't you curious what's going on, too?*' his voice ghosted into her mind via silent comms.

Well, maybe a little, she thought, then commed back, '*No!*'

An amused snort was all the answer she got. All the answer she needed to ascertain that her reply hadn't fooled him.

Asshole, she thought.

'*I heard that,*' he answered. '*Maybe check your transmitter settings?*'

Petrified, Suzy stumbled to a sudden halt, her hands flying to her mouth like she'd actually said it out loud. Quickly, she set her BCI-comms to 'Explicit commands' to stop her drunken mind from sending out any more random thoughts.

Thankfully, he didn't pursue the issue, reporting instead, '*Another man just left the first store and is heading your way. If you time it right, you can slip in after him.*'

Right ...

She quickened her steps. From the right, a middle-aged guy, gaunt and ashen even by Plutonian standards, ambled over. Like those other people who'd sparked the colonel's attention, he carried a box filled with groceries. Once it became clear he was heading for the same door, she skipped a few steps and held it open for him.

"Thanks," he murmured. It was a nicety devoid of feeling.

Still, she smiled a happy smile and channeled her inner Chávez as she returned, "*De nada.*"

As he squeezed past, she got a good look at the box and its contents. As she'd expected, it was full of foodstuffs. Cans, mostly. Some hardtack or whatever.

The shop was a small hole-in-the-wall, nothing special. A few refrigeration units, several shelves filled with cans and other reusable containers. One corner held a freezer preserving large chunks of fish and the like. In the front, a table with fresh produce—mostly baked goods, roots, and mushrooms—provided a tripping hazard. Gosh, those cinnamon buns sure did a nice job of covering up the stuffy smell prevailing in there ... They also made Suzy's mouth water. Must have been a remnant of channeling so much magic. She'd always had days like these after major exertions. Days, when she could just eat and eat ... like a hangover. A magical hangover. Was there such a thing?

'*Did you notice anything strange about the stuff in the*

box?' her invisible puppeteer questioned as she followed the guy inside.

'*There was dust on it,*' she reported with an inner frown. '*And not just on some stuff, like some packages had been on the shelves for a while, but on all of it. Like that stuff has been in the box for a prolonged period. Didn't he just buy this at the other place?*'

'*He did.*'

What in Hecate's name was going on here? Even though some distant part inside realized the tipsiness made her blabber box bold and her thoughts slow, she couldn't do jack shit about it. With some luck, her heightened metabolism was already working to reduce the fog tripping up her mental capacities, and all this would soon make sense again.

Suzy headed for the magazine stand next to the tiny counter just as the man set his box down on it and turned to the bored-looking youth minding the store. He declared in a low, defeated voice, "I'd like to sell this, please."

"Sure," the pimple-faced redhead replied, as if quoting from a script he'd rattled off a gazillion times. "But you know I can't pay full value, right?"

"Yeah, I understand," the man answered in the same monotone.

With a nod, the redhead exchanged the box for a cred-stick. He waited for the man to leave before setting the box down behind the counter. Suzy gave the display a gentle push, and it spun lazily around its axis.

'*Another one coming your way,*' *Federov announced.* '*If the exchange is similar, you leave afterward. No need to hang around and elicit suspicion.*'

'*Roger that.*' She spotted a comic book slide and stopped the display. Normally, she would have just snatched the thing in passing, but with her reflexes slowed considerably, she didn't want to risk making an ass of herself by possibly grabbing empty air.

The shop's doorbell rang. Another man with a box entered, and the whole exchange from before repeated itself.

When that customer had left, the redhead finally looked her way, snapping, "Hey, this ain't a library. You gonna buy that or what?"

"Nah, seems kinda lame." She slid the slide back into its place and added, "But those cinnamon buns sure smell nice. How much are they?"

"There's an AR tag," he replied with that annoyed, snotty tone Suzy absolutely hated. "Can't you read?"

"No, that's why I prefer the picture slides." She smiled sweetly. "So, how much?"

He rolled his eyes and told her.

"Cool; I'll have two," she slid one of the coins over the counter, and he handed her a paper bag.

Behind the counter, boxes lined the wall, stacked several atop each other. From what she could see, there were only minimal differences in their contents.

"Love the customer service," she told him with all caps irony as she turned to bag her merchandise herself. "Keep it up, *amigo*."

Pimple-face snorted derisively. She let the doorbell drown out the sound.

An amused chuckle tickled her insides. '*I see what you're trying to do,*' Federov chided her, '*but you really don't sound like a Plutonian.*'

'*Well, sorry to bump your ego there, but you're wrong. I'm not trying to sound like a Plutonian,*' she answered in her thoughts as she bit into the first bun. '*I'm just trying to* not *sound like a Martian. Besides,'* she had a look around before heading for the other shop, *'what does a Plutonian sound like, anyway? You can't tell me that in a nation just about encircling the rest of our solar system, all people sound the same!'*

Gosh, that cinnabun was good. Still warm too.

Either he had no answer, or he didn't care for her shift into snotty teenage attitude. In either case, her head was hers alone all the way down the length of the plaza and into the next shop.

She stopped just inside to have a look around. Since she'd never been there before, that should be a perfectly natural behavior, right?

Well, this shop looked much the same as the last one, except that it had about thrice as much shelf space. Besides the groceries, there were also several sections featuring everyday items and luxury goods. Once she'd gotten the lay of the land, she headed directly over to the counter.

"*Sveiki!*" With the enthusiasm of a drunken chick, she beamed at the shifty-looking fellow manning it and held up her baggy, asking, "You sell coffee, right? 'Cause I just got these at that other place, and they're really good, but then I thought, 'Gosh, you know what they need? They really need some coffee!' You got coffee to go, right?"

With a lax motion, she leaned onto the counter, right into his space. A series of unvoiced responses ran across his face before he settled on "Sure" and pointed at the board, decorated with coffee beans and steaming cups of liquid goodness, listing the available options and prices. "What do you want?"

"Oh!" Suzy blinked, like she'd totally not seen it. "Yeah, cool! I'll have a cappuccino. Like, a large one ... or no, a middle one. And do you have sprinkles? I looove sprinkles!"

More suppressed movement on his face as he replied, "No sprinkles. This ain't an ice cream parlor, lady."

"Oh, too bad." She sulked for a second, then declared in a bright and happy voice worthy of Rivers, "No problem. You got extra flavorings?"

Shifty Dude pointed at the board. "You see any extras on there?"

Suzy squinted at the hieroglyphs her BCI helpfully translated for her, and said, "You know, I'm not that good with ... ahem ... reading. Are there?"

He rolled his eyes. "No!"

'You're overplaying,' Federov's voice cut in sharply. *'Next customer's coming.'*

"Well, okay." Suzy shrugged and took another bite from her cinnabun. "Just the cappuccino then. Please."

Some ways behind her, the doorbell rang. With a deep breath of obvious relief to soon be rid of her, Shifty collected her money, then set a cup under the coffee machine, and started it.

A plainly dressed woman approached the counter and gave the purple-haired drunk a sidelong stare.

"Oh, sorry." The girl moved aside and pointed at the machine, noisily warming up. "Just waiting for my coffee. You go ahead."

The woman seemed slightly unsure. Shifty Dude reached underneath the counter and set a box onto it, saying, "You here for your order, right?"

Mrs. Nondescript nodded and did the hand-eye gesture of flipping something over. The till beeped in acknowledgment, and the man pointed at a transfer pad, saying, "Thumbprint, please."

While she followed the instructions and collected her box, Dude reached over to retrieve Suzy's cup.

The witch decided to forego the sweetener and quickly popped the lid on so she could leave the shop at the same time the woman did. Again, she used the excuse of holding the door to get a good look at the box's contents.

As soon as the door had closed behind them, she asked, "Hey, sorry to bother you, but I looove those cookies. Didn't see them in the shop, though. You know where they're kept?"

The woman shook her head and asked, "You actually like these? They're basically hardtack."

"Yeah, but my *wujciu* used to put them on the table." Suzy skipped a step to keep pace with her. "Always said a kid's jaw needs the workout to keep pronunciation clean. So it's a bit of nostalgia for me, you know. ... Hey, if you don't like them, why'd you buy them?"

"Never said I didn't." She kept her eyes ahead.

'*What are you doing?*' Federov hissed.

"Right." Suzy nodded, "Hey, wanna trade?"

She held out the baggy.

"No."

"But you don't even know what's in there." Suzy pouted.

"Well, I don't need to." Mrs. Nondescript shook her head. "Go away."

"Well, how about I give you coin for them? Let's say ..."

'*What's way too much for that?*' she asked Federov, then relayed the number.

The woman stopped dead in her tracks and eyed her suspiciously. "If you want them so bad, why don't you go back to the shop and ask for them?"

"Ahem ... well, to be honest," Suzy averted her gaze and gnawed at her piercings before whispering, "that dude was looking at me all funny before you walked in. Kinda gave me the creeps."

She answered the woman's raised eyebrow with a helpless shrug and a nice "Please?!"

With a sigh, Mrs. Nondescript looked inside the box, clearly tempted, then back the way they'd come as well as ahead to where she was going. Finally, she shook her head and pressed through clenched teeth, "Sorry, can't help you. Now leave me alone if you know what's good for you."

CHAPTER TEN

RUFFA\\ THE OSA

LIGHTBEARER, *EN ROUTE TO THE KUIPER BELT*

Ruffa studied the three OSA representatives, with whom Senoxes had finally managed to arrange a holo-meeting. One woman and two men, all of them wearing somewhat similar uniforms and sour expressions on their repulsive Human faces.

As Evron introduced himself and his superior, the commander did his best to acknowledge the Humans in that pleasant manner he'd learned under Thallamon's direct observance. As usual, it felt like a needless chore. Tuvil, who stood to the side, gestured to let his superior know that their communication officer had implemented a discreet lock on the Humans' signals and was now monitoring any private channels linking them, too.

"And what do the Velorians want?" the male with a monstrously large wad of hair clinging to the skin beneath his nose asked.

"As you might have heard, the Plutonians are stirring up resentment toward our presence at the Space Gate." Ruffa did his best to sound concerned. "We're expecting them to strike at our facilities there any day."

"So what?" the woman interjected impatiently. She seemed the most unwilling to have this conversation.

"We are neighbors," Ruffa pointed out. "The fact that the DMZ is strengthening your back is the only reason the Plutonian Republic hasn't yet surrounded and squashed you. Therefore, it should be in your best interest to preserve it."

The Humans exchanged quick glances. The woman shook her head, but it was the younger man who spoke next. "Well, yes. But what would you have us do? Our military forces are spread thin as it is for exactly that reason."

"Still, we could use any vessels you might be able to provide," Ruffa said. "As you know, the Plutonians tend to arrive with overwhelming force, and having them encounter more resistance than they're expecting might drive them away without a fight."

Resounding laughter bellowed out of the hairy one.

"Good luck with that plan," the woman deadpanned. "We'll cheer you on from the sidelines."

They weren't even considering his proposal with any semblance of respect or interest. Heat flared up in Ruffa's folds. He kept it under control, holding his disdain and anger back. Who did these savages think they were?

"Why don't you ask the coreworlds for help?" the hairy one interjected. "They're your allies, *daniete*?"

Ruffa motioned for Evron to take over. These negotiations weren't going to go anywhere, so he might as well use them as a learning experience.

"Well, yes, but their ships will have to get here first," Evron implied neatly that they'd been granted help without lying outright. "You're here now. And we can offer you some of our advanced weapon technology. It would upgrade your ships to a level far beyond anything the Plutonians have. Wouldn't such an advantage more than outweigh lending us some of your assets?"

This made them consider for a moment. Ruffa glanced at the private exchange ostensibly held behind his metaphorical back.

—[Secure channel: General Nowak, Senator Sviliziz, Station Commander Janusinska]—

Senator Sviliziz: Maybe that could actually help.

Station Commander Janusinska: Don't be a fool, Andrei! They'll throw our ships and people at the Plutonians and give us zilch for it!

Gen. Nowak: Besides, the Plutonians honor their deals, as long as we play by the rules. You want to give them an excuse to pull out all the stops?

Station Commander Janusinska: And they're Human. Not like these wig *siris* with their freaky eyes. You see a soul in those? I don't.

—

The younger blinked and took a deep breath before declaring, "I'm very sorry, Mr. Evron, but I don't think we can help you."

"Not even with a bit of intel?" Evron tried to pursue the lost cause, unaware of the immense disrespect these idiotic creatures were spouting where they thought no one but them could hear. "We would gladly pay for information on troop movements and such, your sources might be able to provide."

Before the woman could flat-out decline, the younger man gestured at her, and she gave him an imperious stare.

"If you'll excuse us for a moment, please," Sviliziz said.

Evron glanced at Ruffa's passive face and nodded. "Sure."

As the images of the three Humans froze, the commander gestured for Tuvil to overlay the conversation that had replaced these negotiations so that Evron might hear the despicable comments as well.

"The Plutonians are kicking our asses," the young man argued with fervor. "We agreed to at least hear them out. An alliance with the Velorians could strengthen our position."

"Or it could destroy any chance we have at getting anything worthwhile out of high command." The hairy man crossed his massive arms. "We all know this is coming to an end. We lost ten factions within the last two years, half of them to surrender rather than defeat. Even the core can see the writing on the wall. We fought hard and honorably. The PR is ready to acknowledge this and move their focus onto the aliens. If we cut deals now, we have a chance to gain full citizenships within a decade."

"No, we should hold out just a little longer." The woman tapped her chin. "If the aliens are shopping for help, they'll surely enlist the cories."

"Pah!" The hairy man waved it off. "You didn't believe that, did you? The coreworlds are twiddling their thumbs, as usual. Even though the DMZ was never formally added to it, they don't want to break the Kuiper Contract. As long as they don't interfere with us, we don't interfere with them. Period."

"For now, yes," she agreed readily. "But if nothing else, Bogdanova's propaganda makes the EMMA look bad, and her move against the DMZ will have to be addressed in one form or another. Especially once that alien ambassador leans on the tech lobbies. We all know how dependent the inner worlds are on their toys."

Hairy man nodded his agreement, and she continued, "Once the ESF does come this way, high command will be eager to free their assets from fighting us and add our troops for good measure. We're right next door, after all. That's where and when we should lend a helping hand."

"I don't know." The younger Human frowned. "It seems so ... wrong to cast aside all we've fought for. Shouldn't we do more than look for the best way to cozy up to our enemies? Shouldn't we endure? This alliance might be the turning point toward true independence!"

"The Plutos are less of an enemy than the Velorians," the woman countered haughtily. "They're Humans! They're our cousins! Unlike the Cories, they understand the struggle out here and what it takes to survive. They care for their own. The aliens blow up their own to keep their secrets out of Humanity's hands. And the Cories would love to make us a second-rate fiefdom barely scraping by. Like they did to the Commonwealth. No, we can expect neither understanding nor equal footing from either of them. All such an alliance would provide us with is a deeper ditch to fall into."

"*Da*," the other man agreed. "If they hang us out to dry, we'll truly be alone. We're not here to assess whether this is a partnership worth forging, Dimitri; we're here to gauge how desperate the Vellies are. We did that. Now, let's pretend we're divided and will think about it. Bow out gracefully, so they don't decide to retaliate by sending some missiles our way out of spite or something. Then we'll talk about everything else in a wider circle tomorrow."

The younger one snorted. "Please, missiles we can deal with."

His student looked to Ruffa. The tips of Evron's ears appeared white from how hard he'd squeezed them against his skull. The commander shared the sentiment.

"Petulant vermin!" he cursed. "Why won't they cooperate? This makes no sense at all! They've fought the Plutonians for centuries; it's all these three should know. Why would they decide now, of all times, that it's not worth it anymore? Humans are witless idiots!"

The younger Velorian opened his mouth as if to contradict, but thought better of it as their view of the 'private' channel was replaced with the open one. A rune flashed to indicate the reconnect inquiry. Ruffa straightened and shook off all visible emotions. He would have liked to tell these pests exactly what he thought of them, but it wasn't worth it. Thallamon might still need them for something, and their willingness to throw in with the Plutonians might turn them into perfect conduits to spread misinformation down the line. After making sure Evron's face wouldn't give their knowledge away either, Ruffa touched the rune.

"Cmdr. Ruffa, Mr. Evron," the hairy Human realigned himself with his screen to face the two of them, "we're sorry, but we won't be able to help you at this time. If ...," he glanced at his younger compatriot, "should we come upon intel you might be interested in, we'll be in touch, of course."

"Of course." Ruffa nodded the Human way slowly. "And there's nothing I could do to persuade you to help?"

"We could provide money to strengthen your cause,"

Evron tried again. "You could get hardware and manpower from Neptunian space."

In the hairy one's smile, a strange blend of amusement, pity, and something else Ruffa couldn't interpret combined as the man's voice hardened away from the formulaic apology, and he said, "Listen, Son. If you have the funds, why don't you just go and get yourself some clone mercenaries to augment your clone troops?"

"The answer is no," the woman added. "Good day, Sirs."

"Good day." Ruffa's voice turned cold and clipped.

The line went dead.

Tuvil waited a few minutes before reporting, "The signal shifted. We would have to reestablish a connection to listen in further."

"That's fine, I've heard enough." His superior waved the suggestion away. "These apes won't help. They're not worth any further effort."

"Are ... you mad at them?" Evron asked as if he actually cared for their welfare.

"No. If they would rather jump into their enemies' fire than work with us, they're too dumb to be of any use in the first place." Ruffa shook out his folds.

Once they finally let this whole diplomatic dance play out and could claim this system openly, he would gladly take a task force into OSA territory. It would be poetic irony if nothing else. It would also be one of the last targets, as inconsequential as they were.

"Maybe we should consider buying some Human clones," the commander mused as he stepped out of his office to look down at the subdued bustle on the *Lightbearer*'s bridge. "Seeing as how the Plutonians will try to outnumber us, it might be a consideration worth pondering."

"Aren't Human clones very low quality?" Evron asked as he followed in his wake. "Hardly more intelligent than animals?"

"They are. But we're not looking for intelligence when swarming the enemy with bodies." Ruffa let the idea ripen in his head as he thought it through aloud, "Plutonians like to board enemy vessels and installations. Maybe we should make a point of emulating that tactic. They won't expect that."

"I see. But why buy them? Couldn't we produce such low-quality clones ourselves? And much faster?"

"We're already running all the *Lightbearer*'s cloning facilities at maximum capacity." The commander did some quick calculations. "Even with optimal biomass usage, we likely won't be able to match the Plutonians' numbers in time. And it will behoove us to preserve our own troops for more important tasks."

Another idea came to mind. Human cloning was a messy, unsophisticated business. Getting him close and personal with it might just shift Evron's perspective to see the ugliness of Human existence more clearly.

"Yes." The commander refolded his ears to underscore the finality of his decision, as he declared, "Evron, you're in charge of this. Tuvil will assist you with the research and provide the necessary funds. Find us as many Human clones as you can, preferably to be picked up along the way or in the border region close to the DMZ. Ensure the sellers don't realize it's us making the purchase. Thallamon has established an extensive network of Human shell corporations for precisely such purposes. Since you'll invariably deal with criminals, they should be accustomed to identity-concealing protocols and not give them much thought. Still, be aware of the current prices and drive a hard bargain. Everything else might attract suspicion."

His student looked at him with wide eyes and drooping folds.

"You'll do fine." Ruffa gave him a small smile. "Consider it a fun side project."

CHAPTER ELEVEN

THEA\\ THE ENEMY

WHEN GASIN REMINDED HER OF THE APPOINTMENT, Thea was back to fuming in an instant. Too bad, really. After punching a sandbag until her knuckles, knees, and shins were bloody, sleeping it off and redoing the whole thing time and time again, today, she'd almost felt fine for an hour or two. Only for the blasted computer system to rain on her parade.

"You have an appointment with Col. Federov in half an hour concerning your new posting," the uncaring synthesized voice informed.

Was it just her, or had even high-and-mighty Eve Baileywick caved in and made her pet-AI sound like a broken computer module from 200 years ago? To satisfy the Plutonians, of course. Whatever it took to please those abrasive, idiotic technophobes!

And Federov ... that slimy, stone-cold, overbearing son of a diseased Terran whore! He was the center of it all. The reason her whole life had gone down the drain. Things had been hard enough before he'd appeared out of nowhere with his damn circus flyers and whisked Suzy and Jamaal away to that Velorian ship! Then he'd had her little brother beaten bloody, stunned her unsuspecting lover, and thrown them both in jail. He'd made her man look like a pussy and somehow gotten the admiral not only to keep him and his monkeys on the ship but also to place him at the top of the food chain. And then he'd taken Wire and Xin too, had thrown them in some torture crucible for fun. He'd made Tank his enforcer and got her man's thoughts all jumbled. To the point where Tank had ended their relationship and accepted a screwy Venusian second in Thea's stead!

And now it was to be her turn. Whatever shitty posting Federov had planned for her, it would surely be miserable. She already was a laughingstock. Now he would make her a doormat, too. The lowest of the low. He'd surely make her disappear in some insignificant auxiliary assignment or whatever.

"No," Thea murmured as she rolled out of bed and jerked up her pants. "You're not gonna get rid of me that easily!"

She would show him. She would make him regret that he'd ever set foot on this ship and messed with her unit and her life.

With an angry motion, Thea slapped a magazine into her sidearm and chambered a round.

He would so fucking damn regret it!

As she slid the piece into the back of her waistband and pulled her shirt over it, burning fury was replaced by cold certainty. After she'd gone in, one of them was not gonna leave that nice, roomy office Baileybitch had provided him with. And it wouldn't be her.

"Come in."

The female voice was the first clue that something was terribly wrong. When Thea entered the antechamber to Federov's office, Vestergaard just stepped into the same room using the inner door. Behind the major, the office lights blinked out as the door swooshed closed.

Fuck. What was going on?

"Where's Col. Federov?" Thea asked, sudden doubt stiffening her stance and pushing her voice into a slightly higher register.

The gal with the horrendous facial burn looked up from a dataslide to study the other, saying, "He's on holiday. I'm his substitute for a day or two."

"Oh."

Shit, what to do now? Even though she was ugly as sin, this Plutonian hadn't done Thea any harm, right?

Vestergaard gestured at a samovar sitting on a refreshment table as she stepped closer. "Why don't you make yourself comfortable? Have a cup of tea on the colonel."

Right, okay ... This would give her a chance to turn her face away from the prying eyes of the other woman while she took a moment to think this through. Just as Thea bent down to reach for one of the metallic mugs, a face-slapping alarm ran through her. What if Vestergaard saw the bulge of—

The all-too-familiar *click* of a safety being switched off cut her thought short and ramped up her panic.

"No sudden moves." Vestergaard's voice had turned cold. "Pull out that gun with two fingers and deposit it on the ground. You should know the drill, *daniete*?"

Luna, this was bad. What if they threw her in the brig now? Or Facial Burns called in backup to have Thea roughed up as well? Maybe she could surprise—

"You have a sniper pointing an unknown firearm at your head from a distance of about 127 cm. Are you sure you want to follow that train of thought, Corporal? Or are you just desperate to have me redecorate that wall over there with your brains?"

Thea swallowed dryly and pulled out her gun with two fingers before lowering it to the ground at a snail's pace. Vestergaard never moved, didn't even make a sound except for her steady breathing. And even that seemed slowed down considerably.

"Good. Now turn around and kick it over."

As the Spartan followed the command, she whispered, "How did you know?"

"I'm a sniper, Corporal. It's my job to read a person's intentions right off their body and have them pegged as armed or unarmed within three heartbeats. If I don't, my team might be dead faster than you can say 'Oops.'"

Instead of bending down to collect Thea's gun, Facial Burns had the door to the inner office open and kicked the piece deftly inside without even looking. The door closed again. With a slight motion of her chin, Vestergaard indicated a chair next to the refreshment table. She ordered, "Sit and tell me: what were your intentions here, exactly?"

"I ... I thought I could surprise him." Thea sat down, put her hands in her lap, and looked away. "Give your precious colonel a piece of my mind. Karma. Always comes back around, you know?"

"Karma?" The major lifted her good eyebrow. Then she laughed. "*Da*, I'm sure he knows quite a few ladies with that name. Might be with one right now. But what in the void makes you think you could have surprised him of all people? He's the one who taught me to be aware of my surroundings."

She walked over to grab the second chair and pull it to where she'd been standing—well out of reach. "Computer, show her that simulation Col. Federov and the infiltrators did for fun three days ago."

A vid popped up in front of Thea. Federov was being stalked by six shadowy figures. They couldn't fool him. It was a massacre. Didn't even take him a minute to dispatch them all. A cold shiver ran down the Spartan's spine.

"Oh, and if you'd managed it by some miracle, you would have been lucky if I, one of my snipers, or one of the infiltrators found you first." Vestergaard turned the chair so the back faced Thea, then slipped onto it the wrong way around, her gun now loosely in her hand. Would still get her if she jumped up. "If we'd felt charitable, that is. The others might not have been so quick about it."

Another shudder. Damn, this had really been an awful idea. Maybe it was a good thing that Federov wasn't here ... But, Luna, what would Vestergaard do with her now?

The Plutonian's voice softened just a tad, her eyes darting to Thea's lap as she demanded, "Show me those hands."

Refusal seemed futile, even though shame was now the largest part of Thea's internal world. Her thighs tightened briefly to squeeze them in, but then she breathed out and lifted her hands. Facial Burns studied the broken, slightly mended, and rebroken skin for a handful of heartbeats before she decided, "Listen, you didn't actually do anything yet, and I've sent my superior away so he could clear his mind, not to fill it with more issues once he returned. So I'm going to make an exception here and not report you."

Thea looked up to find a raised index finger pointed her way. "But. Should you ever try to hurt my friend for real, and by some miracle survive it, I will be the one who finds you first. And I won't be feeling charitable. Quite the opposite. Do we understand each other?"

"Y-yes, Ma'am."

"Good. Now, I'd advise you to sit down with someone who's good at talking about shit like this to get your head back on straight. I'm not that person. You might want to try Barbie. She's an expert on feelings and fucking and all the ways those are supposed to work together or not. You know," Vestergaard gestured vaguely, "talk whore to whoremonger or whatever. She should be in one bar or the other. Then, when you're feeling better, but at the latest two days from now, report to your new superior. The details are on the slide. You can claim your sidearm a week from now at the provost's office. Dismissed."

Federov's second pointed at the table. Heat raced up Thea's neck all the way to her hairline.

Whore to whoremonger ... right. Luna, this was so embarrassing ...

"So, what shitty, dirty duty has he given me?" She slowly stood up and grabbed the slide to have a look.

What the ... that couldn't be right, could it?

Thea froze, too jaded to hope it was real. "Is ... is this a joke?"

"No." Vestergaard stood and returned the chair. "Col. Federov was of the opinion that you might not be treated fairly and with respect should he assign you to a Plutonian squad, and since your ex was so eager to get rid of you, he thought that this assignment might serve your qualifications and interests best while keeping you out of Thompson's way. So he pulled a few strings."

Her whole world shifted once more as Thea stared at the dataslide again, at the two words that defined, maybe, the best possible future she could have dared to wish for right now.

"Medical Assistant," it said. "Report to Dr. LaMont regarding further instructions."

"Thank you." A single tear ran down Thea's face.

Maybe it was relief. Maybe it was just the aftereffect of the panic she'd felt only minutes ago. Perhaps it was even hope. She wouldn't have to choose between a crappy day-to-day existence among people who hated her, who called her a whore to her face, and leaving her little brother to fend for himself in some other, alien solar system.

"Don't thank me," the major said with an audible smirk. "Thank karma."

CHAPTER TWELVE

SUZY\SERGEY\\ INTERESTING OBSERVATIONS

While she'd been on her little errand, Federov had changed bases. As Suzy entered the backroom of a tiny bar on the opposite side of the plaza, she found the man nursing a cup of tea while doing something in AR, which she couldn't see.

A tropical volcano theme prevailed, with dark sand crackling underfoot, actual palms thriving under bright yellow lights, and red-glowing cracks in the floor and walls. Given the dark tan the waitresses in their minuscule bikinis sported, the ceiling lamps probably emitted a healthy dose of UV light.

"Hey, I still had food at that restaurant!" she complained as she slumped down opposite her warden at the faux-wood table.

Shit, was it hot in here ...

"And you still do." He shoved over a thermo bowl. She hadn't seen it sitting behind the oversized coconuts holding spices and cutlery.

For a whole minute, he didn't even look at her.

Finally, Suzy threw the paper bag onto the tiny tabletop, saying, "Here, I brought you a cinnabun."

He ignored it, instead snapping, "I told you to be inconspicuous!"

The giddy lightheadedness slowly evaporated like fog in sunlight. Still, unwilling to be cowed, she retorted, "I'm a tipsy foreigner with purple hair and eyes. My trying to be inconspicuous would be suspicious as fuck! Besides, you could have called around to see if one of your infiltrators is on leave right now. You didn't have to send me."

Suddenly, a smile stretched his lips. "Void, you're amazingly confrontational when under the influence. I'll have to remember that."

Ah, shit. A cold hand ran down her spine.

Fuck, she would regret this so hard later ...

"Don't fret; I like it," he accepted the bag and started to nibble at the remaining pastry, "as long as you keep that attitude to personal outings."

"Yes, Sir," she murmured.

"Sergey," he corrected. "While we're enjoying ourselves and our free time, call me Sergey."

Was he for real? Or, more to the point, did he really have an agreeable side, or was her damn mouth just digging the deepest fucking hole she'd ever found herself in? ... Also, who would enjoy this spy shit they were just doing?

When he didn't recall his offer, she finally returned, "Suzy. I'm ... Suzy."

"Well then, Suzy, enlighten me. What do you think is going on?"

She'd already thought about it on the way over and felt almost eager to share her speculations.

"It's a sort of robbery, isn't it? The shops are run by the

same owner, right? They basically sell the same stuff. The second one just has a few extra aisles holding nicer wares. So, the ration slips, which should guarantee an affordable basic living for these people, are used to stock the shops. The owner gets full price by selling shit no one wants over and over, while the people who should get their food for basic fare are somehow coerced into reselling it at a bad price. They probably go to another, completely different shop after this for their food. I mean, they're obviously not in it for themselves or by choice. The woman I talked to was tempted to sell me her crap cookies but was too afraid to do it, right?"

"Right," he said. "That was very dumb of you, by the way. Very unprofessional."

"Well, I'm not a trained spy! I'm not a trained anything. All of this," she gestured, "is out of my depth, damn it!"

He just raised an eyebrow in time with his mug.

"Anyways, if I were in those people's shoes, I wouldn't want to spend my remaining money on these thieving assholes as well, right? So I would go somewhere else for my actual purchases."

Federov—No, *Sergey*—nodded encouragingly.

"And the owner gets paid a certain amount per ration slip when turning them in?!" she continued. "By the state?"

"*Da*." He smiled. "You got it."

"But how would they coerce these people? I mean, these are free citizens, right? They don't have to do it."

And there it was again, that glaring naïveté. And just when Sergey had been so positively surprised at the girl's understanding. But before he could chide her, she glanced aside.

Realization and the echo of pain weathered long ago crossed her features as she murmured, "Oh. I see. They probably have in-your-face arguments ..."

"Yeah."

"That's so mean." The girl observed his reaction.

Was she trying to probe *him* now?

Interesting.

"Does it make you mad? I mean, you're out there fighting to keep the community safe, and then there are these assholes taking advantage of it, bleeding it for their benefit. When they're stealing from the state, they're stealing from everyone, not just their direct targets, right?"

He felt like laughing. Instead, he leaned back and crossed his arms.

"You have to have full Plutonian citizenship to get issued these ration credits," he explained. "Which means all those civies did their Basic 3. Unless they all shared horrendously bad instructors, they learned to be proficient in hand-to-hand and to handle knives, guns, and whatnot. They should be perfectly able to defend themselves. They could join forces. They could leave this place and start anew. But they don't. Tell me ... those miners you worked with. You think they would have accepted that kind of exploitation?"

When she merely shook her head, he continued, "This isn't about the state or the community. This is about a few meek sheep who won't defend themselves. So, no, it doesn't bother me. And you shouldn't let it bother you either. Emotions make for bad decisions."

Suzy Magecraft covered up what she obviously experienced as a misstep on her part with a delicate cough, saying, "So you think we should all just ... clamp it down?"

"Only if you want it to explode later." He shrugged.

"Emotions have their place; they're important indicators. You can harness them," he leaned forward to give his words more impact, "but you should never, ever let them take control of you and your decisions. There's a reason you have such a nice, well-developed prefrontal cortex, and it's not to make your forehead look pretty."

Heat rushed up her neck and into her cheeks at the rebuke, but she kept her eyes downcast and held her tongue. This time around, the girl didn't seem as enthusiastic about eating and only turned the thermo bowl around in her hands for a few minutes, never opening it.

Finally, she asked, "So, what do we do about it? Call the provosts?"

As this was a federal crime, it would fall squarely within the station provosts' jurisdiction. No need to bother station security. Not that the girl would appreciate the distinction ... or even care about it.

"Not that simple, I'm afraid." He thought back to the nicer shop. That one even sported a few shelves holding luxury items. Neat stuff. "Do you think none of the victims ever tried that?"

Suzy looked up sharply. "You're saying the provosts are in on it?"

"It stands to reason that at least the one in charge of this section or that particular brand of crime has been paid off to ignore what's going on." Sergey opened the notes Diaz had provided him with in his AR vision and tried to discern who that would be.

Hmm. Wasn't McEntire after all.

"Could still be McEntire. He has final say on everything." Diaz gestured at Magecraft's thermo bowl. "Are you still eating that?"

She shook her head and pushed it over.

"But it's unlikely," Sergey pointed out. "Then the provost bringing it to his attention should have become suspicious and ratted him out."

"Reported him," the provost corrected as he set aside his faceshield and dug in. "Wrongdoers rat each other out. But yeah, I concur."

"Right." Sergey smiled at the distinction. "So, could you go to McEntire and make him raid the shops?"

Diaz stopped midspoon to consider. Finally, he nodded.

"Probably." He quickly gulped down the rest of the girl's stew. In response to his superior's questioning gaze, he explained, "Sorry, haven't eaten in two days."

Up until now, Magecraft had silently followed the exchange, except for answering direct questions. Now she asked, "Mars...men! Why?"

Diaz shrugged. "I was busy."

"And where are your troopers?" Sergey took back control of the discussion.

"You mean my security detail?" An amused twinkle glimmered in the other man's dark eyes. "Securing everyone else's whereabouts, so I can move unhindered, of course."

"I see," the colonel said. "Why the hesitation before? About McEntire."

Their provost leaned back with a deep exhale. "Because I have a very good idea of how all of this is going by the provost major. McEntire is due to retire in another year. He's already running a cushy number, lets his second do much of the day-to-day. Also stopped hitting the pavement a good while back. The fact that he was the first responder on," Diaz's dark eyes darted to the witch briefly, "that other crime scene seems to have been a mere coincidence."

"Interesting," Sergey mused, "but not conclusive. Could he be grooming the next rotten apple?"

Diaz studied his superior for a long moment before he acknowledged the hidden probing with a minuscule smirk and responded, "Greasing two provosts seems a bit excessive for such a small operation. Last I heard, they're rather expensive. No, I suspect McEntire prefers to be blissfully unaware."

"As long as nothing too drastic is going down in his department?" Sergey added.

Naddi's soon-to-be second nodded curtly. "Exactly."

Common ground established, the colonel returned the nod. He waited for a few heartbeats and leaned in to indicate he was shifting topics before declaring, "Well, in that case, I guess we'll have to wake dear old McEntire from his magical slumber. Your boss is back from holiday; want me to call her in to do the kissing?"

"Better not." A slight wince distorted Diaz's features for a second. "She'll be mightily annoyed at that. I'll do it. Just give me a few hours to collect some incriminating vid footage and transaction figures."

"You have access to all that?"

The other man rubbed the armor over his right thigh. "McEntire is happily shoveling all the investigatory work into my lap. Probably wants me to be the asshole calling IA."

"Or maybe," Sergey waited out the waitress setting down the drinks he'd ordered before continuing, "he's honestly hoping we're wrong and that you won't find anything after all."

"Right." Diaz snorted as he raised his mocktail. "To honest people making honest mistakes."

Sergey held his gaze. "To good provosts doing a good job."

"Ahem, cheers?" Magecraft added her glass to theirs, and they all drank in unison.

CHAPTER THIRTEEN

RIVERS\\ SENSIBLE ADVICE

Riv fell into bed exhausted and raw. Not bodily, mind you, but if her brain were able to display muscle soreness, it would burn like a bloody bitch right now. Ever since Baileywick had taken over and doubled the sensor team's training two days ago, coming up with increasingly elaborate challenges to be solved in ever-shorter timespans, things had started to go downhill. Fast.

The doorbell rang just as she was dozing off.

"Hm?" she called.

"Riv, are you there?"

The scientist blinked open one uncooperative eyelid. "Fee? What are you—"

She glanced at her BCI clock.

AH, FUCK!

Panic jolted through her. She'd been asleep for three damn hours! And she hadn't even realized it!

"Come in!" she yelped.

The door opened and Fee strolled in, all dolled up ... well, for her standards, that was. No doctor's coat or scrubs, her hair kinda styled into something almost resembling a hairdo, and there was even a hint of eyeliner and some subtly applied powder prettying up her face.

"So sorry," Riv mumbled as she rolled her unresponsive body out of bed. "I just closed my eyes for a second, and—"

Fee crossed her arms. "You forgot!"

"No!" Riv lied as she slid into her boots. "No, I didn't!"

Damn, why hadn't she cued an alarm for this?

Fee gave her that look.

"Okay, fine, I did!" Riv confessed with a sigh. "Baileywick is riding us hard, okay? I only just got in. I'm trashed. Maybe we could reschedule?"

Again, that look. Right, she'd really pushed this off for a while now.

"Okay, forget it, I'm fine!" With jerky motions, she tightened her boots and jumped to her feet.

Fast ... that had been too fast ...

Riv fought off the slight vertigo and straightened, covering it with a broad smile. "Let's go!"

"Don't you want to ..." Fee gestured up and down the other woman's slightly rumpled attire.

"And make you wait?" The younger one pulled at her jacket and trousers to straighten out the smart cloth as best as she could. "No way! Besides, I'm starving!"

They made their way to *The Beak* in a mixture of relaxed silence and small talk. It didn't really matter what they talked about. This was just about spending time together.

"So," Fee said with a frown as they entered the bar. "You're not looking well. What happened?"

"It's fine." Riv waved it off. "It's just all these simulations. They seem pointless. I mean, we're not getting any better."

"And why's that?" her friend inquired as she led them away from the gaming tables to the right-side windows.

With no entertainment playing on the empty stage and few patrons overall, a peaceful air of murmuring sociability hung in the air.

"Because we're already doing a great job!" The scientist slid onto the bench in an unoccupied booth and called up the AR menu.

"Are you now?" Fee slipped in opposite. "Hey, isn't that your new teammate over there?"

The younger one looked up and glanced over to where her opposite had indicated. "Yeah, that's Montoya. She's okay. But, I swear, most days, she appears more like a robot than Eve!"

"So you like her or you don't?" Fee's attempt at a covert glance was hilarious.

"You know, that spy gaze doesn't work when the thing you're holding up to your face is mostly translucent, aye?" Riv pointed out with an involuntary grin.

Still, she knew Fee would poke her about it until receiving a satisfying answer, so she confessed, "I'm not sure, actually. First, I thought she was a bitch. Then she was all nice and forgiving, and I thought she might be baiting me for some reason. But nothing ever happened. She does know what she's doing, and she works seamlessly with her team. I just don't fit into their structure. I'm not sure how to be part of it."

Fee cocked her head. "Because you're the lone genius?"

Yeah, she knew Riv too well ... even with all that time spent apart, some things never changed.

"I'm just not good with people." Riv shrugged and placed her order. "Not in the long run, anyway. And I'm not a genius, I'm just good at regurgitating facts."

Fee placed her chin on her hands. "Could have fooled me."

"Ha. Ha." Riv wasn't in the mood for a psych eval. "Besides, it doesn't matter. We're getting along well enough."

"You mean, you're working in parallel instead of hand in hand?"

"Well, yeah, kinda ... But it works, that's what counts, right? So, how's Xin doing?"

"You're changing the subject." The doctor waved the menu out of existence and leaned in. "Listen. You're one of the most intelligent people I know, but you're behaving like a giant dummy right now. You know, avoiding the issue won't end well. He's either gonna come up with some devious plan to break you down and build you back up with your head on straight, or he's gonna shove you off his bridge. The captain can't afford to have his deal with the Plutonians rattled by one uncooperative cog in the machine. If you don't learn to play with your team ..."

She let it hang there. Riv shook her head. "He can't do that. He won't."

"Sure he can!" Fee's eyes widened for emphasis. "And why wouldn't he? You're just some inexperienced stranger, a mule-headed youngster threatening the well-being of his crew. You know what counts more than anything in that equation."

Dryness conquered the 'inexperienced stranger's' mouth. This was so frustrating. This whole situation. It was all such a mess! Oh, how she yearned for those easier times back when. Just for a second, though. Then she pushed those dumb, boring thoughts out of her mind. Let them go with a sigh.

Shit, Fee was right.

"Besides," the older woman's voice lowered, "Why is this so hard for you? You have no problem ensnaring all these guys for your personal pleasure. So don't you dare argue that you're a social imbecile."

"That's different." Riv crossed her arms.

"How? You want the same thing and agree on some basic rules to get there, right? How isn't that exactly what you should be doing with Montoya and her team?"

"Well ..." Riv didn't actually have any good counter-arguments.

Didn't matter, since Fee wasn't finished. "Also, how did you get where you are now? How did you gain your knowledge? Just by reading and memorization? All on your own? Or did you maybe have a few good teachers and mentors along the way?"

"Of course I had."

Damn, she knew where her friend was going with this.

Ah, fuck ...

"And can you discover anything worthwhile in any field, if you're convinced that you already know everything?" Fee raised an eyebrow.

"No," Riv answered dutifully.

"Well then." Fee gestured over to where Montoya sat. "There's your mentor. Go and learn what she has to teach you."

"But—"

"No 'but'. The time for buts has passed. As the older one, I'm putting my foot down. Because I care and I don't want the captain to crush you beneath his! Now, I'll tell you about Xin when you've proven to me that you can swallow your pride and be a team player," the doctor said, standing up. "So go and make a connection. Lay down some ground rules and ascertain what you can add to the equation. I'll be at the bar."

After five minutes of procrastination stewing, Riv took a deep breath and rose as well.

ARGH!

It was such a bother whenever Fee spoke sense and left her in a bind like this.

CHAPTER FOURTEEN

SUZY\\ QUESTIONABLE ETHICS

"Let's head out too!" Federov waved for the waitress as soon as Diaz had left.

"What?" Suzy blinked. "Why?"

"So you get to see some more interesting places." That glittering in the colonel's eyes made a return. "I did promise to show you how to party right."

He'd also said he might show her a brothel or two...

Ah, Marsdust, why couldn't he just have allowed her to stay aboard the shuttle with the others? Fuck, this night got more and more ... just ... plain weird!

"Don't look so glum, Suzy." He brushed down his uniform, even though there were no crumbs or anything on it. More like a reflexive gesture, maybe. "It'll be fun!"

Right, fun ...

With a sigh, Suzy paid her part of the bill and followed Federov out. A relaxed, yet purposeful march down the length of the square, down a promenade, then looping back down another, with a few dips and glances inside some back alleys and dead ends, and down another corridor, they finally found their way out of the section.

"Did we get lost, or did you just case that second shop?" she dared to ask when they finally settled into an elevator.

Federov merely smiled at that as he asked, "So, what do you like better? Women or men?"

She got the not-so-hidden hint and pleaded, "Can't we just go have some more drinks and call it a night? I'll even promise to get hammered, and—"

He gave her that look.

"Okay, listen," she rubbed the light throbbing at her temple, and words suddenly rushed out of her, "I've just had a one-night-stand, so I really don't need or want this. If you do, I'll just go back to the shuttle and give you your space, okay? But this is totally weird, and I'm not going to visit a voidforsaken brothel with my warden!"

For a dreadful moment, silence fell. Then a hearty belly laugh filled the small space, and the man's hand smacked down on her shoulder.

"Actually," he confessed once he found enough air to do so, "I was planning on leaving you there, so you could enjoy yourself while I broke into the shop. But now I think it would be much more fun to have you tag along."

She blinked. "Wait, what?"

The elevator paused between levels as Federov used his leverage on her shoulder to turn her toward him. All jokes and jabs set aside, his expression stripped down to a core of determination and fun expectation, he asked, "Tell me, Suzy Magecraft, do you actually want to get back to the shuttle and snore away a few hours, or do you want to come with me and have some fun?"

Fuck, did she? This was one of those moments, right? If she helped him out here, he might like her more. This might help her in the future. But she might also get into trouble big time ... Ah, Marsdust, she was already a war criminal!

What could a bit of petty breaking and entering add to that? Besides, Federov didn't seem like the type to get caught. And even if he was, he could always claim to be investigating, right? Were they still investigating? Hadn't Diaz taken over that task?

"Depends." Suzy narrowed her eyes. "Why do you want to break into that store again?"

"To steal the good stuff."

What?

Before she could mouth the question, the elevator started back up. It pinged open on the 'main fun-deck' as Chávez had called it. Federov didn't move.

"You have a translation program installed locally, so you can read Plutonian script?" he asked.

"Yeah, sure." She felt strangely unresponsive. Had he just said what she'd heard him say?

"Good. Then disconnect your BCI from the station's matrix now. Many people will do that right here, so they can't be traced while enjoying themselves."

'Enjoying themselves' ...

"Is ... Is that what this is for you? Fun?" She hardly noticed the doors closing back up. "People are being robbed systematically, and you want to join in?"

His eyes narrowed dangerously, and his tone turned frosty cold. From one moment to the next, the nice, congenial guy coaxing her into drinking more than was good for her, evaporated, and the grim reaper spoke, "I'm not joining anyone, Suzy. We're stopping this crime. The records of your observations, bolstered by whatever Diaz manages to retrieve, are more than enough to shut this operation down for good. What I'm going to take has already been stolen. I'm merely rerouting some of it. To put it to good use. If we leave it and they get raided tomorrow, it'll only be placed into evidence."

"But, won't it be redistributed to those people who got screwed over?" She felt a bit of weakness rushing to her knees. Magic begged to kick the weakness aside and take over. To flame up in her hands and electrify this sudden danger out of existence. She pushed it back. If set free, those unbridled emotions would do her more harm than good. At least in the long run. At least that he'd gotten right.

"No. They have no claim to luxury goods, no matter how much they might appreciate the compensation." The ever-present gloom painted an almost demonic edge on his face. "I know people who do. Our people."

"Right ..." *Shit, this was so wrong.* "And if it impacts the raid? What if the provosts show up, only to find the place ransacked and decide someone might have planted the evidence?"

"That's why we'll stay away from the front room and only go after the storage room in the back. The logs will show it's not been disturbed." He was almost blasé about it. His voice changed back to a beacon meant to lure her in, "Besides, the other evidence will probably be enough in any case. There's always a matrix trail."

"You've figured it all out, haven't you?" She shook her head. With the alcohol almost gone from her system, everything came back into focus with painful intensity, "While I pranced around these shops, you made plans to rob them. You had me risk my neck to get you this evidence just so you could make a profit off someone else's crime?! I mean—What the fuck?"

"Whatever gave you the impression I might be some sort of paladin?" he asked.

"And what about me?" A new fear raced through her bones. "And Jamaal, and Xin? What are you planning to get out of *our* crimes now that you've got us under your thumb?"

"Now wait a min—" he started, but she cut him off.

"You've been pretty determined to get me drunk! Pretty good at it, too. So I gotta wonder, what you really want to drag me into that brothel for?" She crossed her arms. By now, her fists weren't enough to stop the purple lightning. Her armpits didn't fare much better.

"Stop!" he ordered, his eyes intense, filled with a sudden fire threatening to burn as bright as her magic. "Before you cross a line you'll regret crossing. I might have done a lot of things you'd consider deplorable, but I've never laid a hand on a woman without her consent, and I never will! And if I didn't understand where you're coming from," he stepped closer, "I would consider corporal punishment for this lack of respect right now."

"I just spent several days exploding rock with my mind." She straightened. "Are you sure you could take me?"

He didn't reply. He didn't need to. His eyes narrowed, and in her head, his voice echoed back from the past.

"I'm not afraid of magic," it said.

Right. The image of the Velorian mage crushed beneath his feet, the taste of blood, the feel of it on her skin, made her almost vomit. Her neck remembered the hurt of that taser hidden in his right hand. And she also remembered how easily he'd decked Rupert. Fucking Rupert!

Okay, Girl, calm down ...

Escalation of this situation would mean a very bad outcome, no matter who won. But she was done cowering. She was done tucking her tail. Whatever his motives were, however wrong her reading of the situation might have been, if she rolled over now like a little spineless loser, she would only open the door to exploitation. Maybe not exploitation of a sexual nature, but he would continue ordering her around and use her as his personal gofer.

Suzy took a deep, shuddering breath and stepped back. One slow, clearly defined single step. Head held high, she guided her hands to her sides and reined her magic back in. "If I've misjudged you just now, I'm sorry." She did her best to keep her voice calm and level. "Having said that, and knowing that I'm not aware of all Plutonian laws and rules, I'm rather certain that all of this," she gestured between them and at the elevator, "a warden ordering his charge to accompany him, threatening to make her go to a red light district, while actually getting her drunk, and in that frame of mind send her to spy on what you had clearly pegged as a crime in progress—without any backup, I might add—only to then get her involved in another crime, is all very much exploding your authority over me. You're supposed to ensure I'm not getting into more trouble, right? To keep me on the right side of the law?"

Something shifted in his stance. A small seed of doubt, hopefully.

Emboldened by not being cut off again, she continued, in a soft, almost imploring voice, "You protected me when Rupert crossed the line from teacher to bully. His magic, I can at least try to counter. Your authority, I can't. And I'm not dumb enough to think Garin would choose my side over yours. So, please, don't be a bully, Colonel."

Federov let that sink in. For a devastatingly long five seconds, the rings in his augmetic eye were the only thing moving about him. Then the thin line of his lips sloped into a small smile. An echo of self-deprecation ran over his features so quickly, she might have imagined it.

In any case, he nodded and said, "I accept your apology. And I acknowledge that I might have overstepped the boundaries of my authority. Truth is, I've never been a warden before, and I didn't plan on wielding this power over you on this trip. All I wanted was a day off. Taking you along was a whimsical excuse, and I thought I might as well get to know you better. Like I would do with a subordinate. But, of course, it's not that simple, is it?"

"No, I guess it's not."

"To be honest, I never planned on anyone wielding this power over you." His stance softened somewhat. "I couldn't let what you and Robbins did on that Velorian ship stand, but I wasn't planning on getting you convicted of anything. I only acted to save face in front of my troops. That I took you out quickly wasn't just a defense against your magic. That was me going light on you. If I hadn't ..."

"Your people would have beaten me senseless just like they did Jamaal," she realized, her mind flashing back to the miners almost lynching them. "That's justice for you?"

"It's the unofficial way, and we would have been perfectly satisfied, but then Thompson marched in and made everything complicated. What's one idiot splitcock more or less? None of my people would have cared. But with Thompson yanking my chain and the admiral storming in, I couldn't turn a blind eye to your crime anymore."

He stopped and pressed his lips into a tight line.

"You really didn't want all this." She bit her lip. A lump had formed in her throat. Curious feelings she hadn't even realized were there, now bunched together into a dizzying soup of conflicting emotions.

"No, I didn't. And I just want you to know that." He took a deep breath. "I'm sorry you were caught up in this."

She swallowed. A single, unasked-for tear flitted down her cheek. Suzy brushed it away quickly and said, "Thank you. For telling me, I mean. I accept your apology."

Thankfully, he ignored the tear and let her have a minute.

"Well, I did get to know you better," he backtracked their conversation, "and I like the look a fully erect spine has on you."

"Thanks." A short snort, then she smiled back, saying, "Listen, I just ... I need clearer rules. If this is a private trip, if we're sharing drinks on a first-name basis, and maybe even get into trouble, then I'm not your ward right now, right? I'm a sort of equal. In my book, that means you give me all the information *before* you ask me to commit a crime ... or solve one."

"What you want is to be respected." He nodded. "I understand and concur. It has never been and never will be my intention to belittle or take advantage of you or your situation. All of today's confusion seems to be caused by my not noticing that you share the same misunderstanding about my original troops and me that almost every one of you coreworlders seems to have."

Suzy just stared at him. Was he actually opening up? Did she dare to ask for more?

"What misunderstanding do you mean?"

For the next ten seconds, he clearly considered his response. Finally, he murmured, "Listen, if you really want to know, then follow me. Should you choose to stay ignorant and ... innocent, then return to the shuttle and do whatever you want. This is neither an attempt at blackmail nor exacting a price, but it's also my day off, and I choose not to spend it standing around in an elevator cabin discussing life and shit."

With that, he opened the elevator doors and marched out into the 'fun quarter'.

Suzy took a deep breath. Her fists clenched and unclenched almost on their own as she considered her options.

... *Ah, fuck!*

CHAPTER FIFTEEN

SUZY\\ WHAT'S AN S-PLATOON?

THEY SETTLED DOWN IN A DIMLY LIT BOOTH INSIDE THE most luxurious strip club the witch had ever seen. After ordering and receiving a whole bottle of top-shelf vodka—which he paid for with four Plutonian ration coins—from a beautiful middle-aged waitress in a plain yet classy outfit, Federov asked the woman for privacy until further notice.

He poured them both a good measure, but didn't raise his glass. Instead, he looked at Suzy, saying, "You don't need to drink. I just ordered this for propriety's sake. So, what do you know about me and my original platoon?"

Was the colonel already back to stone-cold business?

Suzy took her eyes off the half-naked girl performing a gravity-defying pole dance on the nearby stage to study his face. Hey, he was cheating! While his face and natural eye were focused on her, his artificial one clearly observed the strippers ... what an unfair advantage.

"For about four years, you were the commanding officer of the 'Iron Wings'," she said, "a void walker platoon from the Second Plutonian Regiment. The Second Regiment itself was one of the founding—"

"Stop," he interrupted. "You have clearly read the notes we made available. But I didn't ask you to recite history or the contents of my file. I asked what you know. Here's a hint: we're talking about an S-platoon."

She frowned. What did he want to hear? After almost a minute of contemplation, she still couldn't come up with anything that felt like the correct answer.

"Well," she finally thought aloud, "from what I can remember, the 'S' stands for 'specialists' or simply 'special.' So I guess that means you're all really good at your jobs, right? ... I'm sorry, I really haven't had time to familiarize myself with the intricacies of the Plutonian military."

"Please, by the Void, stop apologizing for everything!" he moaned. "I know your schedule and responsibilities, and that you don't have time to take a deep dive into organizational charts that don't include you. I've asked this question to point out one of your blind spots. See, officially, you are correct. S-platoons are supposed to be filled with the best. Unofficially, a smart and seasoned leader like General Phoenix knows to keep the good ones with the normies so they can inspire them to get better. In that case, the S-platoons get filled with what we call 'bad apples'."

Before Suzy could voice the question, he clarified.

"By that, I don't mean rotten to the core. I mean rogues and those who are smart enough to know how the system works and exploit it. Cunning enough to commit even serious crimes without being observed. Are you starting to get where I'm going with this?"

Suzy licked her lips as she started to frame her whole situation from this new angle.

"Wait, you mean those who can't be caught and convicted, even though everyone knows what they've done? You're all pooled together to minimize your chances of spoiling the others. That's why you have so many provosts attached. Fuck."

When he nodded, she grabbed her glass and downed its contents in a single gulp.

Federov finally focused both his eyes on her, calmly raising his glass and saying, "*Nastrovje*," before downing his own drink.

He took his time refilling their glasses, maybe to give her the opportunity to collect her thoughts.

"But that ain't all?" she asked.

"No." He set the bottle aside calmly. "Our kind of S-platoons tend to get the really nasty and hard missions. Not only black ops but also those where high casualty rates are expected. Our unique talents often help us to find unique solutions. As a kind of compensation, we enjoy a certain leeway and extra pay."

"Okay." She hardly noticed her fingertips ripping apart her napkin into tiny pieces. "But what does all this make you, then? Some sort of unofficial crime lord? And where does this leave me?"

Sergey let out a hearty laugh. "No, I'm definitely not some kind of kingpin. More like I'm in charge of making sure my people don't get too ambitious. And this knowledge doesn't change your situation, only how you might look upon it."

"Only how I might look upon it, huh?" She leaned over the table. "But then, what exactly is and has been my place in this officially unofficial mess of an organizational structure? I really need to know what's in store for my future."

"Yeah, I know." The small muscles around his eyes tightened slightly. That was all.

For several minutes, they both studied the dancers in silence. Maybe he couldn't give her an answer because he himself didn't have one. He'd been pressed into this situation, too, hadn't he? By now, the napkin pieces had piled into a small red mountain on the white tablecloth.

"This is how I see it. Apparently, I misjudged your readiness to act. So I'm giving you a choice, and the decision is final. I'm not willing to revisit this topic. You can either stay my ward and I won't curtail your freedom more than is absolutely necessary. Nor will I or any of my people ever pressure you into doing anything immoral. Though we might ask you from time to time if you want to get in on certain things. You can then decide on a case-by-case basis. Just always make sure you're not caught with your fingers in the cookie jar. Or you decide you want nothing to do with all of this, and I find you a new law-hugging, *boring* warden. There are some possibilities among the new troops. You would probably have seven perfectly uneventful, highly structured years of closely observed ten-hour shifts, regulated mealtimes, regulated sleep times, and regulated piss breaks. And of course, no chance to break the law. Your choice."

Right, like that wasn't totally exaggerated. The twinkle in his good eye hinted at the fact that he'd phrased it completely over the top by design. The Plutonian was teasing her. And simultaneously, he wasn't.

There was no real choice here. Not for someone like her ... She'd completely lose her shit and go nuclear in a totally regulated life within no time. Suzy tidied the napkin scraps into a neat pile.

Then she took a deep breath and said, "In that case, I wish to remain your ward. And I'd like to get to know you and your people better. Though maybe you could not throw me in at the deep end and expect me to swim, please?"

A genuine, warm smile appeared on his face.

"And sir—I mean, Sergey—I would totally appreciate a regular opportunity for some hoverboard training. Jamaal could use it, too, and I have this cool new space board that I hardly got to try out at all. And—"

"Okay, okay!" he interrupted her. "Remind me again when we're back on the *Gateshot*. I'll find you some time. You don't need to attend every bridge meeting. But that's enough talk about work. Let's concentrate on fun and R&R."

As he said this, he raised his glass again. They clinked and drank in unison. Damn, this really was the good stuff.

Federov reached out and started arranging the red scraps into a grid pattern.

He held out his hand, saying, "How about we start from scratch? I'm planning to break into the bigger shop's storage room once it closes. My goal is to relieve the owner of as much of the really good stuff as I can hover out of there and get back to our ship, where I'll throw a big party before we leave for the Gate. I'd like you to come with me, because two sets of eyes are better than one, and it'll basically double our take. I won't hold it against you if you'd rather stay out of it. You're free to wait it out in whatever setting you prefer, as long as you're back on the shuttle before it disembarks. However"—he lifted his right index finger—"I will take it personally should you rat me out. I will make you regret it. And that has nothing to do with the balance of power between us. Are we clear?"

"Crystal." Suzy smiled, for once with as much bravado inside as she projected on the outside. She peeled the label off the vodka bottle and tore it into twelve equal pieces. Six of them she folded neatly; the other six she rolled into little balls.

Now that he'd laid it all out on the table, she felt like she had a much more nuanced measure of him and his people. Of her place in this fucked-up picture. Federov wasn't just the grim reaper or the big shot colonel; he was a man, flawed and selfish in his own right, but overall decent. He understood her. She respected him for that, just as he seemed to respect her a bit more now.

She could work within these boundaries.

The witch held out her improvised game pieces. Sergey picked the folded ones and set one down on the red tic-tac-toe grid.

They leaned back in their seats, played a few rounds, and watched the show.

Their scores were tied when he finally asked, "So, what else do you want to know before you decide if you're in or not?"

"What will happen if we get caught?"

"Nothing." He cleared the board and motioned for her to start the next round. "With all the shit that's been going on in the provosts' office on this station, we would have enough leverage to be let go without any mention of it anywhere."

"Blackmail?" she clarified, placing a ball in the lower corner.

"I guess you could call it that." He shrugged and blocked her on the left. "Would it bother you after what you've seen today? To do it to the people responsible?"

Would it? What had she really seen? Except for one scared woman and a handful more angry people? Rows of boxes, stacked several atop each other, came to the forefront of her mind—the dust on them. The perpetrators were getting complacent, so this had been going on for a while now. Been done to a lot of people.

"Besides," Sergey nipped at his drink, "we won't get caught. This'll be a laughably easy operation."

"Done it a million times?" she teased, placing the next piece above her first.

"Not exactly. But often enough." He shut down her winning line by claiming the upper corner.

"I see." She nodded. Then froze as a particular detail that had slipped her mind came rushing back in with a vengeance. "Shit, what about my tracker?!"

"Oh, please," he waved her sudden panic off, "Only Garin and I have the safety key needed to check your whereabouts. Anyone else needs a judicator's blessing to get access. And by then, the data will have been mysteriously corrupted. Garin won't care as long as we find her a nice bottle of something to make it worth her while. Look out for top-shelf brandy; she likes the aged stuff."

Suzy blinked.

"Anything else?" he asked, tapping expectantly beside the board.

She placed the third little ball in the center. "So, if we left it, that stuff wouldn't go back to the community, wouldn't get redistributed?"

"Unlikely. Very unlikely." He turned his head to look at her, his one dark eye softened. "Are we breaking the law here? Yes. Are we hurting anyone by doing it?"

Pause.

"Anyone who doesn't deserve it?"

Oh, the second one had actually been a question directed at her. Suzy shook her head.

"No," he confirmed, letting the folded piece of paper dance across his mechanical fingers like a poker chip. "And that's the difference. I'm not claiming to be Robin Hood.

I'm saying that, sometimes, it's okay to take your cut if life offers it on a silver platter. This is such an opportunity."

"I see." And she did. "And we're gonna throw a big party for everyone before going through the gate?"

"Sure. This mission will be hard enough. We can use the distraction." His lips twisted in displeasure when he realized she'd won either way. He blocked the full row on the left.

"Yeah, I guess we do," the witch murmured, chewing briefly on her piercings. With a nod, she placed her piece in the upper corner and completed the winning row. "Okay, I'm in. Let's do this."

CHAPTER SIXTEEN

EVRON\\ ATTACKED

Lightbearer, *en route to the Kuiper Belt*

When Evron got back to his quarters that day, he felt sick to his core. As Ruffa had promised, Tuvil provided all the help Evron might need to complete his task of acquiring Human clones. As well as a deep insight into how this 'business' was run.

Ziffin chirped, a feeling of tentative concern stroking its master.

"It was horrible." Evron let himself fall onto a couch, happy to say this out loud and relieve his soul of the burden of what he'd seen. "This is so barbaric! And I thought our cloning facilities were gross! The way the Humans pound out these sorry meatpuppets is ... wrong!"

A shudder ran all over his body as the images returned in a flash.

"You know I never liked it." He gladly hugged the warm, furry comfort of his companion to his chest. "I made a point of staying away from the facilities on the *Supreme*

Salvation. Ruffa giving me this task seems more like a punishment than anything else! Oh, Balance! You think he knows? What I told Jake, I mean?"

As he lifted the chrryn to look into its face, Ziffin's large eyes blinked at him rather confusedly. Punishment itself, it might understand, but its master talking about it as applying to him was probably too far of a mental bridge to cross even for this clever little thing. Evron wished he could speak with Jake again, tell him about this. Did the coreworlder know what was going on out here at the fringe?

"Ruffa doesn't understand how different from each other the Human cultures are." Evron pressed his pet back to his chest. "He still thinks of them as one unified whole, with pieces warring for dominance maybe, but still ... And it is confusing. The fact that the OSA is at the same time so similar to the Plutonians that they'd rather throw in their lot with them, and so different that they've been battling each other for lifetimes. I wonder if Velorians would be like that, if the Haslar hadn't come. Or, if we were before they made us a standardized unit in their empire, like all those other races. I heard it said that the Haslars optimize everything. Themselves, their slaves, their planets ... do you think it's true that they redesigned their central solar system way back when?"

With its master's mind relaxing as it wandered down that rabbit hole, the chrryn purred contentedly.

"Some say they didn't let us go as a reward, but because they realized our species is failing, even before we did," Evron murmured the highly unpopular, almost treasonous idea, like someone might be listening in. "That they judged us broken and therefore unworthy of their protection. Some say independence is overrated and that we had a better time when we were enslaved—more opportunities, a clear purpose. I don't know. I feel like I'm a slave, in any case. Expected to perform my duty, punished if I don't. Now I've made all these connections, placed orders for Human beings to be delivered like cattle. I feel soiled like never before."

His hands caressed the blissfully ignorant little being rubbing up against him. "I wish I were you, Ziffin. I wish I didn't know all that I learned those last few weeks."

Large black eyes loomed in his vision. The tiny rune on the chrryn's forehead lit up lazily, and an overpowering feeling of contentment washed over Evron. Tiredness followed in its wake.

"You're right," he murmured and closed his eyes. "Some rest will do me good. I need to be fit for those magic chores."

Evron couldn't even remember falling asleep, but the lights in his quarters had shifted to a dimmer setting as they usually did whenever he tried to rest. First, he wasn't sure what had woken him either. Then he realised with a start that he wasn't alone any more. Gentle footsteps were all the warning he got, then Erestral loomed over him, playful concern on his face.

"Evron," he purred. "Are you all right? You missed our appointment; I got worried."

Evron couldn't move without touching the other. Erestral's face filled out his whole vision.

"I'm fine." he glanced around. "I'm sor–How did you get inside my quarters?"

"The door was open," the other lied as he cupped Evron's right ear with a gentle hand. "You look ... unhappy. Maybe I can help with that."

A strange feeling flooded into Evron. The sensation was very close to sharing Ziffin's feelings, but it had a steely aftertaste. It felt forced upon him rather than something one of his senses picked up rather randomly. Was the other trying to influence him magically? As he attempted to dissect the feeling, he found himself locked into place by something invisible, a strange confusion taking over his mind. Like, moving was just too much of a bother. Sidetracked by this peculiar occurrence, Evron realized what Erestral was up to only when the other's lips pressed against his.

Balance, no!, he thought, but his resistance ran against … something.

Why couldn't he move?

CHAPTER SEVENTEEN

SUZY\\ COOPERATION

As Federov had promised, the break-in was laughably easy. While she exploded the shop's cameras from a distance, he bypassed the security system and opened the doors. Then they just dragged all the good stuff onto pallets and hovered them out. He'd organized a set of overalls that made them look like delivery people, while base caps obscured their faces for all the other cameras. Cueing her when to look and where to reveal the least bit of identifiable profile, Federov guided them through corridors with little traffic back to his shuttle. A brief, large-scale camera outage in the docking area would obscure exactly where the stolen goods had ended up.

Henri helped with the loading, while Nick and Ludmilla stayed oblivious to the whole thing.

"Shit, that was intense! You really do know how to do this," she marveled as they threw the overalls into a nearby recycling unit for instant breakdown and reuse, before returning to the *Lady Godiva*.

"As I've told you." Her warden smirked. "I learned a thing or two in my time. You'll get there."

Suzy laughed. "I'm not sure I should."

"Your loss. In any case, I think I failed to get you truly and lastingly drunk." He waved open the airlock and let her enter first.

"Yeah, sorry about that." She wasn't sure she meant it.

"You feel like giving it another try?"

"Thanks, but ... I think I've had enough excitement for a week or two." She fell into one of the comfy chairs and rubbed her eyes. "I'll take a raincheck, if you don't mind."

"Sure. I'd say you've earned it. Wait ..." He held up a hand and turned his head like something had caught his attention. After a few seconds, he met her eyes again with a young boy's smile plastered all over his face. "Feel like watching a raid tomorrow?"

She blinked. Damn, Diaz worked fast!

The colonel allowed Suzy to pick the venue this time and seemed quite pleased with her choice of a table outside a tiny bistro. Right next to it, a row of planter boxes backed by trellises marked the boundary to a Venusian eatery. From here, they could see both shops without being easily spotted themselves. Also, there was breakfast to be had.

While they enjoyed their hot beverages, munched on pancakes, and waited for the party to start, the girl finally asked, "So ... this Plutonian community business ... what is it all about? I mean, I understand ecological and structural interdependence, obviously. But the way you see it is different around here. On Mars, we're still comparatively individualistic even though we face the same environmental dangers."

"Yes, and that's why coreworlders have such a bad rep

in the PR," he said. "Because for us, on the whole, you're egocentric, while we're community-driven. Out here, everything's much farther apart, so we have to be. When outside help is several days away most times, cooperation makes survival possible. And you know the worst enemy of cooperation, Suzy?"

"Egotism?" she guessed.

"Right. Not individualism, mind you, but the hubris of thinking your view of life counts more than the needs of others. When you disregard everyone else to benefit your ego, you disregard the whole—which you should further—by being part of it."

Not to seem 'egocentric,' the witch forwent the opportunity to argue against his perception of coreworlders in favor of digging deeper into the Plutonian mindset.

"So, you think you should lose yourself in the pursuit of everyone else's goal?" Suzy took another sip of her hazelnut-flavored cappuccino. "But who decides the goal, then? If everyone is just a small shape to be colored in, to make one pretty picture in the end? And how does that square with our behavior last night?"

"You misunderstand." He shook his head. "Everyone is good at something. It's our duty to bring this to the table for the benefit of all. We all shape the goal according to the dangers we face. I don't especially cherish the thought of flying into some unknown part of the universe, fighting void-knows-what without any chance of backup or supporting logistics. However, my superiors believe I'm the right person for such shit. It's why they keep promoting me and why they give me these missions."

"But ... didn't the admiral ask specifically for you?"

Sergey snorted. "Sure he did. But do you really think the most influential person in the solar system agreed to it because she felt pressured by a desperate man heading a semi-private 300-soul mission or that she would have agreed to it if she felt this would do nothing but uselessly lose her assets? I don't think so. I would have been on the short list for this trainwreck in any case."

"So why were you so unhappy about it, then?"

He stared into his cup thoughtfully for a moment. "Just because you're good at something doesn't mean you want to do it all the time. That's the hard part about working together—you have to make sacrifices to exist as part of a community. Sometimes you have to do the things nobody else will do," he looked her straight in the eyes, "... or can. I may not have magic, but I'm willing to do and have done a lot of things others would consider ... distasteful and worse. The higher you stand in a community—or are placed —the more sacrifices you have to make. Most people aren't willing or able to deliver what's demanded of those in leadership."

Suzy nodded, and they kept eating in silence.

After a few minutes, she asked, "Hey, ahem ... Can I ask you something else? It ...might be personal; I'm not sure."

"Shoot."

"Ambassador Bogdanov said that ... if I wanted to know about the places where magic users are imprisoned in the Republic, I should ask you about where you grew up. What did he mean?"

He stilled. A strange mix of emotions ran over his features as he stared into the distance. Finally, his eyes refocused on her, and he said, "My dad was an investigator. A provost. It's how I know how they operate. He was good at investigating, not so good at ignoring. Not so good at accepting defeat, either. I don't know the details, because my parents kept them from my sister and me, but there was a case. Someone he couldn't touch legally, no matter how hard he tried. So when he wouldn't let go and they couldn't kill him, they got him reassigned to CRS 147/CHS. Everyone who knows of it just calls it 'Purgatory'. The worst hellhole I know of."

Federov's right eye blinked suddenly, and he paused to take another sip from his cup.

Suzy simply waited until he continued, "Got my eye poked out there by a bunch of other kids my age. Voidsick SOBs, the lot of them. The station is both an ore refinery and an asylum for the criminally insane. And it made people ... lose their minds. They just ... faded away. Strangest thing. Like something leached away their essence. Just believe me when I tell you everything is better than what happened there."

"Did it affect your parents?" the girl asked after a moment.

"A bit." He shook his head. "Isn't what killed them if that's what you're asking. They died in a transport accident."

"Oh." The witch cleared her throat. "Yeah, my mom too ... well, maybe."

He raised an eyebrow at that, asking, "Maybe?"

"Yeah ... I ..." She stopped to gnaw on the studs in her lower lip. This, she hadn't told anyone yet. But it felt like she should. Maybe not for his benefit, but hers. So she continued, "I have this journal, from the alien mage, the one that tried to suck out my magic and kill the whole ship."

Sergey nodded, and she waved vaguely, saying, "It's very sparse. Not much in terms of explanations or diary stuff. But right before my mom died, he had this whole ritual figured out and wrote down considerations on optimal test subjects. On the day of her death, he drew up an iterated version and ..."

Suzy swallowed hard. Sergey merely nodded again. He got it. What she tried to tell and how she felt about it. Somehow, he could see right through her. And, for some strange reason, in this moment, it felt good. It felt good to be seen.

The moment lingered, then her opposite cleared his throat and gestured at the gaps in the trellis, saying, "Here they come."

One of the three provosts heading a group of other people with see-through face shields and riot gear limped slightly.

"That's Diaz, right?" she asked, and the colonel confirmed her observation.

The raid was quick and brutal. From what the witch could discern, they gave the two shopkeepers a good whacking before parading them into custody, while securing the merchandise and evidence with minimal damage. All around, people watched openly as well as from behind half-raised cups, bowls, or glasses. Some even cheered.

"You know what time it is?" Sergey obviously didn't mean the numbers on the clock.

"I'd guess it's one of the busier times of day?!"

He nodded. "Shift change. Around here, probably the busiest."

She took another look at the faces of their table neighbors.

"They want everyone to know this happened. That justice will be served. That it's over," the witch murmured.

"Yeah." He gave a slight smirk, like he knew a joke no one else did. "A part of societal balance has been restored."

One of the non-provosts stepped out of the nicer shop

and leaned close to Diaz. Judging by his stance, the provost listened intently. Then gave a small jerk. He froze for a few heartbeats while the other man gestured. Finally, he cut him off with a swift movement of the arm, took over the conversation, and pointed back inside the shop. The other man's face showed clear unhappiness, but he nodded and walked back inside.

"You didn't tell him," Suzy realized with a start.

"Not in so many words, no." Sergey took another bite of pancake.

"But he knows."

"Of course he knows; he's a clever man," the colonel replied calmly. "It's what he will do with this knowledge that interests me."

Ah, shit!

"Don't worry, he won't rat us out." Sergey seemed completely convinced.

She shook her head. "How can you know?"

Sergey just smiled. "Keep on learning, and you'll get there too."

Before Suzy could respond, another group entered the scene. Four soldiers, headed by another provost, this one a heavyset and slow individual, walked up to their colleagues. As they approached the first shop, he pointed at one of the station's provosts. A quick shouting match erupted. Hanging back, Diaz gave a slight nod, and the soldiers rushed forward to take down the indicated provost. The guy seemed eager to resist, but had little chance against the overwhelming odds. Following a minor but confusing scuffle, the soldiers paraded the cuffed provost off the plaza.

"Guess Diaz did have a use for those troopers after all," Sergey commented. He drained his mug. "Come on, let's head back; I'm beat."

CHAPTER EIGHTEEN

EVRON\\ TURNING THE TABLES

LIGHTBEARER, *EN ROUTE TO THE* KUIPER BELT

"I know you like me." Erestral's words seemed more of a suggestion than something he actually believed. "And I'm tired of this waiting game. Let's do something about it."

A mindbender. Erestral had to be a mindbender ... or at least use some ritual or spell to force his will onto his victim. He was getting desperate, was he? Seems that desperation made him bold. Evron reached out to feel for his pet. The steady randomness of content relaxation told him that Ziffin was asleep somewhere nearby. Maybe it had fallen off the couch and curled up on the carpet again. Barely minding the other Velorian's fingers running over his clothes, Evron took hold of the connection and sent out a sharp poking sensation.

Ziffin! he thought. *I need you! Scratch that son of a Haslar's eyes out!*

Nothing happened. Nothing but a slight shiver in his

pet's dreams. Erestral's fingers slipped inside Evron's collar and, with a few gentle tugs, the shirt fell open.

"Balance!" the mage hissed in surprise, leaning back from his victim as revulsion dominated the overengineered patterns of his eyes.

The scar. He'd seen the scar. Shame flamed up inside Evron as the realization of what Thallamon had the scientists do to his offspring flashed over Erestral's face. After all he'd done here, all he'd learned, this moment reduced him right back to that quivering idiot standing in front of the mirror, pondering his self-worth.

No. This was it. He would not stay down and let this piece of freggog-shit extract another sample of his genes against his will!

With an expenditure of will he'd never managed before, Evron caught the swirling dark emotions, the rage at his helplessness, the disappointment, the shame provoked by his weakness, and sharpened them all into an invisible knife. He drove the knife into his connection with Ziffin.

GET UP AND HELP ME, DAMN YOU! his mind screamed at the little creature.

A shudder ran through the chrryn's emotions as it was rudely slapped back into reality. Even with its limited understanding, it seemed to at least comprehend that its master was being attacked. With a cute little growl, Ziffin charged into the air and slammed into Erestral's back, sinking its tiny but sharp claws and teeth into the Velorian's neck. Erestral yelped with equal parts surprise and pain as he jumped up and tried to reach the unexpected danger.

His hold on Evron wavered, and the other Velorian pushed against it with all his might. Something shattered, like a pane of glass he couldn't see, only feel. A deep breath rushed into his lungs, dispelling the fog of confusion clinging to him.

Getting a hold on its wings, Erestral ripped the chrryn off of him and threw it into a corner.

In one fluid motion, Evron jumped to his feet and slammed his fist into his distracted enemy's face. The mage went down, confusion written all over his body and wafting off of him in fretful waves. Ziffin tumbled, then righted itself midair and came sailing back. It landed on his master's shoulder with a furious hiss at the downed mage.

"Asshole!" Evron deftly kicked Erestral where it really hurt, before the other could manage to get up again or cast another spell. "You got nerves to attack me like that."

"I ... I didn't attack you!" The mage's plea seemed insincere, as surprised anger superimposed itself in his voice. "I just tried to make you feel better!"

"Right, sure." Evron looked back at the couch, then touched his ear. Something small and hard fell off his folds, and he studied the combination of metal and crystal. Runes were carved all over it. Haslar runes. Anger rushed in like a ruja—blinding, overpowering anger born of indignation.

"YOU USED A HASLAR-FORSAKEN SLAVE DEVICE ON ME?!" He kicked Erestral again, even harder this time. Blood spurted out of the other's nose, nicely complementing the seeping wound on his neck. "You will not get away with this! I'll have your head for this!"

Erestral's eyes widened again, and he held up both hands. Power built up between them.

"Don't you dare!" Evron opened his folds to full display and grabbed a stone-carved statue from the table. "You so much as spark at me, and I'll cave your head in!"

Clearly perplexed by this unforeseen turn of events, Erestral froze mid-motion. His eyes and folds moved rapidly as he considered his options. Evron turned his folds forward, rendering their full display in an even more aggressive light. He'd never stood up to anyone like this, but he was done with being toyed with. He also remembered Ruffa's lessons. Removing a bested foe would only give him new trouble. It would make Berestul come down hard on him. The primary mage might even try to kill him, should he learn of this.

"I'm giving you one chance to get out of this alive," he growled at the downed mage. "You're gonna tell me what your progenitor is up to. Every little detail. If I'm satisfied that you're telling the truth, I might let you go. Or do I need to use this on you?"

He brandished the slave device.

"You don't even know how to use it!" Erestral's folds shivered.

"I'm sure I can figure it out." Evron smiled his best cold smile. "Can't be that hard."

After a forced swallow, Erestral pushed back his folds as far as they would go to indicate his surrender. With his dominance established, Evron relaxed his ears slightly.

"Talk fast," he ordered. "I've got lessons to get to."

As the winner closed his shirt back up, the mage told him what his progenitor had tasked him with and how he'd gotten frustrated once he realized Evron wasn't as easy a target as he'd hoped. It seemed he'd used the device in a similar way a few times before, though never on another Velorian. At least that's what he claimed. Since it didn't make a difference either way, Evron let it stand. Erestral seemed to have been as honest and forthcoming as could be expected in this situation.

Finally, Evron nodded.

"So, this is how it's gonna play out." He held up the

device once more. "We'll both pretend this never happened. No, even better, you'll tell Berestul you succeeded and have a good feeling that our ... merger produced the desired result."

This should give them a week or two before Berestul piled pressure on Erestral to try again.

"I'll keep this as insurance. Should you try another attack on me or tell anyone what actually happened, I'll inform Ruffa about everything. I'll present this to him as proof. And just so we're clear, I'll prepare a log to be released to Ruffa and Thallamon should anything happen to me. So don't think having me fall prey to an accident will help your situation."

A flicker of helpless anger made plain that Erestral had entertained exactly that option for a moment or two. This was not going his way at all. And like Evron before, there wasn't much he could do about it.

"And I don't imagine I need to spell out what I'll do to you if you tell anyone about my shame," Evron growled.

"N-no," the other agreed.

"Good." Ruffa's student stepped back to be safely out of reach as he gestured for the mage to get up. "Always remember this moment. You're my bitch now. Say it! Then get your ugly folds out of my space."

CHAPTER NINETEEN

RIVERS\\ PLUTONIAN COLLEAGUES

The next day, Montoya stepped away from Baileywick, who sat in the XO's seat, to address their section. "Okay, Team, Ms. Rivers and I have a new idea we'd like to try."

While she talked, the VR consoles' configuration changed. Four consoles became five, with two on each side of a pit and one console set higher in the back, allowing the person sitting there to oversee the pit as well as face the command chairs.

"Ms. Rivers and Ens. Nakayama," Montoya pointed at the Plutonian officer whom she considered her unofficial second, since she'd previously served with the lanky, dark-haired man and therefore knew his strengths and weaknesses, "will man the internal sensors, while Lt. Mirak," she gestured at the remaining Plutonian, a broad-shouldered, slightly older gentleman, "will work with Lt. Okoro to monitor the external ones. I'll supervise and direct. Does everyone understand their new positions?"

"Yes, Ma'am." Everyone saluted, even Riv.

"Good, then get comfortable with the new setup. We'll

do a few trial runs before Ms. Baileywick starts the simulation." Montoya nodded to Riv, a certain ... hopefulness in her gaze.

Their talk in *The Beak* last evening had been interesting to say the least. Especially after they'd started ordering drinks. Seeing more of her private side, Montoya's mindset and viewpoint, had certainly helped Riv understand the Plutonian way of doing things. And she'd been amazed to find how much common ground and interests they actually shared. Truly working together would be a whole different level, of course. Still, Montoya's idea to have Riv concentrate on a part in which her scientific background and extensive understanding of the *Gateshot*'s layout and systems would be put to good use and keep her away from the part she'd already screwed up so bad might just work. Now, the coreworlder would only have to get out of her own way and work hand-in-hand with Nakayama.

Here goes nothing, she thought, as she sat down at the console next to Montoya's and started configuring it.

Nakayama leaned in to ask in a respectful tone, "Tell me what you're doing, please, so I can understand your approach."

"Sure," Riv gave him a quick overview of the different filters she'd prepared and explained why they worked and for what. Nakayama nodded, asked some follow-up questions, and then turned to his own console.

"So ... what's your approach?" the scientist made herself ask and listen attentively to the answers, repeating some of them back to make sure she understood and wasn't inferring from her own perspective.

Just pretend you need to write a paper on this, afterward she thought. *Like it's some sort of anthropological study.*

It quickly became clear how they should divide and double-check their findings for optimal output.

"Okay, how are you set up here?" Montoya had finished going over the preparations for the external sensors and leaned in between the two of them.

Nakayama gestured at Riv to do the show-and-tell.

Their supervisor nodded along, finally declaring, "I see. I like the division of labor; just make sure to always double-check each other. One person can easily miss an important detail. Also, this is very combat-directed. Who's keeping an eye on possible breaches in the ECLSS?"

Riv knew by now that telling Montoya that GaSIn monitored the Environmental Control and Life Support System, and that the ship's AI would alarm them if anything were amiss, wouldn't fly.

"Oh, right." She gestured to create another holo-screen between those they were already monitoring. "That's paramount, so we should certainly keep it front and center."

"*Da.*" The lieutenant smiled and patted her shoulder. "Very good. Let's do this, then."

She hurried up the steps to configure her own console and double-check the connections to her team's output, before strapping in and declaring, "Ms. Baileywick, we're ready."

"Good." The ship's master tapped away at her console. Around them, a slew of other people appeared, all of them frozen midmotion.

Next to her, on the captain's chair, a facsimile of Glen, on the verge of sipping his coffee. On the main screen, stars blinked away merrily in the distance. The scanners' start-up configuration showed no planets, stations, or other signs of life in the vicinity. According to the readout on a tiny section of Riv's screen meant to keep her apprised of the overall situation, the ship was moving at travel speed through empty space. All markers were in the green.

Baileywick nodded. "Let's start."

A sudden rumble went through the ship, and their captain swore as a few drops of hot liquid splashed his hand. All the other crew members started to move too. The tiny *Gateshot,* on which GaSIn would normally display whatever the person in command deemed essential, including impacts on the hull and some such, flickered out. Glen looked up like he knew something was wrong.

His emerald eyes searched the new station for answers and stopped on Montoya. "Sensors, what was that?"

Then he gazed over to his right. "Ms. Baileywick, where's my display?"

"Triangulating the source of the disturbance," Montoya reported, as her fingers flew over her console. She ordered, "External Sensors, search for hull damages and determine the nature of the disturbance. Internal Sensors, scan for possible internal sources and damage."

Nakayama called up several prepared queries, asking Riv, "You want the source or the damage?"

"I'm sorry, Captain." Baileywick gave one of the standard simulation excuses. "It seems GaSIn has some problems with the automatic triangulation programming."

"I see." The admiral turned back to Montoya. "Sensors, you're my eyes and ears. What's happening?"

"Doesn't one result from the other?" Riv murmured back, as she considered the queries and filters she might use. "Let's just both go for both. That's your redundancy-thing, right?"

The lanky, middle-aged man's smile held the serenity of someone way older than he could possibly be. He nodded.

Montoya's triangulation appeared on their stations just

as the team leader called out, "Captain, the disturbance appeared on the starboard bow section."

She rattled off the exact section and size. A new tiny model flickered into existence in front of the captain, a red point indicating the spot.

"And what is it?" He'd licked the coffee off his strong hands and secured a lid on the mug.

"External hit producing minimal impact damage," Okoro reported behind Riv's back. "Forwarding details now."

Montoya glanced over the incoming data and relayed, "Captain, we sustained impact damage. The hull is heating up at the point of impact. Cameras in the vicinity show no source for the disturbance."

"Anything our hull can't handle?" Glen asked Lustig.

"Negative," the chief engineer informed. "Damage is within secure parameters. Hull integrity at 10 %."

"No internal damage," Riv added.

Montoya relayed this.

"Good." The captain seemed restless despite his words. "Captain to Engineering and Ship Security, check out the damaged section."

Gosh, he was so lifelike ...

Three more tremors ran through the outer hull with enough force to slightly shift the *Gateshot*'s position in space.

"Attachments to Airlocks 12, 18, and 24." Okoro's voice grew alarmed.

Riv instantly shifted her focus to those positions, only remembering to inform her neighbor of the fact when she'd already opened feeds from the internal cameras and sensor data monitoring them. Heat sensors reported a tremendous increase on the outside of the airlocks, and their integrity decreased ... but Riv couldn't see anything happening. Then the cameras' output fizzled away into white noise and went dead.

"Possible intruder alert!" she declared, looking at Nakayama for confirmation. "I think we're being boarded!"

The Plutonian frowned at the sensor readings and the dead camera feeds for a split second before turning his head toward Montoya, saying with a firm voice, "I concur."

"Captain, we're under attack!" the lieutenant reported. "Three possible sites of enemy intrusion!"

"Comms, send security teams to these locations!" MacAllister ordered. "Sensors, how many intruders?"

Riv shrugged helplessly as she tried different cameras nearby, other wavelengths, and every other means to get eyes on the situation she could think of.

Montoya stared at her subordinates for a moment before declaring, "Unknown, Captain. External, why can't we see any boarding vessels?"

"Nothing on the scanners," the Plutonian in Riv's back replied, like repeating this fact held the answer.

Well, actually, it did ...

"Magic," Riv murmured. "It has to be magic."

"Come again?" Nakayama asked.

"Sensors, I need more information," the admiral barked.

"Aye, Captain," Montoya acknowledged and turned back to her team. "Ms. Rivers, you have something?"

Oh, right, they probably hadn't encountered this before. Magic was still pretty rare, especially on a scale like what Suzy could do ...

"Most likely, they're using magic," Riv repeated, louder this time. "That's why we can't see them. Technology has a hard time recording magic. It messes with cameras and sensors to a point where they become useless."

"Cannoneer to Sensors, I need more data!" a harsh voice called on their shared team comm. "I can't just spray our outer hull with ordnance! I need a target!"

"Sensors to Cannoneer." Montoya remained calm where Riv felt like screaming at the guy to take a number. "We're on it. Stand by."

When the team leader caught Riv's gaze, the coreworlder was sure the Plutonian didn't believe her, that she would rebuke her for wasting precious time with esoteric nonsense. But Montoya paused with her mouth slightly open to take a deep breath and consider.

She turned to Okoro instead. "Lieutenant, can you corroborate this idea?"

"Sure." The team's newest addition nodded. "Magic messes with sensors and cameras, as she said."

Montoya blinked and rocked back slightly.

"So, you're saying we're blind and deaf to these intruders?" The lieutenant's voice held a mixture of disbelief and horror.

"No, not entirely." Riv scratched her head. "We just have to ... circumnavigate the problem. Think outside the box."

"The magic probably has the intention to disguise," Okoro jumped in. "Like Mr. Maverick's shuttle."

"Well, I don't know anything about a shuttle." His neighbor seemed hesitant. "But we can still feel their presence. They triggered our outer hull's pressure and heat sensors, so they're not entirely invisible to us."

"We can still track their effect on our ship and equipment." Montoya's eyes widened. "Internal, you two search for anything that might indirectly report on a being's existence, ... like fluctuation in air pressure, ambient heat, or vibrations. External, have engineering bombard the spaces outside the attachment points with radar waves and try to map the vessels' shapes that way. Modulate the frequencies until you see something."

"Aye, Ma'am."

As concentration reigned and the hurried motions of fingers on AR controls prevailed all around her, Riv felt surprisingly happy at sharing the immense workload of adjusting, running, and combining the results of all these search queries and filters. Montoya kept all those demands for information at bay and satisfied them as soon as her team came up with the appropriate data, which had the nice side effect of preserving everyone else's focus on the critical task of locating the enemy.

Soon, Okoro and his neighbor revealed the boarding pods' shapes and turned their radar waves farther outward in search of the mother vessel. Riv and Nakayama, meanwhile, revealed and tracked the different boarding parties until security had neutralized them.

The simulation ended with the comm chatter dying down, the rest of the bridge crew freezing midmotion, and Eve rising with a satisfied smile.

"Very good." She nodded as she walked over. "You won. And within a satisfying timeframe, no less. Your teamwork has improved considerably, and your attention to detail was commendable. Lt. Montoya, you directed and delegated with a deft hand, yet still managed to listen to and engage with all the important facts shared by your team. Ms. Rivers, you brought your knowledge to bear without trying to override anyone else's work or opinion."

The ship's master went on to give each team member a detailed performance analysis, ending with, "Keep up the good work. You have a ten-minute break, then we'll start on something a little more challenging."

Right ...

'A little more challenging' turned out to be just about doable. Every simulation after that one became increasingly more complex. After weeks of probing and prodding, Baileywick knew precisely what they could and couldn't do and began lashing them into shape with subtle glee. Still, that evening, Riv's spirits soared high. For the first time in a long time, she felt like they might actually succeed in this.

"Well," Baileywick judged after the final brainteaser had left the sensor team reeling and the simulated *Gateshot* half destroyed, "You're getting too tired. Your performance is taking a dive. As far as I'm concerned, you have the rest of the day off. Please report at the same time tomorrow for more elaborate and broader simulations so we can build on your communication breakthrough. Now, does anyone wish for any changes to the new console setup?"

Riv shook her head. It was strange, but she had to admit it worked. Even her amygdala, which had been rattled by the constant noises of people behind the scientist's back, was getting desensitized.

When no one else spoke up, Montoya straightened and said, "Since this is the first time we've worked in this configuration, I recommend trying it out for a few more days, just to be sure there are no drawbacks, which we haven't realized yet. Unless anything comes up in those, I'd say this is what we're going with."

Again, the blue-haired woman smiled. "Very good. Dismissed."

No sooner had she disappeared than Riv smirked and held out a fist to Montoya and Nakayama each. After a quick exchange of tired glances, they both bumped them.

Okoro low-fived his neighbor, saying, "Man, I feel like a shuttle just flew through my brain."

"*Da*," their team leader agreed. "Who wants to go to *The Beak* for a quick debrief and some drinks before catching rack time?"

Everyone did.

When Riv blinked her eyes open in the real world, however, their taskmaster stepped up next to the little group.

"Ms. Rivers, please walk with me for a few minutes." Eve gestured in the general direction of the door.

"Of course, Ms. Baileywick." The scientist nodded her goodbyes to the others, mouthing "I'll catch up," and fell into step beside her.

Only when they'd cleared the general area did the ship's master start the conversation, saying, "Ms. Rivers, I'm very pleased to see that you managed to find common ground with Lt. Montoya and her people. The addition of Lt. Okoro appears to be having a positive effect on the team dynamic. I do hope that the five of you will build on this foundation to become a completely coherent entity."

"Thank you." Riv nodded. "We'll do our best, Ma'am."

Eve smiled at that formal address. Her whole body shifted subtly to indicate a more private, relaxed tone. As did her voice.

"I'm concerned about your overall workload, Heidi," she confessed, her tone free of judgment, her hands behind her straight back. "You're doing so much, and the sudden increase in population puts strain on all your areas of responsibility. You've already had to increase the output of the vertical farming and aquaponics. I've noticed that you lost weight and missed meetings, often because you were double-booked. Your work hours have increased significantly, and I fear that you're not getting enough rest."

"It's fine." Riv shook her head as the happy high she'd been on quickly died down in response to this new problem. "It's just a phase. Once everyone is settled and the VF is producing optimally, it'll calm down."

"Are you sure?" The ship's master stopped to face her. "Even with the increase in personnel, the *Gateshot* is still only at around 13% capacity. She would be able to house even more people, be it in far less comfort, should it prove necessary. If we found ourselves facing the conundrum of taking on as many refugees as we possibly can, would you be able to give them adequate attention?"

"You mean, in case those women we're searching for are actually prisoners of the Velorians and we manage to free them?" The scientist clarified.

"For example."

"Well, in that case, the *Gateshot* would only be a drop in the bucket, right?" The redhead frowned. "In those ten years, the Velorians must have taken millions of people."

"Indeed." Some emotion Riv couldn't quite pinpoint crossed the alien's face. "But this was the largest vessel Marshall could conceivably build given the timeframe and resources agreed upon. Especially considering the other parameters. Besides, other possible occurrences could lead to an increase in the number of people aboard. For example, we might find ourselves taking on refugees from another disabled ship. Could you handle that?"

Riv took a deep breath. She could really do without Eve questioning her like this, but the ship's master had a point and every reason to ask. Her feet itched, and she turned to walk on. This time, Eve matched her pace.

"Also, don't forget that you haven't even started with

your most important task." The blue-haired woman reminded her gently. "Analyzing alien life to further Human understanding. That alone will fill up your days once we can collect some specimens for you."

"You could just give me all that knowledge," Riv pointed out, more to draw out a response than because she was interested in being spoon-fed such information by an alien data source of unclear motivation.

"I could." The other woman merely smiled. "But then, no one in your home system would accept it without confirmation by one of their own, would they?"

Yeah, she'd seen right through that diversion.

"You do have a lot of qualified scientists on your team," Baileywick pointed out. "You could delegate that task. Considering our interview beforehand, I'd have judged this particular task to be most dear to your heart and inclination. I never would have imagined you'd be so adamant about being part of the bridge crew. Have your values changed?"

"No ... Maybe." The scientist gnawed on her bottom lip. Finally, Riv whispered, "Listen, Eve. I ... ahem ... I see your point. I'm trying to do it all, and it won't work. I'm just Human. I only have 24 hours in a day. I get that."

The ship's master nodded gently.

"But I can't leave the bridge!" Riv demanded with a stern tone of voice, before softening it for some hard-to-voice concessions. "I'll ... I'll delegate more of the day-to-day in supply to my direct subordinates and release the oversight of the civilian element to someone else. Would that be sufficient for you and the captain?"

Eve smiled. "Yes."

CHAPTER TWENTY

EVE\\ SPECIAL CONSIDERATIONS

Repairing Glen's hand was hard. Even with her subroutines and programming helping out, there was so much to monitor and consider while steering the myriad of tiny nanites to mold her student's flesh on this second appointment. Eve felt immense relief once the last nerve had been stitched and Dr. Fox looked up from her scanner, declaring, "That's it. I think you're done."

Thank the balance! Eve thought.

She'd been cautious not to show her inner distress. She knew how hard this had been for Glen and the last thing she wanted was to instill doubts within him. So she clamped down on the strain and smiled, saying, "Wonderful. Then I'll call them back now."

Glen met her gaze. Something was up. Was he seeing through her little charade? Or was there something else on his mind?

Eve waited for Dr. Fox to leave before she asked, "What is it, Captain?"

Glen experimentally opened and closed his hand,

murmuring, "It's so strange to know there's nothing wrong with it anymore. I'll keep waiting for it to spasm again."

"That won't happen," she assured him.

He nodded. "There's something else I'm just waiting for."

She raised an eyebrow questioningly.

"What happened with Antolov ..." Glen visibly groped for words, "... was unfortunate. I understand why he had to be removed, and a younger version of me might have even done something similar. Heck, if he'd proven to be as bad for morale as Federov seemed to believe he was, I might have intervened."

She cocked her head, and he continued, "What irks me is that Federov brings out the best as well as the worst in people. His and ours. We need to keep an eye on that."

"I do keep an eye on that," she chided mildly. "You placed my responsibilities with the crew and the ship, so that's where I concentrate my efforts."

"I know." Glen stood to pace her office. "And I trust you."

"What irks you is the fact that Federov didn't give Antolov a chance to do him or his people wrong," Eve guessed. "He just assumed it would happen and acted accordingly. It's the 'guilty unless proven innocent' approach you disapprove of more than his methods, isn't it?"

Her captain froze and considered.

"I guess that is the larger part of it," he finally agreed.

"And you're afraid Federov will hold more sway over your own people, even those you have a history with, when all this is said and done?!"

Another long pause, like he genuinely didn't like to admit the truth of her assertion. Or maybe he wasn't sure she'd hit the right spot after all. With a deep exhalation, he nodded and resumed pacing.

"It goes even deeper than that," he confessed. "If Federov's methods are this slick, what do you think we should expect from his superiors?"

"The high marshal has a rather colorful reputation." Eve thought of the wild stories she'd collected during her research. "It's hard to say where exactly the kernel of truth lies within the grand myths about her. But the Plutonians consider it highly dishonorable to break a deal once they've agreed to it."

"Oh, please!" He whirled to face her, his eyes full of sly knowledge she didn't possess. "You know as well as I do that there are a million ways to skin a cat. And just as many ways to interpret even the most straightforward of agreements."

Something clicked deep inside her mind. Datapoints fell into place. Something he'd said or done previously. This was more to him than thinking through a possible threat. No, Glen enjoyed the challenge of knowing that he might be outplayed and figuring out how he could stack his odds regardless.

Fascinated by this revelation, she took note as he continued, "Bogdanova said it herself; the *Gateshot* is just a minor piece to her. She'll give us our shot at the gate; I don't doubt it. I can live with her enforcer running all over my ship. As long as he's busy with the training of his people and all his little side projects—"

"... some of which are actually yours." For some reason she couldn't quite name herself, Eve delighted in pointing it out. Maybe she'd fallen into matching his mischievous tone on reflex.

He waved the interjection away. "Aye, they are. Not that I could take them back now, even if I wanted to."

Other discussions had revealed his judgment of Federov's interventions as being ambivalent at best. As with Antolov, Glen seemed to regard the likely results as satisfactory, even though he disagreed with the Plutonian's methods.

"Still." He marched back to his starting point and leaned onto her desk to face her squarely. "I just want to make sure that, when the time comes, we can take a shot to positively nuke our bullseye."

He pointed at the spot on the wall where she kept her stash of precious gems. "You already showed me those keys to the kingdom. Don't you think we should talk about the rest?"

"The rest?" She smiled her shielding smile.

He wasn't fooled. "The *Gateshot* is only running on a small percentage of what she can deliver, right? Now, I'm no mechanic, but I'm rather certain that if you have something with a constant energy output beyond any Human measurement and channel that into a vessel of one kilometer at its longest axis, you can get a lot more out of it than we currently do."

Eve kept smiling. It might not have been proper, but she liked making him work for it. She liked the velvety register his voice fell into whenever he knew he had no actual grip on her and tried to sway her by sweet-talking. The change coming over his demeanor in these instances was ... tantalizing. And maybe, just maybe, she also enjoyed giving him some payback for the pain his stubbornness had caused her. Ever since they'd settled their battle for dominance and established both their responsibilities toward each other and their crew, it was gone.

Still, given the unconventional nature of their arrangement, predicting how far she could go or what she could say and do remained a matter of trial and error.

"Come now, Honorable Guardian," he said, sitting back opposite her and steepling his fingers. They'd played this game before, and he clearly enjoyed it just as much as she. "Why aren't we operating this ship at its full capability?"

"Because I deemed it too dangerous to unleash its full potential while other Humans might witness."

"I understand." He nodded. "Running on so much energy would have been noticed. We would have had all kinds of entities pursuing us."

"Yes. It's a leap in technology that might split Humanity right down the middle should any one faction gain possession of it." Eve took a deep breath. It still made her queasy considering the implications, even though he'd already convinced her and the rest of the conversation seemed more of a formal dance than an actual discussion. "The Great Neutrality would disapprove. Which is why I originally decided to only remove the dampeners once we'd passed the gate and didn't run the risk of anyone sharing intel on it."

The question glittered in his emerald eyes before rolling off his tongue. "Didn't you trade Marshall this knowledge?"

"Not exactly." She smirked. "There are several spaces and systems on this ship he never got to see. I designed and outfitted them entirely myself and left them out of the specs. He understood well enough that without a Venerable One, these wouldn't do him much good in any case and agreed to the exclusion. Officially, in any case."

Not that it hadn't been fun to counter all the clever intrusions he'd tried.

"Officially?" Glen had an inkling of the complicated cat-and-mouse games which had shaped his teacher's relationship with the Martian AI governor and knew how to interpret the comment.

"I'm 99.968 % sure he didn't get past my security measures."

Glen laughed. "99.968 %, heh?"

She shrugged in that nonchalant way he found so amusing at times.

"Be that as it may." Her captain leaned back to mirror her. "Once we're truly on our break for the gate, no one can stop us to snoop. And if we don't have that extra capability, we might get stranded or destroyed instead of going through. Also, we don't know what awaits us on the other side. Federov could be right in assuming we'll fall right into a nest of Velorian ships over there."

Of course, he was right.

Eve nodded. This should be all right. She could do this.

"I'll start schooling Dr. Lustig on our Plan B at his earliest convenience."

Glen reached out to grasp her hands and squeeze them gently. "Thank you."

CHAPTER TWENTY-ONE

SUZY\\ FAMILY MATTERS

WHEN SUZY EXITED THE *GATESHOT*'S ELEVATOR, SHE felt the last remnant of tension that Federov might jump out of a crossing corridor and drag her off to another hair-raising adventure, or Diaz come to throw her in the brig once more slowly dribble away.

She'd made it. She was back. Back home. Well ... kinda home.

As the ship's witch entered her quarters, surprised that she was allowed to keep the big, luxurious space, and threw her bag onto the comfy couch in the front room, her gaze caught on one of the pictures adorning her walls. A dome full of greenery. Vertical farming surrounding several skyscrapers under a perfectly spotless architectural masterpiece. If she leaned in and squinted, she might be able to spot the window of the room she'd shared with her sister back on Mars. Elonia. Her home. The home she couldn't return to. The heavy feeling settled in her stomach with the weight of a mid-sized shuttle, and the subsequent yearning left her mind reeling. She hadn't even thought of home in weeks ... she'd always wanted to call her sister again, but there never seemed to be a good time for it.

Suzy plopped down on the couch and reached underneath, feeling for the hidden pocket in the synth-leather lining. There ... She slipped her hand inside and groped for the smooth surface of the object she was looking for. Damn, where was it?

Hm ... maybe this was overkill ... she could just ask Eve for a secure comm line to Mars. But then, she wouldn't want to create more trouble for her sister by openly contacting her. The journalists would be the smallest and nicest crowd looking for the war criminal with a hefty bounty on her head ...

Finally, her fingertips touched the coveted item. Why was it pushed so far in? Hadn't she left it right at the lip for easy access? *Weird ...*

The witch sat up and uncurled her fingers to study the flat, round object about the size of her palm. The pocket mirror was baby blue with wavy white lines edged into it. She flipped it open, her image staring back at her from the upper half, while the lower had been inlaid with carefully drawn runes. Suzy still didn't know all of them.

Personal Connection—Something—Communication—Picture—Enhanced range.

Something fluttered in her tummy. What if Lucy didn't want to talk to her? What if she didn't pick up? Or what if ... *Ah ... fuck it.*

Here goes nothing, she thought, and poured energy into the spell.

"Hey, Sis," she whispered. "Are you there?"

The mirror fogged up, swirling purple energy coalescing behind its surface, like lightning illuminating distant storm clouds.

Hm, that was new ...

As she stared down the vortex for several minutes, her spirit slowly descended to the floor. She let the mirror sink. Seemed like Lucy didn't want to talk to her.

Just as she was about to close the thing, the image finally cleared, and her sister's voice called, "Suzy? Suzy!? Are you there?"

"Yes!" The witch quickly raised the mirror back up to her face. "Marsdust, I thought you didn't want to talk to me! Shit, I'm so sorry about the whole war criminal thing! Please tell me you're not suffering for my stupid mistakes over there!"

Lucy blinked at her, somewhat stupefied.

"War-what? Are you ... What do you ..." Her amber eyes hardened. "Shit, Suze, what happened? What did you get yourself into this time?"

"You don't know?"

"Know what?" Lucy's voice reached new heights as she patted her white-blond hair.

"Damn, you look like you fell out of bed," Suzy muttered. "Did you have your hair cut? You look even more like a politician now. Have you lost weight? Your face is all slim and—"

"Oh no!" Her sis pointed an accusing index finger at her. "Don't you dare change the subject on me! I've been worried sick about you! I try to call, like, all the time, and you never answer! Now you tell me that you're a war criminal? How can that be? There isn't even a war! Not yet, anyhow ..."

Suzy narrowed her eyes. "What do you mean, 'not yet'?"

"Hey! You first!" Lucy set down the mirror and adjusted it as she sank back into her chair.

Even with the changes—different pictures on the wall, less tacky wallpaper and drapes—Suzy immediately recognized their dad's office. Well, former office. She still had to remind herself from time to time that he was gone.

"Well?" Lucy grabbed a comb from one of the drawers in the under-desk cabinet and started straightening out her tresses. Sharp indentation marks on her face suggested that she'd probably fallen asleep atop several dataslides and maybe a stylus or ruler. "Fess up, Sis!"

Someone had been practicing her assertiveness ...

"All right, all right!" Suzy gestured placatingly. "Let me just get a glass of water while I tell you."

As she laid out the whole mess as succinctly as possible, while dialing down the shittiness as much as was believable, Suzy grabbed some food and a drink. She found a good spot for the mirror and made herself comfortable on the couch. Even before she'd finished speaking, Lucy turned to open a holo-screen. As she typed away at it, she confessed, "I didn't hear about any of this. And there's no mention of it in the matrix."

"What? That's weird." Suzy leaned in. "Wait! Stop searching! Just in case. ... I mean, you're a public figure now and all. If this hasn't come up yet, that's good. Don't risk it by showing too much interest."

"Oh, don't be paranoid." Lucy waved, but the gesture held a subtle strain, and she quickly turned off the screen. "Marshall has all my connections encrypted government-style, and his security chief is always checking if things are all right. Pretty sure he's swiping for bugs regularly. Doesn't want to alarm me or anything, but I'm not blind, you know? I'm not an idiot!"

"I know." A knot formed in Suzy's throat as she saw her baby sis sit there, all prim and pretty facade, behind that enormous desk in an oversized office. The emblem of the mage guild on the wall suddenly seemed to loom, heavy and oppressive, like it might fall without warning and crush her.

Suzy shook the disturbing image off and asked, "Hey, how is everything? Are you ... okay?"

"Sure." Lucy smiled that brave smile which said she was soldiering on and didn't want the other to worry. "Just ... a lot of work, you know? Being the grand mage, is ... exhausting sometimes. Daddy always made it look so easy ..."

"Because Daddy pawned off half his work on us and ignored most of the rest," Suzy only half-jested. "Don't be such an overzealous perfectionist. You'll work yourself to the bone."

"You mean, like you?" The yellow lanterns of her sister's eyes shone with inner understanding. "Yeah, I'm sure you're not tackling all that responsibility by yourself. Now that you can openly live out the truth of your witchiness, you probably established a coven to help you with all that magic stuff and find a way through the gate."

"Witchiness?" Suzy giggled.

"Witchiness, witchdom, witchever." Amusement reestablished the laughlines and exuberant delight in Lucy's features.

Suzy kept up the wordplay, and they goofed off until they were both wiping tears from their eyes and holding their aching tummies.

"Fuck, I missed this," the older one confessed after catching her breath.

Nostalgia heavy in her voice, Lucy agreed.

Suzy ordered GaSIn to drone-deliver her a beer and fell back onto the couch, saying, "Okay, your turn. What have you been up to?"

What Lucy told her sounded like she was redacting heavily, but then, Suzy understood. She couldn't tell her sister half of what was going on on her end either. Still, it felt weird to perform this tightrope act when, in the past, they'd shared just about everything. Made her wish she could breach the widening gap between them with a hearty jump. Fat chance of that. Lucy was a politician now, it seemed, rubbing elbows with some of the most powerful people in the system as she accompanied Governor Marshall to whatever official outings he decided to drag her to.

"And what about Steven?" Suzy finally pushed their conversation to a more girly matter. "Are you two hitting it off?"

Color crept up Lucy's neck.

"Uhhhhh" The witch set down the empty bottle and ordered another. "Tell me everything!"

"Well, we ... are an item." Her sister smiled coquettishly. "He's really ... ahem ... you know ..."

"Attractive?" Suzy grinned. "Charming? Sexy? Good in bed?"

"Sweet," Lucy cut in. "We're taking it slow, but ... yeah, I think this could last. He's also super supportive and has started to take a lot of the day-to-day problems off my plate."

"Good!" Remembering that she'd been the one to nudge her baby sis to finally take a chance on the guy, and seeing the happy glow on Lucy's face, made a warm feeling bloom inside Suzy's chest. "So not everything's bad and stressful over there."

"No ..." Lucy glanced away, before confessing, "The bounty has been retracted. You could come home."

Suzy swallowed hard. Silence fell between them. But this time, it was the smothering kind.

"I'm sorry!" Lucy held up both hands. "I shouldn't have said anything. I don't ... I mean, I do, but ... ah, fuck, Steven is great and all, but I want you home so bad, Suze! I know it's selfish, but I just can't help it, okay? I miss you! There are days when I think I can't do it. Sure, everyone wants to help, but I always have to ask myself what they're hoping to get out of it, you know? You were always right here, like a part of me. I could always count on you. And now ... you called to say you're leaving, didn't you? You'll be gone after this, and I won't know what happened to you until you make it back, Mars-knows-when," she quickly wiped her eyes with one lavender sleeve, "or maybe not ever. There's so much that could happen."

"No, I ... I'm not leaving yet."

Lucy's conclusion hurt, but then Suzy really hadn't called for so long ... what else was her sister supposed to think?

"I'm sorry I didn't call," she hurried to say. "I'll do better, okay? I'll try to call every other day and definitely before we leave! You can tell me all about what's been happening, and maybe I can help somehow, but ... I really can't come home."

"No, of course you can't." A sad smile turned all the laughlines in Lucy's face into ironic counterparts of themselves. "You have to get them through the gate. That's important."

"No. I mean, yes, but ... that's not all, Luce." Suzy felt like crying too. "I fucked up, like, *big* time. I'm a felon now, with a tracker on my leg and a super-scary warden on my ass! If I so much as try to escape ..."

For a nerve-wrecking second, she actually considered it. Considered waiting for the last minute and then teleporting away as the *Gateshot* flew off to bring honor to her name. But she couldn't teleport all the way back to Mars. That was ludicrous. She would have to steal a ship from the dock or whatever. Ditch the tracker. But she'd never make it out of the Plutonian Republic. Even with all that emptiness in between ... The Plutonians would be guarding their border and the vicinity vigorously. With the danger the Velorians might pose and all. And even if she did manage to get back to Mars, despite possible pirates and having no idea how to navigate there, or where to get food, water, and oxygen for the journey ...

"Even if I made it home," she whispered, "they'd just extradite me. Do you know what they do to magic-wielding felons out here?"

Lucy shook her head.

"Well, let's just say it ain't pretty." Suzy opened her new beer to wet her dry throat. "I dug myself a hole I can't escape, Luce. I'll just have to fill it back up with honest work and return home a free woman."

Or maybe with work that wasn't entirely honest. ... Who knew what else Federov was going to drag her into ...

Her sister nodded. "I understand. I'm sorry, I shouldn't even have brought it up. I know it's ... impossible."

"I miss you too, Luce." Suzy gently touched the mirror. "And I already promised to do everything I possibly can to get back home in one piece. Besides, I'm still not sure how to even leave ..."

Lucy perked up. "What do you mean?"

"I mean—"

The doorbell rang. Suzy looked up. *Ah, Void, what now?*

"Ahem, one second, Sis." She held up an index finger to her lips and opened the vid feed showing her front door with a hand-eye gesture. Her BCI projected the image to what seemed like a spot in midair, and Suzy swallowed.

"Who is it?" Lucy asked.

Thea stood in the corridor. And she was wearing the red dress. Even though Suzy had just gotten some two days ago, her lady parts throbbed in happy excitement at the notion of what would happen once she opened that door.

No. No, she couldn't. Not now.

"No one." The witch forced on an easy smile. "GaSIn, please tell my visitor that I'm already sleeping and not to be disturbed."

Lucy wasn't fooled. "Suuuuze!?"

"Doesn't matter!" Suzy shook her head. "You're more important right now. This conversation is more important. Besides, I'm off-duty. Unless there's an emergency, they've gotta respect that."

Tentative color returned to her baby sis's face. They shared a long moment of silence, during which Suzy watched Thea protest, then plead, and finally walk away with her head held high as if to mask the disappointment in her stride.

"So," Lucy retraced their conversation, "what do you mean, you can't leave?"

"I mean." Suzy closed the vid feed and fell back onto the couch with a sigh. "I just can't figure out this damn gate! I've deciphered most of the runes, but it just doesn't tell me anything! It's like ... I mean, I have no clue how this ritual works."

"How what works?" Lucy leaned onto the desk, her head in her hands, and put on her thinking face. "Like, what is this ritual you keep going on about? Where did you get it? What is it supposed to do?"

"Well, open the gate, of—" Suzy stopped herself. "Wait ..."

What if she'd gone about this all wrong? What if ...

She palm-slapped herself. "URGH! I'm such an idiot!"

"You are?" Lucy frowned.

The witch jumped off the couch and started pacing as puzzle pieces snapped together in her head.

"Have you ever seen a mining ship?" she asked.

"A what?" Her twin sounded completely confused now. "What does that have to do with anything? And where are you going?"

"Oh, sorry." Suzy turned the mirror to face the room. "You see, I worked on this mining ship ..."

Lucy blinked.

Suzy gestured the unspoken question away, saying, "Why isn't important. The thing is, ... everything around there is labeled. All the tools and stuff. Because most of their crew is a transient workforce, so everything people absolutely need to know when working with that stuff safely is written right onto it."

"Okay ..." Lucy still seemed unsure of where this was going.

"So, I happen to know that the Velorians didn't build the gates. They just found this one."

Her sister's eyes widened. "You think there's more than this one?"

Oh, right ... she wasn't supposed to know. *Damn ...*

"Well, there has to be two to get you from one place to another, right?" Suzy argued. "Besides, these things are, like, super-old, right? And, as cosmic timeframes go, Humanity has only been a very recent thing. So why would anyone travel all this way to an empty solar system to build this thing here, in the first place? If you can only build one set, wouldn't it make more sense to do it somewhere you actually want to go regularly?"

"Not necessarily." Lucy bit her lower lip. "Maybe they needed resources? Or maybe to test it? I mean, there's a lot that can go wrong with such a large magical item, right? You wouldn't want to destroy your own solar system in case it doesn't work ... like, in an explosive way?!"

"Right ... Hadn't thought about that. Thanks for the nightmare fuel."

"Still, if you're right and some alien race connected parts of the known universe with these things to make it easier to move around, and even get to some super-remote, uninteresting backwater solar systems like ours ... Then what?"

"Well," Suzy tapped her chin, "if I were a super-smart alien race working on easier travelability, why would I build something only very few individuals would be able to figure out how to use?"

"Maybe it was common knowledge back when, just not here and now?" Lucy suggested, "Needing a mage to activate it is a roadblock in itself."

Suzy pointed at nothing in particular as she continued, "Not in a society where magic is way more common, which I'm starting to believe is just about everywhere but here."

"Okay, if we accept that premise, then what's the conclusion?" Lucy crossed her arms and leaned back. "That there should be some sort of magical manual on the thing, explaining how it works?"

"No, don't you see?" Euphoric energy bubbled up inside the witch as she grabbed the pocket mirror. "I've been trying to decipher the inner workings of the gate, how it *works*, instead of how to *use* it! It's like these mirrors. I still can't read all the runes you put on them, but I don't need to. I just need to feed energy into it, and the runes establish the connection for me!"

"But ... these are just mirrors. Relaying a bit of sound and pictures," the expert in Lucy cautioned. "You're talking about a giant ring floating in space, that can open a wormhole of some kind and have entire ships fly through! The complexity of that spell must be ... staggering. It must cost so much energy!"

"Exactly my point!" Suzy laughed. "As guys would say, size doesn't matter. No one person can possibly provide this much energy. Therefore, it must come from somewhere else. So it has to be more like flipping a switch than doing actual work."

"Okay ... but then how do you find and flip the switch?"

The witch beamed. "Exactly!"

CHAPTER TWENTY-TWO

GLEN\\ ALL TOGETHER NOW

After Federov, Suzy and Nick returned from the plover, Glen had Eve implement a large-scale VR simulation to assess the whole crew's performance and ability to work together. ... Well, not the civilian element, naturally, but both the military and bridge crew were put through the proverbial wringer in several hours' worth of reaction drills, riddle-solving, and outright combat simulations.

Afterward, Glen decided to share dinner with Eve, Nick, and Suzy for some pleasant distraction before the COs would announce and discuss the results with a rested exec crew the next day. On second thought, he also invited Federov.

"So," the Plutonian started the conversation once he'd finished his bowl, "you finally got your bridge in order and your crew straightened out, I hear."

"Aye," the admiral said. "It seems we're finally getting somewhere."

"How did they perform?"

"Satisfactory." Glen dipped his fingertips into his beard to scratch his jaw. "Yours?"

"The same." The colonel handed his bowl to Nick as the other man started clearing the table. "Some have longer ways to go than others."

"Would you like me to draw up individualized VR training sessions?" Eve offered.

After a moment of silent consideration, the Plutonian licked his lips and said, "I'll have to take a deeper dive into the results of the simulation first. But I'll keep the offer in mind."

"Of course."

"So, Captain." Federov turned back to Glen. "Would you say the Plutonian system has its merit, then?"

Time to eat some crow.

"Indeed it does," the admiral allowed. "It's a tool not easy to utilize, but once understood, very handy."

Federov barked out a laugh.

"Overall I thought your new troops fared rather well," Nick interjected. "It seemed that you had those simulated boarding parties under control fairly quickly."

Their new military commander shrugged. "We're working with what we've got. Their training is paying off and all the personnel we've shuffled around has mostly been integrated. They'll get the job done, I guess."

"I'd say you're modest in your evaluation." Glen remembered the stats Eve had provided. "I've seen veteran troops with worse performances."

"You mean coreworld troops?" An amused glint in the Plutonian's natural eye hinted at his intention to tease rather than offend. "Plutonian standards really are more stringent, then."

"If you say so." The admiral smiled good-naturedly.

"Well, be that as it may." Federov turned to Eve. "Those boarding parties, were they representative of what we might actually encounter on the other side of the gate?"

Drones flew in through the outlet in the ceiling to collect the dirty dishes.

"That depends." The alien robot followed their departure with her gaze.

"On what?"

With a smile, she refocused on her conversation partner. "On who you manage to piss off once we're there."

Low laughter rumbled out of the Plutonian's chest. Glen wasn't sure he'd ever seen the man this relaxed before. This was certainly a good sign.

"In any case," Federov continued, "I think I'd like to fight some more of those creatures. And it makes me interested in facing the puppeteer instead of the puppets."

"I thought you don't revel in fighting just for fighting's sake?" She opened a box of expensive chocolates she'd brought and picked one out before sliding the rest to the middle of the conference table.

"I don't." He took possession of the sweets and claimed one made from dark chocolate. "But I do enjoy deepening my skill sets."

"Well, in that case," the bonny lass batted her eyes at him almost coquettishly, "let me see if I can fit your curiosity into my schedule."

Federov smirked at the underhanded jibe.

"Here, this should go nicely with the chocolate." He set a glass bottle onto the table. Within, a translucent liquid emitted an eerie blue luminescence.

"Is that the glowy vodka you said was a tourist trap?" Nick picked it up to study the label.

"Cherenkov vodka." The Plutonian nodded, then shook

his head. "No; the cheap stuff with the high prices, that's the tourist trap. This one's a decent brand. You'll like it."

As the XO frowned at the Plutonian symbols, which were almost too small to read, he asked, "It's not real radiation, is it?"

Federov snorted. Suzy giggled. Glen and Eve merely smirked. The admiral pulled five tumblers from his desk's lowest drawer and passed them over.

"Right." His young friend stopped trying to make sense of the writing and opened the bottle to distribute the alcohol evenly. "So, that duel was something else, wasn't it? Will the provost major recover?"

"I'm sure he will. Somewhere else." Federov accepted a glass. "Antolov has been relieved of his duties for medical recovery. I hear he'll be reassigned to some other sorry platoon a good while after we're gone."

Nick nodded. "How does Thompson's new second do?"

"Efficient, but he's still of a mind to prove himself."

When he didn't elaborate, Suzy chimed in, "And Thea's in medical now?"

"It only seemed prudent to augment the medical staff with combat-ready people." Federov glanced at Eve. "I've heard rumors that there is no such thing as the Jupiter Conventions where we're going."

"No." The alien studied the content of her glass with distinct interest. "And while most races agree that even enemy healers are too valuable to injure or kill, none extend such prescriptive protection as Humanity does. Therefore, I wholeheartedly agree with your consideration."

As did Glen. Though he was curious if the scuttlebutt claiming Federov to have at least some romantic interest in Dr. Fox might have been a contributing factor in his decision. In all honesty, the admiral had to admit that the

Plutonian was performing his duty with a deft hand and an admirable understanding of the whole system, creating win-win situations wherever possible. Having asked for him seemed to turn out to be a blessing after all. But then, they were still seeing eye-to-eye. The intelligence and determination Federov displayed also deepened Glen's conviction that he would make for a frightful enemy.

"However, I'm still not quite sure what to do with your other mage convict, once she pulls through." Federov accepted a glass. "The CCG won't take her."

"Witch," Suzy interjected.

"Excuse me?" Federov glanced over at her.

"Ms. Yun practices magic intuitively, so she's a witch." The young woman's gaze dropped to the tabletop as she added in a quieter voice, "At least by Human definition..."

The Plutonian shrugged. "Semantics. No matter what we call it, Ms. Yun can wield magic. That makes her an uncontrollable risk and precludes her integration into a regular unit. The fact that she can't remember her military training doesn't exactly help, either."

"You're a colonel now." Glen took a cautious sniff of the glowy alcohol. "Maybe you could use a second aide?"

"You're both an admiral and the captain of this ship and you don't even have one," the Plutonian retorted. "Maybe you should employ her. She started off as your problem, after all. My responsibilities have to end somewhere."

"Well, it's your good name that she won't break her contract." Nick smirked. "Don't you want to keep a close eye on her?"

"Hrmph." Federov lifted his glass.

"Ahem, about Ms. Yun." Suzy leaned in. "I could use her help."

Glen and Federov looked at her.

"For what?" the XO asked.

"I need her magical sight." Suzy combed a few free-flowing purple tresses behind her ear. "To see the gate better. I mean, the Plutonians are now part of the crew, right? So my magical authority holds, doesn't it?"

"Ahem." The admiral exchanged a brief look with Federov. "Basically. You stand outside the ranking and can, in magical matters, overrule anyone but me and your warden. If Ms. Yun is a resource you deem necessary to have for opening the gate, that puts her under your supervision."

Federov opened his mouth with the clear intent to intervene.

"For now." Glen held up his index finger. "And for this specific purpose only."

The Plutonian's eyes narrowed, but then he just shrugged. "Explain what you need her for."

"I've been going about the gate all wrong." The ship's witch seemed suddenly abuzz with excitement. "I've been trying to understand how it works, but that's not the point! I just need to know where the door control is. For that, I need to see how the energy flows. Here." She pulled a round piece of metal from her pocket. Tiny markings had been scratched into it. "You remember this?"

"Isn't that the coin you tried to learn that teleportation spell with?" Nick held up his hand, caught it when she flipped it over, and studied it closely.

"Right! And I had the ritual wrong." Suzy's purple eyes widened. "Xin took one look at it and told me that the energy didn't flow right and which symbols I should have a closer look at."

"So your new plan is to have Ms. Yun look at the gate

once we're there and hope to then figure out how to open it?" The XO raised an eyebrow. "By looking at it?"

"Ahem ... yeah, basically." Some redness crept up the lass's neck. "By looking at it through her eyes, to be exact. I can connect to her in my dreams; I just need to figure out how to do it when we're awake."

For a few heartbeats, everyone just stared at her.

"That's our plan?" Federov turned to Glen. "We go there and *hope* she figures it out in the moment? Under fire?"

Before the other man had had enough time to formulate any kind of sensible response, the Plutonian turned toward Suzy, continuing in a level voice, "Several man-of-war and their escort ships will be risking their crews' lives to get us there and you don't know how to get us through? You've been working at this for months and somehow looking through another person's eyes is your great breakthrough?"

"I'm sorry, but I'm all out of ideas." The witch's eyes narrowed as strained panic flooded into her connection with Glen. "Besides, all manner of aliens seem to be using it. It can't be that complicated!"

Federov opened his mouth, but before he could say anything, she held up one hand and purple lightning burst out to engulf it.

"Look at it," she demanded. "Look at it with your augmetic only. What do you see? You see nothing, do you? Because it's like looking through a camera. All I can see on these pictures," she displayed an assortment of snapshots, all showing the Space Gate, in her open AR. They washed across the table like a tidal wave. Her eyes never leaving the Plutonian, she stabbed her index finger right through them onto the tabletop, "is a bunch of alien symbols I can make almost no voidforsaken sense of! Until I can actually get a look at the thing, I'm as blind to the actual opening mechanism as your right eye is to my magic. I understand that this is a giant leap of faith; I understand the risk and the danger."

The Plutonian simply raised an eyebrow at that.

"Okay, maybe not as fully as you all and I know that this is not what you want to hear." She glanced at Glen, Nick, and Eve in turn, her lower lip shivering slightly. "But that's why I need Xin. To stack the odds. Hecate gave her some sort of third eye, which, sure, I possess too, but I hardly ever manage to open it by myself. When Morgan had me in that circle on his ship and tried to suck my soul out, Hecate gave me a glimpse of what there is to see. It saved my life! I could see where the energy flowed and how it worked to create the ritual that imprisoned me. I still don't understand all the symbols' meanings, but I didn't need to then, to disturb it and to free myself. Just like now." Her voice took on an almost begging quality. "I just need to be able to see!"

Nick frowned, clearly uncomfortable, and looked at Glen. Eve leaned back to indicate she wouldn't intervene and mirrored the XO.

With a slow outtake of air, Federov crossed his arms and also looked Glen's way. "Well, I can't say I'm thrilled with all this. But I cleaned up enough of your backlog disasters, Admiral. This is a magical matter and I'll adhere to your rule—in this instance. So it's your decision."

The captain took a deep breath. He swirled the blue glowing vodka around and around in his tumbler, staring at the poisonous color. This was a tremendous decision. It seemed so ludicrous that this was what their journey had come to. Faith. Pure and simple faith. Faith in his young friend that she could figure it out. Faith in the Plutonians to hold up their end of the bargain. Faith in Federov that he wouldn't try to take over his ship should he consider whatever happened too risky for his people. Faith in everyone involved to do their best and get them there.

His instinct told him to go for it.

"You know, Colonel." Glen smiled. "I remember our discussion about your plan to get that container from the pirate station. Your plan was to board it, with no idea where the contraband was, walk through the entire station like you owned it, find the thing, and extract it. No exit strategy, no exact intel, just faith in your people's skills and your knowledge of places like it."

An echoing smile tugged at Federov's lips. He felt the hint dropped on him like an anvil.

"I wasn't convinced of that plan." Glen shook his head for emphasis. "It seemed too ... simplistic to actually work."

With a snort, Federov leaned back in and grasped his own tumbler.

"And Suzy," Glen continued. "I remember the first discussion we had about magic. You told me that you're not especially good with the intricate stuff, but that you have more raw energy than any witch has a right to. Since then, I've seen your understanding grow. You've done some truly exceptional things. But ..." He lifted a finger and Suzy's eyes widened even more. "You've always done them as a response to danger. You're right. You aren't very good at rituals and spells. What you excel at is instinctual magic. Doing the right thing when the pressure builds."

Tentative happiness crept into their strange connection. It was a slowly blooming pride in herself, a hardening of her resolve. This above all told Glen which decision was the right one to make.

"So, yes, I have faith that you can get us where we need to go. We'll do it your way."

Suzy clamped her hands into her lap, probably to keep from jumping up and hugging him. Bloody hell, what a precious lass she was.

"Well." Federov winked at their witch. "Seems that you do have a way to counter my authority. For now."

She laughed.

Glen lifted his glass. "To simple plans working out!"

"To simple plans working out!" they all echoed and drank in unison.

Some sort of purple drink would have made the toast perfect.

CHAPTER TWENTY-THREE

SUZY\\ FRIENDS AND CONNECTIONS

"My tracker's bigger than yours." Jamaal wiggled his eyebrows as he stepped into the elevator to meet up with Suzy.

She laughed and shook her head. "Enjoying your new freedom, are you? Hey there, Amigo."

The large Spartan shrugged and gently set down his cat in her outstretched hands, saying, "Absolutely. Also, I have to report to my CCG squad in an hour. I told them I'd collect Wire on the way. Seems to me that she could use a friendly face before she gets thrown into the next shark tank."

The elevator started off toward Hangar 4.

"You're absolutely right." Suzy rubbed the little warrior behind his tiny ears. "I'm sure she'll feel better once she gets a look at this precious cutie!"

"Ha. Ha." The marine's tone of voice was ironic, but his dark eyes twinkled with amusement. "Hey, did Thea talk to you?"

"You mean, did she hit me up for rebound sex?"

He coughed delicately.

"Yeah." Suzy sighed and enjoyed the furry warmth in her arms. "She tried, but luckily, I had an important call and sent her away. Gosh, it would have been awkward talking to Tank after *that*. I don't think she would have given me a heads up beforehand, and I only read your message the next morning ..."

"Yeah, she probably wouldn't have."

"So, what are you gonna do?" The witch nipped at the piercings in her bottom lip. "I really don't envy your position."

Thea's brother took a deep breath and continued staring at the door. "I told her she'd been a giant idiot and that it had only been a matter of time until Tank got wise. She stormed off. When she hadn't returned after half an hour, I called Nick and we went to share a few drinks with Tank."

"Uhhhh ..." Suzy grimaced. "That's mean. You're familially obliged to have her back."

"Familially?"

"It's a real word. You can look it up." She scratched the kitten's back, and Amigo rolled to redirect her hand to his scrawny belly.

"Whatever." He sighed and said, "Besides, I have her back ... but I'm also familially obliged to tell her when she's being a giant cunt, right?"

"If that's how you feel, you should have told her, like, waaay earlier."

"Yeah." He scratched his neck with an air of awkward unease. "I guess we all behaved like idiots."

Suzy wasn't sure what to reply to that, so, instead, she asked, "And what did Tank say?"

"He was surprised that I hadn't come by to beat him up." Jamaal smirked, a sad undertone prevailing in the gesture. "I let him pet the ankle-scratcher as we reminisced about the good old times. After a while, we decided to let it go before completely destroying all the good memories by second-guessing and including our idiocy in hindsight."

The witch grimaced again. The 'ankle-scratcher' purred. It was the most adorable sound!

"Not you too!" Jamaal poked her ribcage. "You're supposed to be our big, bad super-witch. Can't have you get all googly-eyed on account of a tiny furball!"

"Well, Chávez was right." Suzy giggled. "Amigo is a chick magnet."

"Doesn't help if the chicks are more interested in patting my pussy than those parts that actually need attention!"

"I wouldn't pet those in any case," she returned sweetly.

"Why?" He leaned down. "Afraid I'd get too big for your itsy-bitsy lady parts?"

Suzy elbowed him in the ribs, and they laughed it off.

Mars, this was nice.

The door opened, and they crossed the corridor to enter Hangar 4. The transport hovered outside the energy barrier. Probably waiting for clearance to land or something.

"C12 is that way, right?" She pointed to the left.

"Right." He headed that way. "You seem more relaxed."

"I got a new plan. I think it's better than the last one."

"You go, Girl!" He slapped her back and it made her stumble. "Tell me all about it over lunch tomorrow? If they let me leave, that is?"

"Sure." Suzy rubbed the patch of slightly throbbing skin. They reached the AR line indicating safe distance to the landing in progress and stopped. "So, how do you feel about joining a Plutonian penal brigade?" she asked.

The Spartan shrugged. "Well, after that pesky little witch gave me an earful, I realized not all Plutonians are giant assholes. So I'll give them the benefit of the doubt, see where it leads."

Gosh, he'd almost made a 180. Good for him!

"I like your attitude," she said, and, with some regret, handed him back his cat. "I'm sure it'll work out."

"Yeah, just gotta be humble and shit, right?"

He set Amigo onto his broad shoulders and the small kitten dug his tiny claws into his uniform with a cautious "Meow!"

"Ah, talking of a-holes." Jamaal indicated a spot with his chin as his voice lowered to a whisper, "Not going to start liking that particular Plutonian anytime soon, no matter what you say."

Suzy turned to find Federov marching their way. Her warden glanced at the transport shuttle, stopped several meters off, and gave her the come-hither with his index finger. He looked grim.

"Uh-oh." Her friend only half-jested. "Did you do a no-no?"

"Not that I'm aware of ..." Doing her best to ignore the sudden apprehension chilling her bones, she sighed. "Later."

"Later." As the soldier turned back toward the shuttle, the witch walked over to Federov.

"Colonel."

"Ms. Magecraft, there's something we need to talk about." He set the tone of the conversation as 'official in nature.' "I didn't want to ruin the mood at dinner the other day, and I don't feel that it merits an appointment. It's just a question I'd like you to answer."

"O ... Okay."

Shit, what was this about? The hardness in his gaunt face definitely warned her of the fact that she should consider her response to this mystery question wisely and that it might turn out very bad for her, should she even think about lying.

"During our boarding action, I asked if you could do mind tricks," he reminded her. "You said 'no'. So, how come you can now connect to someone else's mind? Did you lie to me back then?"

The real question, of course, was whether she could have changed that situation's outcome—if he'd blown up a ship and killed its crew unnecessarily. Had she cost him his prize? *Really thin ice ...*

"As I recall," Suzy started hesitantly, "you asked me if I could get that captain to stop the self-destruct sequence. Like, by changing his mind somehow, swaying or controlling him, right?"

He nodded, his gaze on hers intense, unyielding, and unreadable.

"And I couldn't. Still can't." She shook her head. "What I'm hoping to accomplish here is the magical equivalent of thought-comming someone and asking them to share a vid feed of what they're seeing. They have to do the sharing; I'm not out to trick anyone or control their mind. That would be wrong on so many levels."

The rings in his augmetic eye turned as he inspected her.

"Good," he delivered his verdict. "I don't suppose we need to address what will happen should your views regarding that specific notion change, do we?"

Wait a minute ...

Another thought occurred to her. If there was a bounty on everyday crooks and pirates, bringing in a whole Velorian *ruja* had to be worth something. Something substantial, even ...

She straightened, squared her shoulders, and crossed her arms. "Unless it's a Velorian and you can cash in on their changed perspective, you mean? Maybe you should check your hypocrisy before threatening me on implied moral grounds."

Unperturbed, he leaned closer, his voice dropping in volume and temperature, as he stated, "On the contrary. It's you, Ms. Magecraft, who should check her impertinence in her conduct toward her warden when talking formally and/or in a public setting. I'm not your coreworld captain, and this type of disrespect can easily net you lashes."

Suzy swallowed hard and her stance wilted self-consciously, as she whispered, "Yes, Sir. I'm sorry, Sir. I was out of line."

"Indeed."

His eyes narrowed dangerously as his gaze pinned her to the spot for several more seconds. Then he relaxed back, smirked ever so slightly and said, "Just remember you're not the only one I'm sworn to protect."

"If I fall off that cliff, I probably deserve it." She remembered the Velorian mage he'd slaughtered and shivered. "Just make it quick and painless, please?"

Federov merely raised an eyebrow.

She shrugged. "Just trying to sound tough."

"You're getting better at it. Though, if I remember correctly, I've already advised you to work on your naivety. Where you're taking us, there is no JC. And no one has forbidden you from doing any research. Just don't forget which side you're on."

What the fuck?

Had he just said what she thought, he'd said?

Suzy only stared at him in shock, needing a moment to let that sink in.

"Furthermore," he continued, "I had an idea this morning about how you might be able to take a look at the gate in advance. I'll look into it."

He pointed to the shuttle, whose engines were just shutting down. "Come on. Let's go welcome our new responsibilities."

And just like that, the tension between them dissipated. Suzy breathed out her remaining jitters, and he snorted quietly.

When they reached Jamaal, the AR line faded away. The transport shuttle's door opened, and Diaz and four troopers escorted Xin and Wire out. The women looked like freshly freed survivors of a concentration camp: gaunt and pale, shading their eyes from the brightness, but with a hopeful spring in their step. Relief flooded their faces as they looked around the hangar.

"Xin!" Suzy ran up the ramp to envelop her friend in a deft hug. "Welcome home! It's so good to see you!"

"Whew!" The other woman breathed out explosively. "Good to see you too!"

She hugged back, her grip surprisingly strong, considering her skeletal exterior. Other passengers started to berate them for obstructing the way. Diaz pulled Wire aside and waved for the hungover fault-finders to move past. They quickly piped down once they saw Federov looking on with crossed arms.

When Suzy and her friend parted, Xin said, "See, Marika, I told you someone would care enough to show up."

"Yeah, for you," the other woman murmured.

"Hey Wire." Jamaal waved with just a tad of embarrassment. "I'm here to ... ahem ... accompany you to your new gig. Well, our new gig."

As he gestured to the tracker on his leg, Wire's eyes widened.

Federov stepped closer, asking, "Provost, have they read and signed the agreement?"

Diaz nodded and produced two dataslides.

After quickly scanning them, the colonel nodded.

He held out two trackers and said, "Care to do the honors?"

"Sure." Diaz gestured for Wire and Yin to move off the now-empty ramp and sit on a container nearby.

"Since you finished your chores and accepted the plea deal, which was co-signed by your captain," Federov explained, "I'm now fully in charge of your destiny. Whatever you do within the next five years has direct consequences for my reputation, so I highly encourage you to think twice about every possibly dumb idea which might come to mind," he glanced Jamaal's way and sighed, "On second thought, get a neutral opinion as well."

Xin sat and pushed down her sock, her golden eyes intently studying the provost's faceplate as he fitted the tracker to her ankle. A tiny smile played on her lips suddenly, but quickly disappeared as Federov addressed her.

"Ms. Yun."

She straightened and stood. "Yes, Sir!"

"You'll be Ms. Magecraft's magical assistant until further notice. She explicitly asked for you to help her with her task." He gave both of them a severe stare. "That means she's your superior, and I'm hers. The two of you will work relentlessly on this. If I hear that you're taking advantage of this constellation by goofing off instead of working, I'll find you something else to do quicker than you can say 'ups.' Do we understand each other?"

"Aye, Sir!" Xin nodded quickly.

"Yes, Sir!" Suzy saluted. "I'll work her to the bone, if necessary."

Federov snorted, but there was a twinkle in his good eye as he waved over some information to their BCIs.

"Rules and regulations regarding your new status," he informed Suzy. "... and the details on your assignment," he told Xin.

Meanwhile, Diaz had fitted Wire with her tracker, and she, too, stood as soon as the colonel turned to face her.

"Ms. Delacroix, you and Mr. Robbins are to join the 218th penal brigade, also known as the Crimson Chain Gang, who'll accompany us on this mission. You'll report to Staff Sergeant Bawker and direct any questions about this assignment or resulting orders to him. You're only allowed to bring questions to me if they pertain directly to your plea bargains. Am I making myself clear?"

"Crystal clear, Sir!" Wire saluted.

Jamaal saluted, too, but not as fervently. They both nodded, as if responding to an incoming data package, and gestured to file it away.

"Here are the details on your new assignments, and here," an almost warm tone crept into his voice, as he held out two small envelopes, one to Xin, one to Wire, "that's also yours. Remember where you came from, but don't pay it too much homage. This is your new life; make it count."

With that, he turned and marched off. The four penals watched him go, speechless. Wire patted the envelope, then gave a small cry and ripped it open. A set of small, simple earrings fell into her cupped hand. Her lower lip trembled.

"See." Xin squeezed the other woman's shoulder. "I told you he's not that bad."

With a low snort, Diaz leaned back slightly and crossed his arms. He turned to Jamaal and Suzy. "You two got this?"

"Sure." Suzy gave him two thumbs up. "Thank you, Provost."

He gave a sharp nod, threw another glance at Xin, and left with his four troopers.

"Fuck me, but he's got a nice ass," Xin murmured so only Suzy could hear. With a lot less reverence, she opened her envelope, pulled out the delicate golden necklace with the small heart-shaped pendant she always wore, and put it back on.

"Who, Federov?" Suzy's eyes widened. That guy was, like, waaay too creepy to have these thoughts about him.

"No, Silly!" Xin giggled. "That provost with the complicated name and the hurt chaining up his leg."

"Diaz? Oh, right ..." the witch smirked and waved Wire and Jamaal goodbye as she led her new aide toward the elevators. "Yeah, I guess he's okay. Has kind eyes. And he's smart, I think. You want him for a quick banging or more?"

A sharp pain went through Suzy's torso as Xin bruised her friend's ribcage with a deft elbow slam.

"Hey!" the witch protested. "I'm your new boss!"

Xin merely smirked a nonverbal challenge.

"And you're surprisingly strong for a walking skeleton." Suzy rubbed her side. "So, I gather hell got a lot less daunting after we talked?"

"You could say that." The other woman breathed in appreciatively. "Gosh, it's nice to be warm again. Can we go eat something while you tell me how exactly you had me slotted to be your new assistant and what you expect me to do?!"

The witch laughed. "Sure."

CHAPTER TWENTY-FOUR

WIRE\\ THE NEW SQUAD

"So, how come we get actual, physical trackers?" Wire finally broke the strained silence, which had followed the exchange of safe pleasantries. "Why not BCI tracking?"

"Oh, they do that, too." Jamaal seemed hesitant to answer, like he'd never thought about it before. "I got these rules and regulations to read, and from what those say … and don't say, BCI tracking is the norm. I guess we get this pretty jewelry for psych reasons."

"So we don't forget we're penals." Wire sighed as they started off toward the elevators.

"Among other things." The dark-skinned man shrugged, but the gesture wasn't as easy-going and relaxed as she'd come to expect from him. "I'd say it's to remind us to work hard for our freedom. But it's also a warning to others. See, all penals have a warden. So attacking a penal without good cause is kinda asking for the warden to show up and hammer you into the ground. Or a provost to show up in their stead. And, Boy! Believe me when I tell you, you do *not* want to get on a provost's bad side."

A smirk stretched her lips unbidden. "So you still act before you think it through?"

Jamaal laughed. "Maybe."

He called an elevator, and his voice softened as he asked, "So, ahem ... How are you, Marika?"

"I'm— uhh!" She caught the kitten just in time. The cute little fellow had tried to jump from Jamaal's shoulder onto hers only to miss the landing and tumble forward. "Hey there, Little Guy."

"Meow!" The gray-and-black speckled furball blinked up at her with giant blue eyes. Its soft, warm fur tickled the bare skin of her hands, and she couldn't help but scratch its fluffy ears. The kitten purred and fell back against her midsection, paws in the air, so she continued down its belly.

"I'm better." Wire smiled in honest appreciation. "Being back here is ... strange. If I could, I'd just pack up and leave, I think. But staying isn't the worst I can imagine, anymore, so ... yeah, I'm good."

Jamaal nodded. "Knowing Federov, whatever he had the two of you do over on that plover must have been tough. Cold storage or something?"

"Yeah."

Gosh, that cat was so warm and fluffy!

"I thought I'd never feel warmth again," Wire confessed. "We had to live and work there on minimal rations. Then I was attacked by local thugs running a scam on the place, but Xinyi came through. She saved me. After we got some healing time, the rest was almost a breeze. We shared a tent, which greatly reduced the discomfort. Also, she had a great trick: she would warm up two meals in the evening and slip one inside her sleeping bag, much like a hot-water bottle, then eat it at body temperature in the morning. Once I started that habit too, it got way better."

The other Spartan scratched his neck, asking, "She's really not the same now, is she? Because of the amnesia and shit?"

"No. No, she isn't."

As the elevator slid open, they entered in thoughtful silence.

"So, are you still mad at her because ... you know?" he asked.

"No," Wire spoke out loud what she'd long since decided inside. "Kurt had it coming. I was the fool for falling for him. She did what was necessary."

It still didn't ring entirely true, but she was getting there. One day at a time and shit.

The doors closed on them, and Jamaal took a deep breath.

"Gosh," he said. "would you look at us? A year ago, if you'd told me we'd be in a situation like this, I would have laughed at you. And now, Kurt is dead, Nines is a different person, we're convicted felons, and ..."

"... and you're a cat daddy," his conversation partner inserted as he faltered.

"Yeah..." He gave a little smile. "Also Tank broke up with Thea."

What?

Wire blinked several times to transmit her utter confusion, before she blurted out, "How the hell did that happen?"

Jamaal told her the whole thing, ending with, "At least that's what I've heard. I wasn't here for it, so you might want to talk to Mo or Savoy for the details ... or, you know, ask the ex-lovers themselves."

"Luna, the world really has gone nuts." Wire shook her head. She still couldn't believe it. "And we're gonna work in a Plutonian penal brigade. Shit, they're gonna eat us for lunch!"

"Na, don't worry." Jamaal squeezed her shoulder. "They're not that bad, once you get to know them. ... well, most of them. Amigo is a Plutonian too."

"He's a kitten. Kittens are universally cute and grown cats too self-important to identify with any nation." Wire gave a tentative smirk at her own jest.

He laughed.

"My point stands. Just be nice and respectful, and they're likely to return it." He touched his stomach. "Had to learn that the hard way."

As they traversed a corridor mostly populated by Plutonians in their almost black uniforms, Wire's thoughts became a strange kaleidoscope of almost unrelated facts and feelings. Jamaal seemed lost in his musings and didn't press for more conversation.

They finally arrived at the indicated door just as two guys wearing black bowler hats with copper chains as hatbands walked out.

"You the new guys?" one of them, a slim blond fellow, asked, as he straightened to the full extent of his Plutonian build. "Spartans, heh?"

So much for Jamaal's optimism ...

"Yeah." In response, the other Spartan straightened a little. "Does it matter?"

For a terrifying moment, Wire thought they'd start a brawl right there. That the glittering in the Plutonian's eyes meant trouble. After all, if two felons got into a fight, would the wardens and provosts even care?

But then the man leaned back slightly and broke into a wide grin.

"Nah, just messing with ya." He waved it off. "Whatever you were before joining the Crimson Chain Gang, it's history."

The other man nodded, adding, "Prove your worth, don't act arrogant, and no one's gonna give you a hard time."

"Exactly." The blond guy held out a hand, first to Wire, then to Jamaal. "I'm Khalil Florimonte, you've been assigned to my fireteam. This big grouch here's our squad leader, Staff Sergeant Jim Bawker. Don't mind his perpetual frowning, he got shot in the head once, must have blown his good humor right out the other side."

SSgt. Bawker, a broad-shouldered older man, scowled at his young companion. Then he glanced at the Spartans' trackers and lifted a dataslide for a quick consultation of whatever was written there, while declaring, "Was only a graze and contrary to what my corporal might have you believe, we're an orderly, reputable unit, so don't take his cue and think you can slack off and be all buddy-buddy. As penals, we have to show stronger discipline, higher willingness to sacrifice, and superior manners than regular troops. We're here not just to do our duty, but to earn our freedom. Do you understand, Troopers?"

Almost by reflex to his drill sergeant voice, Jamaal and Wire saluted, shouting, "SIR, YES, SIR!"

"Good!" Somewhat mollified, Bawker nodded and looked back at Florimonte. With a flourish, the other man produced two hats like those the two of them were wearing. The squad leader proceeded to present them to the newcomers, one after the other, with clear reverence, explaining, "Here, these are yours. They're not just part of the uniform; they don't just show everyone where you belong; they're a symbol of your second chance at life and the honorable tradition of this unit. Keep them in top shape. Defend them with your life. Also, unlike the rest of the issued gear, these are yours to keep. Should you die in the pursuit of your freedom, we'll cut the chain and send them into the void with you. Once you earn your freedom, you'll cut the chain yourself and take them home."

Wire accepted the bowler and felt out its unfamiliar stiffness. The chain tinkled faintly as she turned it over and found her name stitched to the inside.

Home. Where was home now? Did she even have anything left but this?

"Any questions so far?" Bawker asked.

So many ... none of which had a place in this setting.

"No, Sir," they answered in unison.

"Good." Bawker gestured at the door. "We got hit hard in our last engagement, so we're left with four bunks to fill. You can take your pick. Uniforms and other items have been provided according to your scans. The first drill to assess your readiness and familiarize you with the use of our equipment will take place in one hour. Get presentable. Corp. Florimonte will provide all the details, answer any questions, and get you settled. Dismissed."

"Sir, yes, Sir!" they replied.

"Oh, and," the frown alleviated slightly as Bawker regarded the kitten, "is this your cat?"

"It's mine, Sir." Jamaal retrieved the little furball. "I'm told Amigo here is the descendant of a family of highly distinguished rodent deterrents."

Behind Bawker's back, Florimonte laughed soundlessly.

Jamaal lifted a small tag at the cat's collar. "I already talked to the ship's master, and she mapped out a section around these quarters in which she allows him to roam free. GaSIn will keep him contained within that perimeter."

Their superior scratched his chin for a moment and

nodded. "Fine. You care for him and make sure he doesn't get underfoot. If I get any complaints regarding that cat ..."

He let it hang there for Jamaal to jump in and promise, "You won't, Sir. I'll see to it!"

"Good." Their new squad leader nodded and left.

"He's actually a nice guy once you get a few vodkas into him," Florimonte took up the conversation as soon as their superior was out of earshot. "While on duty, he has to be a hardass, though. And he will recommend lashes if you step out of line, so better be on your best behavior."

Jamaal raised an eyebrow. "Like you are?"

Florimonte grinned.

"I saved his bacon more often than he cares to admit. I get more leeway than you newbs." He waved open the door. "Come on in and meet the gang!"

Some knot deep inside Wire relaxed. She could do this. This was a world she knew, a world she was comfortable with. Maybe this wouldn't be so bad after all. She placed the bowler on her head. It fit perfectly.

CHAPTER TWENTY-FIVE

SERGEY\NADDI\\ HONEST PEOPLE

"You really liked him, didn't you?" Sergey pointed at the bottles next to Naddi's glass.

A single light over her desk dimly lit her brand-new office. Several neatly labeled, unopened boxes stood stacked against the wall. A cupboard waited to be filled. Stacks of dataslides, which had probably accumulated during her time away, had been brushed to one side of the tabletop. The scent of new carpet and furnishings thickened the air.

"Hmpfh." She gestured for him to sit. "You forgot how to knock?"

With a shrug, the colonel sat. "I knocked; no one answered. I was worried."

"Right." Her voice wavered slightly. With her, it could be a sign of either tiredness or overindulgence. "You didn't think maybe I wanted to be left alone?"

"In that case, you would have locked the door and engaged the privacy settings." He leaned over to lift the bottles one after the other until he found one with some liquid left inside. Naddi frowned, like she wanted to stop him from taking it, but then retrieved a second glass from under her desk and slid it over.

They drank in silence.

"So, you got rid of Antolov," she finally murmured. "Sneaky to use the Spartans. What did you give them for it?"

"Did Diaz tell on me?"

He'd known she would figure it out sooner or later.

"Nah." The fossil filled up her glass once more. "Didn't need to. You were pretty eager to see me off. Haven't seen you sign a vacation slip that quickly in all our time working together. So, what did you give them?"

Sergey told her about the *Gateshot*'s newly established fight club, and she laughed before saying, "Sure, I can do that. They know the rates?"

He nodded.

"Fine then—as long as they don't overdo it. Get people sent to medical or start drunken brawls."

"The Spartans?" Sergey *pff*ted.

"Won't only be Spartans there, right? They don't have enough left of those to fill a fireteam."

Her colonel waved it aside. "They'll be good. If they aren't, we'll dish out a few lashings and everyone falls in line quickly enough."

"Certainly hope so." Naddi sighed. "So, Antolov is gone, the Magecraft girl is back on track, you got your solids and your fun. I get Diaz, right?"

"Sure." Sergey thought back on the man's performance as de facto leader of the provosts for the time Naddi had been away. "He did well. And managed to get his license renewed, yes?"

His provost major nodded, handing over a dataslide. "Begrudgingly took the exam and passed with flying colors.

I don't even think he had to study for it. Got a little judicator in him, that one. Or a private eye. Different way of thinking. I need that in my second. Bellarosa was all right, but she wouldn't have managed."

"Was a good provost, though." Sergey lifted his glass and they toasted the dead in silence.

Silence stayed on for a few minutes like an old friend before Naddi agreed, "She was."

They each followed their own trains of thought for some time.

At some point, Naddi murmured, "You know, maybe I did. Like him, I mean."

Her thoughts seemed to linger on the miner's foreman, whose bunk she'd shared. But then, she shrugged and continued, "But he's too good for me—an honest, hardworking soul. In the long run, I couldn't make him happy. He deserves better."

Yeah, Sergey knew what she meant. People like them weren't suited for the life a miner, an administrator, or a shopkeeper might enjoy.

"But it's nice to glimpse this other side to life once in a while," she continued, her eyes way too heavy with knowledge and understanding as they settled on him. "So why don't you go and find that nice lady doctor of yours? I'm sure she'll be much better company than this old, washed-up hag."

Didn't take her new second long to turn up once Sergey had left. Naddi kept her office doors open. Some conversations needed to be had. Young people like Sergey and Diaz were maybe more eager to fill in the voids between the lines.

They needed to hear certain things, needed to say them. Like some intangible baggage, they collected these thoughts and carried them around, just waiting for that time and place where they could unload them on others. Naddi didn't carry so much anymore. At some point in life, one realized the futility of it. Most words were merely social glue; the act of exchanging them was nothing more than a deeply ingrained mechanism to show appreciation for each other's company. They deepened relationships not by their meaning but by their sheer number. Maybe that was why Naddi didn't have more than a handful of somewhat deep connections anymore. Or perhaps that was because, by now, she'd survived most of those she'd gifted inordinate amounts of words to.

"Provost Major." Diaz wore his uniform without the headgear, the top three buttons of his jacket undone to reveal the dark shirt beneath. An underlying tension in the muscles of his handsome face betrayed the relaxed facade he tried to project.

"Provost." She performed the appropriate gesture. "Care to join me?"

"Sure." He entered the antechamber and walked over to the WaDis. With a glass of water, he settled into the chair Sergey so recently vacated.

She leaned back in her seat, asking, "You want to get on a first-name basis now that you're my second?"

He averted his gaze to the fingers pinching the very bottom of his drinking vessel and smiled. "Only if you do. Besides, I haven't agreed to it yet."

"There's nothing to agree to. I gave you a new position you're perfectly qualified for, and the colonel signed off on it." She shrugged. "The paperwork should be filed tomorrow."

"I see." Diaz leaned back as well, purposefully mirroring her. "And I understand now why you and the colonel get along so well. Both of you know people and have a keen sense of observation. You both like to kill several rodents with one stone."

Naddi nodded for him to go on.

"He likes you not just because of your skills and experience, but for the moral flexibility. And even though it might sound a little self-centered, I can't deny the feeling that my inclusion in recent events also carries a message."

The man's brown eyes focused on hers with the urgent need to know his exact place.

She sipped her drink. "And what would that be?"

"That, should I fail to follow your lead, I might end up like Antolov." The idea didn't seem to frighten him. It was more like an observation delivered by a scientist. "That he's perfectly capable and willing to enlist outside help to do his dirty work for him. That he can entangle Spartans, mages, my superior, and me in his schemes without much difficulty. That I will be expected to cover his ass."

Naddi smiled. "That's why I like you, Adrian. You don't need to be told everything in so many words. It's very refreshing."

His utter fearlessness was also a nice touch. A blade which could cut both ways, certainly, but then ...

"Do you know why I prefer an intelligent subordinate to a rule-hugging moron?" she put her thought into words.

"Because you can use their intelligence to your own ends?" he tested her right back.

"No." She turned her glass in one hand. "Because I'm too old to babysit idiots. And because I don't care for the paperwork and retraining process whenever the nature of this job, the fact that we're attached to an—," Naddi stopped herself and shook her head, correcting, "that we're attached to a mission like this, or the colonel's 'schemes' do the Darwinian thing and sort them out. So, just for the fun of it, let me now point something out that's perfectly obvious to both of us."

Her second-to-be gestured for her to go on.

"There are the rules and there's what's right, what makes sense. Antolov didn't understand that, but we do. Federov does as well. His predecessor didn't. That's why Antolov and the guy, whose orders cost Federov his arm and almost his entire squad, are not sitting where we sit right now. But I don't need to tell that to the only survivor of Penderghast-43, do I?"

The man's entire face darkened as his gaze slid off into the distance. Despite her inquiries, Naddi still had no fucking clue of what had actually happened during Diaz's last assignment. But when noone wanted to talk about an entire station going offline for several days, only to then explode into a cloud of minuscule pieces for no apparent reason, or about the one lone survivor barely clinging to life and raving mad with dehydration and blood loss when found in a badly damaged escape pod, ... well, one didn't have to be a genius to know the magnitude of bad shit that had happened. And she wondered, not for the first time, if the reason for his silence on the matter could be found in an external order or threat, or an internal damage too deep to contemplate.

"No," he finally agreed. "And if we'd had superiors like you and the colonel, that might have never happened. So many good people could still be alive ... which is why I'm willing to stay. I'm even willing to look the other way when I judge it appropriate. Under one condition."

Ballsy.

Naddi raised an eyebrow. "Which is?"

"I don't like to be in command. So if something happens to you, it'll put me in a position I wouldn't like." Diaz's smile felt threatening somehow. "The best way I know how to avoid that is by making sure nothing happens to you. Which is part of my job as your second, in any case. It also means there's one thing I can't ignore. One thing the colonel and I will not see eye to eye on." Diaz stood and started collecting the bottles on her desk into an empty box. "I don't think it's appropriate of him to enable your addiction and I won't tolerate it. If you want me to stay," he gently placed the box onto her desk, his voice still calm and collected, "then this here has to go. I know you think drinking helps, but it doesn't. It makes you less of what you are. It not only dampens the bad memories but also your skills. It erodes your control and your good judgment. It makes you trip up and think you're all right when, really, you aren't."

Defensiveness raged up inside her with an intensity Naddi hadn't felt for years. How did this pup dare judge her on her personal choices? How did he dare presume to know better what was good for her? Had that pesky doctor talked to him?

She stood and narrowed her eyes. "You don't know me."

"Of course I do. Just like you know me. Like you extrapolated what's not in my file." Her unexpected opponent squared his shoulders. "Takes one to know one, right?"

He bent over to exchange his full glass of water with her almost empty one.

"You had enough time to find a suitable candidate for the job, someone who actually wants it. Someone compatible, willing to look the other way. With your track record, you're bound to have collected enough favors and connections to get such a person without the red tape," he voiced the truth deep in her heart. "But you decided you wanted the broken guy, the former CI, the recovering addict. Why?"

She caught his hand on the verge of removing her glass. "You seem to have all the answers. Why don't you tell me?"

"Because you're an intelligent woman, and times are changing. Your way of life is quickly losing its feasibility. It's not just Federov looking your way now. His warding hand might not be enough in the future. And not just that." He gestured with his free hand at the still-unpacked boxes, the office at large. "This change in surroundings removes a lot of those pesky triggers—new office, new quarters, new corridors, new routines. It offers the opportunity to squelch those cravings before they dig new roots into your day. By and large, you've been cutting back."

He couldn't be such a good observer and this daft at the same time, could he?

"That wasn't by choice," Naddi retorted. "Dr. Fox blackmailed me."

He leaned in closer; she could smell his aftershave now. It was a pleasantly subtle mix of sandalwood and bergamot.

"Then why didn't you go back to your old ways as soon as your leg was healed up?" he asked.

Hadn't she? Naddi took a mental step back and reevaluated the last weeks. How much had she been drinking? She honestly couldn't remember. Fuck, if he was right, that meant ...

His eyes narrowed briefly. "Your subconscious has been tricking you."

Quite suddenly, he laughed. He actually laughed. She'd never heard that sound coming from him before. And at her expense ...

To the void with his fearless, contradicting nature! But,

void, he was right ... How could she have missed this? And, more importantly, had this notion that she wanted him, of all people, not been born of instinct but self-trickery? Had her subconscious sought him out as the means to a very different end? If it had ... how could this inexperienced youngster see it so clearly when she couldn't?

Blind spots. After 87 voidforsaken years, she still had blind spots. Starflashed, she retracted her hand.

"It's a good sign," he was quick to point out. "It means you're ready for the next step."

The next step ...

Diaz let go of her glass and opened his palm invitingly. "Like all important journeys, just one step after the next, right?"

He made it sound so easy. He had no idea ... or maybe he did. And why did he even care?

"You would rather leave than be my second, but you would stay to be ..." She shook her head. "That makes no sense."

"No, you misunderstand." He straightened. "I've never had a superior I respected as much as you. What I had was a good friend forcing me into a similar choice when I needed it. That's why I'll stay, and that's why I'll help. That's why I'll be your second only as long as I'm allowed to be your sponsor, too."

Her sponsor.

This irreverent youngster wanted to be her sponsor! Was trying to blackmail her into sobriety ... Now she'd seen everything. Question was, could she get a good replacement in time? Probably not. Did she want this chance? Did she?

"Fine." She grabbed the almost empty glass and set it next to the bottles, then pushed the whole box his way. "You have a deal."

CHAPTER TWENTY-SIX

SUZY\XIN\\ THE LOOOONY CAN

"Wait, you're honestly sending my assistant over to another ship heading for the DMZ to join some black-ops shit and fly a spy run to the gate?" Suzy had to take several steps to keep up with the soldier at her side.

"Sure, why not?" Sgt. Jake Echohawk, the newly minted leader of the infiltrator squad, flashed her his patented 'bad boy' smirk. "They're just gonna take a little peek at the pie, that's all."

The witch exchanged a quick gaze with Xin, who was walking on the man's other side, and crossed her arms in open defiance, saying, "At the heavily guarded, magical artifact surrounded by ships and troops and alien mages?"

"I haven't heard of another Space Gate popping up in the vicinity." He stopped to call the elevator and cocked his head in faux pondering. "So ... yeah."

Suzy leaned in and narrowed her eyes. "Are you fucking nuts?"

He sighed and stepped into the small cabin, saying, "Listen, these guys do it all the time. They're professionals.

They've never been caught. Your aide will be perfectly safe. Besides, it's more ludicrous to wait until the *Gateshot* is in the middle of a battle before taking the first peek, isn't it?!"

"He's right, Suzy." Xin stepped in next to him. "Besides, it will be a good test to see if we can establish and keep that connection at a great distance."

"We only just managed to get it going while both of us are awake," the witch cautioned as she followed. The door closed, and the elevator took off toward the hangar.

"I was told as much." Echohawk ran a hand down his braid to where his dark-brown hair ended slightly below the shoulder line. "But you had a week to practice, and these guys need to be on standby for the actual thing, so they can only give us a limited window. And they'll have to get your aide acquainted with their tech."

Suzy lifted her chin. "Why?"

"Because it's a tiny vessel, about as big as an old-world tank and just as cozy." The infiltrator's voice dropped to that soothing pitch moderators of late-night shows liked to use. "There's no extra seat for passengers. Everyone has a job to do. Still, the whole thing should only take a few days, then you can pick up right where you left off."

The golden-eyed woman nodded. "I'll be happy to learn and work according to their instructions. I don't want to be a burden."

"Xin!" The witch tried to convey—with a handful of frantic gestures—that she should support Suzy's argument, not stab her in the back.

But Xin had no eyes for her. Instead, she was studying the soldier between them with intense focus.

Was she into this one too? That woman really needed to get laid ...

Echohawk barely suppressed his smirk. Given that he was supposed to be a top infiltrator, he probably meant for Suzy to see it.

Asshole.

Suzy glared at him. He ignored it.

"Besides," he pointed out cheerfully, "I'm just the errand boy here. It's the colonel's order, so there's nothing anyone can do about it."

A stray purple tress fell in front of Suzy's left eye, and she blew it away.

Marsdust.

"Here, you might need this." He handed Xin a towel. "You'll understand later."

"Okaaaay." The other woman frowned. "Thanks, I guess."

He smiled some more. "You're welcome."

The small transport shuttle was already waiting for them and, after a quick hug, Xin jumped inside.

"See you soon!" she called through the rapidly closing gap in the airlock door. "Don't worry, it'll be fine!"

With a heavy heart, Suzy waved. Jake stood with her until the shuttle had flown off, and then some more.

"So, how exactly does this work, anyhow?" The soldier tapped his temple. "You just think it and it happens? Like a magical BCI connect?"

"Actually..." Suzy started in professor mode but then deflated. "Yeah, yeah, that's pretty much how we figure it feels like."

"Could you do it with me?" He cocked his head.

"Do you have magic?"

"No, I don't think so."

"Well," she scratched her neck, "then I don't think so, no. It seems to be a prerequisite ... maybe."

Echohawk raised an eyebrow, asking, "Maybe?"

"Ahem ... yeah, to be honest, I'm still figuring this out," the witch confessed. "So it probably is a good idea to test all this beforehand. With the distance and all ..."

He must have heard her hesitancy, as he prodded, "What's the problem?"

"Nothing." She shook her head with as much resolution as she could muster. "It's fine. Just ... needs some fine-tuning, that's all."

How was she supposed to explain that seeing the world through someone else's eyes, especially such strange ones as Xin's, left a lot more room for interpretation than she'd realized? When Suzy thought of the multi-colored strangeness that was her best friend's perception, the mere echo of it left her mind reeling. How the other one could be so chill about it was beyond her understanding. For Suzy, it carried the distinct feeling of tripping all the time. So weird ...

So, yeah, it was probably a good idea to have Xin scout out the gate ahead of time. But what if Suzy didn't manage to make the connection when she was so far away? And, even worse, what if she did and she couldn't make heads or tails of what Xin was seeing? And what ...

"What ... What if something happens to them?" she whispered.

What if she'd just found herself a set of proper eyes and this rushed excursion killed Xin before she could help Suzy with the *Gateshot*'s desperate problem?

"It won't." Echohawk's strong fingers stroked her back reassuringly before settling on her shoulder. "I haven't ever seen one myself, but I know those vessels are made with top-of-the-line stealth technology. It keeps all the heat inside, no emissions of any kind to detect, scrambling tech up to their ears, and its size and shape make it very hard to detect via traditional methods."

"Traditional?"

"Visual and such." The man smiled grimly. "Don't worry. They've already flown several circles around the gate. Where do you think all that intel about the state of the Velorian stations is coming from?"

"Void, I hope you're right." Suzy pressed her lips together tightly. "For all our sakes."

Xin ran a hand over the tiny vessel's hull as she studied the artwork adorning the black sphere's entry hatch. A tin can with four heads sticking out of it, the name of the vessel, *The Loooony Can* was artfully drawn underneath and sported four 'o's.

There were a lot of remnant colors glinting all over this vessel. It must have been home to a multitude of strong emotions over a prolonged period.

"It's beautiful," she told the squat man with the white buzz cut, observing her with narrowed eyes. "Thank you so much for letting me catch a ride on your ship, Captain."

The subtle strands of brooding color wafting about his short frame dispersed somewhat as he nodded and opened the hatch.

"So, I was told that you'll teach me to man one of the stations?" She ducked to glance inside the tight space. While the craft had three stories, one was given over almost entirely to machinery, most notably the heat collector, and seemed to be hardly more than an access corridor for repairs. The remaining two were interlocked for maximum use of limited space, and even the *Gateshot*'s chief engineer would have had a hard time standing upright anywhere inside. A sense of overwhelming intimacy clung to all surfaces, almost like a tangible presence. Not in a bad way, it just ... existed. Might be that no one but her even gave it any notice.

"Damn right!" he assured her. "In my *Can*, every man has a job to do; there's no room for useless hitchhikers!"

She nodded. "I understand, Sir. I'll be happy to work according to your instructions."

"Good." Some of the dark color faded as he gestured inside. "You'll take the bombardier's position. It's the easiest to learn in a pinch and the least essential during a reconnaissance sweep. Strap in down there, and I'll explain the defenses."

Xin followed his instructions, working the instruments to the best of her abilities. After several simulations, he nodded, somewhat mollified, and told her to get some rest.

The *Sanji Merabti*, a frigate carrying 86 souls including *The Loooony Can*'s crew and a platoon of voidwalkers, made her way to the DMZ's border within two-and-a-half days. A lot of time to get comfortable with the bombardier's controls and the *Can*'s tiny space ... well, as comfortable as one could get with that anyway.

When Xin was called back to the hangar for the real deal, nervousness finally made an appearance. In about half an hour, she was to find out how much worse it would be being cooped up in there with three other people and nowhere to go for at least 48 hours.

"Sorry, they couldn't find you a female crew on such short notice," the copilot and navigation officer, an older gentleman with a myriad of beige and plum colors gently churning around him, remarked, not for the first time.

"It's fine." Xin fingered the buttons on her boilersuit self-consciously. "I'm not ... particularly shy, I think."

"You think?" The sensors guy, a bright-eyed young man with the build of a fairy, raised an eyebrow. "Shouldn't a pretty girl your age know if she can handle doing her business within arm's reach of three strange guys?"

"Well ..." Xin tightened her grip on Echohawk's privacy towel. "I can't remember ever being in a situation like this, so ... we'll see."

"Feel free to use that as a blanket, first. *The Loooony Can* has been cooled down to freezer status," the copilot said as he joined the captain in his outward inspection of the vessel. "Enjoy the chill while it lasts; with four people practically sitting in each other's laps, it'll get hot in there fairly quickly. And the heat storage can only contain so much. It's set to keep us from cooking in our own skins, not to keep us at a balmy temperature."

"I hope you're as all-around attractive as your face suggests." The sensors guy winked to indicate the joke. "I've had to look at these two geezers' deepening cracks and perspiring craters for long enough."

"Youngsters these days." The captain shook his head in faux exasperation. "No respect for their elders anymore."

His second merely smiled, like it was an old joke, almost part of a ritual, and the sensors guy winked at Xin once more.

"Just joking. Come on, we have to get in first, anyhow."

He motioned. "Let's get comfy and start on the pre-flight checklist."

As the tiny hatch opened with a hiss, frosty air wafted out of *The Loooony Can*. The sensors guy shivered, then gave a start, and squeezed inside. Suddenly, Xin was very grateful for the cold resistance she'd developed while working in storage. With everyone on the crew being at least a head smaller than her, not having been a born and bred Spartan was also a plus. Height definitely did not count as an advantage in this job.

Like well-oiled clockwork, the remaining two strapped in next to them just as they'd reached the end of their checklists and continued with the inspection of the navigation and flight setup. Within minutes, they were good to go, and the *Can* hovered into position for takeoff, the hatch only closing at the last second. With everyone sitting almost on each other's laps, voices were kept down, and concentration seemed a palpable creature sitting on everyone's chest. Still, Xin cherished this new experience, so far removed from anything else she'd yet encountered.

"So, you're a magic wielder?" the sensors guy whispered once they'd cleared the traffic zone and his work boiled down to keeping an eye out for space debris and such.

"Well ... yeah, I guess." That remained a strange thought, even after all of Suzy's training. "But mostly I just ... see things."

"Like a void priest?" Copilot asked as he programmed a course for the gate.

"I don't know." Xin shrugged. "I've never been a void priest, so I don't know what that's like."

The captain started laughing heartily.

"You're such an oddball," he finally declared. "I'll call you Oddball from now on."

"Is there a reason you don't call each other by your real names, or is that just because I'm here?" Xin inquired with a smile.

"Mostly because you're here." A dark streak rushed over Sensors' body, then briefly jumped over to the other two.

"But also because it's rare to survive this gig as long as we have," Captain added as he accepted the course and engaged their PUs on max. "So it's easier just to call each other by station."

It took several hours for them to reach the DMZ, more than a day to reach the gate. Some time before, they conducted another quick check and then turned off a significant portion of the machinery to enhance their stealth. Xin stared through her periscope at the large shapes soon looming outside. Velorian ships looked very different. Not necessarily their overall architecture, but the impression of their existence. They felt ...

"So, what can you see that we don't?" Sensors whispered and leaned over, his cheek almost pressing against hers.

"They look ... busy," Xin mused. "And some of them have these remnants of light, which I've come to associate with magic. That big one is positively humming with it."

"Shit. I know it from pictures. That's the *Lightbearer*." Captain didn't seem happy about it. "Second largest ship the wigs have in the system. The fact that they sent it here is a statement."

"What's the largest again?" Sensors inquired, his eyes now glued to his controls.

"That ambassadorial vessel orbiting Earth, I forget what it's called." Captain scratched his white buzz cut.

"*Supreme Salvation*," Copilot supplied.

"Is that the Alzheimer's talking?" Sensors quipped.

"No." Captain snorted. "Just never seemed important. It has been moored there since these fuckers sweet-talked the cories into trading and established their presence there."

"And the *Lightbearer*?" Xin asked. Even though it became hard to keep it in sight, she still couldn't take her eyes off of it. Something about this ship called to her.

"Behaved more like a trading vessel," Copilot said, wiping sweat from his forehead. "It's been all over the system the last few years, so we've been briefed on it. Packs a lot of firepower, so let's not stick around to test it. We'll have a visual on the gate within ten minutes. Maybe you should get your connection going, Oddball."

"Those stations are still where they were last time," Sensors pointed out. "But some of those ships over there are new."

"Five *goutas*, eight *rujas*, one unclassified," Captain acknowledged. "Could be a small battlecarrier or a med ship. Do a deep scan as we pass that one on the right and update our logs."

"Aye, Sir!" Sensors went to work. "Active or passive?"

"Stay passive for now," Captain ordered.

"Must have gotten reinforcements from the other side." Copilot shook his head. "I hate that they can just do that. Makes all the intel, which we risk our lives for, second-guessable."

Captain shrugged. "It is how it is. Oddball?!"

"One second," Xin murmured as she let herself fall into meditation mode and reached out for the incorporeal connection she'd trained up with Suzy.

Her friend was there. As soon as the witch felt Xin groping

for her mind, she pushed from her side, and the connection snapped into place. Even so, it felt weak and easily disturbed. Maybe the immense distance did take its toll. Or it could have been the stress of the situation. Suzy's mind did feel unsure and highly excited at that strange point of contact they shared.

"Got it," Xin reported.

"Just in time." Copilot gestured. "There it is. Looks intimidating, doesn't it?"

As they passed out of the unclassified Velorian ship's shadow, the large circular frame hanging in space appeared in the window. It was sturdy, ancient, and ...

"It's so beautiful!" Xin murmured as the runes glowed in the distance, a myriad of colors swirling from rune to rune, lazily enveloping the gleaming metal, interlacing, and pulsing.

'*Yes, it is,*' Suzy whispered in her head, as awestruck as her aide. '*This is ... unbelievable! Just from the pictures, I could have never imagined ... THIS!*'

'*Do you understand how it works?*' Xin asked her in her mind.

'*I ... ahem ... I'm not sure*'

On her end, Suzy grabbed a dataslide and started jotting down what she was seeing and what it might mean. While Xin could feel her friend's thoughts pulsing and jumping, she could only speculate as to their content.

Meanwhile, Captain leaned their craft into a wide arc meant to circle the alien artifact. Even without a clear reference to its size and the craft being positively tiny compared to everything else gathered here, the gate itself was massive. Even the *Lightbearer* was easily dwarfed by its circumference.

'*What kind of ginormous ships was this thing built to*

accommodate?' Suzy took up Xin's musing as if she'd heard it. *'I bet you could fly* Wayfinder *through!'*

'What's a Wayfinder?' Xin asked.

'Only the largest station I know!' Suzy still sounded awestruck.

As they circled around and the other side came into view, the mesmerizing colors persisted.

'It has several layers,' Xin pointed out to her friend. *'There's the more vibrant colors, then the pastels, and then, underneath both, this muddy, mothball flavor. See?'*

'I'm still not sure how you see flavor.' Suzy felt like she were shaking her head. *Even though I can sense it, too.'*

'So, could the vibrant colors be the ... ahem ... user interface—for lack of a better word—and the more dampened stuff the underlying mechanism?' Xin guessed.

'Maybe ... I'm not seeing an obvious on-off switch, though.' Suzy fell back with a sigh.

'Wait, let me try some magnification here.' Xin felt for the focus wheel and zoom ring, turning both until the gate positively loomed in her vision, once again sharp and crisp, but with the added bonus of immense magnification, then slowly moved the purely optical periscope to get a more detailed look of everything. Shortly after, *The Loooony Can* passed the outside and started another circle. Tension slowly built inside their tiny vessel with every second they spent in enemy territory. By now, Xin experienced it as a relentless prickling sensation wafting over her skin. Despite the heat, goosebumps shivered in its wake.

'You see that very faint halo?' Suzy gnawed on the piercing in her bottom lip. *'I think it's ... energy the gate sucks in from its surroundings. That must be how it gets its power.'*

'But there's only empty space around,' Xin pointed out.

'There's energy even in the void,' the witch disagreed. *'I've seen an alien mage harvest it once. I think I did it too. It was a bizarre feeling.'*

'It seems to collect in these grooves, then run through the runes underneath, and finally surface on those three over there,' her aide pointed out.

'Makes sense. That one over there is a transformation rune.' Suzy was still jotting down stuff. *'And the two sets over there ... Destination and starting point, maybe? Or designations of the two gates? They are connected with each other, in any case. Then these two neon runes on the top have to be the switch. They just have to be!'*

'Good. Then how do we flip it?'

'You could try pouring energy into it, but then the Velorians might spot you.' From Suzy's side, a bit of fear surged through their connection. *'We'll have to chance it. Come back.'*

"Okay," Xin said out loud as she let the connection to her friend slip away in favor of the here and now. "I've got it; we can go back now."

"About time," Copilot muttered. "This place always gives me the creeps."

Captain snorted again as he toweled off his face with one hand while keying in a new course with the other.

"Let's do another sensor pass on the *Lightbearer* while we're here," he ordered. "Youngster?!"

"On it." Sensors redirected his instruments as the *Can* swung back around. "Also, I can't penetrate that unclassified's hull ... maybe we should do another pass with active scanners?

Captain considered it.

Xin fiddled with her periscope to get a better look at the massive ship's outer hull. A single, dark-blue shape near the front of the ship drew her eye. As she zoomed in, she could just about make out a humanoid form standing at a window. Suddenly, its color shimmered into an alarmed red, and the shape leaned forward intently.

"Oh no!" Xin called. "I think they saw us! We have to evade!"

She let go of the periscope and hurriedly centered the targeting system on the ship as she'd been instructed to in training.

"What?" Captain's eyes widened. His colors started churning. "Are you sure?"

"How do you know?" Copilot asked.

"Energy build-up in the *Lightbearer*'s beam banks," Sensors advised.

"Shit!" Captain tapped away at his console, and the *Can* lurched sideways violently. "Oddball, deploy decoy! Evasive maneuvers!"

A purple beam flashed through the space they'd occupied only a heartbeat ago. With the push of a button, Xin dropped a decoy and it sped away.

"Let's hit it!" Captain decided and turned their PUs to max, while Copilot came up with a new course. "Hold your fire, Oddball. We might be able to slip away unseen."

"Aye, Sir."

Weaving through the oncoming rain of beams, they quickly left the Velorian ships behind. The *Lightbearer* spit out a few fighters, and they made short work of the decoy. Afterward, their pilots seemed unsure of where to head and shoot, so, after a few heart-pounding minutes, *The Loooony Can* got away clean.

. . .

"Not enough coin in the void!" Sensors breathed out in relief half an hour later. "That was close! How did they see us?"

"Bad luck, I guess." Captain put in a heading for Plutonian space. "Better have those seals double-checked when we're back, just in case."

Xin didn't say anything, but a gnawing suspicion crossed her mind. She'd seen the Velorian mage at the window, seen his energy. What if he'd seen her, too?

CHAPTER TWENTY-SEVEN

RUFFA\\ DECISIONS

Lightbearer, *at the Space Gate*

Something eased up inside Ruffa as they finally reached their destination. Still no sign of the Humans. Senoxes had provided some chatter, indicating their ships would meet up in the vicinity in a few more days, or maybe a week hence. So they had some time left.

"That last shipment of clones was considerably better than the other ones," he complimented Evron as they left the hangar after the inspection of this latest shipment. "I especially like the enhanced specimens."

"Yes, that dealer had a more sophisticated process, which is why they took longer to produce and were almost double the average price of the others." The younger Velorian's voice couldn't quite hide the pained distaste inflicted on him by this particular task.

Still, he'd toughened up considerably since leaving his home on the *Supreme Salvation*. Not enough to voluntarily comment on the enhanced batch. Not that he needed to; his superior had received all the numbers and relevant figures in his final report.

"It's still very crude in comparison." Ruffa gestured for his student to follow as he chose to take the long way along the outside of the ship. "But they'll do what we need them to do. How many did we get in total?"

"About 10,000."

"Good." The commander nodded. "I'm very satisfied with your completion of this task. Your studies are progressing nicely, and I hear from Berestul that you're also applying yourself exceedingly well to your magical training. All of which I'll be more than happy to mention to your progenitor."

"Thank you." Evron bowed his head slightly, his ears folded in respectful attentiveness. "Ruffa, may I ... talk to Jake again, please?"

Something about his face had changed. Ruffa couldn't quite pin it down, but the younger one held himself straighter. He almost oozed self-respect and the first inklings of deep-seated authority. Yes, this trip had done a lot to straighten him out. He also seemed to have rebuffed Erestral's advances, since they'd disappeared almost overnight. So there was no reason to permit Evron another talk with his Human other than to reward him. And as a mere reward, it seemed too dangerous. Nonetheless, Ruffa gave the request earnest consideration.

"I'll have to check with Thallamon," he finally decided. "It's not entirely my call to make."

"I see." The other's folds retracted slightly. "I would be very grateful if you could persuade him to allow it."

Ruffa studied his student for a long moment, then merely nodded acknowledgment, promising nothing. Evron knew better than to push. They walked in silence for a few dozen paces, glancing through the sporadic windows into space to observe the ships gathered around the three stations. This was all they had to work with. Unless more reinforcements arrived through the gate, this would have to be enough.

"What kind of ship is that?" Evron stopped to study the unfamiliar shape.

"It's the first of a new type designed as a fallback plan should our current handling of Humanity stop working." Ruffa's eyes looked over the embodiment of what he thought would have been a better plan from the start. "This battle will give us an inkling on the design's feasibility and possible weak points to be adressed before these are built in larger quantities."

Evron frowned. "What is this plan, exactly? What is the ship supposed to do?"

As the commander explained, his student's face and folds shifted to hide unease and pity behind a bland veneer. Moments like these proved that there was still a weak spot for the Humans inside him. Well, as long as it didn't interfere with Evron performing his duty, that would just have to be accepted. It would dull and harden in time.

"They're just cattle." Ruffa turned to walk on. "Don't waste your pity on them."

"I wonder if that's what the Haslar said when they enslaved our ancestors," Evron whispered.

Ruffa stopped and turned back to face him. Before he could challenge this absurd comparison, his student leaned forward in sudden concentration. His whole demeanor shifted into alertness as his eyes scanned the empty space outside.

"What is it?" The commander hurried back to see what he'd spotted.

"I ... I'm not sure." Evron shook his head. "I thought I ... felt something. Someone. It was very strange, like ... golden sunlight ... or rain."

He touched his cheek like he might in fact find it wet or burned.

"Ruffa to bridge." This might have been nothing, but there had been suspicions of hidden spy drones, maybe even crewed vessels crossing their space. Shooting a few beams that way couldn't hurt. "Release detection strike on coordinates provided by Evron."

He nodded for his student to give an estimate of the area he'd felt the disturbance come from, and a moment later, beams cut through it. Nothing.

Or was there?

"Bridge to Ruffa, we're detecting cloaked movement in that area. It's hard for our beams to keep up with its erratic flight pattern," the *Lightbearer*'s captain reported. "We're releasing fighters now."

The fighters swarmed the area with commendable speed, hunting down the disturbance.

"It was a decoy," the captain reported a short while later with a hint of frustration in his voice. "We're still searching for the actual vessel."

Evron continued to stare out at the stars, his gaze drifting this way and that with single-minded concentration.

Finally, he shook his head, saying, "I think they're gone. I can't feel them anymore."

Something in his voice made Ruffa look up from the scanner console's data flowing from the bridge straight to his personal computer unit. No, he must be mistaken. His student wouldn't chance his people's survival by letting the Humans escape on purpose. That was just silly.

After all, he'd been the one to point them out in the first place.

"Ruffa to bridge," he called. "Anything?"

"No, Commander, I'm afraid we lost them." The captain sounded decidedly unhappy. "We're directing the fighters into a dense net search pattern, but I'm not harboring much hope. If the enemy flew off with any decent speed, they're long gone."

Of course they were. Pesky rats.

"Analyze the scanner's data, send a copy of the raw data and your analysis to Tuvil," Ruffa decided. "Let's make sure that we can spot them next time."

"Of course, Commander."

Ruffa cut the connection and gestured for Evron to follow as he lengthened his strides, saying, "Berestul tells me he needs you for the ritual to keep the gate closed. I'm not sure about it, but then there's not much you could do on the bridge."

"I'll perform my duty as you see fit," the younger one declared confidently.

"Do you have any objections to merging your mind with the other mages? As I understand, a ritual of this nature inherently holds a significant risk for all involved."

A small part of Ruffa hoped Evron would give him a good excuse to keep him by his side. He didn't trust Berestul with his student's safety.

"What else would you need me for?" Evron frowned. "I don't have enough experience to command any part of your troops, or fight, or advise you on the progress of the battle."

"Thanks to your studies, you have a far deeper understanding of military matters than most of those rujas' captains."

"But no noteworthy experience in leading or handling such a vessel." Evron folded back his ears in uncertainty.

"Your self-reflection and modesty do you honor." Ruffa swallowed down a sigh. "Still, I would argue that you have equally small, if not less, experience in performing magic of this magnitude. You could plan and coordinate the Human clones' deployment. It would only be fair to give you this assignment, since you also obtained them."

As the tips of Evron's folds whitened, the commander realized his mistake. But it was too late.

"No, thank you. I'll ...," Evron swallowed, "stick with the mages."

Ruffa refolded his ears to show acceptance when he wanted nothing more than to overrule his student's decision. But then, that was what Thallamon would do. What he had done for countless rotations. Even if this proved a mistake, it was Evron's mistake to make, not Ruffa's.

"I'll inquire about that call," he promised and dismissed his student.

CHAPTER TWENTY-EIGHT

SUZY\\ BRIBES

"So, that's it, hm?" Lucy asked. "The big goodbye?"

"Yeah." Suzy sighed and licked her lips. "Everything's set. We'll be on our way tomorrow. It's strange, you know ... this feeling. Like, a point of no return."

She leaned back on her couch. The comfy cushions met her slight frame and yielded, just about swallowing her.

"Are you nervous?" Lucy combed through her hair with one hand.

Like Suzy, she nursed a large cup of joe. Her white-blonde tresses were tousled, and she still wore her PJs. As it was the middle of the night in Elonia, she sat in bed, comfortably propped up amidst a small army of decorative cushions. The bed itself seemed a far cry from the old bunk bed the two of them had shared not so long ago ...

Well, she was the grand mage now, so she'd probably upgraded. Had she left their old room intact, or had it been given over to some other purpose by now? Would it seem small and insufficient after all Suzy had been through and all the places she'd seen? If she ever came back to it, that was?

"Nerves? No, not really ..." The witch shook her head distractedly as she tried to pinpoint this strange feeling inside. "It's more like ... there's nothing else I can do and no other way but forward. Xin and I trained to exhaustion, and I have a plan ... well, kinda. And I'm supposed do R&R today, so ... yeah. It has a somewhat fatalistic flavor, maybe. You know what I mean?"

Lucy nodded and said, with a smile, "Yeah, I think I know that feeling. It's like you're itching inside to do a million things more, but you also know it won't make a difference at this point, and you urgently have to recharge while you can."

"Exactly."

They sipped in silence for a while, until Lucy prompted, "So, you got a day off."

"I was *ordered* to take the day off. Like most of us. We had this big feast for the entire crew this morning, and I even got the colonel to chip in with much of what we ... ahem ... 'acquired' on the plover."

Suzy winked for emphasis, and Lucy chuckled.

"Gosh ... my tummy's still working on all those goodies," the witch continued. "It was terrific! And afterward, the captain gave a nice, rousing speech and ordered everyone but a few unlucky souls to take a day off and gather their energy."

"Makes sense." The younger twin reached outside the frame to retrieve a coffeepot for a refill. "So, is there anything you still want to do before you leave? You know, just in case?"

Suzy quickly stopped herself from chewing on her piercings. It was a bad habit and totally grossed Lucy out.

"Wellllll ...," she confessed, "there's one thing I'd like to do. But I can't."

Lucy set the coffeepot aside. "And why's that?"

A million reasons ran through Suzy's head, but she voiced none of them, because, if this turned out to be her last day, in this solar system or any other, all of them lost their sway pretty quickly.

"You're right," the older sister said, smiling cautiously. "Maybe I will go and do it."

"Then go." Lucy's fingertips touched the glass gently. "You kept your promise, and there's not much more to talk about at this point. So please don't waste your free day on me. It'll only make it harder to say goodbye."

"I'm still full." Suzy patted her tummy. "Too full for ... that."

Lucy laughed in honest amusement. It made a beautiful glimmer twinkle in her honey-colored eyes and detracted ten years off her face.

"Then go ride your hoverboard, first!" She winked. "Go feel free."

"Good idea. Thanks, Sis." Suzy touched the mirror back as she tried to put all the love and good wishes she felt for her twin into those last few words. "Goodbye for now. Be safe."

"You too." A single tear ran down Lucy's cheek. She didn't mind it, holding Suzy's gaze instead as she pinched the mirror's edge between two fingers.

They shut their devices at the same time. Slowly, gently.

A deep, shuddering breath, a few tears, a hard knot in her throat. And that was it. She'd said her goodbyes to her sister. It had been hard, but not as hard as she'd feared. So, yeah, how about she rang up Jamaal for that race they'd been meaning to repeat?

A few hours later, when her inner clock told her that it should be early evening, Suzy stepped out of the shower, happy and refreshed. She stared at the tracker adorning her ankle. Time to see a guy about a thing.

Federov looked up when she peered through the doorway connecting the deserted antechamber to his office proper.

"Ms. Magecraft, what can I do for you?" He gestured for her to come in and set the dataslide he was holding on a neat little pile on one corner of the almost empty, gleaming desktop.

"So this is the new office?" she asked as she wandered in, surveying the space. "Nice."

One of the bowler hats the CCG guys were always wearing hung on the back wall; its chain was split in the front, with a very faint accumulation of dust on the upward-facing side. A sidearm hung next to it, and a picture of a family. A buff woman wearing the hat, a man, slimmer and smaller than her. A boy of maybe ten or eleven and a girl about one or two years younger. The kids had inherited their father's hair color and build, but the lines of their faces also clearly mirrored those of their mother.

The most eye-catching by far were the two flags pinned to the wall right behind the colonel, their flagpoles crossing. One was the Plutonian colors, the other one his regimental banner. They were the same as in his antechamber, the provosts' office, Garin's antechamber, the mess hall, and probably every other Plutonian office and such ... except for Bogdanov's office and those belonging to the CCG, she'd imagine. Was this the original regimental banner? It looked just a tad more ... ornate. Suzy squinted and cocked her head.

"What?" He followed her gaze and glanced over his shoulder.

Suzy remembered his bit about better not disrespecting her warden, so she straightened and asked, "Permission to joke, Sir?"

"Granted," he agreed.

"I was just wondering." She winked. "If I look at you from just the right angle, will you have flag wings instead of iron wings?"

He merely snorted.

The rest of the back wall was filled with a small assortment of weaponry: some guns, but mostly bladed weapons. A few more pictures, mostly Sergey with Yelena or other soldiers from his old platoon, softened the overly martial theme.

"Aren't you taking the day off?" Suzy tried for some more small talk.

"In about half an hour." The colonel's eyes followed her drifting course and wandering gaze. "I've got to make sure everything is prepared and in place for tomorrow."

"Right." Suzy nodded. "So, everyone seemed pretty happy about those extra delicacies we contributed to the party this morning..."

Federov took a deep breath and leaned back in his seat. "Ms. Magecraft, I do want to get to my time off. Just spit it out, already."

"Sure, sorry."

With a sudden onset of stage fright, the girl fished in her pocket. Should she give him one or two? If she gave one, it might not be enough. If she gave two, he might expect her to stick to that price in future negotiations, and it might get costly over time ... but then, this was a special occasion. And she wanted this. So much so that she'd have given him three or five, but that would have shown desperation. It might give him ideas on a weak point he could slam down on, should he ever feel like forcing her cooperation. No, this had to be smooth. And the right amount. Of money as well as honesty.

So she set down two drinking ration coins on his desk and slid them over, doing her best to keep any emotion off her face and out of her voice as she murmured, "Since it's anyone's guess if we'll survive the run, I'm planning on enjoying myself tonight. I would very much appreciate it if you were ... too preoccupied with your leisure activities to check up on my whereabouts."

Federov raised an eyebrow.

"I won't leave the ship and I'll be fit enough to kick all the *parrucche*-ass I can tomorrow. You have my word on that."

With a slow smile and an almost proud twinkle in his good eye, her warden reached over and palmed one of the coins, leaving the other untouched, as he said, "Well, how fortunate for you that I have plans and will probably be too drunk to check up on anyone tonight. However, if you get into trouble, this deal is invalid. Got it?"

"Aye, Sir!"

"Good. You did remember who else has access, *daniete*?"

"*Da*." She smiled and retrieved the second coin. "Already took care of that."

He nodded and picked up another dataslide, dismissing her by way of inattention. Suzy left, her soul soaring with the success as well as shivering with the notion of actually going through with this.

CHAPTER TWENTY-NINE

GLEN\\ RUMMY

Contrary to his own orders as well as his best intentions, Glen spent most of this last day in his office before giving the new bridge one last inspection. He was just done with his final round of the ample space and stood next to his new chair when the doors opened. Light footsteps entered, and he turned, expecting his ship's master to make an appearance. Maybe she had another question or something else to discuss regarding their wee ace in the hole. But the small, cautious voice belonged to someone else entirely.

"It does look nice," Ms. Rivers judged as her moss-green eyes glanced around. "Still gets me how much bigger it is now!"

They'd managed to complete a few simulations, but since this had been one of the last construction sites to be finished, everyone was still getting used to it ... including the ship's captain.

"Aye." Glen nodded.

"Maybe we should have run one more simulation." The young lass fidgeted nervously.

"Na." The seasoned admiral laid a gentle hand on her shoulder. "It would have only tired everyone out. This is the time to rest up."

Her body tensed briefly under his touch. Just as he meant to pull back his hand, though, the lass relaxed, even leaned into the contact slightly.

She gifted him a smile and asked, "So why don't you?"

He merely shook his head with a hint of self-deprecation.

"Right. Well... I was thinking, ahem. We... The only times we ever sit together are for official meetings and official scoldings," she said, producing a deck of cards and a bottle labeled 'Ginger Wine' from behind her back. "I hear you play a mean hand of Rummy. Would you care for a game? Just to wind down, no wager or nothing."

Glen laughed. "Who told you I played Rummy?"

She gnawed on her lower lip as if unsure if she should say, before muttering, "Nick might have made a mention of it. Something about you playing with your daughters?"

"With my youngest one, Caley, aye." He held out a hand and she passed him the cards. "She likes to play for hours. Getting crushed by her is just part of the fun."

Rivers smirked at that.

"Is it that hard to imagine me losing after those defeats you already witnessed?" He winked congenially.

"To be fair, those were mostly bad luck," she said. "... and some bad calls on the part of your subordinates. Me included."

"Well, no one's infallible. And you worked hard to get better. I appreciate that."

She glanced away briefly.

"Are these the Plutonian 'most wanted' cards I've been hearing so much about?" he asked and shook out the package to take a look at the faces Plutonian high command was willing to pay substantial bounties on.

"Yeah, I didn't pack any, so I had to borrow." Redhead Rivers shrugged. "Interesting concept, to say the least."

"Aye. Well, with two poker decks, we'll still be two wild-cards short of a complete Rummy set."

A slow smile spread on her face. It made all the freckles speckling her nose and cheeks dance, as she challenged, "Only makes it more interesting, wouldn't you say?"

He laughed. "Right you are. Well, let's go to *The Beak* and see if this old man remembers the rules of the game."

"Maybe we should head for your office instead." She fell into step beside him. "I wouldn't want you to lose face if the Plutonians start their betting and you cost them precious ration coins ..."

Now, who was back to her cocky superiority? As long as it didn't interfere with her duty anymore...

"I'll risk it. A captain has to show some presence before a battle, and I've dawdled around here long enough."

The guards saluted and opened the inner door for them.

"Hey, what's that?" Rivers stopped to inspect the bronze bell hanging in a small alcove within easy reach of the guard. Then her eyes glanced upward at the large plaque. Both items were inscribed with their ship's name and the date that should have been either that of the official christening ceremony or their maiden voyage. Since the *Gateshot* had never been christened, it had been decided to memorialize the date they'd so rudely been forced to flee Helper1 half-finished.

"Old Earth tradition." Glen's fingers stroked the plaque reverently. "Used to be that all ships got a bell and a plaque. But it's not all that common on Mars, and Eve's people don't do it at all, so she hadn't included them in her original design. But in the PR, they apparently still stubbornly cling to this tradition. Col. Federov labeled not having these a severe breach of protocol and had them made."

"That's ... ahem ... awfully nice of him."

"Not really." Glen laughed. "He also instructed the guards to ring it every time I, Cmdr. Sheridan, or anyone else of note, enters the bridge. And to any and all ceremonies. It'll be annoying as hell once the shit starts flying. So I think of it more as a bit of light-hearted revenge."

Rivers grimaced. "Well, then it's petty."

Glen shrugged. "Or maybe it's both. I've come to think of the colonel as anything but black and white."

They left the bridge and headed for the elevators.

As they wove their way through the throngs of people merrily enjoying their free time in the *Gateshot*'s primary bar, the woman behind the counter caught their attention.

"Captain!" Barbie set two glasses and two bottles on the steel counter. "I figured you'd show up, so I took the liberty of reserving a central booth for you." She pointed at the one directly at the head of the triangular floor plan.

"Much obliged, Ms. Veltriva." Glen nodded his thanks and took the offered refreshments, setting two coins on the counter. "Where's Dr. Lustig?"

"You'll need him in top condition tomorrow. No one needs me. So I told him to stay in with that cute partner of his and let me take the double shift." She pushed the coins back. "This one's on me. Small thanks for letting me tag along. Hadn't thought I'd get in on any adventures anymore. But then, I never thought I missed it."

"I can already tell that we're lucky to have you."

She laughed. "Cut the charm and get on with your evening, Admiral."

"Aye, aye, Ma'am. Just don't make my men too drunk to work tomorrow!"

She gestured. "Ah, please! I wasn't born yesterday and this is far from my first battle."

"Good to know." He winked and excused himself to make room for other thirsty customers.

Glen led his companion over to the empty booth. After a series of games, of which he won two, and a lot of congenial small talk, his instincts finally decided it was the perfect time to ask that one important question on his mind.

"Say, Ms. Rivers, why do you want to be on the bridge so badly?"

"Honestly?"

He nodded. For a few hesitant heartbeats, the lass chewed her bottom lip and stared at her cards. Then, she set them down to look him squarely in the eyes.

"Because of you, of course." She swallowed. "Because seeing you in action makes me feel safe. It makes me feel like I can do this," she gestured around. "And I'm pretty sure I'm not the only one who feels that way."

He cocked his head questioningly, but it quickly became clear that this was all she would say.

Well, maybe he did have more of a reputation left than he'd realized.

CHAPTER THIRTY

SERGEY\\ GINGER WINE

"So, we're off to the gate tomorrow."

Sergey looked up to find Dr. Felicity Fox standing next to his table. It was the first time he'd seen her wearing civilian clothing: simply tailored, dark pants and a loose-fitting green blouse that accentuated the sparkle in her luminous eyes.

"Mind if I join you?" The color of her subtly applied makeup beneath her raised eyebrow was slightly off.

He gestured. "I'd be honored, Doctor."

"Felicity." She set a large bottle and two glasses on the table.

"*Encantado.*" He smiled. "Sergey."

"*Encantada.*" With a nod, she slipped onto the chair opposite. "This is not a date."

"And why would I think it is?"

"I'm not saying you would; I'm just making sure there's no room for misinterpretation." She opened the bottle and filled up both their glasses generously before toasting. "To surviving this mess. *Nastrovje!*"

"*Nastrovje!*" He clinked glasses with her and tested the

amber fluid. Even though there wasn't much alcohol in it, a natural burn flamed down his throat and warmed his insides. It was quite nice. It took him a moment to recognize the taste.

"Ginger wine?" he asked.

She nodded. "Only have a few bottles left."

"Then I'm honored that you're sharing one with me. Is there a special occasion?"

"Except for us doing a suicide run tomorrow?" She shrugged. "Maybe I just wanted to show my appreciation for how you handled Xinyi and Marika. That you handled it, I mean."

"You still don't appreciate my methods." He turned the glass around in his hands, his eyes on her. "Even though your patients are fine and everything turned out rather well?"

She glanced away. "At least you did something about it. And you've got them reintegrating. They'll fight their way up from there."

Something was off. Her sentiment didn't seem like a lie, more like it skirted the truth. But, hey, she was sitting here, across from him. Did it matter why?

"I'm sure they will." Sergey held out his glass once more. "To second chances."

"To never giving up," she corrected. What looked like the memory of a painful joke played in the lines of her face.

They drank, then shared a long moment of silence. Felicity's eyes wandered outside the window to where the *Voidhammer* and two of her sisters hung suspended, their escorts gathered around them.

"An impressive sight, isn't it?" he ventured.

Something like distaste crossed her face. "I'm sure you'd

think so." She refilled their glasses. "And I'm not here to lessen your sightseeing experience."

"But?" he nudged when she didn't continue.

She smiled briefly, joylessly. The facial expression vanished as quickly as it had appeared, settling into a bland, slightly sad expression. She shook her head wordlessly.

"You're a pacifist and a healer, not just by trade, but by conviction." He kept his eyes on the glass in his hand, noting her reaction only in his peripheral vision. "Standing on the eve of a battle, especially one this large, must fill you with dread."

Probably why she was here, and not wallowing in her quarters. She'd probably gotten restless. But why, then, pretty herself up to sit across from the embodiment of everything she found so unbearable? This woman was a mystery wrapped in an enigma. Unraveling her became an increasingly tantalizing objective with every one of these more private meetings.

"You probably scowl at pacifists," she murmured. "Sheltered idiots with no realistic understanding of how the universe works. Lovey-dovey kumbaya-singers, unable to defend themselves, that don't even understand how their shibboleths spit on everything you've sacrificed to safeguard you and yours."

Cautiously, she reached out to trace the back of his artificial hand with one soft index finger. The unexpected intimacy of the moment made goosebumps ripple up his arm.

"I used to." He met her gaze head-on and turned his hand palm up. "But then I've never met one like you before. You're highly protective. I think that's why you understand, even if you don't enjoy this understanding, that in some instances, there are no satisfying, peaceful solutions to a given struggle. In a somewhat backward way, people like me, doing the things that we do, building and securing those bubbles that make pacifism possible in the first place."

She nodded, her finger tracing the intricate knuckles and smooth contours. "I see your point. I see the necessity of this mission."

Felicity took a deep breath and glanced outside again as she continued, "A full-on attack on the gate is just not what I signed up for. This will kill a lot of people. It might start a war. I didn't sign up to be on the side of the aggressors."

Sergey's fingers snapped closed and entrapped hers. Surprised by the sudden pinch, she stared at his hand, then at his face. "We're not the aggressors here, Felicity." He kept his voice calm and reasonable, even though the sentiment made him angry. "If someone came into your home, swayed one of your kids to walk out with them, forced another along, and raped a third in the closet, would it all be okay just because they left you a brand-new holo-display? No, even you would take back your kids and kick the fucker out —probably with a lot fewer teeth than he showed up with. We're not the aggressors here. We're just the ones who'll kick them out."

She averted her gaze but made no move to struggle against his hold. She knew he was right, that there was more than black and white to situations like these. As a psychologist, she'd probably encountered more than one abusive relationship, which couldn't be mended with words. Sometimes, there were no peaceful solutions. Still, the hope in her heart was strong and pure. Maybe it was that what intrigued him so much. This view of life, he couldn't afford to entertain himself. The fact that she was obviously deeply conflicted about it as well, and that this argument might erode just a little bit more of her hope away, turned his anger into sadness. Slowly, Sergey opened his pinched fingers and stroked her hand gently between both of his. Felicity accepted the gesture and changed the subject.

As they emptied the bottle over the course of several gently unfolding hours, idle chatter never quite reached the point of budding intimacy again. No life stories were shared, just anecdotes. Some white lies and some muted truths. But that was okay. Even if she'd been up for it, with tomorrow requiring all of his focus, Sergey didn't feel like he could have given her the kind of attention she deserved tonight, so he didn't push for anything. They both decided to retire early, and he escorted her to the elevators and let her have the first cabin. As the doors closed between them, Felicity gave him that special kind of smile, the one that could make a man's heart melt if he wasn't careful.

"That was nice," she said. "Thank you for understanding."

He merely nodded and smiled back.

CHAPTER THIRTY-ONE

NICK\\ A ONE-TIME DEAL

"You have to be kidding me," Nick said, staring at the playing board. No way he could win this game now. But then it was his own fault for playing against an AI with enough computational power to run a small waystation.

Gabe chuckled and moved the final piece into position. "Game..."

The door chimed.

"...over."

Who would come by at this hour? Nick checked the clock—almost 2200. The Human traded a look with his drone. Gabe did that bobbing thing that equated to shrugging in his nonverbal vocabulary and should never be confused with the other sort of bobbing, which meant 'yes.'

"Who's there?" Nick studied the board. Maybe there was still some way he could at least—

"It's Suzy," a small voice piped up outside. "Do you have a minute?"

Nick rubbed his temple. Then he motioned to his left, and the spacious single bed hinged itself back into the wall, messy covers and all. The XO's quarters were only slightly larger than the two-person quarters Eve was still residing in and way smaller than what Glen and Suzy had.

One room held the bed, two chairs set on either side of a small table bolted to the opposite wall, a large hidden locker, and a small couch next to the door. It was really all he needed. An adjacent room held his personal bathroom—a real luxury on any spaceship.

"Sure, come in." The XO stood to face the door.

The bad feeling in his gut intensified when the door slid open to reveal the young woman wearing a cute little dress and unobtrusive makeup. And high heels.

Gabe's central camera eye gave a little *whirr*ing sound as the drone inspected the late visitor and then swung around to examine his Human.

—[Secure channel: Gabe, Nick]—

Gabe: You need help with this?

Nick: No, I'll make her feel better, then send her on her way.

Gabe: Let her down easy, Casanova. No falling for the kid, okay?

Nick: Gabe, she's way too young for me.

Gabe: Plus, she just recently broke it off with Thea, and it's the evening before battle. Emotions run high in you meat sacks right now.

Nick: Relax, I'm not gonna take advantage. You know me better than that!

Gabe: I also know you're easily swayed by a hot chick. And she's a badass, so don't underestimate her.

Nick: Yeah, yeah.

—

Judging by the slightly distracted expression in Suzy's eyes, the drone was giving her a similar pep talk. Probably something along the lines of "Hands off my meat bag!"

When Suzy blinked and glanced away, her cheeks colored prettily. Gabe snorted.

He circled the girl once, then kept his central eye on her until he'd cleared the doorway and turned to accelerate down the corridor. The door closed behind him, leaving the two Humans in awkward silence.

Letting her go first and make a fool out of herself might be a cruel but efficient way to deter her.

But, damn, she did look good. Several months of physical training had almost balanced out her scrawny frame to normal proportions. The high heels lifted her ass, and the neckline of the wine-red dress enlarged her small breasts optically, as well as inviting a generous peek at the tattoo above her heart. Nick felt her eyes roam over his body, still clad in uniform trousers and a white tee. He hadn't expected company, and if he'd known she'd show up like this, he'd probably have put on more.

Their eyes met, and the heat in her gaze was almost electrifying in its unexpectedness. Suzy prowled forward, stopping only a handspan away, gazing up at him.

"I think you know why I'm here," she purred. "At least Gabe gave me an indication that you did."

"Maybe."

Damn, she smelled good. Spicy somehow, but there was still that underlying fragrance he'd become so accustomed to in their shared sweating and training. A memory of him pressing her to the ground in a hold that made her tap out later than he'd expected became laden with the possibility of new meaning in his head. She'd always had an eye on him. Had she enjoyed his body weighing her down too much to give in instantly, or had it just been her determination?

... Well, they hadn't trained in a while, so did it really matter?

Nick crossed his arms, leaning back against the chair that was flush with the table, asking, "You need someone to go have a drink with on the eve of battle? I'm sure Xinyi's free."

"Something like that." Suzy blushed some more, but her voice remained steady and her eyes on his, as she continued, "And I was hoping to calm my nerves a little, but not with a drink."

She stepped even closer.

"Oh." Nick looked around, then thumbed at the table. "Would you like to play a game?"

"Feels like we've been playing one since we met." Suzy smirked, her palms sliding down from his chest in an unhurried caress. "And if you ask me, it's time we stopped circling the board and went straight for the climax."

Damn, he hadn't expected her to be so direct .... It was kind of hot.

"No." Nick swallowed that train of thought. "Not gonna happen."

"And why not?" The lower lip she showed off was the only indication that his refusal had any effect on her.

Nick caught her hands before they could travel any lower. "Because I'm the XO now. I can't get entangled with the crew. Besides, you want some guy to give you a twirl, I'm sure there are a lot of them your own age who would happily oblige."

"But I don't want some gawking idiot who pops his cork as soon as I smile his way. Tried that, wasn't fun."

"Thea has taught you standards as well as talking about

sex, I see." Nick smirked. The Martian girl's bluntness had always been intriguing.

"Maybe she taught me more ... things you would very much appreciate if you tried me." Suzy's gaze wandered to his groin for a long, suggestive heartbeat before resettling on his eyes. His stomach fluttered. She had grown up, all right. "Besides, you misunderstand me, Nick. This isn't gonna be complicated at all. I'm not part of the roster, and I'm not looking to entangle the XO in a relationship. I just want to know what it would feel like to be with you. Once. Before it might be too late."

Nick laughed at that, saying, "Now you're really making me feel special."

With a mischievous spark in her eyes, she pressed herself up against him, just when his hands were at the same level as her breasts.

Damn, no bra...

Nick suppressed the urge to feel her up; instead, he gently pushed her away. "No, Suzy. Please leave. This is not going to happen."

"Oh, come on, this is the end of the line. We might not survive tomorrow. This could also be your last chance to get laid!"

Deciding to turn the tables on her, Nick echoed her expression, saying, "Or I could just go out and find someone else to have fun with."

Suzy stared at him, settling back her weight and crossing her arms.

"You must know by now that you have no flying chance with Eve," she said. "And I haven't seen you being seriously interested in anyone else. Sure, you flirt a lot. From the way you behave, from the way people talk, you're supposed to be a ladies' man. How come you're not following through? Is it because of your head?"

Nick froze. His eyes narrowed dangerously as he asked in a low voice, "What are you implying?"

"I'm implying that maybe during your illness, you couldn't get together enough hormones to ..." She lifted one index finger to stiffness, then let it droop down. "So you started to avoid it."

Heat rushed up the man's neck, and his fists clenched at the insult. He knew she was goading him. Didn't make the blow sting less. Didn't stop his male pride from wanting to show her he definitely had no problem in that regard ... well, not any more ... but then that was what she wanted.

"My hormone levels are fine, thank you for your concern." He pointed at the door. "Now get out!"

She stilled. He could see the wheels spin behind those precious purple eyes. The golden flecks in them seemed to move and glitter. She was sizing him up again, almost settling into a fighting stance. He was so accustomed to watching for the subtle movements of her body by now that he could see it before she realized and corrected herself back into a more temperate stance.

Finally making up her mind as to how to get him after all, she held out her hand, saying, "One kiss. Give me one kiss, and if it doesn't affect you at all, I'll go; no fuss, no complications. I'll never talk about it ever again."

"And if I say no?"

"Ah, come on! You've been the one leading *me* on, flexing your biceps all the time and shit! Now I'm a fucking war criminal facing seven years of being tracked and controlled." She jerked her ankle almost accusingly. "By fucking Sergey Federov, of all people! My world has turned upside down, and I got him to give me this evening of freedom—just this one, mind you—to find some peace. So one fucking kiss is really the least you can do! Besides ..."

Purple electricity encircled the girl's tiny fist. Nick's insides jumped as he remembered all the instances he'd seen her use that. His throat dried up.

"...If you want me to go, you'll have to throw me out." She cocked her head. "You wanna manhandle the little witch?"

This was so unfair ... In a purely physical fight, he'd always win, but this ... She'd brought down Tank with this. He could call for help, of course. Not that anyone would ever let him live that down ... Ah, fuck, what was one kiss? It was giving in to her blackmail that he would resent, but maybe not the kiss. Probably not the kiss.

"One kiss? That's all?" he checked.

"Yeah. But a real one, not the 'you're my cute little cousin' kind. Do it like a man." Her eyes flicked to his shirt again. "Also, I wanna feel your abs."

"My abs?" He frowned.

"You've been baiting me with your midsection since the start. Every time you lean against a doorframe with your forearm, so your shirt rides up just that tiny bit. Or in the gym ... They're gorgeous and I want to touch them, just once. Come on, since you're not attracted to me at all, this won't make you change your mind now, will it?"

Damn, she was right. He had been baiting her a few times ... but having her hands on him while kissing her, that might get dicey after all ... His gaze flashed to her delicate fingers. He knew they were deceptively so; she'd built strength in them since first coming aboard.

"Okay, fine." Nick breathed in deeply. He made it sound like he was giving in. Really, he needed it to calm his heart rate down. Thinking about ugly things would get him through this. Wartime memories came to mind. "But when I say 'no' afterward, you go! No discussion about my hormones or what I might or might not feel! These are my quarters, and it's my right to throw you out."

"Sure." Suzy smiled congenially. "If you want me to leave, I will."

She gave him the puppy eyes. It was the last straw.

"Okay, fine!" he yanked his shirt free of his pants. He wasn't gonna strip, but he wasn't gonna hand her an excuse to get her fingers in low. Suzy's eyes twinkled some more, like she saw his thoughts on his face bright as day. She crept closer.

"You have a beautiful body, Nick," she whispered, blushing prettily.

Could she do this on command? *Damn ...*

She looked up for permission. When he nodded, she slid her hands under his shirt, feeling the taut muscle covering his stomach. "I would love to see more of it ... maybe do some licking and kissing ..."

Not gonna happen, Nick thought.

Though it was getting harder to concentrate. Butterflies followed her touch wherever she directed it, and her eyes were so magnificent, he could just lose himself in them. She was a badass, all right, but she still retained that vulnerable exterior, which drew him in like a flame might attract a moth. But, shit, if this went south and he buckled, Glen would give him the hardest time ever. He was the XO. Off-roster or not, she was off-limits. Period.

Fuck, better get this over with ...

Nick gently cupped her face and bent down to meet her lips. He gave her the slow-burning, sensual kiss he'd perfected with years of practice. The motions came back easily enough. Suzy met it. Adjusting to his rhythm readily, she let him set the pace and pressure. Her lips were soft and supple. Her fragrance filled his nostrils and dispelled the bad memories he'd conjured up as a shield. Her fingers splayed over his midsection, one thumb gently circling the rim of his belly button before moving outward. Then she suddenly gripped his hips, and a small moan escaped her mouth into his. The simple gesture tore at his self-restraint, bypassing the thinking brain and going directly to the instinctual, possessive part of him. Nick's hands tightened on her face, and his tongue sneaked through the girl's parted lips before a conscious thought could stop it. She tasted so good ... his heart pounded in his chest as she pressed herself to him, her hands wandering to the small of his back and his neck respectively. Nick gripped Suzy's neck, locking her into the kiss. He could feel her bare chest through the thin materials parting them. Her left hand slid downward into his trousers. Shit, this was not ... She grabbed his ass, giving another small moan which spurred him on, gluing his lips to hers. Nick backed her up against the wall, grabbed her upper thighs, and hoisted her up. Her strong legs curled around his waist as her hands sought purchase on his neck and hair, before running over his shoulder blades. Her tongue slid over his, the studs in her lower lip enticing him to feel them out from the inside.

Shit, this was not—

She moved her hips, grinding them against him, and a groan tore out of his chest. His pants were suddenly two sizes too small. The damn shirt and dress were in the way. He needed to feel her naked skin on his, needed to ... His hands moved up her thighs, under her skirt. Lace panties, she wore lace panties, damn ...

Nick pulled back. This was not what was supposed to happen. He had to stop!

When he came up from the kiss, he was panting, as was Suzy.

"No," he murmured, still holding her ass in his hands.

"And why not?" Her eyes held a dreamy look, as if she wasn't completely there yet. She blinked free of it. "Look at me, Nick! I'm not a girl anymore; I'm a woman! Stop treating me like a delicate flower! This is not about romance; this is about what our bodies need. And you need it more than I do; I can feel it!"

Nick shook his head.

"Oh, don't give me that crap!" She jerked her hip, nudging the bullseye, and he growled. "You're hard as rock, after ten seconds of making out. You're so needy, Man!"

Shit, she was right. And her skin was so flawless ... Nick's gaze fixed on the spot where the neckline of her dress had fallen askew, exposing half of one small but perfectly round breast. Why was he fighting this again? Oh, right, complications down the line.

We might not survive tomorrow ...

Ah, Fuck! So maybe he did want this, but he wasn't gonna be a twenty-one-year-old's submissive sextoy!

He lifted her higher, so she couldn't reach his groin anymore, and pressed her tender form tight against the wall, leaving almost no wiggle-room as he buried his face in her cleavage, working her exposed skin with his tongue and teeth until she gasped, her pulse jumping through the roof and her eyes closing. She was so soft and delicate ... His right massaged her ass and thigh, teasing her with its close proximity to her panties, as his left slid up to cup her breast. Suzy shivered, her hands seemingly unsure of what to do other than hold on to him. He had her now.

Halting his ministrations, he stepped back and gently lowered her to the ground. Her eyes fluttered open, dazed—like a sleepwalker caught between worlds—confusion softening the fairy-lake shimmer of her magical gaze.

"One night." He let her have a good look at him, at what she wanted. "And tomorrow, this never happened. If you're not a hundred percent sure, you can adhere to that, there's the door."

Suzy licked her lips. To her credit, she did give it a few seconds of consideration before she nodded and said, "That's all I want."

"Okay then." With a thought, Nick let the bed hinge back out of the wall as he all but shoved her onto it. She seemed eager to protest for a second, but stilled when he gave her the sultry look and pulled his shirt over his head. Her eyes widened at the sight of his retrained physique as he joined her, prowling atop her on all fours, his chest brushing hers. One hurried swallow later, her lips reached up to meet his as his right slid down her side, his legs boxing her in.

"My bed, my rules," he whispered as he started to kiss his way down her neck. "And you're not gonna hurry me. You're here for a real man, you said?"

"Oh, yes!" she gasped as his tongue flicked out to wet the dress atop one stiff nipple.

"Good." He gently forced her wrists over her head and pressed them down with one hand, never stopping his mouth's assault on her neck and shivering chest. "And as you noticed, I haven't had any in a long while ..."

Well, at least not outside of a dream ...

"...So I'm going to take it slow and enjoy every last second of it. Are you okay with that? Are you okay with me making you scream first? Before you can run your pretty fingers all over me in return?"

The anemic flickering of tickly purple energy pulled back inside her hands, and she moaned, arching her back in sudden response to a quick nip at her sensitive nipple. As he lifted his hand from her wrists, she let them remain right where they were.

"Mars, yes!" she whispered.

CHAPTER THIRTY-TWO

EVE\\ AT THE EVE OF BATTLE

Assuming her liquid form, Eve slid into the pass-through window to join Konani in her austere, radiation-blocking cell. In her metallic guardian form, she bowed to the alien providing the energy for her ship.

"Venerable One." She smiled. "How are you this fine day?"

"Honorable Guardian." Konani bowed back. "Very good, thank you. I enjoy observing these new ships that have joined us. Are they here to help us pass the gate?"

"In a way," Eve said, studying the Plutonian warships displayed on the screen that covered the entire side wall. "I know this isn't how things are supposed to work, but the Velorians leave us no choice but to attack."

"I understand." Konani nodded. "The fact that they try to limit a guardian's freedom to come and go as she pleases, after trying to imprison me, does not speak well of their intentions. These gates were built as gateways to connect the wider universe, not as barriers to be shut toward some."

Of course, she would say that, seeing as how the

freedom to travel the universe was the central joy of her people.

In an unexpected moment of questioning her access to that well of knowledge at the heart of the Great Neutrality, Eve asked, "Konani, do your people know who built the gates?"

After a long moment of consideration, the alien shook her head, saying, "No. Not as far as I know. Actually, I have never encountered anyone who knew. Not even the guardians. It seems that, with the magic coursing through them, they're hard to analyze. But I've heard it said that they're even older than the Haslar race."

So it wasn't a question of access. Eve nodded, her feelings oscillating between relief and anxiety. How could such an important fact have been lost to time? At some point, someone must have known ...

"Is it crucial to know?" Konani offered her a seat on the slim bench set before the screen. "As long as they work as intended?"

"Probably not." Eve sat down with a gesture of gratitude. "And they don't show any signs of weakening integrity, so it most likely is a moot point."

The alien, who looked like a very muddy Human girl, sat down next to her. "How is your captain? He's come by a few times since we had to stop here, and he seemed ... troubled."

"Of course he is." The guardian forced down a sigh. "All this is not what he expected or wanted."

Konani looked her up and down. "You wish to go to him. You wish to connect."

Eve shook her head with a small smile. "I do. But I've neglected my duty toward you for weeks to serve everyone else. On this day, I'm solely yours. He'll understand my absence."

After all, knowledge exchange was a significant part of the covenant that allowed the energy-giving aliens to be harnessed by others.

And since Eve had thought it better to limit Konani's exposure to the crew until they'd passed the gate, and even had to tighten access again and keep the window to the outside closed so as not to spook the Plutonian dockworkers, she was obliged to make up the difference. Time to rectify this and even the score on her inner accounts.

Additionally, Ambassador Bogdanov had made it a point to visit regularly, discussing various matters with the venerable one. Denying him access wasn't as easy as she would have liked, given that he'd just 'guessed' the correct passwords to enter this locked section of the ship and had known exactly where to go ... Putting an end to his visits, if she even could, would also have upset Konani, since she seemed to have grown quite fond of him.

Still, Eve felt obliged to at least counterbalance some of his rather ... propagandistic views on certain topics.

The two strangers to this system talked for hours, mostly about Humanity as a whole and the *Gateshot*'s crew in particular.

At some point, Konani asked, "Why is your soul at home with them?"

The question made Eve's inner world slam to a halt. She wasn't even sure why.

Finally, she murmured, "I don't know. I just ... like them. They fascinate me. Maybe it's just my new nature. Maybe I would find any new race absolutely riveting were I to encounter them now."

Konani cocked her head in a close approximation of the

Human gesture. She pointed at what she was doing, remarking, "The longer I am in contact with a species, the better I can mirror them. Their way of talking and acting. It's what my people do to better acquaint ourselves with our hosts. It only seems respectful. As you know, I'm fairly new to traveling. Some of my kind, who have done this for longer than they can remember, are said to be able to closely resemble their hosts in outward appearance as well."

Eve had to keep the corners of her mouth from ticking up. 'Fairly new' was still a few millennia. In another few millennia, would she talk about such immense spans of time as cavalierly as the venerable one? What a strange thought!

"Guardians do this as well," Konani continued. "It's probably where we got the idea. I've discussed this with several of my kind over the years, as I enjoy the topic. And even with our long track record, our encounters with your species are very few and far between. So I wouldn't dare claim any relevance to my observations."

She stopped, and Eve nodded for her to go on.

"Some guardians seem more inclined to resemble the people they encounter." Konani picked a few stray clumps of mud from her leg and studied them. "But even with their immense base of knowledge, they will do a bad job in the beginning. Their soul needs to adjust as well as their body. It takes time and practice. I don't think you ever needed this. Because you are in love."

Eve swallowed wrong and started coughing. A red glimmer danced across the dark orbs of her companion's eyes, like a whisper of air fanning simmering coals as she silently observed the guardian regaining her composure.

"I'm in love with Humanity?" Eve clarified the venerable one's meaning.

Konani smiled slowly, declaring, "Love is universal,

Honorable Guardian. It is a valuable feeling to have. It holds together the known universe."

"Yes," Eve replied slowly. "Yes, I guess it does."

They sat in silence for a long moment before Eve murmured, "I'm not sure if it's appropriate, though. I'm supposed to be neutral. Should I really be a guiding force in a Human attack on the Velorians?"

"Neutrality is a vague notion at the best of times." Konani's fingers smushed together the mud as if it were modeling clay. "You are a defender as well as a seeker of knowledge. It tends to be forgotten nowadays, but back in the great war, it was the guardians who united the other species against the dark enemy. It was they who tasked them with building ships suitable for war and outfitting them with warriors. It was they who stood right next to the commanders and captains, right next to the queen.

It was they who filled the ships with intelligence. Because the enemy would have killed everyone and infested the universe with death. In some cases, to protect is to keep the balance."

Eve nodded slowly. "But is it in this case? What if I'm wrong? What if the Velorians' transgression isn't as bad as I fear, and releasing the Humans upon them will have consequences more dire than I could possibly calculate? And what will happen once they encounter the other civilizations? The Haslars, in particular?"

"That might be the wrong question." Konani pushed the clay back into her leg. "From what I glean of Humanity, they're not a race to be taken lightly. They're not a slave race. They would rebel against the Velorians anyhow. They would rebel against the Haslars. So the real question is, how much faster they will succeed with our help, is it not?"

CHAPTER THIRTY-THREE

GLEN\\ BATTLE PLANS

Glen studied the holo-shadows gathering around the holographic conference table. The entire setup was significantly larger than his office, as it was designed to accommodate Gunnarson's flag bridge. To counteract this, Eve had applied some digital magic, shrinking the central holographic display while keeping the other captains and the vice admiral himself at their actual sizes.

He paused for a moment when his gaze caught on a gaunt woman with graying hair pulled back into a simple ponytail, who stood talking to several other officers on the other side of the room. Although he was certain he'd never met the Plutonian before, there was something familiar about her. A brief thought later, a label appeared above her head, reading 'Cpt. Theodora Imrin, CO of the *PDN Sanji Merabti*.'

Oh, right.

Now Glen remembered the recording Gunnarsson had shown Nick and him during their visit aboard the *Voidhammer* to demonstrate a Plutonian bridge crew in action.

When Imrin glanced his way, Glen offered her a friendly smile, and she returned the gesture.

"Okay, so how is this going to play out?" the admiral asked Gunnarson, who stood next to him, while they waited for the last two captains.

"The *Gateshot* has been placed under my supervision." The Plutonian's even tone clearly implied that he tolerated the coreworlder's breach of protocol only because he assumed Glen wouldn't know any better.

Besides, like his ship, the *Gateshot*'s captain had a strange in-between role, not being part of the ranking which clearly defined their roles for everyone else in the room. Glen was actually counting on this fact to allow him to ask some of the questions he wouldn't have been able to get away with otherwise.

"You'll get your orders piecemeal, once they are necessary and time-sensitive," the vice admiral informed the interloper. "Like everyone else you see here."

So Gunnarson and the leaders of the other two battle groups were briefed by the marshal, then relayed their orders to their respective assets. Everything was kept tight to prevent sensitive information from leaking. As a former admiral of the Earth Space Fleet, Glen knew this song and dance from both sides. In the past, he'd both followed and led the familiar steps. Still, seeing the Plutonian efficiency in action did make him feel somewhat rusty. Besides, he'd learned never to assume that he knew what was going on. Assumptions could be just as detrimental as any other lack of information.

"The Velorians will go for the *Gateshot* as soon as they see her," Glen told his counterpart. "They might very well bring all their power to bear to destroy us."

He tried very hard to hit that sweet spot where his voice projected respectful conviction without seeming too pushy. After all, he had no leverage in this situation.

"We have enough troops to keep the Velorian forces occupied until you can make your dash for the gate," the Plutonian said, regarding him with a guarded expression. "The aliens might possess a strange mind and be quick to focus on questionable factors, but they're not dumb. Your ship being the first to try crossing the gate might have naturally painted a large target on you back when you were facing them alone. In this instance, however, your ship is merely one of many. As long as you hang back and let us engage the enemy first, you'll be perfectly fine."

What he didn't say was "We know how to do our job. You clearly don't."

Still, these unspoken words vibrated between the lines and in the slight narrowing of the vice admiral's eyes. Glen's mind jumped back to a discussion he'd had with Eve only a few days ago.

"We can't tell them about the guardians," she'd concluded. "There's a reason my people cultivate our image on such a grand scale. So other races don't try forcing our knowledge from us. The Plutonians don't know all this. They board Velorian ships to capture and study them. They might decide I'm too valuable to let go. And you know what will happen to the *Gateshot*, should I be forced to self-destruct."

"Aye." Glen had glanced apprehensively at her office wall ... at the millennia-old alien spacecraft her people might come to extract with no regard for the Humans populating the ship encasing it. "But if we can't tell them about you, they won't give our part in this enough credence. They'll think we're just a minor piece and it could very well ruin their strategy and badly impact the engagement."

"But we can't tell them why the Velorians want us so bad without explaining the whole thing, can we now?" Eve had asked, the internal struggle clearly visible in her bonny eyes.

So the admiral held his tongue. Gunnarson was an astute fellow. He wouldn't buy any half-baked stories, anyway. Besides, he was correct in his assessment of his own troops. The Plutonians clearly were a force to be reckoned with.

It would just have to be enough.

"It's your call, Vice Admiral," he finally acknowledged. "We'll trust your tactical acumen."

"Hm." The hologram's gaze lingered on the coreworld captain for a few seconds more. Then he turned to start the meeting.

Glen stepped in line as the other captains formed a circle around the battle plan. It was only a first iteration, of course. If one could depend on any universal truth, it was that plans tended to change rather rapidly once the first ordnance started to fly.

After every captain had given a quick and concise status summary on their ship, the vice admiral gestured at the display between them, which aided his words with imagery.

"We'll fly standard battle formation Alpha_14 up to the gate," Gunnarson explained. "Then we'll form a battle line the Velorians can orient themselves toward. While the *Void-*

hammer, *Longsword* and *Kopesh* provide cover and suppress enemy advances, our smaller ships will try to break their formation open. Remember that the *parrucche* like to focus to a point that they'll disregard everything else. Our main goal should therefore be to paint them a target in the man-of-wars, so they stop minding the escorts, then exploit that weakness."

The Plutonian captains nodded understanding as the erstwhile suggestion of how everyone would move played out in front of their eyes.

Glen sighed inwardly.

"Two things to be mindful of." Gunnarsson zoomed in on a particular ship in the Velorian formation. "Firstly, the enemy has a new type of vessel. We're not sure what it's supposed role is. Given its overall size and what we can see of its PUs, it's probably fast and agile, with moderate to heavy shielding. Our experts classify it as a battle cruiser and expect it to be used as a linebreaker. We can't be sure until we see it in action, though. You're each being provided with what limited sensor data we could gather. Keep an eye out for surprise attacks from this vessel and relay any additional data your sensors can gather to the *Longsword*."

"Sir, yes, Sir," everyone acknowledged.

"Secondly," Gunnarsson gestured at Glen, "as you all know, we're running a secondary op here. High Marshal Bogdanova expects us to get the *Gateshot* right up to the gate and give her the best possible shot at going through."

Secondary op. There it was, their place in all this. They were the secondary objective, the babysitting gig. Glen cautiously kept all emotions tightly locked behind his professional veneer as the other captains' gazes briefly fell on him.

"This is how we'll play it," the vice admiral continued. "Since the *parrucche* can't be trusted to hold to the Jupiter Convention, the *Gateshot* will guard our hospital ships as they stay at the edge of the battle. Once we break the Velorian defenses, Mshl. Stenmark will give the go-ahead and she'll make her run for the gate. At that time, everyone not currently engaged otherwise will provide cover. Understood?"

Everyone acknowledged this order as well.

"Good. Now, our main focus is to kick those damn aliens' asses so hard that they'll crawl right back through that gate to whatever hole they've come from." Gunnarson straightened some more. "This solar system belongs to Humanity! The Velorians invaded our home and disrespected our freedom! They've taken space that was rightfully Plutonian and dug a trench that kept us from finishing off the OSA for too long. Too many good people have died over the last ten years because of the tactical disadvantage the DMZ presents. Now they've started to openly attack our diplomats and ships. This is where it ends. We will finally make them regret ever stepping foot into our territory, and we will do so thoroughly!"

Cheerful, inflamed shouts of "Hooray" were uttered and echoed all around. Eyes turned hard and faces set into stern, martial expressions.

Aye, this really wasn't about the *Gateshot*'s mission. They'd never been more than a nice excuse to execute what had probably been a plan in the making for quite some time now. They were just hangers-on.

Glen glanced over to where Nick, Eve, Federov, and Bogdanov stood against the wall, watching. As they were in observation mode, they could see and hear what their superior could access, but were invisible and mute to the meeting's actual attendees. Most captains would have at least their XO listen in like this, to cut down on the need for repetition.

While Nick had his arms crossed and a frown deepened on his youthful face, Eve stood straight, hands behind her back, her face passive. Only her eyes and the very faint touch of her emotions wafting against Glen's sixth sense betrayed her unease. Bogdanov set a gentle hand on her shoulder as he observed with a similar poker face. Their newly minted colonel, meanwhile, seemed caught somewhere between joyful expectation at finally seeing action and trepidation at his new responsibilities.

"The *parrucche* have overstayed their welcome and we don't want them here!" Gunnarson continued. "We never did. So tell your people to put their heart and soul into this. For our home! For all our people, who were attacked and killed needlessly! For the republic!"

Another round of fiery "Hooray"s followed by crisp salutes, some more platitudes and propaganda, and finally the vice admiral dismissed everyone but Glen.

"Listen, Admiral." He turned to face the other man. "Just between us?"

"Of course." Glen waved his observers out of the room and cut all connections, so that only he could hear.

Once they were alone, he nodded and Gunnarsson confessed in an almost congenial tone, "I admire your moxie and willingness to go through that alien wormhole with no idea of what's out there. It's a very Plutonian thing to seek new horizons. But we always depend on our base to be there, on our republic to be our safe haven. You choose to rely on an alien for support. I don't think I could ever ask my people to follow me into such circumstances."

The vice admiral took a deep breath as he considered

his own words. Since he clearly wasn't finished, Glen patiently waited for the other man to continue.

"I can see that you're still concerned with the Velorians' interest in your ship and I'm aware that this is probably not what you'd hoped to get out of your deal with the high marshal." Gunnarsson's lips settled onto a faint smile, like he'd seen more than one of these deals play out. Which he probably had, given his position. "But your mission isn't something she can sell to our people, and you know well enough how things like these go, so I won't insult you by spouting empty niceties."

Glen nodded. "I appreciate your honesty, Vice Admiral."

One seasoned officer to another, Gunnarsson nodded back, and delivered his honest verdict on the situation. "Marshal Stenmark asked me for my estimation of your battle readiness and utility. It was I who advised him to place your ship at the fringe of the battle. I did so for several reasons. Primarily, because its crew has had numerous problems in the past, which I'm not yet convinced have all been thoroughly resolved. But also, because ... if you'll permit me my bluntness," one corner of the vice admiral's mouth ticked up briefly. Glen nodded again, and he continued, "your ship has a rather large backside, which I don't fancy crossing my other ships' lines of fire."

Somewhat taken aback by this perfectly viable yet completely unexpected reasoning, the admiral barked out a laugh. Gunnarson's little tick of the mouth spread into a genuine smile, and he winked, which seemed curiously out of character for the military man.

"Well." Glen shook his head in faux disparagement. "I can see your point there. We wouldn't want her voluptuous design to distract your weapons officers from performing their duties."

"Indeed." The other man's eyes twinkled for a heartbeat more. Then his facial expression and tone of voice sobered as he continued, "My battle group will give you the best shot we can. But. Should the marshal decide to pull back at any point and you've not made it through by then, you'll have to turn around or be abandoned. We'll escort you as far as is permitted by him, but we'll leave you behind should you disregard a retreat order. Do you understand?"

"Of course." Glen straightened. "Your first responsibility is to your people, not to us."

"Exactly." Gunnarsson's eyes held the other's gaze for a loaded moment, before he saluted. "Whatever happens, it's been ... interesting to meet you. I do hope that you make it through and come back with a lot of interesting tales."

"If we make it back," Glen smiled as he returned the gesture, "I'll come by and tell you in person."

Dismissed and standing alone in the suddenly wide-open space of his office, the admiral took a deep breath for courage. He envisioned exhaling all the frustration and setbacks of the previous months and years, as he opened his eyes on a reality he couldn't have imagined in his wildest dreams when all this had started. He turned his wedding ring for good luck and decided, rather on a whim, to pray in the words his nana had taught him by heart when he'd only been a wee lad. The fragile hope of otherworldly help remained a vague solace for a man used to depending on his own skill and effort. But then, why not take all the advantages he could? At this point, they could use every last morsel of goodwill any heavenly creature might be willing to extend.

"Help yourself and be helped." Rupert Maverick's voice was free of overblown grandeur and posturing for once as he emerged from a stray shadow and hovered, uncommonly respectful, next to the door. "Do you mind my joining in? I seldom get granted anything, seeing as how my faith doesn't hold the power yours commands, but ... it does feel nice to pray every now and again."

Unable to find fault or deception, Glen nodded, and Maverick stepped close, crossed his hands on the crystal topping his walking cane, and bowed his head. The high priest of Hecate, if he really held such a position, closed his eyes and moved his lips soundlessly in no language Glen could discern. After a minute, he straightened, and the multicolored swirls of his gaze settled back on his opposite.

"I could bestow a blessing, if you'd like." He gestured at the admiral's right hand. "You did accept the guardian's help, so it would only be fair to receive mine as well."

"Does that mean you're willing to do your part, then?" the captain asked.

"But of course I am. What you're about to do is the reason for my existence." The brown bubbled forth as Maverick's eyes lit up with sudden intensity. "You can't imagine how long I've been waiting for this day. Now that it's finally here, I ..." He paused, his fingertips tracing the intricate hairlines along his cheeks down to the tip of his thin goatee. "Also, it might be the last time I can offer this, seeing as how I'll probably lose most of my magic once we're through the gate."

Every last morsel, aye?

Deciding to let go of whatever Maverick wouldn't say,

Glen nodded and meant to extend his right, but the other man shook his head.

"Give me your left," the con mage prompted.

"Why?"

"Cosmic balance voodoo stuff." The blue in Maverick's eyes predominated for a heartbeat as he wiggled his eyebrows. "In many regards, the guardians and I are polar opposites. So it only seems fitting for me to stand at your left, when you've already given Ms. Baileywick your right."

Whatever that meant.

Glen held out his left and Maverick placed it on the large stone before sealing the top with both of his, declaring, "May Athena, Goddess of strategy and patron of heroes, guide your decisions in battle. May Hecate, goddess of magic, sharpen your instincts, and may your loved ones stand with you to guard your heart and soul in your attempts to reach them."

The cool facets underneath the admiral's hand warmed up as the red light inside the stone flared momentarily from a candle's flame to a bright beacon. In the sudden illumination, Glen could count the bones of his fingers and see the dark swirls converging on his skin, dancing around each other to form a picture. Warmth spread to his heart and head, leaving that fortified feeling an important choice tended to leave once it was decided and merely in need of execution. As the light retreated and Rupert let his hand go, Glen turned it to find a rather realistic tattoo overlaying the familiar lines of his hand: a compass, a sextant, and a key crossing atop each other.

"Don't worry, it's temporary." There was a slight strain to the mage's smile; exhaustion played in the features of his face for a moment or two.

Glen rubbed his palm cautiously. Warmth lingered in the symbols. Otherwise, his skin felt perfectly fine.

"Thank you, Mr. Maverick," he said.

Rupert J. Maverick bowed. "No, thank you, Captain. Humanity needs champions of your caliber, even if she seldom knows it until it's almost too late."

Unsure what to respond to that, the captain tugged his sleeve down. He called in his XO to assemble the exec staff, so he could parcel out and pass on their orders.

CHAPTER THIRTY-FOUR

RUFFA\\ INTRUDERS AND GUARDIANS

LIGHTBEARER, *AT THE SPACE GATE*

Predictably, the Humans sent an ultimatum ahead of their forces.

"This is Marshal Stenmark of the Plutonian Defense Navy, addressing the Velorian commander at the Space Gate," the squat, dark-skinned man dwarfed by the Plutonian flag in the background declared. "You have two hours to disassemble or surrender the illegal fortifications surrounding the Space Gate and remove all your equally illegal military assets from this solar system. If you do not comply, the Plutonian Republic will address your infraction against the rules governing DMZs in Human space by removing them for you. Any aggression against our troops will be considered an act of war, and we will respond accordingly. Stenmark out."

Ruffa waved the message away like a pesky fly.

"Ignore it," he ordered, and replaced the view over his desk with that of the actual threat coming their way.

"Shouldn't we at least respond?" Evron dared to inquire. "Maybe it could buy us some time."

"For what?" The commander stretched his folds. "We know why they're here, they know why they're here, and there is no way we could possibly execute their demands even if we were actually interested in doing so. No, this message is merely a formality recorded for posterity. It's so they can claim that they gave us a choice. Nothing we could say will slow their progress, so we might as well not bother to play their childish games."

With some uncertainty, Evron bit his lip and pulled back his folds at the gentle rebuke.

Ruffa studied the line-up of Plutonian ships entering their sensor range. Even with their own greater technological advantage, he didn't particularly like the odds of this fight. On the holo display, 3 man-of-war lumbered into the gate's proximity, flanked by 10 destroyers, 21 frigates, and 39 corvettes. Luckily, some last reinforcements had arrived just five lightshifts prior. It left Ruffa with 9 goutas, 14 rujas, and 10 crubas to oppose them. With the stations securing the gate and his main force engaging the enemy, it would leave the *Lightbearer* and the new prototype to match the guardian's ship. The prototype had an important role to play, so he couldn't risk having it harmed beforehand.

Given the Humans' less developed technology, it would take them another hour to see what they were facing. Ruffa was already exploiting that head start, readying his troops and devising a battle plan.

"We will meet them halfway." He pointed at the exact spot on the three-dimensional map. "It will give us more time to destroy the Plutonian escort and thwart the guardian's dash for the gate. We should expect them to take full advantage of her superior technology."

"Didn't you say her ship's performance up until now was way below what you had expected?" Evron frowned as he studied the projected movements. "Where is it?"

"Yes, it seems she had to underfold with what little quality the Humans could provide her." Ruffa magnified the tight cluster of ships in all sizes. "She probably hangs back to let the Humans take the brunt of the initial attack. It's what I would do."

Evron opened his mouth, but no words escaped, and he closed it again with a slight shake of his head.

"Talk to me," Ruffa encouraged. "Tell me what you think you see that I don't."

"I'm not sure." The younger one scratched his outer folds. "It's just that ... The Plutonians are unaware of the guardians. Why are they even helping her? Why bring so much force to bear for an entity they have never been taught to revere? What if ... what if the guardian is helping the Plutonians instead of the other way around? Maybe her ship is just a hanger-on."

What a strange concept.

"Inconceivable," the *Lightbearer*'s captain judged. "She's a guardian! Interfering in politics and battles goes against her code!"

"Well, she's doing that in any case." Evron pointed at the map. "At least if you're right and she somehow made the Plutonians fight for her."

"An interesting philosophical debate," the commander said, thereby regaining control of the discussion. "One we can conduct at our leisure once this is over. Now we should concentrate on repelling the Plutonians. In the end, it doesn't matter why they're at our doorstep, only how we can defeat them with minimal losses."

"Very true," the captain agreed.

As Ruffa decided their strategy, Evron stood back and listened intently.

"They will position themselves in a solid line," the commander explained. "While the large ships hold up shelling, the smaller ones will try to dive through the holes in our line and attack from the sides. These corvettes and frigates will initiate boarding actions whenever they perceive a suitable opportunity. So we have to present a solid front and not let them slip through or circle behind. The crubas will release their fighters to counteract Plutonian boarding attempts whenever necessary. The *Lightbearer* will uphold cover shelling until the Plutonians are locked into the fight and unable to assist the guardian. As soon as the opportunity presents itself, the *Lightbearer* and her companions will pull out, so they can engage and board the guardian's ship. We need to make sure it's completely destroyed."

"But ..." Evron swallowed, his gaze wavering wildly. "Wouldn't ... If they come at us in one solid line, wouldn't it be better to extend our sides to envelop them and advance from multiple fronts?"

"If we had matching or greater numbers, yes." Ruffa instructed the projection to show what Evron was considering as he continued, "However, the Plutonians excel at boarding and have the advantage of outnumbering our ships. Once they see us spreading out, they'll spread out in turn, creating an even larger circumference. This overextension will make us vulnerable. With their greater numbers, they'll dive into the gaps between our ships and surround, board, or otherwise dispose of them individually. Even our fighters won't be able to counter the Plutonians' sheer numbers."

On the projection, their ships put up a valiant fight, but were quickly destroyed.

"No," Ruffa said, "we need to conserve our strength by keeping our lines tight and cut through theirs using our more advanced weaponry. Once we destroy their large ships, the smaller ones will be without protection and quickly eliminated."

"What about the new prototype?" Tuvil asked. He'd have to communicate the plan and all orders to the other ships' captains, so he took detailed notes.

"Keep it at the heart of our formation until there's an opportunity to send it against the guardian's ship. Its first priority is to destroy that vessel. All other forces will aid it in that effort." Ruffa set up the projection to show how he wanted the battle line formed. The *Lightbearer* in the center, for it was what the Plutonians would surely focus on, the prototype in its shadow, the other ships surrounding them in a tight formation meant to keep the vermin out.

Evron peered at it. "Won't this cut down on our maneuverability?"

"A necessary drawback." The *Lightbearer*'s captain shook out his folds and rearranged them to show his subordinate acquiescence.

The student matched the gesture, though he still seemed unsure. That was to be expected, of course, seeing as how this was his first real battle.

"Won't our battle line falter once the *Lightbearer* pulls out?" he asked in a small voice.

"It takes some skill not to get bogged down by the

enemy," the commander agreed. "But I expect this crew can handle it."

The captain's folds were quick to display agreement. A dash of pride lingered in the flex. Ruffa turned off the holo display.

"Tuvil, relay the orders. Captain, get us moving," he said and gestured for his student to walk with him. "Evron, you'll have to be on your way to the station and get ready to work with the mages. I'll accompany you for a few paces."

"What weighs on your mind?" the commander asked once they'd exited the bridge.

"It's just ... it feels wrong somehow." Evron's folds tightened. "What ... what will we do with the guardian, Ruffa? We can't destroy her, can we?"

"We'll try."

His student looked at him with the crestfallen panic in his eyes which Ruffa himself had felt when first presented with this possibility rotations ago. Just as he had back then, Evron remained speechless for a good while, restless motions of his folds hinting at the inner struggle to come to terms with the idea. Finally, his folds and posture slackened.

"I've heard stories of a guardian self-destructing ..." Evron's voice hushed in that age-old way stories like this were passed from generation to generation. "Supposedly, he took half a planet with him. She could wipe us all out if she wanted."

"If she wanted. Maybe." The commander rearranged his folds. "Don't give these tales too much credence, Evron. The guardians nurture them on purpose. They've infected a whole universe with the belief that they are demigods, to be revered and feared in equal measure. In this little backwater system, where no one knows what she is, the guardian hasn't managed to oppose us in any serious way. No, she's young and inexperienced, like Thallamon judged her to be. She lacks conviction to do serious damage to us or the Humans. That'll be her downfall."

"But ... she's a guardian, except for reasons of self-defense, she can't do serious damage to anyone; she's not allowed to."

A low rumble went through the deckplates as the *Light-bearer*'s PUs increased their output.

"Who knows what they're allowed to be or do and what not?" Ruffa glanced out the windows they were passing to see that their escorts were already aligning themselves with the larger vessel. "Besides, she could have self-destructed at any time. It would be the quickest way for her to return to the Great Neutrality. If they are just code in a machine that can be transmitted into a new body at any time, it would have been the most expedient solution. The only way out of this system we can't block. So, either it's a lie, or she lacks conviction."

"But then, if we destroy her, we'll just send her back home?!" Evron bit his lip. "And that will be a decidedly aggressive act. Isn't the whole point of not talking to them that her people can't prove we're doing anything wrong in this system? So they don't care? If we kill one of their vessels, won't they feel obliged to retaliate?"

"There's the chance of that ..." Ruffa felt his folds tighten. He hated to have an enemy he couldn't pin down. "Unless they lied to the universe, and they are neither immortal nor connected all the time. But history shows that the Great Neutrality is slow to act, and as long as we can claim we didn't know she was on that ship, we might still wiggle out of it. After all, if she had proof that would get her people to act against us, they would already be breaking down our door. This whole operation, everything we do in this system, is playing for time, Evron. We just need enough of it to alleviate the Great Need. Everything else is secondary."

"I see." His student glanced out the windows forlornly. "But she's a *guardian*, Ruffa. We can't kill a guardian!"

"Evron!" The commander stopped and turned to grasp both his student's shoulders as he replied, "That's what they said when Thallamon first gave the order not to ask her any questions. Acting against her is safeguarding our people! Veloria's destiny lies in our hands. This is a fight for survival. If the guardian forces us to destroy her, then that's what we'll do. For our people's sake."

The younger one bowed his head in silent defeat, his ears drooping.

"I don't like it any better than you do," Ruffa continued, his voice a persuasive whisper. "But it's the only way. Just do your part and don't think about it. The guardian is not your problem; she's mine. You make sure Berestul and his lot bar the way for the Human mage."

All around them, lights started to run down the lengths of the walls to indicate battle readiness. Shutters barred the windows, blocking out the stars.

The young one swallowed and nodded.

Ruffa squeezed the other's shoulders as a sign of silent encouragement and goodbye. "Go now. Your shuttle is waiting in the primary hangar. Good luck."

"And to you." His student breathed in courage and turned to go, then stopped, saying, "Ruffa, if ... if our souls really are failing, like some say ... What if we die this day and are not reborn?"

The commander gave it ample consideration. Finally, he declared, "That is the burden of our generation, Evron. It's why we do what we do. To ensure it doesn't end with us, even if our own souls don't make it. Veloria has to prevail. That's all that matters."

CHAPTER THIRTY-FIVE

GLEN\\ THE WAITING GAME

"Are we ready for action?" Glen asked.

He observed the busy bustle on his new bridge. The Plutonian forces were expecting to engage the Velorian battle line within half an hour. To make sure everyone was sharp and on point when the action started, Eve had advised waiting until now to swap in their well-rested prime shift for the secondary one, which had guided the *Gateshot* well into the DMZ and almost to the gate.

The last mid-flight checks came up green, and everyone strapped in tight. All team leaders reported full readiness. Federov's hologram checked in and added military readiness. Even after many simulations overseeing his troops from a tactical operations center, where he had the benefit of strategic oversight, he still seemed somewhat uncomfortable with the reality of not being in the thick of things. That he was also wearing his void walker armor might have been a symbolic assurance for his troops' sake or his own mind's comfort.

"You'll get used to it, Colonel," the admiral encouraged him. "Took me a while too."

"Aye, Captain." The Plutonian seemed unconvinced but accepting of his fate.

Glen turned to meet Eve's gaze.

She nodded, a determined, almost eager expression hidden under the slight smile that was her poker face. "The *Gateshot* is ready, Captain."

The glint in her eyes told him that she meant readiness for both the Plutonians' plans and their own little insurance policy. Since agreeing on their course of action, the two of them hadn't exchanged more than a dozen words about it. As far as he knew, she'd trained Lustig and perhaps a few others among the crew in untraceable VR simulations to keep it all under wraps and as far off Federov's radar as possible.

In response to Federov's little bridge invasion, she'd cordoned off the CO area with a chest-high, bullet-resistant wall from behind and integrated her station into it at the side. While it did reassure the admiral that he couldn't just be shot in the back without warning anymore, having to look up at her from such close proximity was still something to get used to. Since it would take considerable force to knock the alien robot off her feet, Eve—as usual—was the only one of the bridge crew not strapped in. Even their new bridge guards had to secure themselves in emergency seats when battle readiness was declared.

At the back, Ambassador Bogdanov and one of his bodyguards sat in the observers' corner. To their right, Maverick leaned against the wall, his cat on his shoulders. Suzy's hologram stood with the little group, and even Dr. Fox had decided to attend the crossing of that invisible line marking the official start of what might as well be their last battle via holographic shadow. The fact that, on this occasion, Pro. Maj. Garin had decided to lead the bridge guard herself, while simultaneously keeping an ear on her provosts' comm channels, left the admiral with mixed feelings.

To his friend's right, Nick straightened and said, "Full combat readiness confirmed, Captain!"

"Good." Glen took a deep breath. "Lt. Singh, open a ship-wide channel."

"Channel is open," the dark-skinned man replied.

"Attention All Crew: this is the captain speaking. We're about to reach the hot zone. The position of the enemy's forward defense line is uncertain. So stay sharp, stay ready, stay alert. We're finally here and we will make it through!"

Even though they were probably still well out of range of the Velorian defenses, and would remain back here guarding the hospital ships for who-knew how long, the promise of action electrified the air. It made everyone perk up and tense under high concentration. Lips pressed into a thin line, hands deep into her coat's pockets, Dr. Fox's hologram caught Ms. Rivers' gaze to exchange a quick nod and then blinked out.

"Order from VAdm. Gunnarsson," Singh reported a few minutes later. "We're to guard at the provided position."

Glen observed the designated area light up on the map, dominating one of his displays. "Helm, shift us into Defensive Pattern 2/15," he ordered.

While Ludmilla promptly engaged counter-PUs to slow them down and start the maneuver, the Plutonian warships broke their travel formation to form an attack line. As a result, the distance between the battle front and them quickly widened, as the other ships continued to power on.

"Ms. Magecraft," Glen turned, "confirm your status. Do you have everything prepared?"

The girl's face seemed strained, and a mixture of resolution and dread wafted through their magical connection. Since she'd started actively training this side of her gift with Ms. Yun, Suzy had become better at shutting down involuntary leakage, and this slip eloquently proved her nervousness.

"Aye, Captain." She nodded. "We can start as soon as the gate is in sight."

"Stay ready, then," he ordered. "Just in case we get an opening sooner than expected."

Her hologram saluted and blinked out. Maverick squeezed Bogdanov's shoulder in an almost fatherly gesture, before he and his cat vanished as well.

"So, why did you assign so many soldiers to guard her? Do you expect the wigs to exploit the weak spot or maybe even head for the magic?" Nick addressed the colonel's hologram. Like Glen, he'd strapped in, leaving Eve the only one standing.

"Mostly the first." The Plutonian's face darkened. "Let's just say I'm not very happy with opening up those shutters at the very front of the ship just so that one of our most precious assets can look outside."

"We already discussed this," Glen joined in the conversation, which was taking place first and foremost to keep everyone's nerves in check.

Nothing was as bad as silence. Even if their bridge crew couldn't make out what was said, as long as the command staff talked in even voices, everything was fine. So talk they would, keeping everyone at ease until this battle truly got underway on their end.

"Even with Ms. Magecraft connected to Ms. Yun, she'll probably still need a direct view of the gate to trigger it," he pointed out. "Besides, Mr. Maverick agreed to provide magical shielding."

"Right." A night of sleep didn't seem to have convinced the good colonel any more than yesterday's planning session. "Finally, some practical use for that nuisance. I just hope he can deliver what he promised."

"I'm just glad they can work together after that fallout during your regiment's founding party," Nick commented, one eye on the bridge crew, one on his translucent neighbor. "I guess they really had a heart-to-heart."

"Captain, the Velorians are moving to intercept our battle line," Montoya finally reported.

"That was fast," Glen commented as he zoomed in on what was happening.

"Their ships are equipped with superior sensors," Eve reminded them. "It was unavoidable that they would see the Plutonians first."

"Sensors, any of them heading our way?" Glen checked.

"Not yet, Sir," Montoya confirmed his assessment.

"Well then." The admiral settled back to watch the battle begin. "Let's wait for our dance invitation."

And so, the waiting game began.

CHAPTER THIRTY-SIX

THEODORA\\ INITIAL ATTACK

CAPTAIN THEODORA IMRIN SAT AT THE CENTRAL station of the *Sanji Merabti*'s bridge, monitoring the Velorian line advancing on them as more detailed commands came in. Her frigate had been stocked with two dark spheres and a whole voidwalker platoon. Their orders were as straightforward as they could be: Deploy the dark spheres after the first engagement, find a gap to exploit, and get those boarding parties into jumping distance. She studied the projections forwarded by the battle coordinator on the *Voidhammer*.

"Seems like they got some more reinforcements through the gate," she observed as she checked the holo against the intel provided. "Scanners, what are their numbers now?"

"The *Lightbearer*, 9 *goutas*, 14 *rujas*, that unclassified ship, and 10 ... ahem ..." the lieutenant leading the scanner section faltered to double-check, "... *crubas*."

"*Crubas*?" Theodora asked as she enlarged one of the strange ships. "What are those?"

"Carriers," tactical provided. "According to the latest

intel, they can probably house up to 150 fighters each. Similar size and armor class as *goutas*, heavier weaponry."

"Probably, heh? Well, we'll see what they can do soon enough." The captain scrolled through the spotty information. "Comms, inform our hitchhikers of their possible sparring partners. This should get interesting."

"Aye, Captain."

"Now they have fighter carriers," Theodora murmured. "Peaceful traders my ass. It really is high time senior command opposed them."

Matej, her XO of 19 years, nodded, then said, "And don't forget those three stations in your calculations. They'll be sending ample slugs our way, I'm sure."

"Not yet. We're still too far out." The captain felt her ponytail brush against her backrest as she shook her head. "They know we'll evade easily. They'll save the hardware for when we're pinned down or move too close."

"That's what we hope?!" Matej wiggled his bushy eyebrows. "You know the wigs don't make much sense on a good day."

"Well ..." The captain snorted. "We'll see. May the void protect us."

"May the void protect us."

A light blinked on Matej's station, and he reported, "Captain, all hitchhikers are ready for deployment."

"Good. Let's crack that line open, then," Theodora said. "As soon as that first barrage is taken care of."

Right after they picked each other up on scanners, both sides started shooting. In the void, where ballistic curvature and air drag weren't an issue, sensor range and navigational skill ruled the battlefield. Of course, the wigs had the advantage in sensor range, and some of their ordnance came with scrambling tech, making it harder for countermeasures to pinpoint them.

"Our man-of-wars are deploying widespread defensive beams," Scanners reported.

True to experience, that took care of most shells heading their way.

"Deploy countermeasures!" Theodora ordered.

An explosion lit up the main screen for a second.

"Too close!" Matej chided.

"Sorry, Sir," the weapons team responded.

Theodora noted large explosions in the near vicinity. Two of the corvettes had missed their shots and were severely wounded. One of the destroyers had gotten a nasty scratch on her hull.

"Fuck, those corvettes were part of our formation!" Matej swore.

His superior nodded and ordered, "Weapons, lay SP-03 suppressive fire. Navigation, minimal evasion until we receive revised orders!"

"Aye, Ma'am!"

More explosions rippled over the main screen as projectiles came in and were destroyed in short order. Unfortunately, their return fire had about as much effect as the wigs' strikes.

"Captain, revised orders coming in," the comm station reported. "Ruja_6 is our first target, the *Zjena Mirak* and the *Roy Rodop* our assault group. We're to fly Battle Plan Alpha_4, second position. The *Voidhammer* and the *Albion* will help us shoot a corridor."

"Very good." Theodora gestured at her XO to micromanage the order so she could take a minute to study the engagement map.

Their bridge hummed with acknowledgements and intense concentration. In a seasoned crew like theirs, all stations had performed this maneuver countless times and knew it by heart. Not against Velorian ships, of course. One-on-one, the *Sanji* hardly had a chance against a *ruja*. While the alien ships were roughly the same class and size as Plutonian frigates, their superior armor and weaponry would repel most attempts to best them single-handedly. As part of a well-coordinated assault group, however, they should be able to take it down relatively easily. Once they could get to it, that was ...

"Captain, we've orders to release the dark spheres," the comm team relayed. "They're to slip in and engage *rujas* 3 and 5, then move to break the battle line at Gouta_2."

"Acknowledged." Theodora swiped to another view, ordering, "Weapons, once you're done with our part of the main assault, create an unobtrusive corridor for our spheres. Comms, inform them of their orders. *The Loooony Can* leaves first, then *Treacherous Debris*. Helm, keep the hangars angled away from the battle line and in the wigs' sensor shadows."

"Aye, Captain!"

As the *Voidhammer* and the destroyer *Albion* added to the concentrated shelling on Gouta_1 right in front of their assault group, the aliens were quickly overwhelmed. With more shells flying their way than they could possibly intercept, enough went through to damage them severely. A 60-ton shell from the *Voidhammer*'s main cannon punched clean through the *gouta*'s magazine. The resulting fireball ripped apart the wig ship and sent parts of it flying in all directions.

"Incoming!" Sensors warned, just as their helm violently jerked the *Sanji* sideways.

Several Gs pushed Theodora into her restraints, almost shoving her over the left armrest, as the dampeners failed to compensate for the entire force of the maneuver. Shit, that would produce some nasty bruises ...

"As long as we can still feel it, we're fine!" Matej grunted their mantra as another shock ran through the vessel, sending it spinning off course.

"Debris hit on Aft Section 4," someone on internal sensors called out. "Hangar 1 is compromised!"

"Initiating emergency counter-burn sequence Delta-27!" the steersman added.

In anticipation of the bone-rattling result, Theodora gripped her armrests tightly. Illuminated with flickering red stress markers, the holo-model of her ship danced violently atop her console. Blue flames shot out all over it in a preprogrammed pattern designed to counteract exactly this movement.

"Damage report!" she yelled over the cacophony before the *Sanji* had fully regained her equilibrium.

"Not looking good," their main engineer reported. "Aggregating incoming data. But we're alive for now."

"Hangar 1?" Theodora inquired.

"Half gone, as is part of the hull in Aft Section 4," the man confirmed her fears. "All seals engaged. We're not venting atmosphere."

"*The Loooony Can* was flushed out as Hangar 1 got hit," the sensors team advised. "As did two squads of walkers."

"Status signals coming in," her lead communication officer announced.

"We're being targeted!" Matej pointed at their shared display. "Ruja_6 wants to finish us off, it seems."

"Good luck with that." Theodora gestured. "Any walkers in the way?"

"Survivors are widely scattered, asking for orders," Comms relayed.

"Good. Tell them to back off for now," Theodora decided. "Weapons, let them have it! Concentrate on their bow and break them open so those walkers can get in!"

"Aye, Ma'am!"

CHAPTER THIRTY-SEVEN

JOE\\ INVISIBLE HELP

"The *Sanji*'s in trouble!"

"As are we!" Joe—otherwise known as th captain and main pilot of *The Loooony Can*—had his hands full with stopping the dark sphere's wildly careening motions and didn't much mind his sensors guy's warning.

"Stabilizing ..." Copilot helped his superior's efforts with a deft hand and a sure feel for the controls.

"Shit, something ain't right!" The captain engaged all PUs in turn until he found some that worked.

"Ahem, Cap, there's a big ship in the way!" the loud-mouthed Sensors pointed out the obvious.

The *Sanji*'s sister frigate, *Roy Rodop*, loomed larger and larger on their screens as they hurtled her way.

"I know, damn it!" Joe toggled his controls. "Can't get Unit 5 online!"

With his usual phlegmatic demeanor, their bombardier gave the machinery to his left a deft kick. With an indignant sputter, PU_5 powered up. Joe quickly engaged it at full throttle before it could decide to die on them again.

"Evasive Maneuver_8 is working," Copilot announced with a sigh of relief.

"Fuck me!" Captain pushed them off collision course with the *Roy* and the much larger ship's hull flashed by in a blur of motion.

"Not enough coin in the void," Sensors trotted out the old joke. No one minded him.

"Give me a damage assessment!" Joe ordered as he checked and noted all their PUs' outputs.

"We're banged up good," Sensors declared soberly after running several checklists in a flash. "Damage to our outer hull, several PUs are acting up, and I have wonky readings on the heat storage."

"Ah, not the heat storage!" Captain swore again.

"The *Sanji*, Captain." Copilot had pulled down their shared periscope and now turned it for him to take a peek. "Ruja_6 is after them."

As Joe got a first-eye view of the surrounding space, his mood dropped another notch. Debris littered the void. From the two squads of walkers flushed out with them, he could only spot the transponder signals of a handful who'd survived the combination of high-velocity g-forces and being pelted by random objects. Didn't mean there weren't more, of course. As he watched, the walkers got themselves sorted out and looked around for a destination in short order.

"Maniacs!" the captain judged. Maybe too harshly, given his own occupation. But at least he had a real hull protecting him and his crew.

"How about it, Cap? We gonna dance as well?" Bomba looked through his own peeptube.

Joe met his copilot's gaze. They hadn't even made a complete damage assessment yet.

"Even with the *Roy* helping out, the *Sanji*'s not playing good odds there," his friend and voice of reason pointed out.

"Yeah, well," Joe agreed and plotted a course that would take them to the enemy's aft section, where their torpedoes had the best chance of doing severe damage. "We'd better make it quick, so we can check out that heat storage."

CHAPTER THIRTY-EIGHT

SUZY\\ INTERRIM

For the umpteenth time, Suzy checked the ritual circle she'd drawn on the floor at the front of *The Beak*, where tables and chairs had been moved out of the way, and found it to still be in the best possible working order. But that only made her more nervous.

"I thought you said you weren't going to do a ritual," Pro. Eisengaard-Diaz half-asked, half-stated as he looked on.

Their babysitter for this day, tasked with overseeing the two squads of soldiers provided to them, was the only one still on his feet. Except for the ship's witch, of course. The soldiers, Xinyi, and even Rupert had all settled into the booths lining the front windows and (except for the mage) strapped themselves in using the emergency straps usually hidden underneath the cushions.

"I'm not." Suzy squatted down and extended a hand holding the remaining stump of her trusty crystal, which she'd found back on Helper 1. Then she stopped and retracted it. The rune she'd been about to add a little flourish to was perfect as it was. Xin's sight had shown the energy flow to be unhindered and precisely the way they wanted it. Last-minute tinkering would probably hinder rather than optimize the effect.

She sighed and said, "This is just a little thing I picked up. It helps with focusing and clarity of mind. More of a ... mage stim, I guess you could call it. Not really a ritual as such."

"I see." Diaz nodded gravely, like he could actually make anything out of the assortment of alien scribbles magically engraved into the deck plates. "And what's the problem with it?"

Suzy stood and shook her head. "Nothing. Just nerves, I guess."

As she walked over to slip into the booth, where Rupert and Xin were sitting facing each other, she tugged the crystal back into her pocket. Diaz joined her, and they both strapped in—Suzy next to Rupert, Diaz next to Xin.

Silence fell.

Rupert and Xin seemed to see enough outside the large, unshuttered windows, but they were the only ones.

"Penny for your thoughts," the witch murmured as she studied the outline of her teacher's face. He watched the ships battling in the distance with intense focus. The brown in his eyes mostly prevailed, only briefly flickering with gray accents now and then. He shook his head slightly, never once glancing her way.

"It's so colorful." Xin lowered her binoculars and hugged herself. "I'd never have thought so many people dying could look this ...pretty."

Her face contorted as if she were disgusted by the mere thought of what she'd just uttered. Probably the only reason the Plutonians watching over them didn't immediately rip her a new one. That and her highly respectful, hushed tone of voice. Still, Diaz inched a tad closer, his eyes on the two squads of soldiers waiting it out with them.

Provided half by Tank and half by Federov, they seemed as unhappy with their forced inactivity as Suzy was. And given the intense strain on their faces as they followed the official feed showing what was happening too far away to be seen with any clarity, their nationality didn't seem to make much of a difference regarding their outlook on this battle either.

Merely observing the glimpses caught by external Plutonian cameras of the hell that was a large-scale space battle shook Suzy to the core. She would have liked nothing more than not to look. Given that these were real people, risking and losing life and limb out there, at least in part on account of the *Gateshot*, she didn't dare.

Instead, she tried to swallow down the increasing sickness pooling in her stomach, as projected casualties rose by the minute. Finally, Dite jumped into her lap and purred reassuringly, rubbing her cheek against Suzy's. Thankfully, the witch buried her whole face in the fluffy purple fur and let a few of the tears stinging her eyes escape into it, biting her lip to hold down the sobs. This was not what she'd envisioned when she'd left Mars. And this was only following the reports from a distance.

She suddenly dreaded the moment the *Gateshot* herself would fly right into the thick of things and she'd see it all up close.

Then a more earthy note mingled with Dite's subtle, floral perfume. Or maybe it was a spontaneous memory. Because suddenly, Suzy found herself reimmersed in that moment of quiet happiness when she'd woken up that morning in strong arms, Nick a steady, protective presence at her back. A single, perfect moment without pressure, demands, or stress—one in which she had everything she wanted.

Life is precious, she thought. *Life is beautiful.*

This was what she was fighting for here and no one would take the opportunity for more moments like this one from her.

Suzy drew in a deep breath, and with the scent came renewed resolve, loosening her clenched muscles and melting the icy tightness in her chest.

"I can do this," she whispered, almost inaudible.

A soundless purr vibrated against her cheek.

CHAPTER THIRTY-NINE

THEODORA\\ ROLLING

THEODORA STARED AT THE MAIN SCREEN WITH tightly clenched teeth as Ruja_6 bore down on them. The enemy vessel was too fucking fast. *Voidforsaken alien technology!*

"Our kinetic projectiles have little effect," her tactical station advised.

"Disengage and run?" her XO offered an option.

"And present our already battered aft section to them, so they can gut us?" the captain countered. "Not a great plan."

"Sensors, where's our assault group?" Matej barked.

"Realigning to our changed position," the team leader reported. "The *Zjena Mirak* has no clean shot, we're in the way. The *Roy Rodop* is closing the distance."

"Holdout time?" Theodora demanded.

"Three minutes."

"Any fighters in the vicinity?"

"No; at least not ours."

"Three minutes; we can do that." She nodded. "Helm, roll us over those big chunks of debris on Vector_3. Let's duck those slugs and eject *Treacherous Debris* and the remaining walkers into its shadow. Just in case."

"Aye, Captain!"

"Tactical, keep up the barrage. Shortly before we're there, mix in a sensor jammer to disguise our offloading."

"Aye, Captain!"

"Comms, advise all friendlies in the vicinity of the jammer and tell our hitchhikers to stand by for rapid evac."

"Aye, Captain!"

As fingers danced over consoles, orders were broken down and executed with commendable speed. With everyone focused on their tasks and her XO supervising, Theodora considered their options and possible outcomes. They'd had worse odds ... they'd also had better.

"Three more hits," Sensors advised. "Sectors 3, 4, and 8. All minor damage. No hull breaches. Two enemy fighters destroyed. Three more breaking off the assault run."

"All hitchhikers ready for evac," Comms added.

"Ejecting jammer probe ... now," the weapons station informed. "Discharge in 10 ..."

"Evac!" the XO ordered as the *Sanji* entered optimal distance to the debris.

On her display, Theodora followed the tiny dots, each representing a voidwalker being flushed into space with enough velocity to make any untrained body barf by merely looking on. Those guys truly were as tough as soldiers got. Aided by the ship's rapid roll, the ensuing inertia swiftly carried them out of the immediate danger zone and toward cover. The dark sphere went last, with a slight delay, so it wouldn't ram into the boarding troops.

"... 1!"

"Have all our weapons ready to go as soon as we can see the enemy again!" Theodora ordered.

"Yes, Captain!"

White noise overtook all the *Sanji*'s sensors as highly radioactive particles flooded the surrounding space. Using jammer probes was always a double-edged sword. Especially so in a tight formation with their ship hurtling blindly while other players moved all around them, equally blind. She just hoped the wigs were as vulnerable to this as intel suggested. Theodora closed her eyes briefly.

"May the void be with us," she murmured.

"Amen," Matej agreed under his breath.

Ghostly silence reigned for 48 seconds, as half the stations were forced to wait out the jammer's dispersion. Extrapolating from their previous sensor feeds and guesstimating the other ships' movements, the lead steersman stopped the *Sanji*'s roll and turned her to face what he hoped was the direction the enemy would be coming from.

CHAPTER FORTY

JOE\\ BOMBARDMENT

"That Cpt. Imrin is batshit crazy!" Joe couldn't quite hide his admiration at her boldness. "This is the worst situation to throw a jammer I've ever heard of!"

"Well, we'll be fine." Sensors grinned happily. "Mostly."

"Yeah, she'll pass right by us. Okay, change of plans. We'll use that opportunity to swing in close." The captain aligned their craft with the projected course of Ruja_6. "We'll go for the side the *Sanji* won't pelt as soon as they can see again. Let's lend a helping hand here."

"Estimating optimal positioning." Sensors fulfilled the implied order and sent Pilot his estimate of what was mostly safe space to maneuver.

Joe nodded, and as soon as the probe covered their part of the fight in radioactive mist, he punched it. The iffy PU gave him some lip, but he knew his *Can* and engaged auxiliary PUs to balance out the bumpy flight experience.

"Hate to break it to you," Copilot murmured, "but we should stop and check what's wrong ASAP."

"Let's see if we can't gut that wiggy first," the captain pressed through clenched teeth.

"No rest for the wicked," Sensors declared in a disgustingly carefree sing-song.

"Okay, so what are the weak points on this thing?" Pilot asked, then considered the marked plans Sensors sent him.

Rujas were relatively small vessels, only about two hundred meters long, so even with their stronger armor, it didn't take much to destroy them if they could get up close and hit the right spot. And that was exactly what the dark spheres were built for, after all.

"This is interesting. If we get a torpedo in this damaged section here," Joe thought aloud, "it should make a big enough boom to reach their magazine, maybe even chain-react inward to their reactor core. Right, Bomba?"

He sent the picture on, and after a quick glance at it, their bombardier grunted affirmative. The squat little guy wasn't much of a talker, which was a good thing, since his mid-belt accent was so thick, one could slice it.

"Then let's do it." Joe said and turned his head slightly. "Co, tell the *Sanji*, so they won't blast us by accident."

Since they were as invisible to them as to the enemy, they'd have to tell their comrades where they were, in any case. Wouldn't do to become friendly fire collateral.

Pilot swerved the *Can* inside the wig ship's energy shield, shadowing the larger ship's hull on their way toward their destination. ETA: one minute.

"Jammer mist is clearing," Sensors reported.

All around them, wiggy point defenses and larger weaponry realigned. For a fearful second, Joe thought of their tub's malfunctioning heat storage, and his palms tingled as he gripped the controls tightly. But all the turrets swung around to face the two Plutonian frigates bearing down on the *ruja*. Not one loosed a shot in *The Loooony Can*'s direction.

Slowly, the captain exhaled. With all of them sitting this close, fear was not an emotion he was eager to project. Still, it was Human to feel the pressure, right? He'd known a few chaps with no regard for their own or their crew's safety. Emphasis on 'known'.

"Got an answer from the *Sanji*," Copilot said and glanced over. By the look in his eyes, he wasn't fooled. But then, they'd served together the longest, and they were practically sitting in each other's laps. "They'll pelt the starboard side to give us space and distraction."

"Good." Joe loosened his grip slightly. "What about the other dark sphere?"

"The *Treacherous Debris* hasn't reported in yet, but they were ejected way over there, so they shouldn't be in anyone's line of fire right now," Copilot confirmed what Joe'd already been suspecting.

"Also good. Thirty-two seconds to target zone," Joe called out.

"Confirmed," Sensors called back. "All clear to target zone. No fighters, no nothing."

Suddenly and without warning, the wig ship underneath them swerved deftly. The *Can*'s distance to its hull instantly widened. The energy shield loomed as the dark sphere seemed to fall straight toward it.

"Shit!" Joe slammed in a correction burn.

Passing a ship's energy shield from the inside was a good way to get detected. A large body like their craft smashing through from the wrong side was not something a ship's computer was likely to bury in the myriad of sensor data unnoticed. There was only so much their design could do about it, and the energy rubbing off on them would need a second or two to be dispersed. With their banged-up heat storage, Joe wasn't eager to risk even this small window.

"Wooooow," Sensors whooped. "Easy, Boss!"

Copilot gripped his armrests as their tiny vessel swung around and thrust gravity dumped the weight of a large man onto their chests for a moment or two. Then they'd changed direction and raced back to cover, missing the shield by only a meter or two. No one spoke for the few hurried heartbeats it took Joe to realign them with the wig ship. The last remnants of their overindulgent invisible visitors left; normal thrust gravity reasserted itself.

Finally, Sensors confirmed, "No reaction. I don't think they saw us."

"Void," Bomba grunted his relief.

"Confirming new approach vector," Copilot's fingers flew over his controls as he readjusted the necessary parameters.

"Path is clear," Sensors reported eagerly.

"Locking on target," Bomba mumbled.

"One torpedo should do the trick," Captain instructed. "If you get it right down that hole there."

Bomba grunted.

Captain flew them in as close as he dared.

"Fire when ready!" he barked.

A tiny shudder ran through *The Loooony Can* as Bomba released one-seventh of their usable payload. Captain steered them clear of the *ruja*'s flight path and punched it. Behind them, the torpedo sparked its onboard thruster and sped away.

For all his lack of verbal alacrity, Bomba was a superb shot.

"Bullseye!" Sensors confirmed.

Their bombardier snorted self-indulgently.

For a heartstopping moment, nothing happened. Then flames erupted out of the hole where they'd sunk the torpedo. Massive cracks appeared along the enemy ship's hull. Ruja_6 was gutted. Ripped apart by internal explosions, the ship turned into a cloud of quickly dispersing debris.

Scanners whooped and applauded happily.

CHAPTER FORTY-ONE

JATHEKI\\ BORED

"I'm bored," Jatheki mused.

The seer was getting increasingly unsettled by what he perceived, the strategist by not being included in the fight, and the trickster could relate to both of them for once. So he jerked their shared body into motion.

In one sinuous movement, he bounded over a surprised Suzy. He held out his hand to the other girl, who'd been studying him and his walking cane intently for the better part of an hour now, saying, "How about it, Twinkly Eyes? Wanna take a walk on the wild side and get a closer look at the action?"

Xinyi Yun blinked, the pretty symbols in her eyes churning. Gods knew what she was seeing. Vision spells were notoriously hard to weave and constrain ... just ask dear old Cassandra of Troy.

"A closer look?" the woman echoed, though she did unstrap herself slowly and reached for her binoculars.

Twinkly's gaze jumped from his outstretched palm to his slight bow, and to the mesmerizing play of bright colors churning around his cane. It was what drew her enhanced eyes the most. Understandable, really.

Pro. Eisengaard-Diaz frowned. "Where do you plan to go?"

While the provost did stand to make room for her slipping out of the booth, his body language spoke of doubt and unwillingness to do so. Consequently, he stepped into the new configuration rather than aside. Not actually between Jatheki and his charge, but the intention was there. The intention to protect.

"Well, outside, of course! Where we can see with our own eyes what's happening." The trickster itched to accept the challenge, but the others clamped down on him. They were more interested in actually getting out there than starting a fight in here.

"She's not wearing a spacesuit." Diaz pointed at Xin. "And neither are you."

Maverick glanced at Dite lounging on the table, and she snickered softly.

"Semantics!" He waved it off, then leaned closer to peer inside the man's face shield, saying, "You can accompany us, if you like ... but you're not my mistress's pet, so I'm not particularly enthused to look out for you."

The conflicting emotions playing catch in the human's facial features clearly stated he hadn't yet swallowed the line hook and sinker.

Shame on you, Dite, the trickster jabbed for her alone to hear. *Are you losing your touch?*

Hardly, she purred and stood to stretch her feline muscles languidly. *But I'm just as dependent upon time and timing as you are.*

"It's fine, Provost." Xinyi laid a hand on her unsolicited champion's arm. "I'll be fine. Besides, we might already catch a glimpse of the gate. That's what we're here for, right?"

"*Da.*" Eisengaard-Diaz glared at the mage from behind the safety of his mask.

But he knew his place. And his orders.

"Fine," the provost said. "But you'd better look out for her!"

The trimorph laid a hand on his heart, vowing solemnly, "On my honor."

"How do I contact you?" Suzy asked. "Or are you coming right back?"

The little witch was growing visibly agitated too. She was in way over her head and she knew it. Well ... she'd better rise to the occasion. Jatheki flipped her a coin like the one he'd given Glen. It was just for show, but any performance should be consistent.

"You just think of me and I'll hear whatever you say." He tapped the ground with his cane, and opened a portal to space.

Eisengaard's eyes widened, though he kept his composure. Unlike some of the soldiers, who stared. Little Cassandra licked her lips nervously, then accepted Jatheki's arm. Dite hopped off the table and followed in their wake.

As they bridged reality into open space, the refreshing scent of possibilities wafted all around. He'd brought them out on top of *The Beak*, where they could see the way the ship was heading. The girl gasped. Her knuckles whitened on the binoculars. Panic fluttered through her heart and stance for the handful of seconds it took to internalize that her fragile flesh suit wasn't choking, freezing, or boiling to death. After that, tentative astonishment at the majestic glory of the universe replaced those instinctual human notions, and her eyes grew large as saucers in her effort to take it all in.

Look at her, Dite purred in his mind. *Overwhelming amazement never ceases to delight.*

Jatheki merely snorted under his breath. Then he reached out with his magic, feeling for his connection to the wellspring.

Need my help yet? his companion offered.

Just taking a peek, the seer replied.

A sea of possibilities raged around him as he looked into the future. So many vague and confusing possibilities ... everything from utter defeat and destruction to ... to ... where was the way to the other side of the gate? It couldn't have vanished! He'd worked on this, shaped the crossroads to get everyone needed right here. Where had it gone?

Large yellow orbs studied him. Finally, Dite chided, *Stop fretting. We did everything we were supposed to do. Now it's the humans' turn to act and our turn to have faith in them.*

Right ..., Jatheki agreed and closed his eyes.

The strategist's memory treated them to the feeling of a stiff, salty breeze whipping back her long, silky hair, momentarily alleviating the burn of the midday Mediterranean sun. The flapping of cloth sails and the rallying cries of warriors. The rattling of metal drawn in anticipation, mixing with the creaking of ancient wood cut down to allow passage over the wine-dark sea. The scent of honest sweat, bronze, and leather.

The trickster threw in the sounds of ancient forests, alive with a myriad of tiny beings and enormous beasts. Wet footsteps smacked softly as cold rain dripped onto his face. Fragrant morning mists on dew-soaked meadows roiled in from the seer's mind. As his hands stroked the long grasses and tentative buds, his eyes already saw everything in blinding light—full bloom, and rapid decay; past, present, and future—all one fascinating weave of possibilities.

For a precious moment, all of Jatheki's parts connected and synchronized as their hearts swelled with the yearning for simpler times and places.

Then the trimorph opened his eyes to the darkness of space, the soundlessness of vacuum, the confusion of present times, and no clear future, and he felt as misplaced as never before. Just another wanderer making his way to an unknown destination. With no guarantee of actually getting there.

How intriguing. How wondrous.

He hadn't felt like this in so long.

So hesitant, so weak, so ... *human.*

CHAPTER FORTY-TWO

JOE\\ BURNING VOID

As soon as the *Ruja* was done exploding all over the vicinity, Joe looked around for a safe spot to check out *The Loooony Can*'s mechanical problems.

"Copilot, go have a look. Sensors, comm the *Roy Rodop* and advise them that we'll pull in close for a check-up. Ask where they're going," the captain ordered and swung their craft around to match the frigate's flight corridor.

Just in case their damaged heat sink was starting to render them visible, the sensor shadow created by the larger vessel would hide the *Can*, make it look like they were merely part of it. Should they need to power down their engines for some quick-and-dirty repairs, they could attach themselves to the *Roy*'s hull, and if they found the damage was too great or dangerous to alleviate in a jiff, it gave them a hangar nearby.

Sensors established a channel, then discussed their problem with whatever comm-officer responded. Finally, he said, "We're good to duck into their starboard shadow and attach at Section_12 if necessary. They're waiting on the

Zjena Mirak, which should be another eight minutes out. So we're good."

"Nice." Captain nodded. "Then, while we have the time, call the *Voidhammer* next and confirm our orders still stand."

"Aye, Cap."

"How's that leakage doing?" Joe had to perform some wild contortions to catch a glimpse of Copilot rummaging around on the lowest level of *The Loooony Can*. His colleague shook his head as he toggled switches.

"Nothing much I can do," he said and started turning a valve wheel. "We got lucky in that the heat storage caught that bad bump from when we were flushed out of the *Sanji* —probably some nasty shrapnel. Otherwise, we would be venting atmo. This way, we're just bleeding steam. I'm closing off the outermost chamber. That should help a little, but ..."

He just shrugged.

"We'll not be invisible for very long," Captain finished and considered the output of his console. "Then I guess we also lost the auxiliary PUs in that area, which is why steering's such a bitch now."

"Fuck," Bomba added to the conversation.

"At least all other systems are in the green," Sensors delighted in pointing out. "For now."

"Yeah ..."

Still, a dark sphere was no good if it could be detected. In their business, an easily detectable ship amounted to early retirement. And if their maneuverability was also compromised ...

Copilot kicked off and came floating over to strap back in next to Joe, declaring, "I say we go. It's not that bad."

Sensors nodded agreement. "We did missions with worse bang-ups. We ask the *Roy* for a ride-along now, we'll be the laughing stock of the battle. And miss all the fun!"

Bomba grunted in a way that could have meant 'yes', 'no', or both.

Joe rubbed his skull. In theory, this wasn't a democracy. Deciding if his craft was good enough to fly was the captain's prerogative, deciding to put all his crewmen's lives in danger by running with faulty machinery his responsibility.

"How's the overall battle progressing?" he asked.

"Could be better," Sensor's answer sounded uncommonly hushed. "We lost one destroyer, three frigates, and five corvettes in the first engagement."

"And the wiggies?"

"Two *goutas* and three *rujas* are either destroyed or disabled. Several are being boarded. We got one of the *crubas*, too, but only after it flushed some two hundred fighters. Seems those carriers are getting pretty pesky."

So, still a lot of enemies to go around ... benching the *Can* when she could still make a difference would be shameful and shirking their duty.

"Call it in, tell them we're fine enough." Joe popped his knuckles. "Our orders haven't changed?"

"Nope. We're to go for *rujas* 3 and 5, then move to break the battle line at Gouta_2."

"Fine, then let's get to it while we're still invisible and those damn wigs look the other way," the captain decided.

"Aye, Sir." Copilot went to work with a minuscule smile playing on his thin lips.

Joe massaged his neck with his left as he put in a flight plan with his right. Lacking such amenities as overly cushioned seats, dampener fields, or—void help them—AG, their little tub's rude take-off had rattled his old bones marvelously. Now that he had a moment to feel it out, it hurt like a bitch.

"I want one of those sexy massages once we've completed this mission." He fixed his mind on a positive outcome. "Sure hope that plover's still there when we get back."

"Well, I know one bone they'll not be able to adjust correctly," Sensors jibed. "'Cause it's already too crooked."

"Ah, fuck off!" Captain laughed and swung them out of the *Roy Rodop*'s shadow to peek out at the Velorian battle line.

The space around them was positively on fire. All types of ordnance met countermeasures, beams ripped through empty space as well as through hulls and shells. Fighters and void walkers tried bridging the distances. Everyone was stacked up way too tight. Collateral damage just waited to happen.

Copilot cleared his throat before muttering, "Damn ..."

"Passive scanners are overwhelmed by all the interference in this area." Even the notoriously bushy-tailed youngster's voice sounded unnaturally hushed. "I'll have to wait for a bit of clearing. Can we go the long way around?"

"With broken heat storage? Bad idea." Captain found he still had a hard time keeping their *Can* on course. Those damn auxiliaries seemed to produce some output, but he could neither control nor turn them off.

"Shit, I know," Sensors replied. "But if I can't see them, Bomba can't shoot them!"

At least that much was true. Their bombardier grunted his agreement.

Fuck, for a split second, Joe's mind wandered and wished he could have that mage Oddball back. She'd not only been nicer to look at, but also a much more uplifting conversation partner.

"We're at the edge," Copilot reminded him, all reasonable. "We can afford looping out and around. Would certainly be safer. With all that in the way, they don't even need to see us; the shrapnel will kill the *Can* all on its own."

"True," Joe agreed and corrected their heading again. "Give me some more speed on those main PUs, then."

He just prayed to the void that he hadn't just doomed them all with his bravado.

CHAPTER FORTY-THREE

RUFFA\\ INITIAL NUMBERS

RUFFA STOOD ON THE SMALL OUTCROP OVERSEEING THE *Lightbearer*'s bridge, which allowed him to give direct commands to the captain of his main vessel, and at the same time analyzing the progression of the battle on his console, all while leading the rest of the fleet. As was common in such affairs, the initial engagement took a significant toll on both sides before fighting settled into more of a stalemate. A ruja on the far edge of the line, which had been engaged by several Plutonian frigates, just blinked out on his display.

"Commander, we found the guardian's ship!" Tuvil reported and, at his superior's indication, accessed the console. "It really is where Senoxes said it would be."

The view widened out to show several vessels drifting at the edge of their direct sensors' range—the familiar shape of their primary foe's transportation seemingly patrolling a small area holding five other ships.

"So the dimwit actually managed to gain access to

Plutonian battle data and be useful for once." Ruffa could hardly believe it.

"We trust his intel, then?" Tuvil's folds shivered undecidedly.

"His initial troop numbers were correct, as is this. ... I'm starting to be cautiously interested."

The commander studied the movements of the guardian's ship for a while, his mind already back on the real enemy. Finally, he declared, "It's just as I suspected. She's waiting for the Plutonians to crack open our line for her."

He judged the angles and distances. Sadly, they had only managed to get one of the three stations' weapons operational. As using it would instantly make said station a prime target, and tip their hand as to how dangerous the guarding trifecta really was, the commander judged it prudent to keep this fact hidden. For now.

"Tuvil, instruct every ship in the direct vicinity to engage that central man-of-war."

"Yes, Commander."

Ruffa glanced at the main screen to get another view of the ugly Human design barring the *Lightbearer*'s way. It had angled its long side toward the battle line, and all its weapons piled their inconsequential loads against the superior Velorian shields and counter-beams. Next to the Human flag and the silhouette of a stylized blade painted on its hull, it said *PDN Longsword*.

Well, time to break that old-world weapon in half.

"Captain, did you pinpoint all the *Longsword*'s beam ports?" Ruffa called down to the bridge.

"Yes, Commander!"

"Good. Select a cross-section making up about a quarter of that spinning hull. Cover it with area clearing ordnance to disable as many point defenses as you can, then release the fighters. They're to disable the beam emitters there—at any cost," Ruffa said. He felt his folds spread out slightly, as he continued, "As soon as this creates a safe corridor, have the remaining fighters use it to engage the *Longsword*'s cannon ports and PUs. I want that thing drifting and unable to defend itself. Then shower the damaged sections with everything we have."

CHAPTER FORTY-FOUR

THEODORA\\ DEATH OF A GIANT

Theodora might have missed the moment the *Longsword* died, if not for a sensor tech with a face as white as a bedsheet stuttering "C-Captain, you ... have to see this ..."

When he pulled up the vid feed from a nearby destroyer or maybe even the *Voidhammer* herself, the *Longsword* was already pockmarked with impact craters. Even the escort ships couldn't save it from half the Velorian battle line pelting it. Just then, the *Lightbearer* discharged all her weapons at once. Several super-heavy kinetic projectiles punched through the nearby destroyer *Salacia*, and it exploded. Other parts of the man-of-war's escort fell prey to a swarm of tiny alien fighters diving right for their PUs or other vulnerable areas.

The *Longsword* took the brunt of it, though. At least 18 holes appeared all over its hull. Clean, almost neat impacts. But the slugs' kinetic energy left large, ragged exit craters, spilling metal and bodies out into the void. Much like a sidearm would leave a neat hole in one's temple and vacate most of one's brain out the back. Explosions rattled the remaining husk as its aft magazine and several reactor cores detonated.

"By the void!" Theodora stared in disbelief.

In theory, a man-of-war could be destroyed, of course. She'd just never witnessed it. Nor could she remember hearing about it more than a couple of times over her long career. And never with a finality of what she'd just seen. There were tens of thousands of people on that ship! She just hoped they'd evacuated personnel into safe zones as soon as the oncoming destruction had been obvious.

Matej merely nodded, unable to speak.

As the Plutonian battle line was thrown into disarray, several of the Velorian ships pulled forward. The unclassified moved first, covered by the wig's flagship. Both angled upward, skirting the quickly expanding debris field as they sped away . Two *rujas* followed.

The remaining vessels covered their retreat.

Seeing as how larger parts of the *Longsword* might still hold significant numbers of sealed-in survivors, many Plutonian vessels closest to the scene hesitated to fire on the enemy, even though many twitchy triggerfingers were surely just waiting for a sufficient opening.

"Where are they going?" Theodora whispered.

The sensors team leader swallowed audibly, then said, "They're heading for our hospital ships, Captain."

"No," Matej disagreed. "They want to get their hands on our secondary objective."

CHAPTER FORTY-FIVE

GLEN\\ DANCE INVITATION

As the battle unfolded, Federov seemed increasingly antsy to join in. Glen couldn't fault him for the impulse, as he felt just the same. When the *Longsword* was destroyed, not only the colonel's mood took an understandable dive. Shock settled in on every Plutonian's and most other faces. There'd been so many people on that ship ...

Ambassador Bogdanov stared at the main screen. Even the void priest looked visibly shaken, if not necessarily surprised.

"Can we engage now?" Federov growled.

"Comms," Glen double-checked, "any revised orders?"

He wouldn't think so. The marshal surely had his hands full rearranging his main fleet and would be too predisposed to mind their hangers-on.

"No, Sir," Singh confirmed the admiral's suspicion.

Federov's eyes narrowed.

"Helm, swing out wider, so we can see more of the battle line," the admiral ordered. "Unobtrusively, of course."

"Aye, Captain." Ludmilla gestured for her Plutonian helpers to provide her with a new flight path, and before long, the *Gateshot* moved farther out. Since the battle was taking place right at the edge of their sensors, this would give them a slightly better view of what was actually happening.

"Ms. Baileywick, is there any way to extend the sensor range?"

"I'll see what I can do, Captain." She nodded at the underlying question and pretended to fiddle with the settings for half a minute, before declaring, "This should help. Dr. Lustig, if you could realign the forward sensor arrays, please?"

Their head of engineering played along, confirming the change in short order.

"Lt. Montoya, does this help?" Eve asked.

"Yes. Sensor range increased by 2 %," the Plutonian team leader noted.

Glen studied the slightly enlarged tactical display. Federov's holo leaned in, as if he were actually standing next to him.

"Ms. Baileywick," to further distract the colonel from their momentary uselessness, Glen pointed at the ship that had just overtaken the *Lightbearer*, "can you tell us more about this unclassified ship now that we have it on our sensors?"

Eve enlarged the silhouette and what else their sensors picked up onto the main screen and squinted at it. She took her time studying the rows of numbers rolling by too fast for Human eyes to read before declaring, "I still don't recognize it. As I previously noted, this has to be a new design. Something my people haven't encountered until now."

"Makes sense," Nick agreed. "Given your knowledge, what could be its primary purpose?"

"I'm not yet certain ..." The guardian shook her head. "Maybe I can tell once it moves in closer."

"Seems you'll get that chance rather soon." The XO stared at the battle's center. "The Velorians aren't actually pushing through the Plutonian line, are they?"

Even Jiǎng halted for several seconds to stare before replying, "No, but several are angling away from it, Commander, staying close only where it provides cover."

"They're taking heavy losses. This is a strategic nightmare!" Nick shook his head in open confusion.

"They're Velorians." Federov's voice sounded strained as his eyes moved between Eve, Glen, and the hospital ships on the tactical display. "And they're coming for us."

"Aye," Glen agreed.

"The unclassified passed the Plutonian line!" Lt. Jiǎng reported. "And the *Lightbearer* is hot on her heels!"

"Bloody hell, this could get nasty," the admiral murmured. "How will we get past that ship if she catches up to us?"

"How about we don't give her that chance?" His XO's eyes darted over to the helm.

Bloody hell!

They couldn't let the hospital ships get caught in the crossfire. They'd have another mutiny on their hands in a flash and for good reason.

"Comms, tell our charges to retreat to Fallback Position Alpha," the captain ordered. "Inform the marshal and VAdm. Gunnarsson, that we'll draw the Velorians' attention and fire away from the neutrals. Helm, plot a course to achieve said purpose!"

CHAPTER FORTY-SIX

RUFFA\\ NECESSARY SACRIFICES

"COMMANDER," THE *LIGHTBEARER*'S CAPTAIN cautioned with mounting strain in his voice, "Our shields can't withstand the ongoing strain. Our hull is already taking damage."

"Damage we can easily repair afterward," Ruffa gripped the edge of the tactical display. "First, we need to destroy the guardian's ship. The rest is secondary."

Next to him, Tuvil cleared his throat, saying, "Commander, the governor—"

"... gave me full authority to get this done as I see fit," Ruffa cut him off. "Yes, the gate is a concern, but the guardian is the real problem. We have her in our sights. If we wait, she might escape again."

"And the Plutonians?" his adjutant inquired.

"We just destroyed one of their main ships," Ruffa pointed out. "We can do the same with the others. *After* we've eliminated our primary objective. Look at them, their line is broken. We can mop it up at our leisure."

The captain's folds twitched as he said, "The other two

large ships are maneuvering to bring their main cannons to bear. We won't be able to evade at this range."

Balance, he was right ... This was getting too tight for comfort ...

Ruffa pointed at two already badly damaged rujas. "Tuvil, tell these two to interpose themselves between the cannons and us."

"That would reduce the forces holding the Plutonians off our back" his aide cautioned.

"A necessary sacrifice," Ruffa decided. "All we need is a little more time to get out of this position."

"Yes, Commander." Tuvil's folds tightened briefly, but he relayed the orders as instructed.

One of the rujas dove for the man-of-war closest to it. One didn't. With a confused wrinkle in his folds, Tuvil repeated the order.

The second man-of-war's cannon activated and several heavy mass kinetic projectiles shot their way. Underneath his feet, the bridge crew exchanged a flurry of commands and acknowledgments. Emergency burns lit up a large portion of the tiny *Lightbearer*'s model as the projectiles punched clean through the ship's weakened shield and hull, all the way to the other side. A rumbling vibration shook the bridge as part of the kinetic energy transferred into the vessel. The bridge crew stopped their activity and looked up.

Ruffa studied the incoming system-generated damage reports, but only for two heartbeats.

"We're fine," the commander judged. "And we'll be far enough off to easily dodge by the time that cannon's reloaded. Tuvil, order the rest of the fleet to keep the vermin at bay until we return."

"Commander, we have a massive leak in the secondary energy core cooling system! We can't sustain this!" the captain protested. "We have to reduce speed as soon as we clear the immediate fighting zone!"

"We have to destroy the guardian's ship!" Ruffa's folds extended to half display in an unconscious movement. "Everything else is secondary! Do you understand?"

The captain's folds pressed against his skull. "Y-Yes, Commander!"

CHAPTER FORTY-SEVEN

XINYI\\ FIRST GLIMPSES

Through their strange bond, Xin could feel Suzy's impatience and nervousness. Like icy air prickling on exposed skin. Inside the young woman, panic warred with relief at the prospect of action finally coming their way.

Down in *The Beak*, security measures had been enacted as the battle drew closer to the ship. Up here, Xin could see the Velorian ships heading their way. They bore down on them with a vengeance. As soon as it had cleared the main battle, the lead ship started firing. Beams and projectiles streaked through the magnificent expanse of the void. First, only a few came close to anything resembling accuracy. Those that would have hit, were easily destroyed by the *Gateshot*'s countermeasures. But the rain steadily increased and, with the two *rujas* flanking it adding their share, the deadly rain came closer and closer to the ship's hull.

Xin gripped Rupert's arm tightly in an instinctual need to draw him back as a shell about her size hurtled toward them. It was intercepted way too close for comfort, and the pieces flew on to impact the debris shield, setting the transparent net into hissing and sizzling.

"Shit, get back down here!" Suzy called out to them. "You'll see everything from the windows just fine!"

"Oh, don't be overly dramatic." Rupert slammed the butt of his staff onto the *Gateshot*'s gleaming black hull, and a faint circle of runes and swirls raced away from it to create a circle of about two meters in each direction beneath their feet. "We'll be fine. Best view in the house!"

A domed shield sprang up to cover them. Xin could see it all as bright as day. It was radiant and pretty. And so many interlacing flows of energy ... She could feel Suzy's breath catch at the image, as transmitted through Xin's eyes.

"Xin, I need to see the gate!" The witch interrupted her helper's wandering thoughts. "Can you already see it?"

"Oh, right! Sorry."

Xin quickly turned. She raised the binoculars and the internal mechanism balanced itself to adjust for all the movement. Even though purely optical, it provided a razor-sharp image.

Gosh, where was the gate?

There!

Still, even with twentyfold magnification, the alien artifact in the distance remained elusive.

"It's so tiny!" Xin reported, squinting and straining for a better view. "I can barely make it out with all the colors and stuff ..."

"Fuck!" Suzy said. Xin felt an echo of the motions when the witch unstrapped and went for her circle, ordering, "No matter. Keep it in sight and tell me as soon as you can make out the activation runes!"

"Aye, aye, Boss!"

CHAPTER FORTY-EIGHT

THEODORA\\ BACK-UP

THE HEAT OF BATTLE RARELY LENT ITSELF TO indulging in feelings of mourning or panic. So Theodora pushed them aside for the sake of the present.

"Ruja_8 is moving to engage the *Voidhammer*," the tactical station observed. "Shall we follow?"

"Yes, let's crack them open while they're presenting their back to us." Theodora gestured. "Comms, inform our assault group of the change. Helm, get us there!"

Suddenly, several explosions rippled across their bow. Alarms started blaring, and red icons appeared all over the *Sanji*'s tactical display. Then another series of explosions, these so close that they rattled the whole bridge. One wall caved in, burying several stations and crew with debris.

"What was that?" Matej coughed as he peered through the dust.

For several seconds, the sound of their fire suppression system engaging drowned out the gasps of pain and shock.

The sensor station was first to answer. "Cloaked mines, Sir. Possibly magnetized or self-guided. The fighters must have dropped them in passing."

"Helm, full stop!" Theodora ordered. "Comms, warn our assault group!"

Too late. Next to them, the already damaged *Zjena Mirak* was ripped apart as the mines hit a weak spot and triggered a destructive chain reaction. The *Roy Rodop* managed evasive maneuvers. Their sudden change of direction caused a cascade of tiny fiery dots to appear close to their bow. Most likely, several mines had collided with each other instead of their target.

"Damage report!" Matej demanded of their engineers.

"It's bad, Sir," the team leader informed. "We lost several bow sections. We're venting atmosphere, and the reactor containment is failing!"

Captain and XO looked at each other with helpless anger in their eyes. They'd never lost a ship before.

Just then, as could be seen on the main screen, a massive slug punched through Ruja_7, shoving it off course. For a long moment, the enemy vessel spun aimlessly. Then it powered up all PUs to push its crippled remains against the source of its destruction.

"Shit, they're going to ram the *Loreley*!" Matej's eyes widened. "She won't be able to get out of the way in time."

"Can she push them off?" the captain inquired, more concerned about her own ship's conundrum.

"Negative," the scanner section replied. "Their mass-pushers are busted."

Ah, Void!

"Weapons, pile everything we have on the *ruja*," Theodora instructed.

"I'm sorry, Ma'am," the wide-eyed officer stuttered. "I can't access anything; my consoles are dead!"

"And both backup stations lay crushed under debris!" Engineering added through a vicious bout of coughing.

"Tell the batteries to switch to manual targeting!"

"Aye, Ma'am," the chief weapons officer answered. "But with our shaky flight pattern and so many friendlies nearby, they won't get many shots off."

"Damn. Anything else we can do?" The XO's fingers danced over his controls with single-minded intensity.

"No," the squat engineer replied helplessly. "The *Sanji*'s out of commission, Sir. Only thing still working is the main PUs."

"And we're the only ones in range?" Theodora double-checked.

"Aye, Captain." The sensors officer who'd replaced her downed team leader swallowed. "The *Roy* could maybe come back around in time, but ... well, maybe. It would be close. Very close."

Cold certainty filled Theodora as she glanced around her wrecked bridge, noting the flashing red spots covering most of the facsimile of her ship. No. Too many lives were at stake to risk it. And the *Sanji* was scrap metal anyway. It would be too costly to restore her. Why not give the old girl one last chance at glory?

"Helm, plot a course to intercept. Make it so we ram the *ruja* with minimal damage to the *Sanji*. Engineering, reroute helm controls to my station. I'll keep her on course." Nervous anticipation enveloped her heart. "Comms, open shipwide channel, then warn all friendlies in the vicinity to gain distance."

"Channel open, Ma'am," the wide-eyed officer replied.

"All Hands, this is the captain speaking. Evacuate now! I repeat, this is the captain speaking. Evacuate now! Evac Protocol_4. You have a max of twelve minutes to vacate the blast zone!"

She cut the channel, straightened, and addressed her bridge crew. "That goes for all of you too. Dismissed!"

Everyone who could do so saluted crisply, then followed her command. In short order, steering had been rerouted, and the healthy crew shouldered the injured to file out in orderly haste.

Matej stood and saluted. "Give them hell, Captain."

He'd stay if he were allowed to. But this was too risky. Just in case one CO didn't make it, the other had to take over responsibility for their crew.

"I will." She returned the gesture. "Now get our crew to safety."

"Aye, Captain!"

He was the last to leave and stopped briefly on the bridge's threshold to yell back at her, "Be safe, Theodora. This is not the day you get a ship named after you!"

She forced on a smile through the chills and laughed. "It isn't. Now, get your lazy ass off my bridge, Matej!"

"Aye, Captain."

Before he left, he rang the ship's bell one last time.

As Theodora Imrin studied the collision projections, eager nervousness settled in her stomach. Even having started her 43 years of service as a pilot hardly prepared her for this maneuver. She just prayed to the void that the damn wigs wouldn't flinch at the last second. With all their broken PUs, it would be hard to address any last-minute evasion attempts. And that the *Sanji* would hold together long enough.

"Good girl," she murmured and gently stroked her armrest. "We can do this. Just one little push right at the belly and those damn wigs will be off course. We can do this."

She'd once heard of a captain who'd lost three ships. Not his fault, presumably. The drunken deckhand who'd told her had claimed he'd been tasked with installing all three plaques over the captain's bed, then asked for reassignment to another ship right after. Would she be considered bad luck after this day?

Relief flooded her once the last evac pods were away.

"Proximity alert!" the ship's computer informed. "Counterburn and—"

"Acknowledged. Shut up!" Theodora bit her lower lip.

Ruja_8 loomed on the main screen, the *Loreley* only a small way off now. The destroyer's PUs were alight with the visual signs of maximum thrust. With its heavy mass, inertia proved a fierce enemy. No way she could evade in time.

"Well, that's what we're here for," Theodora murmured and tried rerouting power to one of the broken PUs to gain just a tad more momentum.

Didn't accomplish anything. With the strain on the system, the ship groaned around her. Somewhere in the distance, something heavy connected with something else, sending a faint vibration through the floor and her seat right up her spine. More red icons appeared on the facsimile and a new explosion expanded the hull breach on the *Sanji* bow. As the frigate sped closer to the *ruja*, the wig ship moved to evade. It tried to slip sideways, let the frigate pass, and slam into a different section of the destroyer.

"Oh no, you don't!"

Even as Theodora corrected, she realized there was no more fine-tuning at this distance. Not with their front navigational thrusters gone. It was all or nothing.

So she overset the main PUs to asymmetric thrust, and ignored the blaring warning messages and klaxons informing her of imminent structural damage, reactor overheat, and collision, as well as many secondary nuisances. It was the only way to get the necessary course correction. As she moved to dial them all back up to maximum, the anticipated counterattack slammed into the *Sanji*. Ruja_8 sent all her remaining ordnance straight into the gutted frigate. More vibrations rattled the bridge. Red dots; half her ship disintegrating into space. Still, the wig's pushback wasn't enough. On the captain's display, the projected course lines blinked to indicate both vessels would veer off and clear the *Loreley*'s vicinity.

"Got you!" Theodora smiled grimly.

She'd had a good run protecting her home, and her kids were all grown up and settled—no reason for regrets.

With her final act, Captain Theodora Imrin dumped every last bit of power into the main PUs, and the two ships collided hard.

A sharp explosion of pain was all she felt once the *Sanji Merabti*'s bridge exploded into flame, and the void embraced her.

CHAPTER FORTY-NINE

GLEN\\ UNWELCOME SURPRISE

"They took the bait," Lt. Montoya narrated what Glen could clearly see on the main screen. "Unclassified_1, Ruja_10 and Ruja_11 are bearing down on us. The *Lightbearer* is still some way out."

The captain nodded, saying, "Let's keep them interested so they don't decide to turn back for those neutrals after all."

"They won't." Eve's voice was all calm analysis. "We're the target and the Velorians will be single-minded in pursuing us."

"Do we need to engage them or can we just let them chase us all the way to the gate?" Nick provided options.

"And what would stop them from licking our heels all the way into another solar system?" Federov countered. "Besides, if we get too close, those stations might blast us apart before we can get through."

"Aye." The admiral had seen enough space battles to judge how much damage a station that size could do to a passing ship like his. "Rushing in just because we can is not a great plan. We're a large target. Those smaller Plutonian ships have much better chances at slipping through—and can rely on those MoWs to back them up. Once they take the stations, and the main fleet has mopped up resistance at the main battle line, we can get in there easy."

"Given these projections of their speed versus ours, we'll not be able to outrun the Velorian ships. They'll catch up long before we reach the gate," Montoya interposed helpfully.

That wouldn't be a problem—once they switched to plan B. But the right moment hadn't come yet. Or had it?

"Ship's Master, your recommendation?" Glen's vague words hid the actual question.

"Col. Federov is right." Eve shook her head. "I don't think we can just fly over and through, no matter how fast we are. Eliminating our pursuers while they're on their own is the most logical play. It will also give the Plutonian forces time to clear a path for us, as they promised. However, we could use the Velorians' focus on pursuing us to maneuver them back into the Plutonian crossfire while simultaneously advancing into a better position to race for the gate."

"Now that's an idea we can all agree on, I'd say!" Nick commented, mirroring the mischievous grins and eager nods being exchanged all over the bridge.

Glen thought on it briefly before saying, "Aye, we are. Helm, plan a course accordingly! Tactical, give me options on engaging those ships. Scanners, how's the in-depth scan of that unclassified coming along?"

"This ship seems to be designed for frontal assault, since it has the thickest armor there. But that's about all we can say for sure," Lt. Montoya reported as she parted off a small section on the main screen to show an erstwhile spec of the vessel in question, right next to the camera feed of it spearheading the two *rujas*. The specs only showed the outer layer, maybe two or three levels. Where the sensors had failed to penetrate, a featureless void prevailed. The front section appeared especially empty. All in all, there was little to see.

"It might be an assault carrier." Montoya zoomed in on what she was describing. "There's at least one large hangar sporting a forward-facing ramp and one facing aft, optimally angled to release small fighters or maybe drones. It might be a bigger version of those *crubas*."

"Velorians mostly use multi-purpose vessels; they don't seem to have much of a designated navy, right?" Glen turned to Eve to confirm his memory of what she'd told him.

"Yes. While they were occupied, they weren't allowed one, and what they developed afterward is more of a merchant fleet." She explained. "Their *cruba*-class is an exception. But such designated warships usually serve a supportive role, like the defense of an installation or freighter convoys."

"So this is something new in more ways than one." Nick flipped a copy of the design onto his holo console and leaned in for a closer look.

"Indeed," Eve replied, her gaze fixed on the data streaming across her screen.

Even though her outward appearance didn't give anything away, Glen could almost feel her frustration at being unable to identify what they were looking at.

"Well, whatever it is," Federov decided and crossed his arms, "if they come too close, I'll send over my walkers. They'll take it in no time."

"Take it?" The mischievous glint of understanding twinkled in the XO's eyes as he turned toward the hologram. "So your comrades can tow it on the way out and have a good look at the new design of your neighbors?!

I would have thought you eager to destroy it after what just happened."

"Personal feelings have no place on the battlefield, Commander," the Plutonian retorted. "You should know that."

"I admire your eagerness to get in on the fighting." Glen rubbed the bridge of his nose. "And your business acumen. But your next attempt to capture a Velorian vessel is postponed. We'll try shooting them from a distance, first. Tactical?!"

Lt. Jiǎng nodded and began outlining engagement strategies when the first enemy barrage hit their ship.

"Captain, Plutonian corvettes are engaging the *rujas*!" Lt. Singh called out. "Both are already suffering boarding actions."

Glen and Nick exchanged an almost surprised look.

"What?" Federov said. "We're still under Plutonian protection."

Right.

"Indeed." The captain nodded with a small, thankful smile designed to blunt the colonel's sharp reaction.

And really, three corvettes expertly trapped the *rujas*, thereby forcing an engagement away from the other two Velorian ships. Almost as soon as they'd matched the enemy's speed, they sent over even more voidwalkers and a few boarding shuttles before returning to safe distance.

"Great, that should take care of those rujas." Nick said.

The unclassified, meanwhile, wasn't deterred by losing its entourage, it just continued trying to intercept the Gateshot. Ludmilla did a superb job at jinking, but even her talents couldn't get them free of their pursuers.

"Our weapons have no significant effect on their

armor," Montoya reported a few minutes later. "And they're gaining on us."

"What about the *Lightbearer*?" Glen studied the enemy flagship falling further behind. In space, this didn't mean she slowed down, just that she didn't speed up at the same rate the other ships did.

"Our maneuvers seem to have worked. The Plutonians are hammering them constantly," a tactical officer informed.

"She seems to have taken damage to either her PUs or the reactor system fueling them," Lustig added. "She's trying to make up for it by shooting at us, though. Two ships like these concentrating their fire on one small section—that's too much for our aft energy shields to handle. We need to engage an emergency cooldown, or our shield generators are going to fry."

Well, that wasn't good ...

Glen would have loved nothing more than to dash for the gate and be done with all this, but he also knew the deceptive danger of get-there-itis. They had to be smart and patient.

"How much longer can the energy shields hold?" he checked.

"Five minutes, tops," Lustig replied unhappily. "Any longer and we risk irreversible damage."

Damn.

Well, there wasn't anything viable they could do about it. However, losing them completely wasn't an option, either.

"How long for emergency cooldown?"

"At least eight minutes," their head engineer replied.

Glen opened a private thought-comm to Eve, saying, '*Listen, Eve, this is it. This is where we pull out all the stops.*

We can't risk being disabled right at the gate's threshold! We can't risk getting too beaten up to get through!'

Her eyes wavered as she stilled for a heartbeat, thinking. Trying to override her doubts and her inherent need for secrecy.

With a grim nod, the admiral ordered, "Dr. Lustig, shut it down."

"Captain!" Montoya called with urgency. "The unclassified just released a wave of small crafts. At least ... twohundred of them at once! They're coming in fast!"

"What the—" Rivers' voice sounded confused. "Those aren't fighters."

Eve blinked.

Nick's eyes widened. "It's a boarding carrier!"

CHAPTER FIFTY

JOE\\ CUT OFF

"There goes our ride," Joe murmured as what was left of the *Sanji* slammed against what was left of Ruja_8 and both merged into an oversized, fiery comet swerving away into the void. Ships vacated its flight path in due haste. A swarm of evac pods quickly dispersed to make it harder for enemies to pick them off.

"Damn," Bomba acknowledged.

Everyone stayed silent for a minute. They had a minute. It was only right to give at least that much consideration to void knew how many of the people they'd bunked with over the last few months, who'd just died.

"I liked the crew," Sensors finally broke the reverence. "Especially that cute blonde from engineering. I hope she made it. Was thinking of asking her out."

"Better make sure *we* make it, first." Copilot checked their status. "Shit, this battle is coo-coo-crazy! The wigs just pulled all their mobiles to the center, littered half the void with cloaked mines and fighters, and for what? To get to that strange mystery ship Oddball serves on?"

"Looks like it." Captain sighed.

Their targets had just flown off, engaging their advanced speed for maximal effect, and left the *Can* stranded in a minefield. With no enemies in the vicinity, Joe's crew had been tasked to use the dark sphere's highly sensitive scanners to map as many of the cloaked mines as they could discover. This also gave them an opportunity to vent their busted heat storage.

Meanwhile, the unclassified wig ship, the *Lightbearer*, and two rujas had split from the main force and sped off. As soon as they'd crossed the Plutonian battle line, and there was no point in staying, the rest of the wiggies, who'd headlessly flown right into the enemy line, retreated back to their own. At least they tried to. But being caught in no man's land, with both their cover and heavy fire support suddenly gone, was not a healthy proposition under any circumstance. Especially not with properly enraged Plutonians bearing down on them from all sides. Any wig ship with less than stellar luck on her side was positively hammered with relentless, disciplined fire, until nothing but dust remained.

"Shit, what just happened there?" Copilot asked no one in particular.

"Big dumb mistake?" Bomba answered.

"You're being generous." Joe shook his head at the awe-inspiring idiocy. "Fucking rookie blunder, that's what that was. What kind of moronic asshole leaves their troops out to dry like that? And for what?"

"Oddball's ship?" Copilot guessed, "The wiggies must want it real bad. They have this tunnel-vision problem, right?"

"Yeah, but ... Void!" Joe just couldn't seem to stop shaking his head. The whole situation was so ludicrous. How did these assholes choose their leaders? Definitely not due to experience or merit, if this clusterfuck was any indication ...

"I like it," Sensors looked up from his work long enough to comment. "Good for us."

Bomba grunted agreement.

"Yeah." Joe shifted into a nod, before asking, "Copilot, any news on what we can't see with our own eyes?"

"Well, there's been a lot of colors changed. Seems like we've successfully captured seven Velorian ships."

Sensors whooped loudly.

"The battle ain't won until it's done," Joe cautioned.

"Well, yeah, but with what just happened over there, the tide's definitely turning our way," the youngster jabbed back.

Everyone agreed on that much.

Meanwhile, on the other side of the battlefield, the black coreworld ship left the hospital ships behind with the clear intent to lead the aliens away.

"We better find a way out of here." Copilot commented. "We've charted as far as our scanners can reach—and the heat storage is as cold as we can get it right now."

"Yeah." Captain gently tugged at his controls, praying that the damaged PUs wouldn't make them lurch to either side as he followed the prepared course, which guided them out.

"You know," Copilot mused, "we don't have to go through the mine field. Oddball's ship is swinging around. We could intercept."

The possible flight plan he presented to his superior had them avoid the main battle and head toward the gate.

"And why would we do that?" Sensors didn't get it.

Bomba did, saying, "We still got a sixer."

"Yeah," Captain agreed. "That would look mightily fine in one of those holes the *Lightbearer* already has ... we could decide this battle—do what all these big boats couldn't!"

"We need permission to fire that one," Sensors pointed out.

"Don't think the marshal would mind." Copilot's voice carried a sardonic smile. "As long as we don't bother him with foreknowledge."

Bomba grunted agreement.

The youngster contorted in his seat to stare at all of them in turn. As much as he could, anyhow.

"There'll be hell to pay in front of the JC if we get through this," he finally muttered.

Bomba opened his fist explosively and laughed. "We get there, there's no way we'll miss! We bring that tub down, they don't give us to JC, they give us medals!"

"Right ..." A tentative smirk spread on Sensors' face. "They'll name ships after us, if we make that happen!"

Copilot nodded. "We'll send the damn wigs scrambling like headless chickens! Without their flagship, they'll finally falter for sure."

"Yeah." Pilot took a deep breath. This was what it was all about, why they were doing this damn job. To make an actual difference. What more could he ask for?

Question was, could they make it that far without being detected? What if that side skirmish turned away before they could meet it? Their tiny thrusters weren't built for high-speed chases with ships several kilometers long. Those ships had thrusters several times the *Can*'s size. Had a lot more mass to get moving too ... and inertial dampeners.

"We better time this right." He flipped his controls over

to the new flight plan. "The way I see it, we've only got one shot at it."

"The void gives and the void takes," Copilot agreed.

"For the republic!" they all answered as one. "For our home!"

Pilot turned their craft away from the minefield and punched it.

CHAPTER FIFTY-ONE

JATHEKI\\ WRONGNESS

WITH THE *GATESHOT* BEING AS LARGE AS IT WAS, THE ships gunning for them seemed tiny, almost insignificant. Except for the whiff of death accompanying them. Jatheki narrowed his eyes as the seer reached out to hone in on the unpleasant feeling. It seemed familiar and yet ... not quite.

Without sound, the battle between the *Gateshot*, the pursuing ship sending a continuous stream of boarding shuttles, and the wounded giant limping in both their wake seemed strangely without context or direct impact.

The boarding carrier. The shuttles. That's where it was situated. The festering wrongness nagging at Jatheki's sight. As the *Gateshot* opened up on them, more and more tiny sparks erupted in the distance. Like infernal embers bursting against a celestial tapestry.

"Can we get them all?" Xinyi whispered fearfully.

"I wouldn't think so," the strategist answered with some revulsion carrying in her voice. "It's a numbers game. Throwaway troops. Accepted losses of 60-80 %. That's why they send so many at once. The larger shuttles will probably hold 10-12 people, the small torpedo-like vessels 5-7.

With about ..." with how many battles she'd witnessed, one quick look sufficed for an estimation, "...say two hundred vessels in the first wave, that's 1,700-2,100 enemies in total. Which means anything between 340-840 will board this ship."

Little Cassandra's eyes widened. "That's more than we have people aboard!"

"Yes, and it's just the first wave. I expect more to come." The strategist shrugged. "But boarding a ship isn't easy. Say what you will about the Plutonians, they know warfare. They'll make a good fight out of it."

"But ... so many!" the girl protested. "They can't possibly hold against all of them!"

Jatheki felt his mouth press into a thin line. Dite stroked his calf with her tail. The movement had a wooden feel to it. Worry. Add to that the stomach-turning sense of wrongness stubbornly haunting him, and the trimorph felt decidedly out of sorts. He knew where to place it once the first souls vacated the exploding shuttle crafts and came their way.

The impact made him stagger, and the girl looked up and down his form with obvious bewilderment.

"What is it? What's happening?" she asked.

Nausea crept up on Jatheki as he felt the monstrous, sinful exploitation humanity committed upon its spiritual core pass through him on the way to the afterlife.

"Can't you see it?" He couldn't keep the growl out of his voice. "The wrongness?"

Children. They were dumb, irresponsible children unaware of the destructive nature of their entrepreneurial tendencies. Of the devastating consequences to their sanity.

His hands gripped his cane tighter.

Oh, how he would love to stop this! How he would love

to lash out and rip them all out of their pitiful corporeal prisons and back to the wellspring in one fell swoop!

"Wrongness?" Xin whispered.

The golden orbs of her eyes adjusted to study the far-off battle more closely. The torches surfaced from the golden depths of her irises and stayed, locked into place by an unseen force. She took an inadvertent step forward. And stopped. From one moment to the next, her whole frame froze. She swallowed hard, and tears ran down her cheeks in sudden rivulets. Her breath quickened and stalled.

She could see it!

Jatheki gently squeezed her shoulder. "Don't look too deep into the abyss, My Dear. It's not conducive to your mental health."

As if he'd broken a spell holding her eyes fixed to the unholy sight, Little Cassandra blinked and quickly gazed away. The minuscule torches detached from their places and drifted back into the lazily swirling magical concoction.

"It's ... horrible," she confirmed. "What ... what *is* that?"

CHAPTER FIFTY-TWO

GLEN\\ PLAN B

"It's a boarding carrier," Glen repeated his XO's words as the cloud of shuttlecraft accelerated toward them.

Bloody hell, this was bad. He shouldn't be surprised—it only made sense.

"Weapons, switch to defensive fire patterns!" the admiral bellowed. "Pick off as many as you can! Helm, gain as much separation from those shuttles as possible. All point defenses fire at will! Scanners, relay information on which airlocks are being targeted to the gunners and Colonel Federov's teams as soon as you have an estimate. Colonel, secure and defend those targets!"

A storm of affirmatives rolled his way, and within minutes, the space between the *Gateshot* and the Velorian ships was alight with a redoubled effort to blast away their unwelcome tail. But the numbers weren't in their favor. Those were a lot of shuttles and the *Gateshot* only had so many countermeasures.

"Since when are the Velorians bothering with this tactic?" Nick ran his mouth to cover the stress as his fingers danced over his controls. “I thought they preferred to rely on their superior firepower and accuracy?”

Eve glanced at Federov. “Might be that they’re adapting.”

“Might be. But they can’t have much experience with it, yet. Let them board! Our defenses will make short work of their clone troops.” The Plutonian had relayed his verbal commands and now proceeded to gesture at several someones on his end of the line. His voice sounded grimly determined as he turned to Glen. “Captain, permission to send out walkers to board back!? With the Velorians focused on their engagement on our ship, my people can disable that ugly hunk of metal from the inside before it disgorges more waves.”

“No,” the admiral answered in a steady voice as he stared at the pitiful dent their projectiles and beams made in the overall number of the boarding vessels. “All your troops will be needed to defend this vessel. We can’t spare anyone.”

This wasn’t going to work ...

“Captain,” one of Lt. Jiăng’s helpers called, “both bandits have resumed shelling.”

Of course they had ...

‘*Eve*’, the captain thought-commed, ‘*please. This is the time. At this point, we can’t afford to lose any more crew than is absolutely necessary!*’

She swallowed and glanced away, clearly warring with herself.

“Admiral,” Federov advised, “we can handle a wave or two, but that *parrucche* ship is large enough to hold significantly more troops and shuttles than what we’re seeing right now. This first wave is to test our reaction and defenses.”

“I know.” Glen steepled his hands. “I’m counting on it.”

The younger man frowned but didn't disagree a second time. Maybe he saw something in the admiral's eyes.

"This is a standard boarding tactic." The admiral jabbed at the display. His eyes locked onto Eve. She was the one who needed to understand just how bad this could get if they didn't act now.

"Old ESF pattern," he continued, "they waited for our shield to buckle. Swarming us with projectiles will divert our defenses to allow enough shuttles to slip through, packed with troops ready to seize our ship. But just in case we put up more of a fight than they're betting on, the second wave will be significantly larger."

'*We need to act now*', he added for her ears alone. '*We need to get rid of them and then leg it! The time to play coy has passed!*'

Federov didn't reply; he opted to organize and manage the internal defenses over arguing with the captain.

"Boarding vessels are closing in!" Montoya advised. "ETA to first contact: two minutes."

"Incoming projectiles exceed available countermeasures!" Lt. Jiăng's even voice came as close to panic as Glen had ever heard it. "Energy shield is still down!"

The guardian nodded—a final, decisive gesture.

Thank goodness!

"Ms. Baileywick, execute Plan B!" Glen ordered.

"Permission to connect with the ship, Captain?" she replied, placing the palms of both hands on her console.

"Permission granted!"

Eve bowed her head and her palms sank partly into the console. "Overwriting reduction protocols," she reported.

"Captain," Montoya gasped and shook her head, "Our sensor range just ... increased tenfold! The entire scale changed!"

"Available energy levels emanating from our primary energy source have increased as well," Lustig reported what he'd just been waiting for. "Rerouting to beam banks."

"Lt. Jiăng, you have new countermeasures available." Eve announced in an even voice. "I advise using the emergency pulse wave now, then get comfortable with the grid beam emitters."

"Cooldown complete," Lustig added. "Shield generators powering back up."

"Do it!" Glen ordered toward Jiăng's section.

"Aye, Sir!"

The minuscule smile playing on the senior weapons officer's lips made Glen suspect he'd been secretly trained for this. As the man's fingers flew over his console, he simultaneously instructed his team on how to activate the new functions Eve had mentioned.

As the admiral watched, an energy spike ran from the shield generators through their hull. On the main screen, the almost invisible field flickered as it ballooned outward. Wherever it touched the cloud of enemy projectiles coming their way, they exploded or were shoved off-course unceremoniously. Some of them were even redirected into enemy shuttles by the motion. As it washed over the unclassified, the other ship's energy shield flashed brightly and faltered.

Drained, the energy pulse flickered out at about 5 k distance.

"What was that?" Montoya's dark eyes were as large as saucers and glued to her console's output.

"I told you she's a special ship." Rivers' voice barely held in her bubbling enthusiasm.

"Captain, we can only do this once every half hour," Lt. Jiăng advised. "Due to the recharging cycle. But it should have gained us some breathing space."

Backed by strengthened beam banks and renewed enthusiasm, he and his team were already picking off more of the remaining shuttles. They also used the opportunity to gun for the boarding carrier. Several large holes appeared in the mothership before her own energy shield slammed back up, and another wave of incoming fire diverted Jiăng's attention.

"Acknowledged, Lieutenant." Glen relayed his thanks to Eve with a grateful dip of his head. "Scanners, how many remaining boarding vessels?"

"Ahem ... 62 ... no, make that 58," Montoya reported. "ETA to first target: 34 seconds."

Glen looked to Federov. "Are your people ready?"

"*Da.*" The former voidwalker showed his teeth as he gripped the edge of his tactical display. "These bastards won't know what hit them."

"Good." Glen returned the expression. "Helm, how's our flight corridor doing?"

"New corridor established," Ludmilla reported curtly.

After a quick glance at the helm's datastream, the captain raised an eyebrow at his ship's master.

"We're not faster?" he asked.

"No," Eve returned, her face devoid of explanation.

The admiral merely shrugged.

"Too bad," he said, then commed their ship's witch. "Ms. Magecraft, do you have a lock on the gate yet?"

"It's still too small for Ms. Yun to see properly." The young woman sounded frustrated. "But we're getting there."

"Understood. Tell me as soon as this changes."

"Aye, Captain."

CHAPTER FIFTY-THREE

WIRE\\ BOARDING ACTION

"To your right! Go! Go! Go!" SSgt. Bawker barked as soon as the elevator doors rushed open and disgorged his squad into one of the wider corridors near the aft hull.

Like the rest of her new comrades, Wire legged it.

Well, as much as she could while lugging the ammunition crates. The newly-baked loader—or 'ammo mule' as Khalil affectionately called it—had been given a sturdy battlefield hover carrier to lift the dark-blue crates for her, but it was a pain in the ass to direct. So she did like the other fireteam's mule and manhandled the thing along. Next to her, Jamaal carried the machine gun that would transform some of the ammo belts in her crates into deadly horizontal hail.

"Fireteam 1, go right! Fireteam 2, go left!" their stocky squad leader yelled over the hubbub of boots slamming the ground, equipment being jostled, and weaponry being checked on the go. "Standard setup! And remember the colonel's order: Accept no surrenders! We can't afford to upkeep any prisoners or be tricked into splitting our forces to guard them, just so they can stab us in the back later. No surrenders!"

Yeah, that order didn't exactly sound ... all that legal.

"Aye, Sir!" everyone panted. "No surrenders!"

Helpful AR arrows blinked into existence to indicate their way. With boarding shuttles gunning for them, time was of the essence. They had to secure this entrance before enemies spilled into the *Gateshot*, ready to do damage.

As Fireteam_2 jogged around the next corner and the airlock came into view, the ship was already setting up its defenses. The airlock sat at the center of a T-junction, slightly recessed from the crossing corridor.

"Mule, park it there! ECM and Thrifter, set up the big gun!" Khalil, their fireteam leader, pointed at a barricade swinging out of the left-hand wall, then down the corridor and to the left. "Mike and Judy, grab and go!"

Wire hadn't quite managed to engage the brakes on her carrier when the last two troopers to be addressed each grabbed an ammo crate off the top without breaking their stride. As soon as they'd passed by the airlock, several plates hinged upward out of the floor and slammed into place audibly, creating funnel barriers and trip hazards in one go.

"ECM, you're on the Beast," Khalil ordered.

"Aye, Sir!" Jamaal slid the machine gun off his shoulders.

Hooks extended out of the floor to mount the heavy weapon, and Khalil quickly grabbed one end of the tripod to steady the gun for automatic strap-down. He gestured with the other hand, saying, "Thrifter, you're feeding."

"Aye, Sir!" Lily, a trooper with strawberry blonde curls peeking out from under her helmet, was carrying her own ammo crate. The metal inside rattled as she slammed the sturdy container down next to the gun and popped open the lid. With a *scrape* and *click* another barricade swung out of the wall, and connected to the one shielding the machine gun and its operator, thereby completely blocking the corridor on this side.

Khalil pointed at another barricade, one farther away from the airlock. "Wire, you're directing the ship turrets. Hunker down over there and get connected. I'm your shield. Everything making it halfway through the corridor, you bring down!"

"Aye, Sir, halfway!"

At his cue, a set of AR-controls and several vid screens blinked into existence in front of her. On the screens, she could see Mike and Judy huddling behind their cover, inserting one ammo crate each into wall slots. Halfway between them and the airlock, two turrets descended from hidden compartments in the ceiling. A yellow AR-light indicated the status of the self-feeding process. The ship provided her with a green-lit completed systems check for both guns, and Wire disregarded all vid feeds she didn't need. Those would only confuse her once the action started. The yellow light switched to green. All of this would have been unnecessary on an ESF ship, of course. But Plutonians really didn't like any machine deciding whom to shoot at and whom not to.

"System's engaged. Coils green. Pulse clear. Magnetics stable. Weapon online," Jamaal called out like a pilot going through his checklist.

"First belt clear," Lily called back. "Two to go."

"Two to go," Jamaal acknowledged.

"Hey, Boss, why the weak ammo?" Lily inquired. The twenty-something was a freshie too. Gangbanger with a history of smuggling illegal shit.

"'Cause it will suffice." Khalil's fingertips checked his

belt's content—the only sign of nervousness he displayed. "Velorian clones are squishy targets; seldom armored beyond light vests. They don't like to wear helmets either. Maybe because of the ears. Besides, even without engaging the anti-material setting, this close to the hull, we'd better not risk punching holes through walls."

"Right." Lily nodded.

"Okay, People," Khalil addressed all of them, out loud and on comms. "Everyone look sharp and engage night-vision. Word is the wigs can't see well in near darkness. So it's lights out in three! Fire at will!"

Right then, the airlock groaned under the change in pressurization. A nervous flutter settled into Wire's stomach. Her eyes jumped from the turrets' views of an empty corridor to her own of the door into space. The light died down to where even the Plutonians had to engage night-vision on their helmets. Not a problem for the *Gateshot*'s cameras. Those vid feeds were more crisp and telling than her new helmet's filters could manage. Also, they had heatvision, which was even better.

The airlock blew open. Feet trampled the ground. Jamaal opened up on the figures, stumbling into the dark corridor, tripping over the first holes in the ground. Wire focused entirely on the vid feeds, on the indicators dividing her kill zone from his. He mowed down the first couple. They didn't stand a chance. The ones following moved more easily, maybe because their fallen comrades clogged up some of the treacherous ground. Wire caught those who survived the first half of the junction in the crossfire. Within seconds, heaps of dead and dying clogged up the T-junction. Then everything was over but the pained moaning and gurgling gasps of those still clinging to life.

At the front, Mike and Judy circled their barricades

with their weapons drawn. For good measure, they each threw a grenade into the shuttle and then began to take out the dying. Wire kept an eye out for movement. She was their backup. The sounds stopped abruptly, one after another, and silence fell like a suffocating blanket.

"That took more than I expected ..." Khalil murmured.

"Because they had light armor and helmets," Wire said as she rose to peek down the corridor. "I thought Velorians don't do those?"

He frowned at her. That's when the lights flimmered back on to reveal the whole mess the assault had left behind. Blood and other stuff usually situated within bodies redecorated the hallway. Haphazardly stacked corpses clogged the junction.

"Boss," Mike called, "you have to see this. It's not Velorian clones!"

"No clones?" Khalil squinted over the barricade.

"It's clones, all right." As the other trooper reported, Wire could see it on the vid feed herself, and her eyes widened in time with Judy's following words. "Just not Velorian ones."

"Fireteam 2!" Bawker's voice barked out of their comms. "Get down to the next airlock! Another shuttle is about to dock!"

"Fuck!" Khalil swore. Then he gestured for Lily to cut the chain and Jamaal to shoulder the Beast as he commed back, "Bawker, it's Human clones. I repeat: they're sending in Human clones! Slightly armored—helmets and vests."

A brief moment of silence.

"Yeah, ours too," Bawker reported. "Nothing for it. Get moving, Florimonte!"

"Aye, Sir!" Khalil ordered Mike and Judy to retrieve the

ammo from the turrets and follow their corridor to the next airlock.

All these doors to space were part of a net used by the maintenance staff to access the outer hull. They were necessary weak points, heavily armored and each sporting its own set of outward-facing defense turrets. To comply with the Plutonian mindset, those were now accessed and used via the bridge or, in more pressing situations like a boarding in progress, by a multitude of specialist gunners sitting in some war room or whatever.

Tugging along her ammo cart, Wire legged it to their next point of engagement. It was much like the last one, and they'd just set up the same way, when the airlock blew open. Darkness engulfed them, but both night and heatvision showed only an empty corridor. Khalil kept his cool.

"Wait for them to move," he instructed. "We only have so much ammo."

"Aye, Sir," Wire whispered.

Suddenly, the telltale sounds of small canisters hitting the floor. The *hiss* of smoke escaping. Superheated smoke, devised to render heatvision useless, blanketed the airlock.

"Fire!" Khalil ordered, and Jamaal's machine gun vibrated with the uninterrupted *humm* and *whoosh* of 1,500 RPM being flung out magnetically.

Wire augmented this deadly hail with the two turrets. For several hurried heartbeats, the *pling-pling-pling* of metal hail and slightly wrong *sirr* of ricochets was all they could hear. One large body dropped. Only one. Then, the scratching, scurrying scuttle of metal on metal. Wire looked up.

"On the ceiling!" she warned and reaimed, just as the first enemy exited the smoke cover, clinging to the ceiling.

The man in tactical gear fell to the ground and rolled.

In one smooth motion, he sprang back to his feet and yanked out one of the pre-installed barricades for cover. A small canister came flying. Jamaal, who'd also been aiming for the ceiling, sent a quick burst its way and deflected the grenade. It exploded slightly above and behind the guy taking cover, a mere four meters away.

Wire closed her eyes instinctively, which made her almost miss the two others crawling along the ceiling. They headed straight for the turrets. She aimed one turret on each and let them have it, but the men, completely covered in dark tactical gear, seemed hardly inconvenienced. In a desperate attempt to get them before they got her guns, she turned both turrets on one of them, positively shredding his upper body. Whatever super-fancy armor he was wearing couldn't take that much abuse. He dropped. But it gave the other one a clean shot at her left turret.

Her two squadmates, meanwhile, had thrown several grenades into the airlock and followed up with short, precise bursts aimed at the weak points in the remaining boarder's armor.

It wasn't enough. He grabbed the turret and pushed off the ceiling, ripping it clean out of its mount, then engaged the CCG troopers with his bare hands.

WHAT THE—???

"Mike, Judy!" Wire called. "Fall back to safe distance!"

She couldn't shoot at the guy with her comrades this close, damn it!

The freak slammed his fist halfway through Judy's chest. The petite brunette blinked, as if surprised. Her mouth moved, but either it was too loud to hear her, or no air escaped to form sounds to whatever she'd meant to impart with her dying breath. Her compact assault rifle slipped from limp hands and clattered onto the floor as she fell to her knees. Mike quickly exchanged his CAR for a shotgun. With the wicked spike at its end, he smashed in the enemy's faceshield, then whirled it around to let the freak have the full brunt of whatever the shortened barrels held. The helmet ballooned and cracked. Blood spurted back at Mike and dribbled down the enemy's neck. With jerky motions, the body went down. As the helmet rolled away, it left a bloody stump throwing electrical sparks.

Yikes!

"Wire!" Khalil called, and she refocused on her actual body.

Her boss pointed at the badly burned creature jumping the barricade Lily and Jamaal had been huddling behind a mere minute ago. Lily lay dead, her neck shot clean through. Jamaal punched their attacker in the faceplate, and for a second, the thing almost seemed surprised. Then it slammed the butt of its gun into Jamaal's helmet, and transparent polymer shards flew everywhere. The Spartan staggered back blindly.

"Cover fire!" Khalil ordered. "ECM, fall back!"

FUCK ...

Wire brought up her CAR.

"Go for face and neck!" Khalil already did exactly that. He was a superb shot, but the target wasn't going down easily.

Even at close distance, it took half an eternity of direct fire to get in enough bullets for the thing to falter.

"SHIT!" Wire kept her CAR trained on the downed, twitching corpse. "What the fuck are those things?"

"Cyborgs." Khalil gazed down the corridor, as he helped Jamaal up. "They're Human ... technically. But they get metal embedded in all sorts of places, sometimes even laced onto their bones. Before a fight, they're stimmed up to the gills, so they don't feel pain, have faster reactions, better sight and whatnot. I don't see spikes, so they probably have magnets embedded to be able to stick to the ceiling like that. Jamaal, you all right?"

"I'll live ..." The dark-skinned marine coughed.

"Yeah." Khalil took a closer look at his shattered helmet. "You better keep that on. I know, the shards sting. There, let me get that one next to your eye. Don't move now. ... Okay, here."

Their superior pulled a shard of unreal proportions out of Jamaal's cut-up face and snipped it away, saying, "The medics should do the rest, concussion risk, and such. I already called it in. You keep at the back for now."

"Aye, Sir." Jamaal sounded unusually subdued as he picked up the CAR he'd lost and followed Khalil and Wire down to the airlock.

Mike inched out to meet them. Together, they inspected the burned-out husk of the simplistic shuttlecraft. It was more of a boarding torpedo than an actual vessel ...

"Only a five-seater." Khalil gripped his gun tighter. "Guess we were lucky."

Mike had a long look around, then kicked a badly charred chunk of flesh with metal sticking out of it.

"You think that's enough pieces to make another two metalheads?" he asked. A sort of subdued rage burned in his eyes as he glanced from the corpse pieces back to where Judy's corpse lay out of sight.

"I think so ..." Khalil shook his head. "I'll call it in as a not-sure, though. Just in case one slipped by us."

He seemed to notice Mike's inner turmoil. His lips pressed into a thin line briefly, as he holstered his gun to squeeze the other man's shoulder. "Seal that airlock and grab your gear. We'll probably be needed elsewhere."

"Aye, Sir," Wire whispered and swallowed hard.

She knew the drill; the living took precedence. They would come back for their fallen later, once the ship was safe. Made sense. Had always felt wrong, though. Back in the war, just as much as now. And it left her wondering how many they'd have to recover once all this was done.

And if she would be one of them after all.

CHAPTER FIFTY-FOUR

SUZY\\ BLOCKED

As the *Gateshot* neared her ultimate purpose, Suzy watched through Xin's eyes, eager to catch a first glimpse of the activation runes. After all, who knew how long the gate would need to ... power up or whatever, and be ready for them to fly through? Given the pursuit so hot on their proverbial tailfeathers, every second might count!

Though, with the three Velorian stations hanging suspended around the giant, ancient artifact like stern guardians, who knew when they would make their dash for it? ... Or did Glen plan to just go for it now? Surely, that would be too dangerous, right?

Nervousness fluttered through their connection. Suzy could feel the tightly wound muscles in Xin's back. Her friend knew there was a battle raging behind her. It was hard to ignore. And there was something else ... some ... unnatural nausea pooling in her stomach. Rupert had shown her something. Something bad. Suzy didn't know what, but it was derailing her aide's focus.

Whatever it was, Rupert still watched it. The three

colors churning around his slim form were increasingly shrouded by a brooding black anger.

"Xin, concentrate!" Suzy hissed. "I know he's distracting you, but this is more important right now! This is what we're here for! We need to be ready once everything else falls into place!"

"Right. Sorry!"

Her friend's eyes blinked several times and refocused on squinting at the distant ring. She fiddled with the purely optical zoom on her trusty spyglass. Way too slowly, the gate drifted into sharper focus. More and more details emerged.

In the complete soundlessness of space, the knowledge that a shell or a piece of debris might sniff her out in an instant and she would never hear it nearing set Xin's neck to tingling with increasing restlessness.

"That's what Rupert's there for," Suzy said, trying to calm both their frayed nerves. "We have to trust him. Come on, we're almost there. I can almost make out the symbols on the top."

"Yes, I know," Xin whispered under her breath. She took a deep breath. Another one. Forcing her raging pulse down, she did her best to steady herself as she searched for the three runes they'd previously identified as most likely being the activation switch.

After another nerve-racking eternity, they came into view. First, only the faint glow of magic, from different parts of the mechanism. Then, finally, the shapes took a distinct form.

Suzy breathed out explosively.

"Okay, there are the runes we've identified." The girl's hands opened and closed nervously. "Magecraft to MacAllister, I can see the runes. Shall I try to open the gate?"

A pause. Some strange feeling of thoughtful contemplation. Then Glen answered, "Do it. Let's see if it works and what the stations will do if it does."

"Understood." Suzy nodded to herself. "I'm going to send energy to the runes now."

This is easy, she thought. *It's just like flipping a switch. No big deal.*

This was merely the culmination of months of sacrifice, smashing her mind against a seemingly unyielding problem, and a relentless fight for survival. And they were going in being assaulted and opposed, fighting tooth and nail all the way to the other side ... a very fitting way to end this part of their journey.

'*Stop procrastinating and do it already,*' Rupert's voice cut through the poetic flight of fancy her mind was taking.

"Right." The witch sucked in a deep breath and held it. She focused her mind on the runes. As she sent out all the energy she felt comfortable parting with, Xin's eyes widened.

The flow of energy on the gate shifted. The runes glowed brighter as the artifact pulled in magic from the surrounding area. A subtle wavering started in the space within. Like heated air dancing over a stove.

Marsdust, they were doing it! They were really doing it! ... No, she was doing it. Suzy fucking Lisbeth Magecraft was using her magic to open the marsforsaken Space Gate! Gosh, if Lucy could see her now! This was ... incredible! And so fucking easy!

Suddenly, without warning or sense, a bright flash ran from one of the stations to the gate. Like a laser beam, it smashed into the central one of the runes Suzy had triggered. At its end, the beam turned into a dark rope and wound tightly around it.

"What the—?" The witch gasped and staggered back, right out of her concentration circle. The sensation burning her insides felt like a bodily blow, and as if someone had stolen something from her at the same time. In the distance, Xin staggered as well. Their connection hadn't been cut as such, just ...

"What is it?" Diaz caught her, restrained urgency in his tone.

Xin gazed over to the station. The subdued fire she'd seen there before had easily tripled in luminance.

"Suzy?" Glen's voice sounded over the comms. He was clearly worried. Like he could also feel something was majorly off. "What's happening?"

Marsdust, she'd just had to think it was easy, hadn't she?

"Jinxed it," Suzy murmured.

"Come again?" Glen prompted.

"I'm being ... blocked," the girl said out loud and on comms for everyone's benefit. "I think the Velorians are somehow preventing me from opening the gate!"

A muttered curse ran through her connection to Glen.

"So we can't leave, is what you're saying?" Nick weighed in. "We need to wait for the Plutonians to take out the Velorians, in either case?"

Suzy could feel Glen's discomfort, could feel his hunch pricking him like his seat had turned into a thornbush. He knew time was running out. She needed to do something.

"Fuck that!" she growled. "We didn't come all this way to wait for Mars knows how long that spell lasts. We're getting through that gate! We're getting there, right now!"

"How?" Nick asked.

Suzy pulled up her sleeves and balled her fists as she shrugged off Diaz's helping hands and stalked back into her circle, saying, "Well, I guess I'll just have to get creative!"

CHAPTER FIFTY-FIVE

SERGEY\\ PIVOT

As the panicked comms started pouring in, Sergey stared at the tactical display in mounting unease. What was happening? This should have been a cakewalk!

"Human clones," Brigadier Major Stenson reported. "The Velorians sent Human clones; light to medium armor!"

"They're not even sending in their own species?" Yelena shook her head in disgust. "Damn cowards!"

"Some of my people report cyborg units," the brigadier major continued, marking the airlocks in question on the display. "Heavily enhanced—and an absolute pain to kill."

With a thought, Sergey asked for a vid feed showing those.

"Martins." He rubbed the bridge of his nose as he identified the face they probably all wore. There were only a dozen or so popular genetic blueprints for cyborg clones, all named after their respective original. Martins were top-notch, very expensive one-man armies. To the void with them!

Fuck. His people were getting their asses kicked, and he'd issued weak ammo.

"Ten years, and as far as we know, Velorians never used Human clones before, let alone cyborgs," Yelena commented with a frown. "So what do we do?"

Right. No use in beating himself up. First, they needed to turn this shit-show around.

"We need stronger arguments," Sergey decided. "Something with more force. Rail guns and tubes should do the trick. We'd just have to lure them away from the hull. Order everyone to fall back should a threat not be containable. Most of those cyborgs are basically immune to small-arms fire and conventional explosives. Lev, locate and distribute some railguns and tubes. Armory, send out penetrator rounds and anti-armor rockets. Officers, reposition your troops and organize their supply."

"Yes, sir!" everyone acknowledged. Fingers flew over invisible AR outputs.

"If we fall back now and let this fight drag on, we will have a hard time rebuffing a second wave." Stenson took that tone of voice which indicated he had something to say, on the simple merit of being the senior soldier and having overseen more action than the young colonel. Without disrespect or gloating, just some simple advice.

"I realize that," Sergey nodded his appreciation for the suggestion, "but on the other side of the gate, there's no more backup to be had. Makes sustaining our forces our first priority. Besides, MacAllister's fighting hard to widen the distance. So, hopefully, we'll only have to hold out for a short while, and then we can mop up."

By way of an answer, Stenson nodded and went back to overseeing his troops.

Sergey gripped the desk on which the segment of

Gateshot hovered, all the compromised airlocks were indicated in red, the two parties battling it out represented by icons of different colors. His left-hand knuckles popped quietly, and he eased his grip on his right so his augmetic wouldn't leave dents. Void, how he yearned to be out there and stomp those damn Martins into the nicely carpeted ground himself.

"You know ..." Thompson clearly tried for a similar tone as Stenson's, with very mixed results. "The ship will help, if you let it."

"You mean that AI, which Ms. Baileywick is downplaying?" Sergey couldn't quite keep the deeply ingrained mistrust out of his voice.

The Spartan stepped closer, prompting Yelena to shift ever so slightly in anticipation of having to intervene in a sudden conflict.

"GaSIn is programmed to protect us," Thompson said, all level and factual. "It can access all the internal sensors, cameras, and onboard defenses and get an overview far quicker than any Human. All your redundancies and relying on people takes up time. You know how precious time is in battle. If you need a ghost in the machine to feel safe, you can always ask Baileywick to give you a hand. She's been dancing around so hard as to not step on your toes. ... Maybe you could try matching her flexibility, ... Sir?"

The proposition didn't surprise Sergey. He'd even anticipated this exact argument. But rules couldn't be abandoned just because there was a more convenient way.

As he contemplated a response, his eyes were drawn to the weapons rack holding his own CAR and tube, as well as his whole command staff's guns. They were still clean and unused.

The large man stepped back. "That said, I can provide four fighters in exo-suits. Most corridors are too small as to be conducive to fight in those, but they'll do wonders in these larger maintenance rooms and corridors." He pointed at a selection of hubs for moving parts from the inside to the outside of the ship or whatnot. "If the lighter troops and drones lure the cyborgs there, we take them out. And Stenson has two more suit pilots that could help out."

"Denied. I know what you're saying, Major, but even at record time it would take you half an hour to get suited up and reach the conflict."

Thompson looked taken aback. Sergey's gaze drifted to the unused guns once more.

Ah, fuck it, he thought.

That damn Spartan Gorilla had made a good point. Though Sergey hated compromises, this wasn't the time to let pride stand in the way.

He took a deep breath before announcing to the room, "Everyone, listen up! The setup ain't working. Neither for me nor for most of you. Therefore, everyone who wants to be with their troops is free to leave for the battle—provided you trust yourself to keep up the chain of command."

On many faces, shock and confusion gave way to relief.

"Colonel, what—", came MacAllister's voice from Sergey's station before the colonel muted him.

"Use GaSIn to help with coordinating troop movements, supply runs, etc. But that AI has to keep out of mortal decisions! Lev, you'll stay here and oversee the whole process."

That said, he matched actions to words.

On his way to the weapons rack, he thought-commed, '*Baileywick, you keep out of this as well. Your full attention is needed on the bridge.*'

As he grabbed his weapons, a queue was already forming behind him.

"See? I knew it. You owe me three coins," Thompson whispered.

"Fine," Yelena's voice answered.

Void, this would become one hell of an uncomfortable debriefing.

CHAPTER FIFTY-SIX

SUZY\\ BRIDGING THE GAP

Suzy tried opening the gate five more times. Every time hurt like a bitch, but a little less so. Still, she was getting winded, magically speaking. And she was getting more and more frustrated as well.

Damn it! Hadn't she sworn an oath to the marsforsaken goddess of crossroads? Shouldn't that come with at least some perks that would help her open a fucking *gate*?

"You hear me, Hecate? Doesn't this fall squarely into your domain? Isn't this one of the biggest crossroads humanity has ever stood in front of? Aren't I supposed to be something of your champion? So how about some voidforsaken help? Please?!"

Nothing happened.

Silence prevailed.

"Do you know the definition of insanity?" Diaz murmured as he held out a hand to help her up.

The witch growled. Unimpressed, he pulled her tiny person back onto her feet once she grasped his armored lower arm. Again.

"Wait!" He held her fast when she moved to stalk back into her circle like a boxer into the ring. "Stop and think for a moment."

"I don't have time!" she spat. "I need to get us through that damn gate! Like, yesterday!"

"Yes." He lifted a stalling hand. "But taking a moment to think this through isn't the same as overanalyzing. I'm not asking you to fall back into procrastination. Just stop smashing your head against that invisible wall and take a step back. There has to be a better way, right?"

Suzy took a deep breath and sighed.

"Right," she agreed. "I just— This is so unfair! I finally figured out that it's not complicated at all to open the damn thing, and now someone is making it impossible!"

"Someone? Okay, let's start there. Who or what is blocking you?"

"I don't know!"

This time, when she tugged, he let her go, and Suzy rubbed her face with both palms.

"Well, what do you know?" His analytical tone calmed her inner storm and reasserted reason.

The witch stilled and closed her eyes to replay in her mind what had happened every time she'd tried applying force to the gate.

"I think there's someone on one of those stations," she murmured. "Maybe several someones. They're blocking the activation rune on the gate. So when I put energy in ..."

Suzy let her words run out as she considered what exactly might be happening there.

"They lash out at you?" Diaz asked and pointed at the circle she kept staggering out of.

"No." The girl frowned. "I don't feel like they do. Gosh ... I think I'm slapping myself!"

She remembered the defensive reflection spell she'd mastered.

"Pardon me?" The provost cocked his head.

"My energy comes back. I don't think they do anything more than shield the rune with a reflection spell. That's why the pushback lessens! I'm not wearing them down, I'm wearing *myself* out! Gosh, what an idiot I am!" The witch threw up her arms. "But maybe ... maybe if I also reflect it, like, often enough, it builds up sufficient momentum to shatter that other spell!"

She headed for the circle, but he grabbed her again.

"Wait! What if all that energy builds up and then goes here?" Diaz pointed to the floor.

Marsdust.

Once it had become clear that no corridor fighting was going to break out on this side of the ship for the time being, Federov had pulled his soldiers away to where they were actually and urgently needed. Diaz and Suzy were alone now. But that was no reason to commit suicide.

Suzy swallowed. "Yeah ... you're right. That might not be the best idea. Let's call it plan F for now."

"Okay," he agreed. "So what else could you try? Can't Maverick help you?"

It was worth a shot. And he was Hecate's high priest after all, so maybe this was her goddess's way of helping her. Even if her magic teacher had more of a hands-off approach to imparting knowledge, they *were* pressed for time, so maybe he could be persuaded to help. Suzy's thumb and forefinger pinched the gold coin, and she called, "Hey, Rupert, are you there? Do you have any ideas on how to solve this?"

When he didn't answer, Suzy shifted her mind into Xin's body and looked up at him. The con mage was still staring into the distance, his gaze fixed on the space behind the *Gateshot*. The blackness so hot on their heels seemed to close in, suffocating him.

As the women's combined gaze followed his, they saw the *Lightbearer* fall further behind, while the other ship steadily gained ground. A sense of wrongness and pain rippled through its twisted form, like the sharp reverberation of an impact across a large brass gong. It was so creepy ...

Slugs and beams flew across the tightening gap from both sides.

Suzy blinked open her own eyes and found her heart pounding in her chest.

"Yeah, he's of no use right now ...," she murmured.

Disheartening and depressive thoughts made ready to press in on her, but Diaz cut them short, asking, "Okay, so since those mages are not touching you, you can't touch them back?"

A memory flashed across Suzy's mind. Morgan's ritual. The one he'd killed her father with. It was in his notebook. She could ... No ... no, that wouldn't work.

"What are you thinking?" Diaz prodded.

"I have a ritual. Kinda like a super-creepy, destructive voodoo spell. But I don't have anything personal to connect me to the mage or mages over there." She started pacing around the outside of her circle. "I don't even know who they are ... so it won't work."

"What about Penal Yun? You don't do creepy voodoo magic on her, do you?"

"No!"

Diaz leaned back against a table, arms crossed. "So how do you connect to her when she's far away?"

"Well, I just ..." Suzy blinked, gesturing aimlessly as she was at a loss for words. "... do."

The provost gestured for her to go on.

"Get over there! That's an idea!" Suzy snapped her fingers. "Maybe Rupert can provide a way!"

She'd just have to get through to him first.

CHAPTER FIFTY-SEVEN

JOE\\ CASCADE EFFECT

"Our angle is off," Copilot pointed out what Joe could clearly see on his controls.

"I know," the dark sphere's captain ground out through clenched teeth as he wiped a sheen of sweat around on his face.

It was getting hot and stuffy inside the crammed space again. Too soon. It was way too soon for this. Losing part of their heat storage took its toll. Also, whatever damage the PUs had sustained was messing with the whole flight control system by now. Maybe some broken wiring produced faulty signals which confused the navigational computer or whatever. He wasn't a tech, so he wouldn't know.

"Those ships are rushing by pretty fast," Sensors remarked in that armchair-coach tone of voice his comrades hadn't quite managed to beat out of him yet.

"No shit, Sherrok," Bomba replied dryly.

"If we overshoot, we'll just fly by in their wake," Sensors said. He rarely got the hint to shut up.

"No shit, *Sherlock*," Joe growled, overemphasizing the

correct phrase for Bomba's benefit. He toggled his switches in a vain effort to get more thrust on their portside.

"Running systems check," Copilot informed. His calm, professional tone did the trick, and two minutes ticked by without another word being uttered.

To distract himself, Captain studied the three ships in the distance. His *Can* was heading toward the group at a perpendicular angle and might still be far enough away for even minor course corrections to make a difference—if they managed to input the right ones, that was.

As Oddball's ship jinked for the gate's general direction, the unclassified and the *Lightbearer* pursued them relentlessly. Well, the one in the middle wasn't so unclassified anymore. Given the fleet of tiny vessels it had disgorged earlier, its purpose was now clear as the void. And it proved beyond doubt the wigs' duplicitous nature. What would a species of harmless tech traders need a boarding carrier for? And one of this size to boot? Damn aliens! They'd surely build it to attack Plutonian stations and ships wandering too near the DMZ. Senior Command was right to worry. Right to send a fleet to dismantle these stations. The wigs were way out of line! This was Human fucking space—Plutonian space, damn it!

"Void, that's bad," Copilot's voice cut into Joe's musings. "We got more systems in the red than in the green, Captain."

"Figured as much." Joe took a deep breath and sighed. "Anything you can do about steering?"

Next to him, Copilot frowned as he studied the details on his screen.

"I don't get it," Sensors piped up once more. "This thing is supposed to be super sturdy. We just got a little banged up."

"In just the right place, even the tiniest problem can cause a cascade effect," Copilot muttered. "We could try a complete systems reboot. But that would take five minutes, and if we're really unlucky, the system could just die on us completely."

"And leave us dead in the void?" Bomba sounded unhappy about that prospect. "No help, no nothin'?!"

"Well, we do have that emergency beacon ..." the youngster pointed out.

"You mean the one that'll make us visible to friendlies and bandits alike?" Captain tried another way to regulate the broken PUs. Something had to work!

The smile on Copilot's old face held a strange flavor. An uncomfortable mixture of fatalistic amusement and death-defying anger.

"We've come this far." Captain sighed. "How are the odds?"

Copilot shrugged. "Hard to say."

Joe felt a headache coming on. Dehydration effect. Void, his zero-g bottle was still filled to the brim! As he reached to unclip it from the wall, he considered their options aloud. "So either we're lucky and the system does restart, we can correct course, reach the voidforsaken *Light-bearer*, blow it to pieces, and die heroes when the Velorian's vengeance comes down on us. Or we're unlucky, the system won't restart, we get found out either by the beacon or the heat dribble, and blown to smithereens. Or suffocate. Or we miss our target, and the same shit applies?"

"We could also be both unlucky and lucky," Copilot pointed out. "Get picked up in either of the latter two cases by friendlies—only to become the target of ridicule and pity once our comrades realize the size of the target we missed by a ball hair."

"Yeah." Bomba sounded glum. "Almost is not good enough! I say we restart and pray!"

"Restart and pray," Sensors agreed. "We got emergency oxygen and three torpedoes left. We can do this!"

Concentrating on the pisswarm water running down his throat, Joe felt inside for what his experience and training had to add to the matter.

He closed his eyes for a long heartbeat, then looked at Copilot and ordered, "Yes, we can. Do a hard reboot, now."

His old friend nodded and flipped the switch.

From one moment to the next, every last light and artificial sound ceased, leaving *The Loooony Can* to hurtle through space as a true dark sphere. Four nervous, sweaty men prayed wordlessly for the system to come back up and fast.

CHAPTER FIFTY-EIGHT

SUZY\\ CONNECTIONS

Suzy sat down and connected back to Xin, telling her friend what she needed.

"Mr. Maverick." Xinyi glanced up at the tall mage, who was shielding the two of them from an oncoming rain of ordnance. "Please, Suzy needs your help!"

As he ripped his gaze from the swirling void behind them and refocused from the *Gateshot*'s fight back to the problem at hand, that creepy darkness overshadowing his aura pulled back somewhat.

"She needs to engage whoever's doing the magic on that station over there," Xin continued. "Can't you get her across? Like, for real? You got the two of us out here, right?"

"I did," he agreed, a first trickle of strain carving deep lines around his eyes as the shattered remains of a ricochet penetrator slammed into his shield and sent it rippling. He didn't quite manage to mask his mounting exhaustion with a superior tone, as he said, "But I can't, sorry. To bridge such a vast distance is not especially ... conducive to a human's corporeal integrity, I'm afraid."

"I see," Xin murmured, even though she wasn't quite sure how the scaling effect would work. But then, a few dozen meters was nothing compared to several ten thousand kilometers. And his words rang true. "So how could she get there?"

"Why would she need to?" The blue-eyed part of him was looking through Xin's eyes, directly at Suzy. "Magic can touch without actually being in the same room. It's imagination, after all—bringing into reality what you desire. It binds us to each other and to the universe, if we want it to. If we let it."

"If I have enough power to back it up, that is," Suzy remembered one of his earlier lessons.

Rupert smiled as he slowly curled his left hand into a fist. "Or, if you're willing to take it."

Suzy frowned, unsure of what exactly he meant. But then Xin looked back at the distant brightness in the heart of the station, at the magic lashing out to bind the gate. That was energy. Magic was a form of pure energy.

"Everything is connected," Suzy whispered in Xin's voice.

"Some connections take a special soul to make and use," Rupert cautioned. "But yes, in essence, that's today's lesson. You feel properly schooled?"

"Yeah," Suzy balled her fists, "and I feel very much like sharing. See one, do one, teach one, right?"

Something like actual pride twinkled in the strange being's core as he smiled at her.

Just how to do it?

A gently brooding silence stretched between them as Suzy studied the light in the station—the dark wisps of energy tangled around the gate's activation runes.

After a minute or two of Suzy remaining still, Diaz

edged closer and tentatively waved a hand in front of her face. The gesture snapped her out of her reverie.

"I'm fine," she snapped at him. "I almost got it! Stop distracting me!"

Diaz held up his hands in a placating gesture as he backed off. "Sorry."

The witch lay down in the circle and closed her eyes. She needed to be out of her own head and over there.

Everything was connected.

So maybe, she could move her mind without taking her body along. After all, she'd been doing it all day long with Xin.

Baby steps.

She zoomed out of her own existence, concentrated on Xin's experience until she couldn't feel the floor under her own body anymore, but felt the *Gateshot*'s hull under the soles of Xin's boots like they were her footwear. Engaging all her senses, she smelled the slightly dusty scent of Rupert's cologne, mixed with salty air, which also prickled on her tongue. She could hear nothing. Xin opened her eyes in confusion and saw the reason for that lack of sound. Space. Right, she was in space.

Suzy turned her friend's head to stare at the light in the distance, right there, at the heart of that station, and concentrated on it to the exclusion of everything else. *That's* where she needed to go. Even though she had no idea what or who was over there ... But then, she'd connected to Xin in that dark sphere, such a mind-staggering distance away. She hadn't known what to expect when she'd made that connection either.

What she needed was a focal point, something to cling to.

Upon closer inspection, the magicy light separated into

several distinct ... flavors for lack of a better word. Two of them burned brighter than the rest. And she was suddenly sure that it was there where she needed to go.

Imagination. Desire. Just like connecting her BCI to a distant computer, right? She just needed to connect and get there. Like a VR experience. Like when she was Tank in that memory Eve had shared with her. Like when Eve had been part of her.

There, the leftmost of the bright lights felt ... closer somehow. More Human, less ... alien and strange. That light was her way in. That person was her destination.

And something else ...

Faith.

Magic was faith. Of all things shaping the universe, faith was the most potent. And like with all the important crossroads in her life, she would have to make a leap of faith to cross this one.

"For Hecate," Suzy whispered with Xin's voice, with her voice.

Under Rupert's widening brown gaze, Suzy closed Xin's eyes and felt the connection click into place. And with that, she jumped from her friend's skin onward. Hoping to land in that of her enemy.

CHAPTER FIFTY-NINE

JOE\\ PREMIUM CHANCES

JOE STARED AT THE FLIGHT CORRIDOR HE'D DRAWN UP in his AR, the 'no connection' symbol a flashing red icon in his peripheral vision as *The Loooony Can* continued its powerless hurtle through the void. Another glance through the periscope, combined with his long years of experience with low-tech navigation, confirmed his assessment. He corrected the plan to account for another minute on their old, now invalid course. Their long acceleration had given them enough speed to fly straight out of the battle should they overshoot their target and pass by in the *Lightbearer*'s wake instead of stopping in time to engage her. If they were unlucky enough, they might survive only to be labeled deserters. That would be bitter irony, if nothing else ...

No, this had to work. It just had to.

Joe calculated the correct angles and vectors he would need, then prepared the necessary course corrections for quick BCI input.

He wanted to be ready to punch it as soon as the *Can* started back up.

If she started back up.

Copilot gulped down his nervousness with his own piss-warm water. Joe only heard it in the very slight rustle of his seatmate's clothes. He imagined Bomba had slipped his wife's picture from his suit's breast pocket and was fondling it, even though he couldn't see her pretty face in the darkness. Sensors was the only one openly showing his distress. The nervous beat he tapped on his armrest ground on Joe's nerves.

He was just about to reprimand the young soldier when a deep hum ran through their craft. It quickly rose in pitch as their main reactor started back up. Several hissing noises and the occasional subsonic rumbles or throbbing pulses, more felt than heard, chimed in. Dull creaks and a low mechanical exhale indicated the return of air circulation, just as a faint breeze descended from the ceiling to caress Joe's face.

"Void, YES!" Sensors jubilated and pumped his fist in the air, only to curse like a voidwalker as he hit a steel plate.

A low smooching sound followed by the rustling of clothing and the sharp snap of a button announced Bomba hastily putting away his wife's picture. Copilot's relieved laughter almost drowned it out.

At last, the consoles flickered back into life, and Joe input the flight plan.

"Sensors, complete systems check!" he ordered. "Copilot, double-check my calculations! Bomba, confirm your station's readiness!"

"Aye, Captain!"

From one moment to the next, the small space was abuzz with activity once more. The BCI connection icon turned green and vanished from Joe's peripheral vision. He synced the flight plan on the console with the one in his head. The checklist appearing to his left still showed more reds than greens, but when he gently tested the PUs, they handled much better.

"Still far from perfect," he admitted out loud. "But she'll fly."

Copilot nodded in response to the implied 'Well done', then frowned as he studied his console.

"We got all the important systems running, Cap," Sensors cheered. "Except for our heat storage, of course."

"Weapons A-Okay," Bomba grunted.

"Good." Joe looked over. "Copilot?"

"This flight corridor will still make us overshoot our target," his friend pointed out the obvious.

"Yes, it will. See, I had an idea about that." The pilot engaged the correction PUs and the *Can* jumped sideways to accommodate the hastily inputted new heading.

"With how busted up we are, I think we should overshoot her on purpose." He pointed at the quick diagram he'd drawn up while waiting and was now streaming to all their consoles, "The wiggy has a big hole close to its center over there. If we time it right, we can send off the sixer to go right in, then overshoot her and be in the clear once she blows."

"A long and slow delivery like that is risky," Sensors pointed out. "If she picks up the torpedo on her sensors, she can just destroy it with her point defenses, and we'll be on our way off into space. Doubling back will take tremendous forces at the rate we're going. Could the PUs manage it with how shot they are?"

"She's not waiting to be shot from that angle," Bomba defended their captain's plan, "Would just think it was debris. Ignore it."

"That's what I'm counting on." Joe felt a nasty grin oncoming. "Besides, with our busted storage, chances are she'll see us even better if we try to deliver it all the way.

A torpedo is so small, it should go undetected, especially if we send it in dark, on a timer."

"Doable." Bomba audibly scratched his short, coarse hair. "With good calculation."

"Our velocity will certainly suffice to get it all the way to the center ..." Copilot tapped his chin thoughtfully, then ran a set of calculations.

"I'd say we aim for this hole closer to the front, though," Sensors pointed it out. "See the scans? That's pissing and it's glowing blue. I bet the shell nicked one of the wiggy's reactor containments. It's probably why they can't keep up. And if we hit near one core ..."

He left it hanging there.

"Cascade effect." Copilot smiled. "Smash one, overload the system. It should blow the whole thing!"

"I like it." Captain nodded. "But this will make us overshoot to the front. If we're unlucky, it could get us into the crosshairs of both wiggy ships."

"Way I see it," Bomba audibly shrugged, "*Lightbearer* won't be a problem. And the other wiggy is busy—maybe busy enough to also get blown by us."

"Velorians are hyper-focused." Sensors clapped his hands happily. "It might work! We'd be close enough to turn and try, at least ..."

Joe shook his head. "With how shot our PUs are, I wouldn't bet on it."

"But think about how impressive that would be!" Copilot mused. "One dark sphere blowing the wiggy flagship *and* saving the cories? We'll all get ships named for us!"

"Besides," the youngster's voice turned uncommonly serious, "Oddball's people need us. The Republic offered them protection up to the gate, right? I don't see anyone else in the vicinity who can uphold that promise. We must do as much as we can for them!"

"You're right." The captain hadn't thought of it like that.

He'd been weighing his crew's life against the possibility of destroying the wiggies. That calculation was wrong. The *Gateshot* carried not only coreworld troops and civilians, but a regiment of their comrades. Even running as hard as they could, they were getting their asses kicked. That was a lot of people's lives to outweigh the sacrifice of four suicidal maniacs.

"Let's do it!"

Joe turned *The Loooony Can* onto her new trajectory, his heartbeat quickened by glorious expectation to see the boom of a lifetime. And maybe even survive long enough to blow the second ship as well.

CHAPTER SIXTY

GLEN\\ MASS AND ACCELERATION

Rivers' jubilant whoop tipped Glen off to the good news before Montoya announced, "Sir, the *Lightbearer* seems to have decreased the output of her PUs further!"

Despite her subordinate's breach of protocol, the Plutonian sounded pleased. About as pleased as Glen felt to finally get some good news, especially after blowing their cover by pushing their systems far beyond what Human tech should be capable of. Add Federov's struggles with the boarding parties and military logistics to the mix, and, well ... at least they were making progress on one front. Now, if they could just shake that boarding carrier, too ...

"On the downside," Montoya added, "she has also just exited our supports' effective fire reach and the fleets' main focus shifted to dismantling the remains of the Velorian battle line."

"Also, the *Lightbearer*'s still firing on us." Lt. Jiǎng wasn't sharing the optimism. "I estimate another twenty minutes before we reach dodging distance."

"That's about the time we'd enter the stations' crosshairs," Nick added.

Bloody hell.

"Col. Federov," Glen caught the military leader's attention. "How are your people holding up?"

"We're still mopping up those boarders, which slipped through during our fallback. Especially the cyborgs are a real pain. Resupply is 86 % done. We will proceed to contain and eliminate the interlopers."

Glen's mind churned. Their plan B didn't cover internal enemies. He'd been sure the soldiers could handle those.

Eve joined the conversation.

"I could send 50 combat drones right now." Her tone of voice made it sound like a question. "Another 50 upon activation. But they're all self-regulating."

"You mean they determine whom to shoot?" Federov clearly worked hard to even consider this.

"I can steer them if you prefer," the ship's master allowed.

Federov was just now attaching himself to one of his rookie squads, which had taken some casualties. The deference his people gave the young colonel was impressive. No argument, no crestfallen faces. In fact, the sergeant seemed enthusiastic to relinquish leadership to his superior. Neither seemed the added burden to hamper the Gateshot's military leader's ability to coordinate the battle.

If he just wouldn't be so hard-headed about—

"No!" Federov answered while reforming the squad with himself in the lead, "Ship's Master, I've asked you before to stay out of this. There are several good reasons for it, and none of them have to do with pride. Besides, many high-class cyborgs are equipped with IFF spoofers, so your drones wouldn't know whom to shoot anyhow."

While Eve didn't show any outward signs of feeling slighted or stung by the rebuke, her internal reaction was probably very different, as suggested by a slight sizzling sensation tickling Glen's sixth sense.

"Colonel, we just want to help," the captain added. "Is there anything we can do for you?"

For a moment, their conversation partner seemed to dwell on it. While he did, he hurried his new squad along and appeared to take part in at least two thought-comms, before answering, "Place those drones as sentries on the already compromised airlocks. They are to engage and eliminate everything that passes through until further notice—on my authority. From the moment of placement onwards, they are to neither move nor switch fire lanes. Coordinate their placement with my battle coordinators before switching controls over to them."

He'd barely finished his last words when he gave a series of hand signals to his troops and as one they charged forward, falling into the backs of a group of clones led by two cyborgs.

Bloody hell, GaSIn had marked those as friendlies!

Half a minute later, and without any casualties, Federov's squad had dispatched the clones, and the colonel held up a device he'd cut off one of the cyborgs.

"How did you know?" the captain asked.

"Their movement patterns didn't match any of ours. I'll leave this here for collection and analysis. And, Captain, please just let me do my job."

With that, he ended the conversation.

Had that bloody bastard just dismissed the ship's captain? Again?

—[SECURE CHANNEL: PRO. MAJ. GARIN, ADM. MACALLISTER]—

PRO. MAJ. GARIN: Keep it for the debrief. I'll make sure it won't come to blows, then.

ADM. MACALLISTER: I'm the captain of this ship! Wasn't he the one who always preached discipline, protocol, and such?

PRO. MAJ. GARIN: He's adjusting on the fly. It's how he's used to doing things. And he hasn't involved you in the process, so you can concentrate on the flying.

[CONVERSATION ENDED.]

—

"Captain!" Montoya called before Glen could turn to glower at the bridge guard. "The unclassified released a second wave of boarding craft. ETA seven minutes!"

"How many?" Nick asked before Glen could.

Montoya swallowed. Her voice wavering slightly as she answered, "Minimum 362. ... They're still deploying."

Bloody hell!

"Please tell me you have another ace up your sleeve," Nick leaned in to whisper.

"I'm afraid not," the old man said, scratching his chin.

Or did he?

In a sudden flash of inspiration, Glen fished the gold coin out of his pocket and stared at the two interlocked thistles engraved on it.

Well, it was worth a try.

CHAPTER SIXTY-ONE

EVRON\SUZY\\ INTERNAL STRUGGLE

Evron staggered as something inside him shifted. For a heartbeat or two, he wasn't sure if ...

Had Berestul done something? Was he trying to harm him after all? No, surely he wouldn't divert any energy at such a critical moment. They'd just stopped another attempt at opening the gate. To his left, Erestral adjusted his stance. Had he done something? He'd love the opportunity to get out from under Evron's thumb, wouldn't he?

Why the sudden itchiness inside? Sure, standing in a circle with all those mages, basically being bled for his talent while outside, a battle was raging, left him with a strange feeling of vague paranoia, but ...

"Evron!" Berestul chided as he pushed him back into the small circle. "Stay vigilant! Don't get distracted now. They might try again."

"Right." The other Velorian shook his head. "Sorry."

As Evron studied the magical setup, faint glowing lines flickered before his eyes, running from every mage into his circle, pooling there only to be leeched off into the larger ritual. It all collected in Berestul's slightly larger circle.

There, it combined into a translucent pillar pulsing upward and straight through the metal ceiling toward ... somewhere else.

The gate, presumably.

What the ...?

Evron blinked, and the lights were gone again. What just happened? He gazed around, but no one but him seemed to notice anything amiss. They all had their eyes closed in concentration. Berestul was the only one who opened them now and again to look around, as if he felt some disturbance and tried to pinpoint its source. His garishly overcomplicated eyes snapped to his right once more, and he growled, "Concentrate, Evron!"

What was the guy's problem? Magic wasn't even Evron's forte. Nothing was. He was just ... What was *his* problem? Where did these strange thoughts come from? Evron closed his eyes and shook out his folds, refocusing on his task.

Evron. So that was his name. The world looked different through his eyes. Not as batshit crazy strange as Xin's perspective, but still ...

'*Hey!*' her friend protested. She was still there, acting as the fragile link between Suzy's body and this alien.

'*Sorry,*' Suzy murmured. It was more of an absent-minded reaction than anything else. Most of her mind was focused on what she might do next. She had to do something! That was what she was here for, after all.

While she seemed to ride shotgun in his body, Evron's mind was closed to her. Much like that one time Eve had shared her body, there was a sort of flexible wall between them. This one felt even more unbreakable. Maybe it was the strangeness of his mind ... but then, Eve was an alien too, so ... hm ...

A sudden screeching noise erupted from the right, and as Evron's eyes snapped back open, Suzy found herself staring into gleaming black pearls. The small creature that had contentedly perched on the alien's shoulder until now hissed at her. Not at him. *Her.* She was sure of it.

Runes lit up all over its dark fur, and another intelligence pressed against Suzy and Evron's minds.

Fuck, that thing saw her! It felt her! And it knew she was in its master's body, somehow.

With another screech, a confused mix of rage and concern, the thing scratched the flabbergasted Velorian squarely across the face. Evron cried out in pain and staggered out of his circle. He tried pushing the little beast off his shoulder, but it had dug the claws of its three remaining paws deep into his clothes. So deep, in fact, that it drew blood. The rest of the Velorian mages blinked open confused eyes.

'This might be our chance!' Suzy gasped. *'Xin, try opening the gate!'*

Back on the *Gateshot*, her friend lifted an unsure hand toward the alien artifact. With a fortifying breath and biting her bottom lip, she channeled energy into the activation runes as soon as their bindings wavered.

"Evron! Get it under control!" the leader mage growled. Even though he surely spoke Velorian, the Human understood the words just fine.

"Ziffin, what is it? What's wrong?" Suzy's ride tried in vain to calm his pet.

A comforting calmness left his part of their shared space and entered the creature's. He had a connection to this thing! Must be why it felt her. Maybe why he'd been easiest to connect to. This was so weird. The little furball would hear none of it and in return sent a warning panic.

From Xin's side, Suzy could see the energy distribution in the gate shift. It pulled in more and more energy, and the space at its center started to waver again like heat over a stove.

"Now!" the leader alien demanded. "We're losing the gate!"

"Ziffin—" Evron started.

A blast of kinetic energy ripped the little creature off his shoulder and flung it across the room. It smashed into the wall and fell to the floor in a limp heap. Its mind instantly reduced to a rapidly weakening kernel of hurt and confusion.

"Erestral!" Evron snapped angrily. Not minding his ripped shirt and bleeding shoulder, he whirled around to face the Velorian on the other side of the leader mage.

That one had his hand outstretched and a self-satisfied smirk on his lips. Suzy instantly disliked him. Not just because of the blinding hatred radiating from Evron's mind into hers. Great, maybe they'd keep each other occupied with fighting it out long enough for the *Gateshot* to leave!

But just as Evron jumped to tackle the other alien, the leader mage waved a hand and arrested all movement within his limbs.

"We have no time for this!" The leader's ears did a funny thing and a mixture of fury and fear bubbled up in Evron, as the guy continued, "Whatever your Commander Ruffa might think of me, I'm perfectly aware of the stakes. These stations are practically defenseless and even if the Plutonians don't realize this and smoke us out, your progenitor will have my head, should we let the guardian escape.

So either I keep the gate closed and get rid of those Plutonians, or we're all dead! Well, I'm not going to pass on because some dumb idiot, who has more power than he knows how to use, disturbs my ritual! I'll hold this line until the guardian's ship is destroyed! And you will help me! You will give me all the power I need."

'Practically defenseless', heh?, Suzy thought. *Interesting ...*

Another part of the ritual circle flamed into life. As Evron stared at the strange symbols on the ground uncomprehendingly, Suzy could see ghostly tentacles slithering out from amongst the runes to reach for him. The leader asshole was planning to suck his magic. So Morgan hadn't been the only one who knew how to do that trick.

Weakness filled Evron's limbs with lead, but that only made his fury burn hotter. He'd done everything they'd asked of him, damn it! He'd made Erestral his bitch. This was not how he was going down. But what could he do?

Suzy noticed the weakening in the wall holding them apart, could almost hear his thoughts now. This was so weird. And if she let that damn mage suck this guy dry, she might not have another connection point. He might actually win!

'*Suzy, something's happening!*' Xin's voice sounded strained. '*I almost had it, but now the gate's closing again! It feels ... more final than before. And we'll soon be in range of the stations!*'

'*I know,*' the witch retorted. '*I'm working on it!*'

She'd been in this guy's position, damn it. She knew exactly what to say. She just needed him to hear her.

In a desperate attempt to get Evron's attention, Suzy conjured up Hecate's blade and drove it into the wall between their minds. It made a nice little hole, and she leaned in to whisper, "Evron, let me help you. You might not know how to fight with magic, but I do! I can help you survive!"

"What? Who are you?" his voice echoed back. "And where?"

"A friend." Suzy put all the smoothness of Rupert's voice into it. It wasn't a complete lie, after all. She didn't mean the alien any harm on a personal level. She would be happy to destroy all his pals and this damn ritual circle, but that was another discussion altogether ... "I'm here, with you. Very close. I can help you."

Hesitation lingered between them for a shuddering heartbeat.

"Besides," the witch pointed out, "he's about to eat your soul. What choice do you have?"

Another shuddering heartbeat. This one felt faster and like an eternity at the same time.

"No," he murmured. "I'm not going to die a pushover! I've been one my whole life!"

"If you do nothing, you *will* die a pushover," she retorted.

How stupid was this guy?

"At least I won't have betrayed my people."

"No, your people will have betrayed you!"

He cowered back from that attack, as if she'd actually struck him.

Something Morgan had said came back to Suzy, and she whispered, "If he eats your soul, you can't be reborn. You have no chance to do better next time. You know that, right? You also know it's wrong to stand against a guardian, don't you? I can feel your hesitation! I can feel your pain! You did bad things. That's why you think it's all right to die. You think you deserve it. I'm not judging. I don't care about that.

What I care about are my friends and my crew. Help me send the guardian on her way! Help me open the gate!"

"You're her," the Velorian realized. "You're the Human mage."

"Yeah, that's me. Also, I bested a freaky-powerful Haslar warrior mage. He couldn't bring me down, so your little club of dabblers won't either." Suzy presented her best poker voice to cover up the fib. "Only question is: Will you be around to witness it?"

"Fuck." A single tear ran down Evron's cheeks, and his ears flattened against his skull. "Fine. What do I do?"

Suzy smiled. "Step aside and let me take your body for a spin."

And as his mind retreated deep into himself, she pushed Hecate's key into the hole and turned it. The witch closed her eyes. When she opened them again, she was an alien, sitting half-prone on the floor.

"Not so fast!" She gripped the energy leaving Evron's body ... *her* body, and yanked it, like it were a chain.

Berestul sputtered. His eyes widened, and he staggered a step. Not enough to break the circle, though. *No matter ...*

Sweat covering her brow, Suzy reached out a hand. She had to push hard, like a dozen gravities were working against her. Still, her magic pulsed through her borrowed body's arm and enveloped it in purple lightning. She let loose on the Velorian holding Evron down. Like that little beast Ziffin before, Erestral was flung back and hit the cold metal wall with a bone-crunching *thump*.

That got a reaction.

"You ... disrespectful imbecile!" Berestul raged.

His grip on the ritual wavered. He couldn't hold Evron down, and the gate shut at the same time. His minions started casting nervous glances, anxiety beginning to bloom.

"I think you're confusing me with someone else." Unshackled, Suzy rose, opening her ears to full display. "My name is Suzy Magecraft, and I'm here to kick your creepy, voidforsaken behind all the way back to your home planet. Asshole."

CHAPTER SIXTY-TWO

JATHEKI\GLEN\\ A LITTLE HELP

"I ALMOST CAN'T FEEL HER ANYMORE," LITTLE Cassandra murmured. "It's like she ... distanced herself from me."

Jatheki patted her shoulder reassuringly, saying, "She's probably just busy fighting someone. Give her some time."

The seer could still see the slim connection remaining, like a lifeline wound about this girl's soul, stretching all the way to the Velorian station. Nothing to worry about. Yet.

Behind them, the battle still raged soundlessly. The strategist observed the tides turning this way and that, to finally settle into a steep dive for their side.

"You're so angry." The girl straightened and followed his gaze. "The darkness, the wrongness ... You never told me what it is."

Distraction. She was asking for a distraction. Or maybe she actually wanted to know.

"Clones." Jatheki spat out the word. "It's a vast amount of human clones. Tortured souls in desperate need of salvation."

"Salvation?" Xinyi echoed. "Like ... death?"

"Death is not the end. It's merely a place to rest and mend." Jatheki squared his shoulders. "It's where they need to go to get better."

"Can something this horrible even be mended?" Xinyi seemed highly doubtful.

"Given enough time. Most of them can." The trimorph sighed.

"Maverick, this is MacAllister," the captain's voice echoed around them through the eerie silence as he held his coin and spoke. "The boarding parties are about to swarm us. The *Lightbearer* is shooting at us with a vengeance. It's time to pay for your passage. Do something!"

Xinyi looked around like she might pinpoint the source of the sound. The strategist wanted nothing more than to take up her weapons and rain fire on the abominations chasing them. As did the trickster. Before the seer could object, he lifted the staff. Then stopped.

"You want to do it." Little Cassandra turned her golden eyes onto him. "It's all over you. Vengeance. Desperation. Red burning flames and cold blue steel."

Of course. This close to him, her powers would be heightened. She would be better at interpreting whatever it was that she saw.

He lashed out. As his power funneled through the staff, a golden shield spread from it, sloshing toward the back of the ship like a translucent wave. It spread into all directions and spaceward, racing toward the oncoming munitions the *Gateshot*'s countermeasures had been unable to stop. On impact, they dissolved into nothingness. Dust in a real wind flapping the mage's overcoat and hair around his slim frame dramatically.

Pain flared up inside, and the hand holding the staff cramped. For a heartbeat, the flesh of his fingers turned black as ink, and the nausea of overspending mixed with the sickness of being constantly bombarded by half-crazed souls looking to pass into the afterlife, as well as those chained to their pitiful, unnatural existences, looming in the distance. He forced it down. He was three aspects in one, after all! A little magic use shouldn't even ruffle his hair!

Dite meowed with subdued concern and warning.

Xinyi stared up at him unblinking.

"What?" The trickster turned his head slowly to jest, as if nothing had happened. "Can you taste my distaste?"

Ignoring both the quip and his weakness, the girl demanded to know, "Why don't you? You're here to help, aren't you? Destroying that ship won't just help us but them! Why don't you do ... something?!"

There she was. With all the seraphic surrender it had been displaying recently, he'd almost thought its latest experiences might have shifted this blazingly radiant soul into some detached nirvana. But when the girl balled her tiny hands into fists and narrowed her eyes in open challenge, he could see it again, clear as day. There was the soul he'd watched over for a dozen lifetimes now. Its core remained untouched: to stand up for those less fortunate or powerful, even at its own greatest detriment.

Such a beautiful aggregation of some of humanity's most valiant traits.

"Killing is a free will's prerogative," he said with an air of tortured resignation, shifting the shield to dispose of another handful of metallic chunks eager to rip their ride's hull open. It made his knees wobble ever so slightly.

She studied him further, probably hoping he'd offer a more precise answer without the existential theatrics.

"No," she finally declared. "You're not unchanging! You're not unable to intervene! Your entire purpose is to intervene. You're here to smooth our ride. That blue color trapped inside." She pointed her index finger at his heart, merely a centimeter from actually touching his chest. "It's the one that kicks off change, isn't it? It's the whole point of ... you."

He shook his head. The gesture made all the tiny lines around her eyes tighten, as if she were reevaluating.

"You were touched by death," she said after another brief pause. "When can you do it if not now?"

How ... what ...

Jatheki lifted his prison's hands to look at them, then stared at his reflection in the stone. On the gem's multiple facets, his parts came undone and stared back at him in pieces. One of them, Hades's star fingerprint, pressed against his sternum.

What a thought ... What a marvelous thought!

'*What a stupid thought,*' Dite commented in his head, '*I agree with her in that we should do something, but we're bound to certain rules for a reason.*'

'*Indeed,*' all his parts concurred and power pooled in his hands—humanity's power. '*But what if someone else already made the choice to kill? What if we just ... change the target?*'

The seer pulled in the power to see what lay hidden in the present. His sight didn't reach beyond what he needed to know right now. It illuminated little more than the path they would need to tread.

"Dite, my ever-helpful beacon of chaos," he held out his left, "I would be very pleased to receive your help in this."

"That's what I'm here for," her melodic voice answered out loud. As a woman's gentle hand settled into his palm and another onto his shoulder, his nostrils filled with the intoxicating smell of freshly cut roses and salty air. Power flooded into him, reinforcing his puny reserves with determined fire and vicious protectiveness.

"Thank you," Jatheki said, both to her and the crew, giving him exactly what he needed at precisely the right time.

With an uproar of kinetic force, the mage grabbed the torpedo launched by *The Loooony Can* and yanked it through the hole in the *Lightbearer*. Turning its flight path around, he raced against the thing's programming to reel it in. It entered through one of the holes in the boarding carrier the *Gateshot*'s crew had managed to create while its energy shield had been overloaded.

Right on time.

"Maverick, this is MacAllister." The captain made his voice vibrate with unyielding authority. "More boarding parties are about to swarm us. The *Lightbearer* is shooting at us with a vengeance. It's time to pay for your passage. Do something!"

For a long moment, nothing happened. Then, Maverick's smooth voice hung in the air, saying, "Aye, aye, Captain."

A few seconds later, the tactical display hovering over Glen's console glitched. It reestablished itself, with a large chunk of the smallest dots about to impact their aft section missing. Nick blinked in confusion and punched the console.

Montoya's eyes widened. "Captain, several salvos of munitions just ... vanished off our scanners! Everything between the *Gateshot* and about 14 kilometers in each direction!"

"So he's good for something, after all." Glen allowed himself a small smile as he glanced over at Eve.

She nodded, a very brief echo of his relief playing on her lips.

On his console, he could see Lt. Jiăng's team seizing the opportunity. At least momentarily, Maverick's intervention had freed up a lot of resources. The tactical team aimed every beam bank and gauss cannon suddenly bereft of a target to fire on the nearest boarding vessels. It made a visible difference.

"We just devastated the next boarding wave," Montoya reported a few moments later. "About 72 % of its vessels are gone."

Then the window slammed shut once more, and their defenses were quickly engaged by the next wave of shells. Still, this would make the wave manageable.

"Does that help?" Glen asked Federov.

"*Da.*" The colonel's voice and posture aptly relayed the man's relief. "We should be rid of the remainder of the first wave and in position to deal with what's left of the second by the time those finally break through the automatic defenses."

The admiral's tactical display showed the remaining boarding parties slowly but surely being squashed.

"Very good." He nodded.

"Should we ask Maverick to ... do it again?" Nick ventured.

Just then, the unclassified vessel's center detonated in a startling plume of flame. The tremendous energy of a tiny star unleashed a sledgehammer wave that tore through the vessel's atmosphere, reaching into every last nook and cranny, blasting it apart. The main screen hardly dimmed the brightness of this brilliant flash of artificial sunlight.

"EVADE!" both COs called as they saw several large pieces of debris superaccelerate toward their ship. They knew they couldn't possibly outrun. Everything was already maxed out. Those ship parts would rip their pretty lady's already wounded backside wide open.

"EVE!" Glen yelled. He wasn't even sure what he hoped she could do ...

CHAPTER SIXTY-THREE

JATHEKI\\ DESTRUCTIVE SALVATION

JATHEKI REVELED IN THE DESTRUCTION.

One moment, there was a ship full of suffering souls. Next, a cloud of debris spilled those same souls into the freedom of death. As they raced toward them, Xinyi cried out in startled horror. She ducked behind the trimorph, who threw his arms wide in welcome. Thousands of souls plunged into Dite and him, the nearest gateways to humanity's wellspring.

It was too much for his form to bear. It tore him apart like a desert storm chewing up a snowman.

But Hecate's tattooed bindings wouldn't allow him to dissolve. With the conviction of acid flames, they flared up all over his body and forced his parts back together. Back into their form. Mind-searing pain followed in the spell's wake. Time itself seemed to stumble. With a cry, he staggered to his knees and crumpled. Dite caught him, a luminous form of pure, heartwarming light for the few seconds it took the brunt of the souls to change planes. She shivered, too, a low moan escaping her full lips.

As Jatheki's mind reasserted itself, he found himself

sprawled atop exquisitely strong legs, comforting arms wrapped around him. And her face ... the trickster missed a breath as he beheld the face that had entrapped him so long ago.

"Oh, no!" Little Cassandra panted.

At its aft section, the *Gateshot*'s debris shield flared up as a hail of tiny superaccelerated particles were disintegrated or repelled by the faltering force field. As a small, merciful bonus, this shrapnel had first shredded the last of the boarding shuttles.

It wouldn't be enough.

Jatheki reached for his staff. It flew toward his hand ... and slammed against an unresponsive limb. By the time his fingers closed, the staff had already dropped to the ground. He felt parched, arthritic, beaten into minced meat.

How woefully pathetic ...

A red-golden shield sprang into life just before the first chunks could hit the glimmering black surface. Pretty little runes shimmered all over the void like stars for the painful eternity it took to weather the worst. Then it collapsed.

And with it, the girl who'd snatched up the staff and was simultaneously holding Dite's hand like a drowning kitten.

Xinyi's golden orbs rolled back into her head.

"Oh, no, you don't!" The trimorph collected what little he could and sent a small electric shock her way. "Don't you dare fall unconscious and lose Suzy her way home!"

Little Cassandra coughed convulsively. Her eyes flew back open.

The trickster sank back with a sigh. His cheek connected with his companion's supple, graceful shoulder. A treacherous part of him inhaled deeply to fuel his fading memory. But this weakness was the easiest to overcome.

"Lose the face, Dite," he growled. "It's not yours!"

The heart-stoppingly beautiful woman lounging behind him turned back into a cat, leaving him to slam onto the ground unceremoniously as she hopped away with a snicker.

"Did she just ..." Xinyi's eyes widened as she studied the purple feline. Her voice sounded as slurred and exhausted as the trimorph felt.

"No, she didn't." He couldn't even manage a mild degree of sharpness. "You shouldn't overdo it with the magic, Dear. It drains the body and mushes up your brain."

"Heh." The girl rubbed her eyes as if trying to escape a dream. "Because ... I could have sworn she blazed with so much magic; I'm still seeing white spots all over. I felt it too!"

"Careful, Little Cassandra." Jatheki fought his way back to his feet. "If you buy into it, dear Dite here will have you believe she's the most powerful force in the system. Quite the little mistress of deception, that one."

Dite purred self-indulgently.

"Anything on Suzy?" he inquired.

Xinyi frowned and seemed to listen within intently. Finally, she shook her head.

"I'm sure she'll come through." The trimorph nodded for emphasis. Or maybe to heighten that sublime sense of the universe spinning around him. Such a captivatingly Human feeling!

He held out a hand and helped the girl to stand as well. Everything hurt. Nothing buckled, thankfully. It was quite vexing to feel this ... vulnerable and beaten. Very enlivening as well. The whole affair was also the best thing to happen to him this millennium. With the wrongness righted, the pressure lifted off his senses, and the knowledge that they'd freed so many souls in desperate need, a certain ... happiness settled into Jatheki's leaden limbs.

Still, he'd like nothing better than to snore away a century or two.

'*Don't even think about it,*' Dite purred for his ears alone, '*We have to secure this end of the connection, or it may all be for nothing!*'

'*Indeed.*' He sighed and straightened his clothes as best he could.

CHAPTER SIXTY-FOUR

RUFFA\\ PRIMARY OBJECTIVE

"What just happened?" Ruffa demanded to know. "Did the guardian's ship destroy our vessel?"

Down on the bridge, folds flattened against heads pressing in closer to control screens. Fingers hastily tapping away became the only sound alongside the warning chimes.

"Commander," the *Lightbearer*'s captain cautioned with mounting strain in his voice, "the leak in the energy core cooling system has been widened by the strain of pursuit. We need to slow down and evade! If we pull through the debris field—"

"No." Ruffa stared at the tactical display. "We need to destroy the guardian's ship. The rest is secondary. We're already too far behind. If we skirt the debris field, we'll never catch up to them."

Tuvil's folds twitched as he said, "Sir, we've lost more than half of our fleet by now. The eight remaining crubas are the sole reason why the Plutonians aren't simply overrunning us. They have captured several of our vessels and are sending ships to reinforce the guardian. Wouldn't it be better to rally our troops and fall back into the stations' protection? The guardian will go for the gate. She will come to us. Do we really need to chase her? Also, if we keep giving her ship reasons for evasive maneuvers, our fleet could surpass her and cut off her approach. Right now those ships are being wasted in an unsupported holding action."

"We almost have her, Tuvil." Ruffa gripped the tiny ship on the display and balled his fist around it. "Our best option for destroying that ship just exploded. It's on us now to safeguard Veloria. Even if the Plutonians win the gate, they won't be interested in going through. They wouldn't know how. We have to assume the guardian does. We need to stop her or all this was for nothing!"

With a sigh, he shook out his folds.

"But you're right," he said. "Tell our forces to fall back to the stations and protect them. Any of our ships that won't respond are to be assumed compromised and destroyed. If the remote destruction sequences don't work, have them tagged as hostiles and externally removed. The battle-ready station is to target the guardian's ship—but only fire when they are absolutely certain they won't miss. The same goes for the ships. I want to see the guardian vanish in a concentrated hail of fire!"

Tuvil's folds squeezed shut for a brief moment. Then he bowed to affirm he'd understood and went about issuing the orders.

"Captain, avoid the debris as little as possible," Ruffa said. "And don't you dare lose sight of our primary objective!"

CHAPTER SIXTY-FIVE

EVRON\SUZY\\ TOO NICE

As the Human mage took over his body, Evron felt shoved into the backseat of his own existence. At least he wasn't being leeched for life anymore ... Balance knew what that crazy bitch would do to him after she was done with the others, though. And all because he'd been a coward again. A pushover.

When Erestral hit the wall, Evron couldn't help but feel a petty flicker of satisfaction at the sound and sight of it. He couldn't wait for her to teach Berestul a lesson. She sure felt capable of it. The power suddenly coursing through his body felt enormous. So at least he hadn't been pushed aside by an impostor. This Human might actually have faced a Haslar and survived ...

He'd love to hear that story. One of the almighty Haslars brought down by a mere Human? Must have been one impressive fight. Or a very weak Haslar.

Now that she looked through his eyes, he could see the energy of the ritual snapping at her heels, trying to bind her. The casual ease with which she bent down and slashed out one of the runes kindled envy in his heart. Magic had never seemed like such a gift to him. Until he'd needed it. Now that it bound him, now that it had brought him into this situation, he wished he had her knowledge and sight.

Even with all his authority, Thallamon had never managed to imprison Evron's mind or take over his body. This last refuge had always been his alone. Until today.

Maybe death, even an eternal one, wasn't such a bad alternative, after all.

Freggog, this was treason.

Every blow he let her exchange with the primary mage was a blow against Veloria. Without Berestul holding it closed, the gate would open. The guardian would fly through. The Great Neutrality would come down on them. For what exactly, Evron didn't know. He didn't even know what happened to the women, pregnant or otherwise, who were shipped to Evrolith for their Human genes. Whatever the scientists did to them was likely as pleasant as the rape of his core genes. Still, it was supposed to keep his race alive. It was supposed to be the only path to survival Veloria had left.

So what was Evron doing? Why was he gloating at the mages' destruction when they were the only ones keeping his whole species alive right now?

He had to act. He had to do something to stop the Human.

Anything.

Over at the wall, Erestral moved weakly. She didn't seem to notice it yet. A faint hope bloomed in Evron. Maybe with his body, the Human had also claimed his weakness. Entirely focused on Berestul, she hardly gave the other mages trying their best to keep the gate closed without him any heed. This might work! He just had to take back control. Just a little. Just enough.

Sweat coated Evron's brow as Suzy rallied her magic to finally push this Berestul out of his personal circle for good. Holding off his counterattacks with her shield while keeping her hold on the alien body and the connection to Xin intact was more draining than she'd anticipated. For all hise silly demeanor, this shithead opponent was a fucking strong mage. She was happy the other mages mainly kept out of it. Though from what she could see, he was still pumping them for energy. The ritual was getting messy, though; the energy lines Xin's sight faintly showed her were breaking and getting rerouted all over the place.

'*You do realize that, even if you get through the gate, there will be more of us there, right?*' Evron's voice asked in her head. '*More ships with more mages?! My father didn't think it prudent to send even more here, because of the politics involved, but ...*'

He let it hang there.

'*Your father?*' Suzy thought back, something tingling in the back of her neck like one of Glen's hunches. She shouldn't engage in this conversation now.

'*Yeah. I'm Thallamon's son. The primary Velorian ambassador. You might have heard of him?*' He seemed to be trying for superior nonchalance.

Suzy sidestepped a lash of dark-blue energy. Her teeth tried to bite down on her piercing, but of course, they weren't there. Also, Evron's teeth felt funny.

For a split second, he seemed ready to protest. Instead, he tried hard to sweet-talk her—though it clearly wasn't one of his strengths.

'*Listen, if you just back off, I'm sure we can talk about it,*' Evron said. '*You could always claim me as a hostage, right?*'

A hostage?

Suzy hadn't even thought about it like that. She threw a kinetic blast, and while her opponent was covering himself, caught a glimpse of her borrowed body's reflection in a small reflective pane on the wall. It only showed a small part of his face, but knowing where to place him, she still recognized it.

Damn ... even though she'd only ever glimpsed him once across a crowded room at one of those big balls Governor Marshall regularly threw, the sudden knowledge of who he was, that their paths had crossed at least once before, imbued the whole situation with a strange aftertaste.

He seemed to catch her moment of uncertainty. With a feeling like he was swallowing, he murmured, '*You recognize me.*'

It wasn't a question. Not really a statement either. It held wrapped in it a pondering of ...

'*You said Magecraft,*' he realized. '*You're the other daughter. ... One of the twins.*'

Something rippled through her, from his side. Something like a struggle to put everything into perspective.

'*Shit,*' they both thought.

Berestul again gathered energy for his next strike. Suzy made ready to counter. Suddenly, her sight grew unfocused. Her hands felt numb. Her head started to spin.

What the—, she thought.

'*I'm so sorry, Suzy,*' Evron's inner voice sounded honestly sad. '*But I can't let you succeed. I mustn't.*'

Pain bloomed in her back, directly followed by a ripping sensation at her front. A bloody blade exited Evron's chest. On another reflective surface, Erestral's nasty grin loomed behind her shoulder.

Evron grabbed for her. Not in a physical sense, but for

her mind. He held onto it like a drowning man to a life vest. Not to save himself, she realized, but to drag her down with him. To keep her mind in his dying body. Berestul laughed and flung his magic.

Sergey's words echoed in her head. "You're too nice. Too naive. The next time some random rapey asshole tells you to put on your own cuffs, or else ..., you switch your gun to full automatic or your magic to whatever is the limit there, and let them have it."

'*I'm sorry, too,*' she whispered.

She placed the memory of how it had felt to draw magic from the void front and center in her mind.

Then she flung her soul wide, imagining it as a black hole, an empty battery. As Berestul's magic connected with Evron's dying body, she grasped it, took it in, sucked it right out of his hands.

And she didn't stop.

Berestul's eyes widened as he stared at his hands. He staggered forward. The five mages connected to him dropped first. Lights which marked their existence flowed through him into her. Then the light burning inside their leader vacated his body and dispersed into Suzy. His eyes empty, he dropped limply to the floor.

"Father!"

Erestral tried to wrench the blade from her body, but she merely motioned with one hand to throw him off once more. Infused by the sudden energy, she pushed a head-sized piece of flesh and bone right out of Erestral's midsection. It flew all the way to the wall and slammed against it with a sickening slapping sound.

The witch swallowed hard as the rest of him crumpled to the ground.

Yeah, he wouldn't get up again ...

FUCK!

Evron was still there, full of regret, confusion, and panic. As the knowledge of his imminent death sank in, that all faded away, and one image filled his mind and soul.

A man. A Human. The gentle touch of his lips. The precious ring of his laughter. His delicious scent.

Jake.

Marsdust, she couldn't ...

You're too nice. Sergey's voice whispered again.

No, I'm not, Suzy thought as she stared at the massacre she'd just committed.

Jake's face flickered in and out of her sight.

I'm so sorry.

Was that Evron's thought or hers?

You're too nice. Sergey's voice whispered again.

So what? the witch answered.

As Evron's body gave out and fell to his knees, Suzy forced it to take one last, shuddering breath.

Then she threw off the Velorian grasping at her soul and slammed him deftly into the connection he still had with his pet.

Her cheek hit the floor. Her ear hurt in strange ways and places.

'*Suzy!*' Xin's voice yelled. '*COME BACK, DAMN YOU!*'

Suzy watched as the little furball rose, blinking around rather stupefied. An uncanny intelligence stared back at her in confused horror.

With a smile, the witch closed Evron's eyes.

As the last drop of life dribbled out of the Velorian, she grabbed Xin's offered hand and slipped back through her friend into her own body.

CHAPTER SIXTY-SIX

GLEN\\ LAST MINUTE RESCUE

Glen was sure his ship was about to get her tailfeathers clipped. Badly.

Except it didn't. Red lights blinked on his tactical display. The debris came for them on the vid feed. Then a wave of static disrupted both, and as soon as the picture cleared, all that remained was ... a gently floating cloud of glittering metallic dust.

"Bloody hell, that was close," he murmured. "Guess I'll have to thank Maverick for having our back."

His XO merely nodded.

"Tactical," Nick looked to Jiǎng with confusion written all over his youthful face, "did we kill the boarding carrier?"

"No. None of our shells came even close to the detonation point or could have produced this type of destructive pattern," the officer replied with the clipped tone of someone still looking for answers, then glanced onward. "Scanners?!"

"That ... ahem ..." Montoya seemed flustered by her readout. "With all the interference ..."

"May I?" Rivers offered. "I think I can clear it up somewhat."

The lieutenant merely nodded.

"No need," Glen interjected grimly. "I've seen that kind of damage before. That was most definitely a thermonuclear explosion."

The XO's eyes narrowed. "Who could have sent a fusion bomb so precisely? There's no one else around but us and the *Lightbearer*. You think they accidentally blew a reactor? It would—"

"Captain, you'll want to hear this," Singh cut in.

At the admiral's affirming nod, a slightly panicked voice boomed from the loudspeakers, "Yun to Bridge, there's a Plutonian dark sphere hurtling away from the *Lightbearer*'s port-side bow section. Something's wrong with her! She's in desperate need of assistance."

"Scanners, confirm?!" Glen zoomed in on the mentioned section.

Shit, they were coming up on the gate, fast. It was time to either run for it, hoping the stations wouldn't fire or angle away and back to the Plutonian main force to gain assistance from them. Either way, swinging toward the Velorian flagship to start a rescue operation was definitely not in the cards!

Montoya studied her console for a few seconds, her fingers tracing the screen. Finally, she nodded and pulled up a surprisingly sharp vid feed, saying, "I found them! Squarely behind us, 4 k out. They're leaking heat. Given their highly erratic flight pattern, they've clearly been hit by something."

"We could collect them," Rivers stated cautiously. "Pull them in with our grav engines? Opposite to how we pushed the Neptunian freighter away ...?"

Nick leaned in to whisper, "They probably did just save our bacon."

Ah, bloody hell ...

"Engineering, reel in the dark sphere!" Glen agreed. "Just don't pull the *Lightbearer* up our exhaust pipe while you're at it!"

After he'd glanced at the proposed maneuver, the captain continued, "Comms, call the dark sphere and tell them to make a run for Hangar 5 as soon as we've pulled them close. Weapons, give them as much cover fire as you can spare. Oh, and Col. Federov, your next appointments have been cancelled. Their shuttles broke down due to high-velocity debris."

Lustig, Singh and Jiǎng went about their tasks. Federov checked with someone, then acknowledged.

"Good. Dr. Lustig, did we take any serious damage from all that?"

"No, Sir," their head engineer reported with a happy smile on his face. "Minimal external damage to our pretty lady. The boarders did more damage than the munitions. Many of the aft airlocks are out of commission and the aft shield generators are still under critical strain."

"Seems like the Plutonians got the upper hand." Nick pointed at the overall tactical display. "Several of the remaining Velorian ships are marked 'friendlies' now and the rest of their line is faltering."

"Tell that to the *Lightbearer*." Glen frowned at the large ship still nipping their proverbial tailfeathers.

"I have to correct you there, Commander, but the Velorians aren't faltering, yet," Jiǎng cautioned. "They're falling back toward those stations. Probably to cut us off. I can't yet determine if they'll succeed. And while the *Lightbearer* is falling behind, her fire still forces us to evade, which is messing with our optimal approach path and giving the other Velorian ships time to get into position."

"But they've lost!" Nick said, his voice incredulous. "This is tactical suicide!"

"Velorian single-mindedness," Eve corrected. "They *really* want to destroy this ship."

"Captain," Ludmilla called, "we're getting uncomfortably close to those stations. Shall I proceed or break off?"

Jiǎng's rough estimate of how much fire might come their way if all those defenders let loose on the *Gateshot* chilled the seasoned admiral to the bone. The last time he'd been this hopelessly outgunned, his ship had been destroyed beyond repair and a lot of good people had died. Nick almost included. A quick meeting of their eyes told him the lad remembered it, too.

"We should break off," Nick said. "Our backup is on the way. We've won."

No, they hadn't ... not quite. And they had shown more of the *Gateshot*'s capabilities than Eve would have preferred. Could they trust the Plutonians with respecting the guardian's secrets?

Sudden warmth drew Glen's eyes to his left hand. As he gazed at the tattoo Maverick had conjured on his palm, time slowed down. The busy bustle of the bridge receded, and silence fell. His instinct sharpened to an almost painful intensity as his mind extended. Options, strategies, and possible outcomes unfolded before his inner eye. Then all of it gave way to an intangible knowledge. To instinct. To faith.

His mind made up, the admiral looked up.

Time reasserted itself.

"No. We'll lose all momentum," he decided. "If we double back now, we'll be stranded."

"And then what?" his XO leaned in to argue. "We don't stand a chance against these odds."

The old man raised an eyebrow, saying, "You mean, like we didn't stand a chance ten minutes ago? Besides, I wonder why those stations have yet to take one single shot. Don't you?"

His young friend's eyes narrowed. It was an XO's duty to stop his captain from hurting the crew if he felt the decisions made by his superior were suicidally unwise. Decision made, Nick straightened in his seat and shook his head.

"Damn," he murmured, clearly unhappy. "I sure hope your hunches see us through."

Glen allowed himself a small smile.

Trust was a precious thing.

"Keep going, Lt. Ludmilla," the captain ordered.

"*The Loooony Can* is secure," Eve reported. "She's turning off engines now. Medical personnel are standing by."

"Captain," Jiǎng caught his attention, "we're about to pass into unsafe proximity to the stations. Now."

For a few heartbeats, everyone stared at the main screen. People held their breath in fearful expectation.

Nothing happened.

"Captain, have a look at this," Rivers remarked as she zoomed out on the tactical display.

"Earth," Nick murmured. "That's gonna hurt. I bet the Velorians won't see that coming until it's too late. Won't help us, though ..."

"Captain!" Montoya called. "The *Lightbearer*!"

Behind them, the Velorian flagship vanished in a massive cloud of fire and gas.

CHAPTER SIXTY-SEVEN

SUZY\\ TWO BIRDS IN ONE

Suzy opened her eyes and gasped. The overflow of energy was burning her insides to a crisp. At least, that's what it felt like. It was also radiating out of her, escaping her grasping hold. Slowly, but unstoppable. She had to use it now, or it would be gone! And the gate was ...

'They sealed it!' Xin reported breathlessly. She felt exhausted and as if she were barely hanging on. *'They made the spell permanent. Or semi-permanent ... I think it's degrading at the edges, but it'll hold for a long while. I'm not sure we can break it. I wouldn't know how.'*

'NONONONONONONO!!!', Suzy screamed. Her head spun like crazy. They had to find a way around this. There had to be another way. She—

Of course, there was.

The witch fell to her knees and pressed her hands to the floor.

"Eve, are you the ship?" she gasped through chattering teeth.

"Yes," the voice of her friend and teacher echoed out of

every loudspeaker nearby. Gray-blue eyes appeared on the screens all around.

"I need to connect to you." Suzy swallowed, momentary panic rushing through her at the magnitude of what she was about to try. "I need you to stay connected to the ship. I need you to be the *Gateshot*, every last square centimeter of it!"

"Okay, how—" Eve started, but with her supercharged senses, Suzy had already found the faint essence of her running through the deckplates beneath.

As she linked up, her body stayed behind, just one faraway part of the giant body she was now inhabiting.

The faint wall between Eve and her, which Suzy recognized from their last mindmerge, ripped like paper as she touched it with her power.

Suddenly, they were one.

Eve and Suzy and the *Gateshot*. The part that remained of the witch marveled at feeling every last bit of metal, every drone, every container pressing against the floor. And the people in it! They were connected as well, their BCIs satellites to the matrix flowing through the structure like blood through living tissue. Their weight on the carpets, their warmth as seen by the internal sensors, the displacement of air in their wake, the levels of oxygen dropping ever so slightly wherever a living being passed.

And Konani. The pure energy of the venerable one emanating from that little chamber up front into the machinery. On it flowed, down the whole length of the ship, into the last little nook and cranny, enlivening machinery and systems along the way. Drones servicing the organism like working ants, swarming through the corridors.

Xin as she stood on the outer hull, arms wide, magic

coursing through her in a desperate attempt at opening a gate that wouldn't budge.

The only thing Suzy couldn't feel ...

'*Rupert! Dite!*' she called in her mind. '*I can't sense you! Stop hiding or stay behind!*'

A slow flicker of energy, then two more beings appeared next to Xin. Miniature suns burning as bright as Konani, but with a different fire. A part of Eve gasped as she beheld this sight, felt this fire on her hull.

'*I can see magic!*' she whispered into their shared mind.

'*I can see technology.*' Suzy smiled deep down. '*Now let's cast a spell together.*'

All over the ship, she imagined the runes she would need to steady a ritual of this magnitude. Immediately, the spell took shape and they blinked into existence on the wall screens, the drones, and any equipment that could display them.

"Eve, what's going on?" Glen spoke, and his voice was forwarded without delay.

"Captain, this is Suzy," the ship's witch declared as she took over part of the bridge controls. "The gate is compromised. But I have another way."

"Another way?" A tiny waft of incredulous bewilderment funneled into their empathic connection.

Nick's voice interjected, saying, "Suzy, listen, it's fine. We won. We can take our time now."

Take our time?

Suzy listened inside. The alien magic still roiled and burned. And it was escaping. Trickling away, drifting out of her reach like elusive fog.

"No, we can't," she said. "There's no time to explain, but this is a magical matter. So it's *my* decision to make. And I say we go *now*. Just trust me and hold on tight!"

Her mind turned to Eve as she activated the bridge's 3D holo-output and dove into the as-yet hidden star charts. "Eve, I need a destination. Where's home for you?"

A camera feed of Glen as he stared up at the randomly changing light patterns all around flashed up in their shared space.

"Suzy—" he started.

"Give me a location that's safe," Suzy clarified. "Large enough for the *Gateshot*? Far away from the Velorians waiting for us? Something you remember really well. A place with meaning."

Eve's wandering mind realigned with the witch's goal-oriented mode.

All around the bridge crew, dark shapes rustled. Then the giant leaves were brushed aside and revealed a stunning sight of a starlit sky sporting no moon. Suzy felt Glen experience a small bout of weightlessness as the point of view rose and rose, until there were only stars all around. A small space station of alien design hardly noticeable far to his left.

Home.

For a moment, the feel of blazing sunlight on her feathers and the scent of wet bark and humid earth flickered through their shared mind. Then the intense memory of the first time Eve ever saw the full splendor of space was replaced by a star chart showing the constellations, the space station, and any other objects in the vicinity. Eve locked it in and held it in their mind with single-minded concentration.

Good. Suzy took a deep breath. *Then this is where we go.*

As she envisioned what she wanted her magic to do, the flames of power coursing through her and into the *Gateshot* set her mind alight. Purple fire ran down the length of the ship, all the way to the tips of her wings. And as the phoenix that was Suzy equaled the dark bird of prey that was Eve, reality shifted.

From one moment to the next, the *Gateshot* vanished from the fabric of reality and was flung to that other place.

CHAPTER SIXTY-EIGHT

RUFFA\\ SOULSTEALER

"What happened?" Ruffa barked as the fiery overlay cleared the main screen and the warning lights dimmed back down from indicating a catastrophic failure to merely a ship-wide technical problem.

"Our secondary energy core cascade just failed catastrophically, allegedly due to overheating," the *Light-bearer*'s captain announced with shivering folds. "As I warned you, it might. We're lucky we survived. We have to break off pursuit!"

He gestured and everything went dark for several minutes.

When the power came back online, it was a feeble, minimalistic thing.

"What ..." Tuvil stared at the tactical display. Static interference ran through it and the ships displayed there flickered unsteadily.

"Radioactive explosions tend to mess with the scanners," Ruffa explained without thinking.

"Yes, but ..." His aide pointed at an empty patch of space right in front of their ship.

"Where are they?" the commander demanded as he tapped the display to get a pinpointed readout. "Where's the guardian's ship?"

"Scanning!" The seasoned officer at the sensor station jumped at the implicit command. As his fingers ran over his console with increasingly jerky motions, Ruffa exchanged a glance with the *Lightbearer*'s captain.

"Well?" the captain chided his subordinate.

"I ... ahem ... I ..." The officer flattened his folds against his skull. Finally, he admitted in a small voice, "We lost them, Commander."

"Lost them?" Ruffa growled. "It's a ship of rather significant proportions! How can we have 'lost' them?"

"I ... don't know, Commander. They just ... disappeared," the officer replied in helpless confusion, his fingers still working the controls.

"Have you taken into account the scanner's difficulties with the remaining radioactivity clinging to the ship?" the captain asked.

"Yes, of course, Sir," the officer replied. "Even so. They aren't anywhere in the vicinity. It's like they just fell out of existence."

"A cloaking device?" Tuvil suggested.

"On a vessel that size?" Ruffa rubbed his outer folds thoughtfully. "Not unheard of, but highly unlikely. Besides, why would they only engage it now? That makes no sense."

Also, no cloak could cover a damaged vessel effectively, no matter the sophistication of the underlying tech. No. The guardian's ship had been there, and now it wasn't. There was no reasonable explanation for it, as far as Ruffa could tell.

He stared at the empty patch of space his foe had occupied so recently.

"Advise the stations to feed all available energy into the sensor banks," he told Tuvil. "I want this sector analyzed down to the molecular level! They have to have gone somewhere!"

"Yes, Commander," Tuvil acknowledged.

"And open a channel to Berestul. There is one option we can't scan for."

"Yes, Commander."

"Commander!" The officer at communications turned deadly pale. "Our stations are under attack!"

"What? From whom?" Ruffa widened his display.

A new Plutonian man-of-war and its escort swooped in from the other side of the battlefield, aiming directly at the stations. The retreating Velorian forces were caught between these new pieces and their original pursuers. Even the station sending out fire at a rapid rate wouldn't do much to deter the enemy. This was a tactical nightmare.

Senoxes hadn't mentioned anything about a backup force!

In silent rage, Ruffa watched as several of his rujas and even a gouta started attacking their own.

This was ...

"Commander," the captain folded back his ears in open hesitancy, "the Plutonians are completely ignoring us. It seems the remnants of radioactivity are still masking our presence. The explosion probably tricked their scanners into believing we were destroyed. We should use this opportunity to escape."

"No, we should use this opportunity to fall upon them from behind and relieve the stations!" Ruffa decided.

"Commander, with the damage to the *Lightbearer*'s systems, we don't stand a chance!" the captain pleaded. "We only have one energy core left! That's not enough to power shields, weapons, and propulsion! I'd highly advise not to engage anyone right now!"

Heat ran up and down Ruffa's folds. What should have been a very straightforward task had turned into a disaster. And, now that the guardian's ship—his primary target—was nowhere to be found, the overall situation sank in. How in Veloria's name had these stinking savages managed to overwhelm their superior technology? This was... infuriating beyond belief.

"Commander!" Tuvil's folds and voice wavered as he looked up from a display.

More bad news, was it?

"What is it?" Ruffa demanded.

"Primary Mage Berestul is dead," Tuvil reported, visibly shaken. "As are all the other mages."

A first inkling of fear traveled up Ruffa's spine.

"Evron?" he asked.

Tuvil shook his head.

"I see." Ruffa couldn't believe it. This was... unfathomable. The whole situation was beyond reason. It just made no sense! "Captain, make ready to head for Neptunian space. Advise any forces able to break away to do the same. I'll need to consider this for a moment."

The captain's folds drooped as he acknowledged the order.

With a detached sinking feeling of imminent disaster, Ruffa gestured for his adjutant to walk with him up to his office.

"What happened to the mages?" he asked as soon as the door closed on them.

Tuvil blinked in open confusion, as he reported, "The guards posted to secure the room report no breach. That entire wing of the station is perfectly intact, as are most of the mages' bodies. They report Evron was killed by Erestral's blade, who in turn was torn apart by magic. Some of the ritual runes are burned and blackened. I'm pulling camera footage now. But... ahem... There's nothing our healers were able to do, Commander. For any of them."

Absentmindedly, the lead warrior's fingertips touched the clock on his desk.

What had just happened? How had this day gone so wrong?

"I have the footage now," his aide hastened to report. "If I may?!"

Ruffa gestured for him to forward it to his desk's holo-display, then followed the happening being replayed with mounting perplexity and dread. As Evron fell and closed his eyes for the last time, Ruffa's heart hurt with the depth of his ineptitude to safeguard the young one. He replayed a different section and turned up the volume.

"I think you're confusing me with someone else," Evron said as he rose, his ears on full display, his voice at the same time his and not his, as it had instantly and subtly changed in inflection and tone. "My name is Suzy Magecraft, and I'm here to kick your creepy, voidforsaken behind all the way back to your home planet. Asshole."

Suzy Magecraft.

Magecraft.

A Human name.

Weakness rushed through the military commander at the realization of what must have happened. He strode around his desk and sat down to hide the unexpected emotion. Yet, he couldn't keep it out of his voice entirely as he confessed, "I've heard of this. Old tales claim that the most powerful Haslar mages could kill their enemies from afar. It's why they say rituals like this, which require merging one mind with another, are so dangerous. At least in theory, minds can be invaded. In a ritual like this, it is said, entering one mind enables entering them all."

Tuvil's eyes widened. Clearly, he remembered the same tales of the Haslar bogeymen, hunted to extinction everywhere the master race's reach prevailed, as he stuttered, "Are you saying this was ... a soulstealer?"

"Impossible!" The word left Ruffa's lips before his mind could even fully fathom the idea. "Ludicrous!"

With their minimal magical abilities, there was no way the Humans could birth such a powerful creature. A creature even the Haslar Queen herself feared.

But how could the ship have vanished if not by magic?

And how could he explain this to Thallamon without losing his head?

Three lightshifts later, Ruffa's inner turmoil hadn't settled so much as turned into dreadful acceptance of his fate.

As he paced around his desk, waiting for his connection to Thallamon to be accepted on the other end, a sharp ache bloomed in his chest. He reached out a hand to touch the timepiece on his desk. By some trick of his mind, Evron's face superimposed itself over his own child's image. He'd failed the young one. He'd failed his superior. He'd failed Veloria. The loss of the gate, many of their in-system ships and mages, as well as the guardian's escape to an unknown destination added up to a staggering amount of shame.

Shame upon himself, his superior, his bloodweb.

There was only one course of action that might start him on a course toward redemption.

Only one.

He'd accepted this.

Still, to go through with it had cost him greatly. And he was just getting started.

And he would not go down alone.

His offspring smiled at him from inside the clock—then vanished.

"Ruffa." Thallamon's hologram flickered into existence in front of his desk, towering over the commander. "I read your preliminary report."

The governor's ears showed full display; his eyes were clouded by what Ruffa suspected to be a mixture of grief and fury. His posture hinted at the barely restrained wish to lash out at the subordinate who'd so thoroughly displeased and disappointed him.

Without a word, his lesser knelt, ears folded to the very back, and presented the vial to him. He'd unbuttoned his uniform at the collar and held his head high so that the governor could inspect the fresh wound on his neck. It was an old custom from before the time the Haslar had enslaved the Velorian people. One of the few to survive their long rule. And even though their former masters had not only discouraged, but almost dismantled it, the meaning remained unchanged.

By offering his core genes for Thallamon's use, Ruffa acknowledged utter inferiority. He offered not only his person and possible offspring Thallamon might create with this, but the merger of their bloodwebs. If Thallamon decided to accept, Ruffa's bloodweb—starting with his person and offspring—would for eternity be considered an inferior part of Thallamon's genepool. It was as drastic an apology as any Velorian could offer. The fact that Thallamon had Evron's core genes stored and could have him cloned, or use it to design other offspring with similar purity didn't impact the fact that Ruffa had caused the loss of Evron's soul. No clone was ever the same as the original. So much was certain. Evron, the real Evron, was gone, and Ruffa's genes the only price that might lessen this debt.

And even if Thallamon accepted, he could still demand Ruffa's ears.

Or his whole head.

Neither demand would change the new status of Ruffa's offspring.

The worst possible outcome would be for Thallamon to decline.

As the timepiece changed into dark blue illumination, the governor simply stared.

Ruffa waited.

He'd lost his right to demand or even ask for anything. Even a speedy decision on his fate.

Finally, the governor sat. His ears loosened up by the smallest of fractions.

"Tell me everything," he ordered coldly.

As Ruffa reported, Thallamon's face remained frozen and expressionless.

Still, the commander dared to end with an accusation, saying, "Senoxes played us, Mylord. His tactical advice turned the battle. He confused us on which of our ships had been boarded ... and if I'd known about the fourth man-of-war at our backs, my strategy would have been very different."

"You're right." The governor's folds tightened in displeasure. "And I haven't heard from him since. His junior adjutant tells me that Senoxes was asked to attend a meeting with Senior Commander Bogdanova right before the battle. Since then, he's gone. There are rumors that he asked for ..." Thallamon spat out the following words, "*political asylum.*"

Ruffa's ears shivered. "His bodyguards and primary aide should have—"

"It seems the Plutonians expected this and prevented this failsafe from interfering," the governor cut in, fury once more preeminent in his folds.

His subordinate quickly pressed his own ears flat to his skull. Senoxes' treason had certainly been a factor in his downfall, but it wouldn't gain him any clemency. It didn't lighten his guilt in either his own or his superior's estimation.

Thallamon took a deep breath, as if restraining himself, and stood.

His voice held deceptive calm as he continued, "It doesn't change the fact that we've lost the gate, the guardian, and our face in front of the Humans. Since we don't know where the guardian's ship disappeared to or how, there's nothing much we can do about that. I'll relay a warning to Veloria, so they can deal with it. I'll also advise them to amass more defenses on the other side of the gate, but leave them there for now. No reason to invite our meddlesome neighbors to swoop in a second time. If they persist in playing the righteous victims in all this, they'll clean out our stations, destroy them, and then leave. I expect our people to resist and destroy the stations before that and with as many Humans aboard as they can."

Obviously, he saw Ruffa's impotent anger at just accepting that these barbarians had bested them as he gestured for the other to calm down.

"Even with all the reinforcements Veloria could send us, it would be unwise to show aggression," he continued. "It will only leave us even weaker in number and make the other nations wonder if we'll turn on them next. Besides, why waste the resources if we can make the Humans fight this war for us?"

A strange shift ran over Thallamon's folds and face. He smiled maliciously, saying, "While you might think my actions weak and ineffective, my results are just starting to unfold. This is a political struggle now. It always was. And as much as it hurts me to fall back on this Human notion, your loss is my gain."

He reached out to hold open his palm, his folds flaring to show he accepted Ruffa's genes. With a sudden sinking feeling, the commander set the vial onto his new lord's palm. That the hologram couldn't actually take it at this moment didn't change the meaning of the gesture. It didn't change the new power dynamic at play.

"Observe the Plutonians at the gate. Should they leave, send back a minimal amount of ships to uphold our claim on it," Thallamon ordered harshly. "Also, fix up the *Lightbearer* and then return to Earth. We have a war to start."

CHAPTER SIXTY-NINE

GLEN\\ WHERE'S HOME?

Blinding light erupted around them. Not just on the screens. For either a split second or a small eternity, it seemed reality itself was pure light.

When it passed, the *Gateshot* was dark.

Truly dark.

Glen couldn't remember when he'd last sat in the complete darkness of a power outage.

Normally, there was always some tiny light blinking away somewhere. An emergency light. A console. A small army of indicators. Anything.

Now there was nothing. Not a single source of luminescence. His BCI was working but unable to get a connection.

"Report!" he called out, even though he wasn't quite sure what he wanted reported or how his people could tell him anything without their instruments.

Rustling and whispered words started up all around him.

"Ahem, all the sensor crew alive and accounted for?" Rivers' voice finally called out.

"Aye!" four other voices called back.

This prompted other stations to perform a similar headcount, and after two minutes, they'd at least established everyone in the room was still there and unharmed.

Everyone but ...

"Eve!" Glen unbuckled and felt his way over to her station. "Eve, are you all right?"

She'd dropped next to her console. He fumbled to find her face. Underneath his fingertips, he felt warm flesh instead of cold, unyielding metal. So that was a good sign ... As his thumb brushed over her soft lips, a shuddering breath escaped them.

"Glen?" she moaned.

"I'm here." He helped her sit up. "What happened? Can you see anything?"

"Give me a moment ..."

The faint rasping of skin on skin made him suspect she was rubbing her forehead, but he couldn't be sure.

"Seems we're suffering from a complete blackout," Nick reported. He stepped next to them, the tiny light of his trusty multitool sweeping over Eve before checking the nearby consoles. "Shouldn't we have backup power or something?"

"With Konani aboard, a complete loss of power is ... highly unlikely." Eve shook her head and let Glen help her onto shaky legs. "I'm not sure what happened or where we are. I can't connect to anything!"

A sudden panic rose in her, so palpable that Glen could feel it.

"You don't think the *Gateshot* got completely fried by Suzy's magic, do you?" he asked.

She merely stared back at him, unable or unwilling to answer. Faint noises drew the captain's glance to the door, where Garin and the other bridge guards were just forcing it open. Nick, meanwhile, was making the rounds. A few more handheld lights had sprung up, mainly in the engineering section.

"Well, at least I can't make out any vibrations," Glen commented. "So that's good."

Eve cocked her head at him.

"If our ship were shot to pieces all around us, we'd feel it." The admiral sighed. "Even this deep inside."

"Right," she agreed.

Suddenly, the power just ... returned.

"All systems check out fine," Lustig reported about ten minutes later. "I have no clue why the power was gone or even how."

"Suzy!" Nick exclaimed, then opened a channel. "Sheridan to Magecraft, report!"

"She's down," Eve replied in the girl's stead. "A medical team is already with her."

On Eve's screen, a camera feed showed the bar. Suzy's limp body was just being secured on a hover gurney. Seeing her chest rising and falling on its own calmed Glen's apprehension somewhat. Around her, the ritual circle seemed blackened as if the symbols themselves had started to burn the metal floor. A jumble of chairs and tables littered the walls. Off to the side, Thea Robbins looked over a slightly banged-up provost. His helmet, face mask, and gloves lay scattered all over the room.

"Pro. Eisengaard-Diaz, report!" Glen demanded. "What happened on your end?"

"Ms. Magecraft did ... something." Underneath his professional veneer, the man's voice sounded shaken and confused. "Then the lines and symbols on the floor started to flare with purple fire, and it expanded. Like an explosion. It threw me across the room. Then everything went dark. As soon as I could free myself from the debris, I checked on the girl and called for help."

"I see. Where are Mr. Maverick and Ms. Yun?"

"They were on top of the *Gateshot*, I think."

"Very good, thank you, Provost."

"Aye, Captain." Supported by Medic Robbins, Garin's second cautiously rose to stand.

Glen's BCI advised him of an incoming comm from Dr. Fox, and he accepted.

"Captain," his head medic sounded slightly unfocused, as if she were minding several things at once, "I thought you might want to know: Maverick staggered into the medic bay a few minutes ago and dropped off Ms. Yun. She's completely exhausted but otherwise fine."

"And Maverick?"

"Disappeared." Felicity sounded simultaneously pleased and apprehensive.

"Well, I'm sure he'll turn back up," Nick commented.

"Like a bad penny." Glen nodded. "Thank you, Doctor. Keep me advised of Suzy's status and send me a report on losses and injuries received during the battle."

"Dr. LaMont is already on it," Felicity answered. "Last I heard, we have 29 dead, 35 badly, and 61 slightly injured."

"Acknowledged." Glen waited to hear if she had more to say. When she cut the channel, he turned back to his bridge crew. "Engineering, damage report! Sensors, where are we?"

Someone began ringing the ship's bell with slow, heavy movements, forcing the entire bridge crew into a minute of solemn silence.

"Minimal damage," Lustig reported afterward.

"Nothing we can't fix within two days and with minimal resources."

Another good piece of news.

"Konani's fine," Eve added. "Just confused. It seems she fell unconscious. That's ... highly unusual for her species."

"Captain." Montoya worked her console hard. She shook her head. "The Velorians are gone. Everyone is gone. We're ... not in the Human solar system anymore. But I can't say where we are or how we got here."

The main screen flickered back into life, showing a mostly green planet with several moons in the near distance. Everyone paused in their tasks to look up.

"Any signs of other ships?" Glen studied the image.

Like many others, Ambassador Bogdanov stepped closer to the screen, an almost reverent expression on his face as he gazed at the alien planet teeming with unknown life.

"There's a small space station." Montoya encircled its position on the screen, then overlaid a few stars with a zoomed-in image of an alien design. "Signs of medium traffic coming and going. We're not picking up much else. The planet's surface is covered in colossal vegetation, lacks large oceans, and exhibits few signs of technology. There might be more on the other side of the planet."

"There isn't." The guardian stepped forward, recognition mixing with awe in her features. "This is Karrakii. It's a low-technology world. We're at the edge of Haslar space, practically on the other side of the galaxy! Suzy moved us across 70,000 light-years within 8.47 Human minutes!"

Silence fell over the bridge as this information sank in.

"We did it," Redhead Rivers marveled. Then she jumped up to hug her seatmate and shouted, "We actually did it!"

Montoya opened her mouth as if to reprimand her colleague, but she had already jumped up the steps to embrace her with a relieved laugh.

Glen sat back and watched with satisfaction as Rivers' enthusiasm spread to the rest of the bridge crew. Hugs, handshakes, and pats on the back were exchanged, and some clapped and cheered with relief. Lustig laughed as his teammates, caught up in their euphoria, scooped him up and tossed him into the air several times.

Ludmilla also watched the little show with a good-natured smile, and even Jiăng's lips twitched briefly.

Bogdanov shook hands with both COs and the ship's master. Nick took the opportunity to hug Eve with a cheeky grin. She returned the touch and flashed him a friendly wink.

After pulling the captain out of his chair for a quick hug, the lad turned him toward Eve. A brief moment of indecisiveness, then they both stepped forward and shared a quick embrace.

Side by side, the captain, XO, and ship's master waited for the excitement to subside.

Glen himself wasn't yet sure how he was supposed to feel in that moment. Sure, they'd made it. They had survived and escaped the Velorians. But they weren't where they'd meant to go.

They had overshot their target by a wide margin, and even if he didn't yet grasp the full scope of the geographic mess they were in ... seventy thousand light-years surely meant one hell of a long way back. Had he truly come any closer to his daughters—or had he, in fact, moved even farther away from them? Would they hold out until he could finally reach them?

Lost in thought, he turned his wedding ring on his finger.

"This is the place you thought of," Glen realized. "This is your home?!"

Eve nodded. Then shook her head.

"It was ... in another life," she murmured. "Maybe."

"Will these people attack us?" Federov entered the bridge in time to catch the exchange.

"No, the Karrishians are a small and peaceful people." Their alien friend seemed very confident. "As long as we don't threaten them, they'll seek no quarrel with us."

"Karrishians, Velorians, Haslars ..." Garin had removed her face shield to get an unobstructed view of the main screen. "How many more aliens are out there?"

"My people know of 32 unique, intelligent species that have reached a level of development defined as civilization." The guardian considered the hardened soldier's derailed facial features with mild amusement before continuing: "The Velorians are pretty much at the bottom of the pecking order, and Humanity is officially considered a race colonized by them. So I would recommend treating all other species with respect upon first encountering them."

Federov snorted and crossed his arms.

Nick leaned back, his gaze once more considering the minor miracle on the main screen as he asked, "How long to get to Velorian space from here?"

"At top speed and including the use of space gates ..." Eve bit her bottom lip. "Depending on the route and any delays we might encounter, I calculate one to three years."

Bloody hell.

The captain sighed.

"It's fine. We're here. Nothing to do about it now." He laid a hand on Eve's shoulder and squeezed gently.

"Let's take a moment to reorient and plan this next part of our journey."

"On the plus side," Nick grinned broadly, "the Velorians won't search for us here, right?"

"No, I wouldn't think so," the guardian agreed with a tentative smile of her own. "The Great Neutrality has never heard of any mage performing a teleportation spell on this scale."

"Then we better keep the fact to ourselves," Federov said. "You never know who's watching, *daniete*?"

~ the end (for now) ~

CHAPTER SEVENTY

LUCY\\ EPILOG

Mars, Elonia - Two days after the battle at the Gate

Dressing was a highly automated afterthought as Lucy Magecraft studied reports from various news outlets, hoping to find any word on her sister's fate. Even the grandiose and elaborate self-aggrandizements of the Plutonians offered nothing to indicate whether the *Gateshot* had made it or not.

One of the gazillion alarms her BCI helpfully provided reminded the grand mage that she was running late for her breakfast appointment.

Marsdust.

Lucy brushed down her skirt and legged it. She really shouldn't be late for this one.

"Even in light of the *PDN Longsword*'s destruction, her surviving crew valiantly set forth in shuttles to defeat the enemy ..." she murmured, shaking her head as she speed-read through the third article saying the same as the first two. "What a load of propagandistic jibber-jabber! Just tell me what happened to my sister, damn you!"

"Hm?" Selene Trimara looked up from a stack of notes as Lucy rushed out of her rooms, then hastened to follow.

Catching up was easy for the regal woman with her long, shapely legs and down-to-business gait. On any other day, Lucy felt dwarfed by the pretty brunette. Not today. Her mind wasn't in it today.

"I'm trying to find something, *anything* about Suzy!" The grand mage gestured for the customary stack of problems her aide was sure to have prepared for a quick assessment.

Selene settled in next to her and handed over the dataslides just as the elevator door closed behind them. "You ... ahem ... missed a button there."

Lucy followed the gesture to her lavender dress shirt and sighed.

"Please, allow me." The ruby-tipped golden threads of her earrings tinkled softly as the woman stepped closer and rearranged her boss's buttons with firm hands.

Selene's own purple and white attire was as pristine as ever. One reason why Lucy had made the mage guild's newest tutor her personal aide was the regal authority and presence oozing from every sun-kissed pore and silken strand of hair. It was the perfect addition to counterbalance the green youngster vibe Lucy had such a hard time shedding in most people's eyes. When everyone else in the room was older and more experienced, it was hard to be taken seriously. Selene really helped with that.

"Maybe Governor Marshall heard something," the middle-aged woman tried to ease Lucy's mind. She was good at that, too, most days. Not today, though.

"Yeah ..." Lucy stared at the dataslides, then handed

them back. "Sorry, I can't … concentrate on this right now. Run it by me again later, okay?"

"Sure." Selene refastened the last button and took back the slides just as the elevator opened.

They walked over to Marshall Industry's Tower, Lucy brooding, Selene watching the animals hiding in the shadows of the plants. Even in the lowest tier of vertical farming, a mostly decorative assortment of trees was already blooming again, poised to produce all kinds of genetically optimized fruit.

On the governor's table, fresh produce and delicious pancakes waited for them. Lucy ate some, so as not to offend the cook, but it was one of those days she could have just as easily done without eating.

"You heard." AI Ebbon Marshall was going through the motions of pretending to eat, so his guest and mentee didn't feel weird.

"Yes." Lucy set down her cutlery, thankful for the invitation to talk about serious things now. "I read all kinds of accounts. None of them mentions the *Gateshot*. Have you heard anything?"

The computer program with the face of a moderately attractive middle-aged man looked at his new chief of security, asking, "Aren?"

Aren Kaelos was a blocky, muscular man with a rugged attractiveness designed to make people of all genders take notice. A smoldering intensity lingered in his piercing dark gaze, hinting at a fierce, hidden brutality. Whenever Kaelos looked her way, shivers ran down Lucy's spine. Deep inside, there was something wild and dangerous about the man.

It beckoned her. The darkness of his skin evoked echoes of things burning.

"I know a person who knows a person," he declared. The very faint smile playing in his features did nothing to soften his stern face. "Got a small peek at the *Voidhammer*'s original sensor data. Seems your pet ship just ... disappeared."

"Disappeared?" Against her better judgment, Lucy openly stared at Kaelos.

"Yeah." His gaze sent her insides into a frantic panic. "It just *poof* went away. One moment it was there, and the next it was gone. Have a look."

Above the neatly set breakfast table, a holo output showed part of the battle at the gate. It zoomed in on the *Gateshot*. True to what Kaelos had said, the ship just ... blinked out of existence.

"You think they made it through the gate?" The grand mage gestured for a slow-motion replay and looked on in horror.

"Don't think so. I mean, I'm not a wizard or anything ...," the man's gaze diverted to Selene for a second, then refocused on Lucy, "but the gate didn't do anything and the *Gateshot* wasn't even close to shooting through, right?"

Marshall, as always, seemed untouched by the strange effect his employee had on his guest. He leaned in, squinting as he studied a list of numbers and such, probably sensor data, that accompanied the visual recording.

"This is ... unexpected." Even the governor seemed at a loss for words.

Kaelos shrugged. "I heard some claimed to have seen purple lightning enveloping it before it vanished. There is no debris and none of the radiation a complete vaporization of a ship would produce when it dies, so the Plutonians seem to think it wasn't destroyed."

"What do they think?" his boss asked.

Behind closed lips, the security chief's tongue slid over his upper teeth before he said, "They don't know what to think. Which is probably why they're simply omitting it from all official accounts until someone higher up decides how to handle it."

He stabbed his pancakes like they'd done something to affront him.

"Interesting." Marshall steepled his fingers. The governor's brown eyes matched the full head of dark brown hair falling into subtly arranged waves. There was some salt-and-pepper going on there as well as in the short dark stubble hugging the sun-kissed skin of his strong chin. Even though both men had a timelessness about them, and looked about the same age, the feel of them was as different as could be. Marshall made Lucy feel safe.

"So what do we do?" the girl demanded. "How can we find out?"

Marshall shook his head. "I'm sorry, Ms. Magecraft, but I don't have many connections that far out. My interests seldom go that way. But if the ship wasn't destroyed, it has to have gone somewhere."

Somewhere? That was all she was going to get from the most powerful man she knew? Fucking somewhere???

With a deep breath, Lucy clamped down on her feelings, keenly aware that Kaelos was still watching her. Selene also glanced her way, but with a more reassuring, calm hopefulness.

"Besides, we'll soon have bigger problems than one

missing ship." The security chief devoured another pancake.

His boss gestured for him to go on.

"Haven't you read the news?" Kaelos raised an eyebrow. "How everyone's blaming someone?"

"Well, the Plutonians are mightily happy with themselves." Lucy bristled. "What a big win for Humanity, showing the invaders their place. Pah!"

The man leaned in. "And did you read what Earth has to say about that?"

"They claim the Plutonians were out of line and rally behind the Velorians, naturally." Lucy didn't like the obvious lobbyism at play on Humanity's home planet, but it was hardly a new tune. "Some news outlets speculate that there will be sanctions against Pluto. But since there's hardly any trade between them, I don't see the point. The Plutonians don't care about the coreworlds."

"No, but Earth alone isn't the coreworlds," Marshall interjected gently. "Is it?"

Lucy thought about the Martian reports. They'd been the only neutral ones she'd been able to find on the matter.

"The new EMMA agreement still isn't signed, is it?" she asked with a sinking feeling.

Marshall shook his head. He waved the holo-display closed. "I've already had the first politicians lobbying for sanctions, indicating that they won't sign unless something is done against—as they put it—'the outrageous developments at our outer colonies' borders.' There have been discussions about fine-tuning our agreements to account for the Velorian presence in our solar system. Some want them included in the contracts, especially the trade agreements. Some want the opposite."

Lucy frowned. "Why does this only come up now? They've been here for a decade!"

"It doesn't." Marshall picked up his steaming cup of holographic coffee and took a sip. "There have been agreements and contracts made almost as soon as they arrived. But nothing as solid and comprehensive as rooting it in the EMMA would be. Ambassador Thallamon has worked long and hard to get all his people in place for just this opportunity. All his ducks in a row, as they would say. I've seen it coming and moved my pieces, so Mars can't be outvoted in this. Sadly, all that lobbying leaves the EMMA vulnerable and liable to be split clean down the middle. Which is highly likely to prove just as much of a win for the Velorians as getting all their demands met would be."

Selene's elegant hand played with the centerpiece of the large golden chain around her neck, a Martian diamond in the form of a multifaceted teardrop, as her intelligent eyes jumped from Marshall to Kaelos and back.

"You mean you didn't want the Velorians to gain the upper hand over such a large part of Humanity, so instead, you created a standstill?" she clarified. "A place from which no one can move forward?"

"I'm programmed to mind my people and what's good for them." The AI's voice took on a very subtle, forlorn tone. "Having an alien race with presumably hostile intentions wielding any power over Mars is unacceptable. I couldn't allow it."

"So instead, you let the EMMA die?" Lucy swallowed as she realized the immensity of what fallout would probably come from this. "You'll claim neutrality in whatever happens next. You always said you didn't like how Earth overreached Mars to keep its economy balanced out. So, the Velorians will push for Earth to do something, and without the benefits Mars provides now, Earth will be relying even more on the aliens to produce their technology. They'll move against Pluto, which is insane, given the republic's sheer size! The consequences of either side breaking the Kuiper Contract are simply incalculable. The outer colonies are still angry and impoverished, so they'll jump at the chance to rebuild the Commonwealth and try for independence once more. The Velorians won't be interested in keeping the peace, because a split Humanity is easier to play. They can just step back, fan the fire, and pick up the pieces afterward."

Marshall nodded. Sadness crossed the hologram's features. He knew damn well how many lives his decisions over the last ten years would cost in the near future. But, much like the Plutonians, he didn't consider the rest of the solar system to be his problem. His responsibility lay with Mars, and only with Mars.

Kaelos' tiny smile chilled Lucy to the bone. As did his declaration, "Yes, there will most certainly be war. And this time, with the Kuiperbelt involved, it will envelop the whole solar system. That little skirmish ten years ago will be nothing in comparison."

"And we mages will stand squarely in the crossfire." Lucy blinked quickly to suppress a tear. "The Velorians have mages, so everyone opposing them needs mages, so everyone opposing anyone will need mages! And what better way to weaken any side than to kill their mages! We'll be hunted, weaponized, and dissected for our usability."

Marshall shook his head. "Not on Mars."

"But even if they'd all come here," the grand mage whispered, "Mars couldn't take them all in. Magic's on the rise. I've seen the numbers. It's not just more and more people wielding magic, but they're getting stronger every day! And you don't actually want that ticking bomb on your lawn, either, do you?"

Marshall didn't answer.

The grand mage nodded and, with a sad smile, stood. "Thanks for the heads-up. Now, if you'll excuse me, Governor. I have my own preparations to make."

😃📚 Dear Reader, 📚😃

Oh my God, we made it!

This was the first "season" of the Witch Way Chronicles. The story I ended up needing seven books to tell was initially planned as a single volume. But, what can I say … my characters had other ideas … 😉

Between the first and the second volumes, I had several ideas that clearly trumped my original ones. That's why, for example, I replaced the rather flat, Yoda-esque old man with Rupert (and I will stubbornly insist that my con mage was simply wearing a different face in those scenes. 😉)

And then Jim came along and dropped an entire faction composed of cool additional personnel into my lap. Not only did that generate many exciting backstories in my mind, but it also established an entirely new political dimension.

In Volume 5, I tried to bring all of that together and tie up most of the loose ends. Since I can hardly bring myself to kill off characters, some of them will probably have to fade into the background from Volume 6 onward. And Volume 5 didn't merely grow into a doorstopper—it also came with a somewhat atypical story structure.

I do hope my efforts so far entertained you

either way, and that I managed to surprise you with one or two of my twists along the way. (Especially with the ending of this book— And yes, I had that one planned from the very beginning.)

If you've enjoyed my universe so far, then— please!—leave reviews for my books, gift them to friends, family, neighbors, or anyone in your life who could use a little more magic.

Let's expand that cute little sci-fi niche again!

Yours sincerely,

Kim Nexus

HI THERE, I'M KIM NEXUS!

Welcome to my witching world!

I'm a full-time working mom living in Germany with my beautiful family in a house where each room is designed differently, because we hate boring things.

I'd love to read more than I ever get around to (especially more fiction), and when I do get around to it, I mostly enjoy paranormal romance and science fantasy.

Other interests of mine I always strive to learn more about are learning itself, self-betterment, motivation, bio-hacking, history and the English language.

Find out more about me at KimNexus.com or become a patreon at patreon.com/KimNexus.

👎 Please Review This book! 👍

I know, I know, everyone says it these days, but it REALLY DOES help us Indies out if you take just five minutes out of your busy day and quickly jot down a few impressions.

Tell the community what you liked and what didn't jive, so other readers know if this is the book for them and so that I can make the next one better FOR ALL OF YOU.

Thank you so much!

See whole series
& review on Amazon:

Say Hello 👋

I won't promise anything, since I do have a full calendar, like, all the time now, but if you have questions, suggestions, or found typos and the like, why don't you shoot me an email at hi@kimnexus.com.

Or find me on instagram (instagram.com/knp_kimnexus).

ALL BOOKS IN THIS SERIES

WWC #01 - WITCH WAY TO SPACE

WWC #02 - WITCH WAY TO JUPITER

WWC #05.1 - WITCH WAY TO THE GATE
(PART 1)

WWC #05.2 - WITCH WAY TO THE GATE
(PART 2)

WWC #03 - WITCH WAY TO SPACEDUST

WWC #04 - WITCH WAY TO THE VOID

WWC #03.5 - SUNBURNT

Witch Way to the Gate - Part 2 (*Witch Way Chronicles* #05.2) - Kim & Jim Nexus

---

Author, Spellchecker, Format & Coverdesign: Kim Nexus; c/o Block Services; Stuttgarter Str. 106; 70736 Fellbach

Coauthor, Father of Plutonians & Developmental Editor: Jim Nexus

Coverart: Björn Frost [Give him some love at deviantart or instagram!]

Print: Amazon EU S.à r.l. (For executing print-on-demand center see identification on the last page)

ISBN-13 (paperback): 978-3-949552-37-3

ISBN-13 (hardcover): 978-3-949552-36-6

Formatted with Vellum

www.ingramcontent.com/pod-product-compliance
Lightning Source LLC
LaVergne TN
LVHW041054080826
845145LV00007B/1573